As the heavy music ⟨...⟩ came on quickly. The f⟨...⟩ sun were smothered by ⟨...⟩ Alexi of nothing so muc⟨...⟩ spirit. The shadows arou⟨...⟩ of the trees more ghostly, the currents of the river more still.

A thick blanket of fog rose out of the water. It ascended as an unnatural mass of slowly churning vapors, the sort of effect Alexi had seen only in his nightmares. It swayed and rolled to the haunting music of Lysander's flute, mirroring the notes in coiling tendrils of fog.

Suddenly a dark shape stirred within the vapors.

Ravenloft is a netherworld of evil, a place of darkness that can be reached from any world—escape is a different matter entirely. The unlucky who stumble into the Dark Domains find themselves trapped in lands filled with vampires, werebeasts, zombies, and worse.

Each novel in the series is a complete story in itself, revealing the chilling tales of the beleaguered heroes and powerful, evil lords who populate the Dark Domains.

Ravenloft Books

Vampire of the Mists
Christie Golden

Knight of the Black Rose
James Lowder

Dance of the Dead
Christie Golden

Heart of Midnight
J. Robert King

Tapestry of Dark Souls
Elaine Bergstrom

Carnival of Fear
J. Robert King

I, Strahd
P. N. Elrod

The Enemy Within
Christie Golden

Mordenheim
Chet Williamson

Tales of Ravenloft
Edited by Brian Thomsen

Tower of Doom
Mark Anthony

Baroness of Blood
Elaine Bergstrom

Death of a Darklord
Laurell K. Hamilton

Scholar of Decay
Tanya Huff

King of the Dead
Gene DeWeese

To Sleep With Evil
Andria Cardarelle

Lord of the Necropolis
Gene DeWeese

Ravenloft® BOOKS

Shadowborn

William W. Connors and Carrie A. Bebris

For my father.
C.A.B.

For my father, Donald W. Connors
January 26, 1936 – November 30, 1996
William W. Connors

SHADOWBORN

©1998 TSR, Inc. All Rights Reserved.
TSR, Inc. is a subsidiary of Wizards of the Coast, Inc.

All characters in this book are fictitious. Any resemblance to actual persons, living or dead, is purely coincidental.

Distributed to the book trade in the United States by Random House, Inc. and in Canada by Random House of Canada Ltd.

Disitributed to the hobby, toy, and comics trade in the United States and Canada by regional distributors.

Distributed worldwide by Wizards of the Coast, Inc. and regional distributors.

This material is protected under the copyright laws of the United States of America. Any reproduction or unauthorized use of the material or artwork contained herein is prohibited without the express written permission of TSR, Inc.

All TSR characters, character names, and the distinctive likenesses thereof are trademarks owned by TSR, Inc.

Cover art by Ciruelo Cabral

RAVENLOFT and the TSR logo are registered trademarks owned by TSR, Inc.

First Printing: March 1998
Printed in the United States of America
Library of Congress Catalog Card Number: 96-60824

9 8 7 6 5 4 3 2 1
8074XXX1501

ISBN: 0-7869-0766-5

U.S., CANADA, ASIA, PACIFIC, & LATIN AMERICA Wizards of the Coast, Inc. P.O. Box 707 Renton, WA 98057-0707 +1-206-624-0933	EUROPEAN HEADQUARTERS Wizards of the Coast, Belgium P.B. 34 2300 Turnhout Belgium +32-14-44-30-44

Visit our website at **www.tsr.com**

PRELUDE

608, Barovian Calendar

They speak my name.

The word echoes across the infinite void that separates my realm from the world of man. Through the darkness of space and the ripples of time, I hear them. To be sure, the vast nothingness between us renders their pale voices indistinct. It muffles their chanting to an insectlike buzz, but my acute senses easily distinguish them.

They call to me.

Of course, they do not pronounce my name properly, those pitiful creatures of flesh and blood. Their mouths are as limited as their minds. My name holds sounds they cannot conceive, let alone voice. But still they attempt in vain to repeat the immortal syllables.

I cannot help but laugh.

They do not understand what they say, do not realize the peril in which they place themselves. By speaking my name, they invite me into their world. If I wished, I could follow the trail of their words across infinity and appear before them. I could amuse myself with the ridiculous sight of their trembling bodies. I could revel in the sweet taste of their horror, slake my thirst on their wretched spirits.

But something gives me pause.

How have they come to know my name? Only my most trusted allies know the appellation given me by my genitor so many millennia ago. If these insignificant creatures had the power and the knowledge, they could use my name to destroy me.

I must listen closely.

Their whispered voices chant more than my name. They speak other words, arcane words. They have woven my name into the fabric of an incantation. They seek to summon me.

Do they truly hope to force me to appear before them? Such incredible presumption must be suitably rewarded.

I will destroy them.

I shall respond to their summons. Crossing time and space is not difficult for one with the wisdom to do so. Long ago I learned the secret of navigating the eddies and currents of the universe.

Leaving behind my own realm, I ascend through layers of existence and sweep across realities unimagined by the pitiful creatures who call me. Dark shapes, some nearly as terrible as I, brush past me. But my business is not with them this day. I follow the sound of the tiny voices, the astral path their words cause to unfold before me like a ribbon of light. Ultimately this radiant trail carries me to a place of both darkness and light. It is far removed from my realm, but not so distant that I have not walked here before.

Is that the answer?

Perhaps that is how they learned my name. The wretched woman Shadowborn, who drove me back to my own realm, knew it. She understood power, and, mere speck though she was, she bent the forces of the cosmos to her will. Her eyes saw things invisible to other mortals, and her faith proved strong enough to resist even my power.

I believe I shall linger in this place after my business with the insects is done. I leave no debt unsettled, and the Shadowborn woman has not yet been repaid for her actions.

But first I must attend to the fools who have called me here.

There are three of them, a trio of insignificant whelps gathered around a magical circle into which they propose to force me. I can feel their spell urging me on. It is but a faint tug, one I will break in a moment. For now, however, it amuses me to appear just as they anticipated. I allow the faintest image of myself, a mere shadow, to take shape in the center of their circle.

To their credit, they do not falter. This trio of living, breathing creatures has faith in the frail spells they have woven. If they knew as much as they think they do, they would cry out in fear. They would beg for a merciful death and plead with me to let matters end there.

But they have not the wisdom.

The first mortal is a slender creature, tall and wiry. The aura of authority surrounding him tells me clearly that his will commands this doomed triad. It is his spell that calls me and his voice that first spoke my name.

"Ebonbane," he intones, his voice rich with foolish confidence and paltry magic. "By all powers dark and unholy, I command thee to enter the circle!"

His presumption astounds me.

To one side of the wizard stands the second of this

company, a well-muscled woman with hair as dark as the abyss. Her eyes, fierce and hard, watch everything as only a warrior's do. In many ways, this female reminds me of the cursed Shadowborn. Her spirit, however, is as dark as that other woman's was bright. Her hand rests on the hilt of her sword, a magical blade about which her dark aura hovers protectively. Clearly this blade was made by the warrior for her own use.

This one puts too much store in steel.

The last is a most curious creature. Short and petitely built, there is more to this mortal than bone and sinew. Her faith is strong. Doubtless this one is the minion of some dark god, a servant whose master even I would not dare cross. But this mortal is an insignificant follower; the power she serves will not even notice when I destroy her. The priestling has set spells upon this place, though their nature eludes me for the moment.

Her faith is nothing.

In a moment, I shall dash their enchantments aside. I will destroy them, one and all, before returning home. But I am curious. I want to know more about these lamentable fools. How did they come by my name? And having found it, how did they learn to give voice to it? To be sure, these wretches pose no threat to me, but do they forebode another menace? Does a power equal to me command them?

It seems unlikely.

Still, they have taken a great many magical precautions. Wards, impotent as they are, hang about this place. They have set runes upon the floor, and the tang of mystical herbs hangs in the air. Evidently this trio understands something of the peril I pose.

The wizard steps forward.

"Ebonbane, creature of darkness, servant of the ultimate evil, heed my call and appear before me," he demands.

Once more I am astounded by the ego of this pitiful mortal. He repeats his command, pouring so much magical power into his words that even I sense them pulling at my heart. Ten centuries ago, when my power was less, I might have been unable to resist his magic. But that time is long past. My laughter fills the air. As it echoes from the walls of this abysmal place, I step fully into their universe.

Then I know the truth.

While the wizard's magical wards alone cannot contain me, only now do I see the entirety of their plan. In coming into their world, I failed to notice the steel prison they had built to entrap me. It tastes of the warrior, whose hand no doubt forged it. The magic of the priest hangs thick upon it, too. The spells of the wizard were nothing more than bait and smoke. They knew I would come to destroy them for speaking my name. The wizard laid himself before me as a decoy.

I have been as foolish as a new spawn!

A dozen spells rise up to contain me in this metal prison. Half of them I cast aside, but the others take hold. I am contained within an object of cold matter.

I should have destroyed them the instant they spoke my name. Had I not waited to investigate, but merely annihilated them, this outrage would not have come to pass. I should have suspected that they used my name with hidden purpose.

I howl with rage.

My spirit hammers at the metal shell in which they have trapped me. I batter it with all my will, but it does not yield. The mortals have done their work well. They have lured me into this world, and no act of mine can free me.

The smirks on their pathetic faces disgust me. They think they have triumphed, but they do not know the extent of my power. To be sure, I am contained.

But I am not controlled.

Abandoning for the moment my effort to escape, I focus my will upon the wizard. This was his plan; I can sense it. He is the one to whom the others look. He shall die first, that they might know the folly of their blind faith.

My will lashes out. Like the kiss of a whip, it snaps against the wizard's spirit and ruptures his heart. For the faintest fraction of an instant, his eyes bulge with fear. The first gasps of a startled scream trickle past his lips but are choked off when I drink of his soul. The taste is weak and unsatisfying, but not utterly without flavor.

As his flesh withers and draws tight to his bones, I turn my attention to the warrior.

Her sword flashes into the air. Though she responds quickly, her steel will not avail her now. My power overwhelms her. I tear her soul apart and drain away her life to satisfy my hunger. There is almost nothing to this one. No faith. No power. Just empty rage.

She falls to the ground before I even notice I have destroyed her.

The priest calls upon her god. Prayers pour forth from her lips, filling the air with words both dark and obscene. It is always the way with such creatures. When the end is upon them, they rely upon a power they have probably never even seen to save them. The priest's futile prayers go unanswered. She erects a pitiful magical barrier around herself, but I hurl it aside and inhale deeply of the living vapors within her.

Hers is the sweetest taste of all.

The room is quiet. The echoes of their screams have faded. In time, my rage cools, and I concede that I have no immediate means of escape. I am destined to remain in the realm of man for a time. Having accepted this fact, I determine to learn something of my surroundings. My prison seems stationary now, though I shall learn to move it about in time.

The moment has come for the dead to rise.

I reach out again with my will, tracing the fading outlines of the wizard and coiling mystical energies around his body. A moment of concentration, then a torrent of darkness surges into his willowy corpse. He cries out in agony, but it is only a remembered sensation. He can no longer feel true pain any more than he can know love or happiness. In death, he shall be a creature of the flesh only; the raw, untapped power of magic and the cosmos shall be denied him. He shall rule legions of minions, but only at my command.

The warrior rises next.

Hers is a physical existence. She lived for the sensual pleasures of the flesh and the thrill of battle. The former I will deny her in death, but of the latter I shall give her more than her share. Let her know the strength of the dead, but never again the heart of the living. She shall feast upon life and move as one with the darkness.

The last of them provides the most satisfaction of all.

It is the priest's magic that holds me within my prison. Thus she shall pay the dearest price for her act of treachery. I permit her to retain her power, but she shall pay homage only to me now. I shall be a god in her mind, and she shall do my work in this world. Her will shall be nothing but a reflection of my own, and her faith shall rest only in me.

Now the time has come for revenge.

ONE

626, Barovian Calendar

Scattered clouds, dark gray against the emptiness of a midnight sky, hovered above the cemetery. Shafts of moonlight lanced between them, falling occasionally upon curling wisps of fog that drifted on faint breezes, like restless spirits eternally searching for a place to rest. Dark shadows crept across headstones and tombs that ranged from days to centuries old.

Deep within one of these pools of darkness, Alexi Shadowborn held his sword with care so as not to let the moonlight catch the brightly polished steel. Pressed flat against the side of an old, almost forgotten crypt, he waited.

Alexi had chosen this position because it offered an unobstructed view of almost the whole graveyard. He could see the wrought-iron fence that bordered the cemetery and the cobblestone path that ran between the vaults. He could see the low patches of flowering shrubs, already losing their blooms at the first touches of the coming winter.

But most importantly he could see the freshly turned earth of three new graves.

There lay the bodies of three merchants. Two days ago, they had operated a small chandlery near the center of Brimstadt. Now, in the wake of a terrible fire, they were dead.

More than that, they were bait.

The young knight could not help but pity the trio of innocents—a man, his wife, and their sixteen-year-old daughter. They had done nothing wrong. They deserved the peace of eternal sleep. And he would make sure they got it.

As the distant church bells peeled the hour of one o'clock, Alexi released a low, quiet sigh. He had been standing here since sunset. Between the chill night air and the hours of inactivity, his muscles were beginning to cramp. He had worked them as best he could, tensing and relaxing them without moving, but it was becoming impossible to remain still any longer. He shifted his weight, careful to avoid making too much noise in his chain mail. His limbs complained but were thankful for the activity.

Almost as soon as he had begun to move, however, Alexi froze. Something new had come into sight, something that caused the blood in his veins to run colder than the October breezes around him.

The grave robbers had come.

It was a revolting enterprise, grave robbing. Alexi had difficulty understanding what drove a man to violate another's final resting place. How could the desire for a gold pocket watch or an emerald ring be strong enough to commit one of the church's ultimate sins? Perhaps, he considered, he might think differently had he been born into the lower classes. He had never wanted for anything, never known hunger or lacked coal on a winter's night. But try as he might, he could not comprehend the heinous act.

For the past month, these villains had preyed upon the cemeteries of Brimstadt, violating the sacred graves of the newly dead. They had torn open a dozen caskets, stealing not only valuables laid to rest with the dead but the bodies as well.

Of course, the constabulary had taken steps to thwart them, but the only result had been two more graves for the fiends to loot. After that, Brimstadt's mayor took the problem to Lord Vincent, Alexi's father and the master of these lands. That had been two days ago, the same day of the fire at the chandlery.

The knight's fingers tightened on his sword hilt as he watched the dark shapes move from headstone to headstone. He would wait a little longer, allowing them to make their guilt evident, before striking. They would die quickly, convicted by their own actions. And the name of Shadowborn would once more be praised by the people of Avonleigh.

Alexi did not undertake this mission to attain any measure of personal glory or fame. For the past two years, since being knighted on his sixteenth birthday, he had fought his battles for a nobler purpose. He aspired to become a champion of Belenus, the sun god, and had persevered to prove himself worthy. His blade had won him the respect of friend and foe alike. Already he had taken the oaths of fealty and piety that bound him for life to the service of Belenus. Only one step remained.

In one week's time, the High Mother of the church would celebrate Alexi's Rite of Ascension. During the ritual, Alexi would take his place among the elite Knights of the Circle, and Belenus would accept Alexi as one of his holy paladins.

Paladin. The word rang sweet in Alexi's ears. He

would become an instrument of Belenus, charged with protecting the Great Kingdom in his name. For a warrior, there was no higher calling. He answered it willingly, as his mother had before him.

As a paladin, he would be called upon to face and defeat the enemies of the church—as he was tonight. He watched the shadowy shapes of the grave robbers gather around the resting places of the chandlers. He counted four vandals. They seemed quick, but they moved with an odd, rolling gait.

If they were defenseless, he would give them a chance to offer up final prayers before carrying out the only sentence Belenus allowed for grave robbing. If they were armed, they might put up a good fight—the sort of battle his mother, the renowned Kateri Shadowborn, was said to have taken in stride.

Alexi wondered whether she would be proud of him. He had done all he could to pattern his life after hers. He had studied sword fighting extensively, and yet he found time to read the scriptures, just as she had. There was not a single passage in *The Book of Radiance* that he could not quote verbatim. He wished he could have known Kateri Shadowborn. He wished she had lived long enough to see the infant she bore grow to manhood.

Three of the grave robbers commenced clawing at the freshly turned soil. They made no use of shovels or picks, but tore up great blocks of earth with their bare hands. As grave robbers went, Alexi thought, these seemed remarkably unprepared.

The fourth intruder crouched low, like a wild animal, and twisted his head back and forth. He appeared to be acting as a lookout, but the snorting and sniffling sounds he made reminded Alexi of a slavering dog trying to catch a scent. What manner of grave robbers had he come across?

As if in answer to Alexi's question, the clouds parted for a fraction of a second, and a shaft of pale amber light fell upon the quartet. Alexi shuddered.

These were no mere grave robbers.

Although once they might have been men, the creatures digging at the soil could claim that status no more. Their flesh, gray and mottled like half-cured leather, stretched tightly across bones that seemed unnaturally sharp and angular. Their mouths were elongated, devoid of lips and filled with teeth that reminded Alexi of a viper's fangs. Long, wicked claws—talons, really—topped slender, skeletal fingers. Their eyes were black like those of a snake, but bloated and swollen. Gruesome tattoos, horned skulls the color of fresh blood, adorned their foreheads.

Alexi realized that he stood in the presence of the living dead. Clearly these were ghouls—cannibalistic creatures who hungered eternally for the flesh of the newly deceased. In two years of campaigning, he had never faced such horrors. Though he knew that these creatures were themselves victims, slain by some master of the dark arts and then brought back to serve his unholy needs, he could not help recoiling in disgust. A gasp that was half fear and half revulsion escaped his lips.

At that faint sound, the sentinel's head snapped around. His baleful gaze fell upon Alexi and a terrible howl shattered the crisp autumn air. The four creatures sprang forward at once, like jackals attacking a wounded animal. In an impossibly short time they had covered the thirty yards that separated them from the no longer hidden Alexi.

The sentinel had started from a few yards closer than his foul companions, enabling him to reach the knight first. This cost him his life—or what remained of it. As the creature crashed down upon Alexi, the would-be paladin forced his blade through its ribs with a sickening grinding, cracking sound. The monster twitched spasmodically and released an ear-piercing shriek.

Alexi rolled to the side, deflecting as much of the beast's momentum as he could. Even after impaling itself on his blade, however, the ghoul struck with enough force to knock the knight off-balance. Only the fact that he was braced against the side of the crumbling mausoleum kept Alexi from falling.

As he kicked the now-inanimate body from his sword, the other three ghouls reached him. They lashed out, scraping their talons across the gray metal of his breastplate, but failed to find any exposed flesh.

Knowing that he couldn't allow them to pin him against the wall, Alexi ducked his head low and drove forward with his shoulder. He struck one ghoul in the abdomen and forced his way past the fell creature. The blow would have knocked the wind out of a living opponent, but Alexi knew all too well that these creatures no longer needed air to survive. Still, the impact proved great enough to spin the creature halfway around and cause it to teeter.

As soon as he was clear of the horrid trio, the knight whirled about. His blade swept through the air, flashing as it cleaved a shaft of moonlight, and bit deeply into the neck of the off-balance ghoul. The creature's eyes bulged, but quickly lost any sense of animation that might have remained in them. By the time his slavering companions neared, the decapitated body had already struck the ground.

With half his enemies dispatched, Alexi quickly assessed his situation. He was still in great danger. He knew, from the tales of other knights, that even a single ghoul made a formidable enemy. He held his blade steady, keeping its point aimed at the space between the two animated corpses. No matter which one struck at him first, he would be able to defend himself.

The two creatures came at him in unison.

Alexi stepped to the right and lunged forward. His blade pierced the body of a ghoul, spilling black ichor onto the ground. The creature thrashed about wildly in an attempt to escape the deadly steel but managed only to wound itself further. Alexi withdrew his blade with a vicious lateral sweep, tearing a great gash in the creature's gray-green flank, and the ghoul fell to the ground with a howl of pain. Seconds later, it grew still.

The remaining ghoul showed no sign of fear at the demise of its three companions. As Alexi finished dispatching its ally, the last surviving beast raked its filthy talons across his face. The blow lacked any real force, but the wounds burned intensely. Alexi clenched his teeth in pain and tasted blood at the corner of his mouth.

Before his heart had beaten twice more, the knight realized his peril. A deathly stiffness crept through his body, spreading outward from the lacerations on his cheek. He had only seconds before the ghoul's paralytic poison would leave him defenseless.

Panic threatened to overwhelm him, but the young knight fought it back. If he was going to survive, he would have to keep calm and act quickly.

The ghastly creature reached out for him, seeming to sense that victory lay nearly in its grasp. Alexi tried to bring his sword into play, but the stiffness in his right arm proved too great to overcome. Even as the hilt slipped free of his numb fingers, his left hand drew a long, sharply pointed dagger from his belt.

The ghoul grabbed him in its powerful hands and opened its mouth wide. Needlelike teeth gleamed yellow in the darkness as the creature leaned toward his throat. Alexi saw that the red tattoo on the beast's forehead seemed to glow as if it were aflame.

At that moment, Alexi struck. With the last of his strength, he brought the dagger up, driving the blade through the ghoul's throat and up into its brain. The light drained from the death's head until it looked like a black brand.

The creature shuddered. Its grip loosened, and gravity drew it down to crash on the cold earth.

Alexi Shadowborn was not far behind.

The ghoul's toxin had spread throughout his body now, making even the slightest movement almost impossible. Breathing became unthinkably difficult, and even the beating of his heart was a taxing burden.

Without warning, a terrible pain swept through his body. Even in Alexi's state of virtual paralysis, its intensity forced him to spasm and convulse. Images of death and burial flooded his mind—the ghouls' human deaths, before their corruption. He experienced the anguish of their demises, the suffocating closeness of a casket, the endless cold of the grave's eternal night.

And then a new sensation filled his spirit. It began as a nagging twinge in his gut, but grew quickly into an agonizing hunger. Alexi retched as the taste of rotting carrion filled his mouth. For a brief second, the hunger slackened, only to return even greater than before. Alexi realized that he was vicariously experiencing the ghouls' endless curse of feasting on human corpses.

Then came a series of stabbing pains. One after another, he felt the sting of his own blade as it laid each of the dark creatures to rest.

And then it was over.

He lay still on the cold earth as a chill autumn wind swept through the cemetery. He tried to close his eyes, but found that the toxin made even that simple task impossible. He was utterly helpless now. If any other ghouls lurked in the cemetery, he was theirs for the taking.

As the minutes crawled past, he prayed to Belenus for protection. In some corner of his mind, he wished that the ghoul's toxin also caused unconsciousness. He would lie here now for hours before the venom either receded from his blood or killed him. And all that time he would be fully aware.

Alexi watched the yellow face of Brigit, the moon goddess, trace its nightly arc across the sky. From time to time he thought he saw a dark shape moving about in the graveyard. It was little more than a sensation, something perceived at the very edge of his vision. He strained to redirect his gaze to confirm or allay his suspicions. Perhaps, he hoped desperately, the moonlight was merely playing tricks on his vulnerable imagination.

But when he heard the snapping of a twig and the rustling of leaves, he knew he was not alone.

TWO

Alexi sat up sharply, throwing off his covers and filling his lungs with a sharp gasp. His heart hammered so loudly that it roared in his ears.

It took him several seconds to recognize the familiar sights of his bedroom. He was home, safe inside Shadowfast, his ordeal in the graveyard almost a week past.

His shoulders sagging in relief, he dabbed rivulets of sweat from his brow with the edges of his bedspread. With a shaking hand, he poured himself a glass of water from the crystal pitcher at his bedside. He sipped it slowly, calming himself with a series of deep breaths.

For as long as Alexi could remember, he had been troubled by nightmares. Usually they involved vague fears and shapeless dangers that he could not recall clearly upon waking. Since his battle in the graveyard, however, Alexi's nocturnal enemies had worn the unmistakable faces of the living dead. Night after night, ravenous ghouls loomed over him as he lay sprawled in the dirt, unable to defend himself. Worse yet were the dreams in which he became one of them.

Alexi shuddered at the memory of his encounter with the ghouls. Brigit's reign had never seemed so long as it did while he lay helpless on the cold ground, a hostage to the terrors of his imagination. He never learned who, or what, had hidden in the shadows. By the time the toxin had worn off, his mysterious companion was gone.

Setting down the half-drained glass, Alexi climbed out of bed. His sweat-soaked nightshirt stuck to his body. He shook the soft cotton fabric loose as he walked to the bell cord and rang for breakfast.

From an intricately carved cedar chest he withdrew black hose, a flowing yellow chemise, and a wasp-waisted black doublet. He dressed pensively, his mind still occupied by the ghouls.

Though the grave robbers had been Alexi's first encounter with the living dead, he knew other knights who had faced them in combat. Alexi had heard about ghouls' ability to paralyze their opponents. When their toxin had taken effect, he at least had known what was happening to him.

But he had not been prepared for the horror of vicariously experiencing their deaths and ghoulish existences. None of his comrades-in-arms had ever spoken of such an affliction in the wake of a battle with the creatures. And unlike the toxin, which had worn off in hours, this legacy of the ghouls had continued for nearly a week. Would it torment him forever?

As Alexi laced up his sleeves, he resolved to ask Dasmaria about the experience the next time he had an opportunity. She had faced ghouls in battle before. As his friend, she might be more likely to reveal truths that others would not.

A sharp rapping sounded on the door.

Alexi shook off the dark thoughts that crowded his mind. "Good morning, Ferran," he said as his young squire entered with his breakfast, a generous combination of fruits, berries, and freshly baked rolls.

"I was beginning to think you would never wake up." Ferran placed the tray on Alexi's writing desk.

Alexi glanced up from his laces. "Not all knights would countenance such insolence from their squires," he chided gently. Picking up a silver brush, he watched Ferran in the mirror as he smoothed his hair.

"Not all squires serve their brothers." Ferran stole a plump grape from the tray and popped it into his mouth. "And so long as you let me get away with it, I intend to exercise my privileges as a younger sibling."

The knight rolled his eyes, then turned to regard his brother. The youth reminded Alexi of himself a few short years ago, at least in temperament. In appearance, Ferran shared Alexi's shoulder-length blond hair and pale gray eyes, but the physical resemblance ended there. Ferran was more angular than the muscular knight, his lithe body showing the clean lines of an acrobat instead of the intimidating bulk of a warrior. It was little wonder that young Ferran favored the bow over the sword.

Just as his mother does, Alexi thought. Ferran follows his mother's path, as I follow mine. Though Alexi and Ferran had been raised as brothers, in truth they were only cousins. Alexi's aunt and uncle had adopted him when his real mother, Kateri Shadowborn, could not raise him because she was fighting in the Heretical Wars—the wars that had killed her. Alexi had no memory of his birth mother, and all he knew of his real father was that he, like Kateri, had been a soldier.

Vincent and Victoria Shadowborn were the only parents Alexi had ever known, and they had given him all the love and attention they showed their other two children. Alexi thought of them as his real mother and father, and of his cousins as his true brother and sister, and he felt perfectly natural in doing so. Yet as the day of his Ascension ceremony drew closer, he found himself increasingly identifying with the woman who had given him life.

Alexi returned the brush to its place beside the washbasin and reached for his leather belt and scabbard. As usual, Ferran beat him to it. Without comment, the young squire wrapped the thick black band around Alexi's waist.

"You're becoming a good squire," Alexi said. He resisted the impulse to reach out and tousle his brother's hair. Ferran was too mature for such a gesture. But this morning Alexi felt old, as if the span of years between him and Ferran had doubled. As if his encounter with the ghouls had aged him.

Alexi sat down to break his fast as Ferran fetched a pair of calf-high boots. Once Alexi donned them, the squire buffed the leather with a soft cloth until they shone like black mirrors. All the while, Ferran chattered on in a seemingly endless array of subjects, but Alexi was still too preoccupied with ghoulish thoughts to offer much more than an occasional comment.

As the clock in his room chimed nine, Alexi emerged from his bedroom, with Ferran close behind.

As he stepped on the burgundy carpet that ran along the hall outside his room, a flash of motion sprang toward Alexi. He barely had time to brace himself for the impact when the so-called Terror of Shadowfast hurled itself at him. Still, the reflexes of a warrior proved useful even when his sword lay untouched in its scabbard. He caught the blur in his arms and swept it into an upward spiral.

"Good morning!" shouted a high-pitched voiced.

"Good morning, Aurora," said Alexi with a smile. He hugged his sister tightly and kissed her on both round cheeks. She squeezed him back, wrapping her pudgy arms around his neck.

Alexi lowered Aurora to the floor and wiped away the remnants of her sloppy kisses with the back of his sleeve. "How are you today?"

"Okay," said the child with a smile, "but I think you're in trouble!"

"Why is that?" he asked as they reached the top of a wide stairway. As they descended it, Aurora leapt onto the banister and slid down its long, graceful curve. Alexi shook his head, unable to guess how many times their parents had told her not to do that.

"Mom and Dad are waiting for you in the li-berry."

"It's pronounced 'library,' " Alexi called after her as the little girl dropped off the banister and dashed down the hall.

By the time he reached the library doors, Aurora was already inside. She tried to climb into her mother's lap, but Lady Victoria stopped her with a curt gesture. The round-faced girl pushed out a pouting lip, but finally tossed herself on a plush pillow near the hearth.

"Good morning, Mother," said Alexi. "And to you, Father." The musty smell of books bade Alexi its own welcome. The library had always been one of his favorite places, offering a wealth of lore about the Great Kingdom, the province of Avonleigh, the Shadowborn family, or any other subject he wished to study. It was here that he had studied the scriptures that helped guide him toward paladinhood.

Victoria Shadowborn smiled and stood, unfolding her wispy form like an elegant spider. She was no beauty, having always been tall and gangly, but she was graceful and in her younger days a champion archer. The velvet gown she wore fit snugly at her waist and was shaped to enhance a figure that could at best be described as boyish. Her hair, slightly darker than that of her children, formed amber curls woven into an ornate silver tiara.

After embracing Alexi in a tight hug, she stepped away from her oldest son. With gliding steps she slipped over to the mantel and reached for a long, slender mahogany case. Lifting it smoothly, she carried it to where her son was seated and placed it on the table before him. The gold lock glowed warmly in the firelight.

Alexi cocked his head to one side as he studied the object. He had never seen this particular case before and was taken by its elegance. Golden braces held the dark wood firmly in place at the corners; a gleaming sunburst latch sealed it securely in the front. But nothing indicated what the box might contain or where it had come from.

Ferran leaned forward alertly. His eyes sparkled as they always did when presented with a mystery, large or small. Alexi had to smile at the eagerness in his brother's face. Everyone could see that it was all the squire could do to keep from grabbing for the box himself.

"This is for you," said his mother in a strangely reverent voice. "Your father and I have kept it to ourselves for a good many years, waiting until the time seemed right to make you a gift of it. With your Ascension ceremony scheduled for tomorrow, I can't imagine a better time."

Lord Vincent produced a small golden key from his pocket. It bore the radiant candle icon that had been the mark of the Shadowborn family for generations. He smiled fondly at his eldest son and extended a broad, muscular hand. Light from the fire danced brightly on the key. As Alexi reached out to accept it, Lord Vincent seemed to hesitate. A distant look, which carried with it the impression of almost forgotten memories, came into his eyes.

"I recall a day in autumn when you were Aurora's age," said Alexi's father. His daughter smiled brightly at the mention of her name in the hope that he was beginning a story about her. She stirred on her overstuffed pillow, stroking the golden cat that had found its way into her lap. "The first snow of autumn had fallen, and we were taking a walk in the woods south of here. When we came upon the family crypt, you asked what it was."

"I remember," said Alexi. It was an important day in his life, but he didn't realize that his father had taken any notice of it.

"Have I been there?" asked Aurora. He mother hushed her, and Lord Shadowborn went on with his tale.

"I tried to explain to you that your ancestors slept there when they had grown tired of living. You wanted to see them. I don't think you really understood what I meant."

Alexi chuckled. "No, I guess I didn't."

"We went inside, and you made me read you the names on all the vaults. It must have taken an hour. I had to tell you who each person was and what kind of life he or she had led. When we came to the chamber that bore your mother's name, you made me stop."

"It was . . . different," said Alexi, recalling the pull he'd sensed upon seeing Kateri Shadowborn's name etched in the cold marble. "There was something about it."

"So you said," Lord Vincent responded. "That day

marked the first time I ever told you about your real mother and her part in the Heretical Wars."

"But not the last," Alexi said. From that day on, tales of Kateri Shadowborn, her travels, and her war against evil had been regular bedtime fare for Alexi. Before long, the young boy had decided that he himself would become a holy warrior, a paladin, just like his mother had.

It was this early determination, no doubt, that resulted in Alexi being one of the youngest candidates ever to enter the service of Belenus. Tomorrow, when he underwent the ritual of Ascension, he would become the second youngest paladin ever to join the holy order of the Circle, an achievement bested only by his mother.

"I wish I could have known her," said Alexi softly.

"She visited you as often as she could," said Lady Victoria, the firelight playing across the angles of her face. "But the Great Kingdom needed her more. When the war ended, she hoped to spend more time with you. First, however, she had some mysterious mission to complete. She stopped here on her way south to say good-bye. You were about two at the time. We never saw her again."

"At least, not until they brought her body home for burial," amended Lord Vincent. A somber silence spread like a shroud across the room. Before the mood became overpowering, however, Aurora's voice danced into the air.

"Can Alexi open his present now?"

Lady Victoria smiled. "She's right, Vincent. Let's not have our celebration turn into a wake."

Vincent nodded, moving toward a small table. Alexi noticed for the first time that it held a bottle of deep red wine and several glasses. His father poured wine for each member of his family. Even Aurora received a small splash in a gleaming crystal glass, something that made her eyes sparkle.

The master of Shadowfast raised his glass. It flashed in the light of the fire. "A toast," he proclaimed. The others lifted their glasses as well. "To Alexi Shadowborn, my eldest son, who shall become the second of our family to wear the armor of a paladin and ride under the standard of the Circle. May he bring hope to all the people of the Shadowlands and despair to all the enemies of the Great Kingdom. Belenus willing, his name shall be known and his songs sung in all the thirteen provinces."

Alexi's heart swelled as his family voiced their approval of Lord Vincent's sentiments. He sipped his wine, thanking Belenus for delivering him into the care of such a supportive family. He would do his best to make them proud.

"Yuck!" cried Aurora. "I don't like this stuff!" She held her glass at arm's length and regarded it with a disapproving eye. She turned an accusing glare on Ferran. "You said it was like grape juice!"

As laughter filled the room, Lord Vincent tossed the golden key into the air. It tumbled twice, flashing brightly in the firelight, before Alexi caught it.

He turned it over, admiring the elegance of its insignia, then slipped it into the lock. There followed a faint scraping noise, a sharp click, and the snap of the lock popping open. Alexi slipped the lock from the latch and placed it carefully on the table. Like the key, it was a work of art and deserved delicate treatment.

The lid of the case swung open easily. Inside, resting on a bed of black velvet, lay a gleaming sword. Its slender blade was flawless and untarnished, decorated with a delicate inscription of gently brushed characters. Light seemed to pool up and run along it like quicksilver, trickling into every crevice of the ethereal traces engraved upon it.

"This was my sister's sword," said Lady Victoria. "It even has its own name: Corona."

Corona. The word resonated through Alexi, a warmth that started in his heart and spread like the rays of Belenus.

With reverence, he lifted the weapon from its case. He slipped his fingers into the exquisite pommel, which was in the shape of a striking hawk, and nodded in appreciation. Not merely beautiful, the sword was also a masterpiece of design. It seemed to weigh nothing in his hand. As he shifted it back and forth, it appeared to move almost before he willed it to do so.

Aurora pushed her way past Ferran and tilted her head to read the inscription on the blade. "Those aren't real words," she declared.

"Sure they are," said Ferran, "but they're in the Holy Script, just like the *Libram of Belenus.* Alexi can read it, can't you?"

Alexi bent forward over the blade. As he read the runes, which were indeed in the language of Belenus himself, he translated them for his family. " 'Blazing fire in the east, shining steel from the west, luminous valor from the north, radiant glory in the south.' "

"What's that mean?" demanded Aurora.

"The words tell the story of the sword's making, dear," said Lady Victoria. "Corona was forged for your aunt Kateri by the armorers of the Eastern Kingdom. They used special ore brought by traders from Avonleigh, which they call the Western Lands—that's the fire from the east and the steel from the west. They presented the blade to Kateri as a reward for one of her adventures in their land. My sister took it with her when she rode from the north to the south in order to join in the great crusades against the heretics of the Southern Empire."

As Lady Victoria spoke, Alexi gently swept the sword from side to side, testing its balance and flexibility. Only the weaponsmiths of the east could make blades this light and responsive. The sword fairly danced through the air.

"No one has worn this blade in over fifteen years," said Lord Vincent. "Not since Kateri died with it in her hand." He turned to Alexi. "We have kept Corona for you these many years. Now that you are about to take your place in the Circle, we thought the time had come for you to carry it."

The full magnitude of the gift rippled through Alexi. He held the very weapon that Kateri Shadowborn had brandished in countless battles. Corona, the enemy of all things dark and evil. Bards sang nearly as many ballads about the legendary "blazing sword" as about the paladin who had wielded it.

And now the blade belonged to him. "I'll do my best to live up to it," said Alexi.

"Is it really magical?" asked Ferran. Like Alexi, he had grown up hearing the stories of Kateri Shadowborn charging into battle with the radiant Corona held high.

"Unfortunately, I myself have never seen any sign of magic," said Lord Vincent. "I think the stories of 'the blazing sword' may be slightly exaggerated."

"Magic or not," said Alexi, "I've never held better."

"And I daresay that it's never been held by better," said Lady Victoria. She stepped forward and wrapped

Alexi in a warm hug. "Congratulations, my son," she said. "Great things lie ahead for you."

And tomorrow, Alexi thought, on the day of his Ascension, they would begin.

THREE

The darkness closed in on him from all sides. To the left and right, ahead and behind, even above and below, it was a palpable barrier that threatened to crush the life from him. Alexi released an involuntary cry of helpless despair.

Something surged forward from the darkness, withdrawing from his sight the moment it became visible. He had the faintest impression of a humanoid shape, one with eyes that burned a malevolent scarlet. The sickly sweet odor of corruption assaulted his nostrils, revealing at once the nature of his unseen enemies.

Ghouls.

A sharp pain forced a choked gasp from his throat. Keen talons slashed out from the endless night to taste the soft flesh at the back of his neck. He whirled quickly about, feeling for the wound but finding no laceration or trace of blood. Despite this evidence to the contrary, he knew that the pain had been real.

Dim shadows moved against the eternal blackness in which he stood. Their near-invisibility made him doubt his own senses.

But he knew they were there, just as he knew that the

lingering spirit of every evil thing he had ever vanquished was with them. Just beyond his vision, Alexi could feel them circling about. If he let his guard down, even for a moment, those terrible creatures would attack.

"Why can't you rest?" he cried. "I put you in your graves! One and all you should dwell in the Kingdom of Arawn. Go to him! Go to the master of the dead and leave me in peace!"

The endless abyss of darkness offered no surface to reflect his words. But while his own voice did not echo back, his cries did not go unanswered. Distant, booming laughter broke through the darkness. Ringing like the thunder of an approaching storm, it washed over Alexi and chilled his heart.

He shuffled slowly across the blackness beneath him, muscles tensed in anticipation. He kept his hands out, fists tightly balled, ready to fend off anything that might charge at him. He had heard this distant laughter before, but never had the master of this dark place shown himself.

Perhaps tonight would be the night.

There was a change in the darkness. Something seemed to trouble the restless spirits. Alexi knew that a presence lingered here that had never walked these nightmare lands before.

He whirled about.

A dark figure, perhaps nothing more than an extension of the blackness itself, stood before him. He could not discern it clearly, for its indistinct edges seemed to dissipate even as he looked upon them. Alexi's mind formed the impression of a man draped in nothing but black robes. Like the ghouls, the figure was a patch of darkness against the sea of nothing that surrounded Alexi.

The warrior remembered the night in the cemetery, when he had seen some mysterious shape moving at the edge of his vision. Was this his unknown visitor?

"Who are you?" he cried.

The rippling shape made no reply. It raised a slender arm, folds of dark robes shifting like soundless waves on a midnight sea, and pointed a gnarled, gray finger at Alexi.

As the mysterious stranger made this simple gesture, Alexi's worst fears were realized. The dark shapes of the ghouls, drained of all color in this landscape of gray and black, moved forward. Behind them, old enemies who had fallen before Alexi's blade closed in. Unarmored and weaponless, the knight helplessly waited for his former opponents to repay him for their deaths.

Despair seized him. Alexi sensed that he had been here before, many times, and that this was how the struggle always ended—with his death.

Suddenly he felt a shift in the forces surrounding him. The hooded figure, he realized, was not pointing him out to his enemies. Instead, it was attempting to direct Alexi's attention to something else. He lowered his gaze, following the direction of the figure's outstretched finger.

Corona.

Alexi wore the gleaming sword and its scabbard at his waist. He blinked in disbelief. Never before had he been able to carry a weapon into his final confrontation with the dark remnants of his enemies.

The black shades surged forward.

First came the quartet of ghouls, his most recent enemy. A dozen other creatures, all of them evil to the core, appeared behind them, their images less vivid.

Alexi reached for Corona. The instant the weapon cleared the scabbard, a brilliant flash tore through the landscape of endless black. Light fanned out from the radiant blade in all directions, driving back the evil essences.

Faith swept through Alexi. He could triumph over these fell creatures in this nightmare realm just as he had in life. Through the sword Corona, Belenus would aid him.

He swept the blade at his nearest enemy. As it struck the ghoul, a loud crash sounded.

With a start, Alexi awoke.

He lay safe in his bed. Eyes blinking, he scanned the room. The mirror, his night table, everything was in its proper place.

Except the crystal pitcher. With a wave of regret, Alexi saw it lying smashed on the floor. He must have knocked it over during his nightmare.

He closed his eyes in frustration. He'd hoped that he could awake on the morning of his Ascension, at least, with no disturbing dreams. That somehow the sanctity of this day would keep the darkness at bay.

This dream *had* been different, however. Corona had enabled him to vanquish his enemies. Perhaps its presence signified that he had conquered the nightmares as well. Perhaps today, when Belenus accepted him as one of his holy champions, the heaviness that hung over his spirit would be lifted.

Alexi lit a candle and carefully slipped out from under his bedding to clean up the broken crystal. When he finished, he stepped across the room and opened the shutters.

Instead of the rolling expanse of Shadowfast bathed in Brigit's light, there was only darkness. And a face.

Alexi recoiled in horror. It was so twisted and evil a visage that his heart froze. In a fraction of a second, it vanished.

Liquid darkness poured into the room through the open window. Alexi tried to step back but discovered that the thick, viscous liquid had already flowed around his ankles. Like amber clinging to the legs of an unwary insect, it held him fast.

He cried out as the incredibly cold blackness rose around his body. Gritting his teeth in agony, he felt it pass his knees. By the time it swirled around his waist, he had lost all sensation in his feet.

As it reached his chest, his heartbeat slowed.

In a last attempt to free himself, he thrashed back and forth frantically. But his efforts proved futile. The all-powerful evil of the night had won. Alexi's triumph in his dream had been nothing more than a fleeting illusion.

In the seconds before the darkness rose above his mouth, Alexi's fear overcame him. He screamed in unbridled terror, forgetting the courage and valor that was the heart of a paladin.

And again he was in his bed.

Alexi sat up with a jolt, his heart pounding hard enough to explode. He glanced wildly about his room, unable to believe its perfectly mundane state.

His breathing slowed as he realized what had happened. He'd merely had another nightmare. Or, more accurately, a nightmare within a nightmare. When he thought he woke up, he'd actually still been dreaming.

As a cold autumn breeze drifted through the open window, he reached shaking hands toward the pitcher of water on his night table. When his fingers touched nothing but air, he looked down.

And saw the shards of smashed crystal littering the floor.

FOUR

Alexi raised his head as the last words of his whispered prayers passed his lips. He rose from his knees, making a circle with two extended fingers to end his entreaty to Belenus. His muscular form, made even more impressive by the gleaming ornamental plate armor that he wore, seemed to fill the entire chapel.

His supplications were simple and direct. He prayed for guidance; he prayed for direction; he prayed for the blessing of his god. In just one more hour, the eye of Belenus would reach its zenith in the sky. At that moment, the roof of the great temple would open, and he would be officially accepted into the Circle. He would become a paladin.

And Alexi would prove himself worthy of the honor. He would do the work of Belenus no matter where it took him, and wield Corona in the name of his god.

Even as he imagined the life upon which he was about to embark, Alexi heard someone else enter the chapel. He turned slowly, expecting to see a member of the sisterhood who tended the Great Temple. To his surprise, however, the warrior found himself facing the silhouette of another figure in armor nearly as grand as his own. The black shape of a diving hawk adorned a red surcoat. He recognized the armor immediately.

"Dasmaria!" Alexi's face broke into a smile.

At the mention of her name, the other knight lifted her helmet. The light of a dozen votive candles splashed the silver highlights in her short-cropped locks. As the helmet came completely clear, a single long coil of inky black hair fell free, draping itself across her shoulder like the tail of a lounging panther.

From nearly the first moment he'd seen her, Dasmaria's features had captured his attention. They were fine and angular, as if set into place by an artist whose eye for beauty was matched only by a keen sense of precision. Her piercing eyes glowed so darkly that they looked like opals against the rich olive complexion of her skin. She was a child of the southern provinces, where the gaze of Belenus was hot and unyielding.

Dasmaria stepped toward him and hesitantly leaned forward to plant a light kiss on his cheek.

At the unexpected show of affection, Alexi's pulse quickened. He caught her gaze. "Did that mean what I hope it does?"

She shook her head. "It's for luck," she said, stepping back. "That's all. I need more time to think about . . . the rest. You understand?"

His spirit deflated a little. After years of campaigning with Dasmaria, Alexi had grown to feel more than friendship for her. When he admitted his feelings two weeks ago, the news had taken Dasmaria by surprise. Alexi had never seen the practiced warrior flustered until that moment, when she'd stammered that she needed a chance to examine her own feelings.

He grazed her cheek with his fingertips. "Take all the time you need, Das. I'm in no rush."

She broke off their gaze, turning to set her helmet on a nearby pew. "So—" she cleared her throat—"today's the day." She turned back to him and smiled. Her teeth were bright against her dark lips. "You've worked hard for this, Alexi. I know you'll make everyone in the Shadowlands proud of you."

"As will you," he said. "The next opening in the Circle is yours."

"I hope so." Her face clouded. "I only hope it won't be your place I'm taking."

Alexi knew exactly what she meant but was reluctant to pursue this line of conversation. The Circle comprised thirteen members, one for each province of the Great Kingdom. Alexi would take the place of Sir Kendall, who had fallen in battle just over a month before. If there was a warrior Alexi had admired as much as he did Kateri Shadowborn, it was Sir Kendall. His death was a loss that the Great Kingdom would long remember.

"I'm too stubborn for that," he said.

Dasmaria rolled her eyes. "I'm surprised you aren't dead already," she said. "Sometimes I wish you would take a few minutes to think before charging into battle."

"And sometimes I wish you'd stop planning strategies into the ground. Occasionally you have to put your faith in steel."

Dasmaria raised her hands in a gesture of truce. They could continue this debate for hours, she insisting that he was reckless and took far too many chances, and he complaining that she took an interminable amount of time to decide upon the perfect strategy for any given encounter. While Dasmaria would never admit it, Alexi felt certain it was this dichotomy that had drawn them to each other as comrades-in-arms. When they combined their talents on the field of battle, few enemies could stand against them.

"I have to go," she said. "The pre-Ascension service starts in a few minutes. But I wanted to see you first, to let you know how proud I am of you."

He reached for her hands. "Thank you," he said. "I'll see you after the ceremony?"

She nodded, then stepped away and retrieved her helmet. As Alexi watched her walk out of the chapel, he imagined their future. With Dasmaria by his side, he could conquer anything—even his nightmares.

In the distance, a bell tolled. It struck eleven times, reminding Alexi that he was but one hour away from becoming a paladin. As the last resonances of those heavy carillons faded toward silence, Alexi knelt once again to complete his final series of prayers.

"May my lord Belenus find his servant Alexi Shadowborn worthy to serve as one of his holy champions . . ." he began. As he said the words, a shadow crept into his heart.

Nerves, he thought, and began again.

When the sun had nearly reached its zenith, Alexi rose. At the door of the chapel, he paused and took a deep breath. The next hour would define the rest of his life.

He was ready.

Without so much as a backward glance, he strode into the bright sunlight. As he walked across the open courtyard toward the great domed cathedral beyond, he noticed from the corner of his eye a dark shape at one of the cathedral's narrow windows. A second glance revealed nothing unusual about the opening, although he felt certain that only a second before he had seen a dark, hooded figure standing just beyond the sun's rays.

More nerves, Alexi thought.

* * * * *

The Ascension ritual had actually begun at dawn. As the Eye of Belenus first appeared in the sky, the High Mother had begun to pray on Alexi's behalf. One by one, in an order dictated by their position within the church hierarchy, the other sisters who served the cathedral joined her. This was a private time for the sisterhood from which even the paladin candidate was excluded.

Several hours later, other worshipers arrived in the cathedral. Present members of the Circle, knights of the Great Kingdom, nobles of the provinces, and family members of the candidate all gathered to invoke the blessing of Belenus.

With the sun a scant fifteen minutes from its zenith, the two youngest members of the sisterhood, neither of whom were more than ten years of age, opened the great golden doors of the cathedral. They were dressed in sparkling golden gowns and carried bouquets of yellow and white flowers. On any other occasion, they would have drawn the attention of every eye.

But today did not belong to them.

Alexi stepped into view, his ornamental armor gleaming brightly in the light of the countless candles illuminating the inside of the dark temple. For the first time, he saw the crowd that had come to celebrate his Ascension. The sight fairly took his breath away.

At the far end of the temple, beneath a vast bronze dome, sat the bier upon which Sir Kendall's body lay. He was clad in burnished armor that was even more ornate and brightly polished than Alexi's. Phantom, the great sword that he had wielded in battle, lay atop his body. The blade was broken, a mark of the blow that had ended his life. Kendall's standard, a gleaming golden starburst on a black background, hung behind his body; thirteen lamps, each tinted a different color, hung above the fallen hero. Only twelve of them were lighted.

Just in front of this somber scene stood twelve knights, nine male and three female, in fine armor. Their own distinctive standards hung behind them. These were the surviving paladins of the Circle, the men and women who waited to welcome Alexi into their order. There were no more beloved champions anywhere in the Great Kingdom. Alexi knew each by reputation, although he had met only three of them. The idea that they all gathered here in his honor humbled him.

To the side of the ring of paladins stood Ferran, Alexi's squire. In his arms, he held the folded standard that would soon fly beside those of the other knights.

A great mass of men and women—no fewer than five hundred, all told—filled the pews of the cathedral. These were the most important members of the gentry and nobility, gathered from around the Shadowlands to see one of their own undergo the Rite of Ascension. They wore their finest clothing—silks and satin, fine brocade, plush fur. An untold fortune in gems and jewels sparkled throughout the august company. Even Alexi, who was about to take a vow renouncing worldly goods, was impressed by the display of wealth and elegance laid before him.

As he strode slowly and solemnly forward, Alexi's gaze fell upon his family. They sat at the front of the cathedral, in the presence of Prince Patrick, the king's own representative and heir to the Alabaster Throne of Avonleigh. Lord Vincent stood holding Lady Victoria's hand. Both beamed with pride as their eldest son moved slowly closer. Aurora tugged at her mother's fine silk gown and pointed at Alexi.

Next to the Shadowborn family, Alexi saw Dasmaria. She still wore her ceremonial armor, sans helmet. Always the picture of calm composure and careful dignity at formal occasions, Dasmaria met Alexi's gaze. With only the faintest hint of a smile, she winked at him. The uncharacteristic display so startled Alexi that he wasn't sure he had actually seen it. When he looked at her again, Dasmaria had resumed her normal stoicism.

A few more steps brought Alexi to a point some fifteen feet from Sir Kendall's bier. For a moment, he forgot all about the assembled crowd and the honor he would receive today. He knelt and bowed his head, offering a silent prayer for the memory of the deceased paladin.

As Alexi finished his prayer, a petite door opened at the side of the cathedral dome. A petite shape appeared in the portal and stepped slowly into the light of the candles.

The High Mother had arrived. The moment of Ascension was at hand. Alexi drew in a deep breath.

As the High Mother stepped slowly forward, her ever-present cedar staff in hand, a hush fell over the crowd. Not only was the silence a sign of respect for the person believed to be the very mouth of god, but it was also a function of her presence. Something about this slender woman—an inner radiance—made everything else pale beside her.

As she passed the assembled Knights of the Circle, they dropped to one knee. When her gradual, deliberate steps brought her to a place between Alexi and the body of Sir Kendall, she raised the cedar staff high. All heads bowed in anticipation of the words to come.

"My children," she said in a voice that carried like the reverberations of a hunting horn, "we have assembled here today for the holy Rite of Ascension. Before the Eye of Belenus closes on this day, a new paladin will join the Knights of the Circle. In all the hundred-year history of the Great Kingdom and its matron church, the Ascension has occurred only twenty times. Today, we gather for the twenty-first."

After a pause, she continued. "History will long remember the twenty-first Ascension. Never before have two members of the same family been accepted into the ranks of the most holy Circle. When Alexi Shadowborn swears the oath of Ascension this day, he follows in the footsteps of his mother, Kateri Shadowborn, crusader of the Heretical Wars in the south and tamer of the Sea Raiders in the north. The fifteen years since the Circle lost Kateri Shadowborn have done nothing to erase the memory of that great warrior. To this day, the bards sing of her valor and recite the stories of her adventures.

"But enough of the past," proclaimed the High Mother. "This is a day for looking forward, not backward."

With that, she raised her great staff into the air and spoke a word in the language of the gods. The golden sunburst affixed to the cedar pole flared with magical amber light. Gasps of wonder swept through the crowd at this rare display of magic.

"Alexi Shadowborn," called the High Mother, "step forward."

At the mention of his name, Alexi rose to his feet. As commanded, he walked toward the High Mother, stopping when he stood less than a yard away from her. They exchanged exaggerated, formal bows, and Ferran moved quietly to stand beside his brother.

"Alexi Shadowborn," intoned the High Mother, her commanding voice sending a shiver of anticipation down Alexi's spine. "Why have you come here this day?"

"High Mother," responded Alexi, his mouth dry, "I have come to take my place among the Knights of the Circle."

"It is a great honor that you seek." Despite the fact that her words were part of a standard litany used at every Ascension since the original thirteen knights were sworn in a century ago, her tone was warm. "The Knights of the Circle are the ultimate defenders of the Church of Belenus and the Great Kingdom of Avonleigh. They ride at the head of our armies and undertake the most formidable quests in the land. Do you understand this?"

"I do." Alexi felt the gaze of a thousand eyes upon him, but found that he could not tear his own from the glowing head of the High Mother's staff. The magical aura so captivated him that he could scarcely blink.

"Do you, Alexi Shadowborn, reaffirm your devotion to the radiant Belenus, his most holy church, and all its traditions?"

"I do."

"Do you reaffirm your oath of fealty to the Alabaster Throne, his Royal Majesty King Christopher, and the thirteen provinces of the Great Kingdom?"

"I do."

"And do you, Alexi Shadowborn, accept the duties, responsibilities, and obligations incumbent upon a Knight of the Circle?"

"I do."

"Then hand to me your blade, Alexi Shadowborn,

that I may bestow upon you the greatest honor any warrior may strive for in the Great Kingdom."

Alexi drew Corona cleanly from its scabbard. The gleaming steel caught the candlelight and reflected it back onto the walls of the cathedral. Holding the blade flat across his hands, he presented it to the High Mother.

The High Mother allowed a smile to touch the edges of her mouth. Perhaps she recognized the sword, but Alexi could not say. She grasped the pommel, not seeming to notice the weight of the weapon in her thin, frail hands.

She nodded, and Alexi lowered himself to one knee. He bowed his head, his heart hammering. He waited anxiously for the touch of steel on his shoulder and the words of Ascension.

"Let the Eye of Belenus look upon us!" cried the High Mother. At her magical command, the top of the great dome folded outward, opening itself like a bronze blossom. A gust of wind swept through the cathedral, extinguishing the thousands of flickering candles.

At that moment, a shaft of sunlight should have fallen on Alexi, the High Mother, and the body of Sir Kendall. Beyond the now-open dome should have been a crisp blue sky and the blazing eye of Belenus himself.

Instead, there was only darkness.

For a second, panic gripped Alexi. As gasps of fear and cries of alarm ran through the crowd, the warrior remembered his dream. He remembered throwing open the shutters of his bedroom window and seeing only the fluid darkness that lay beyond. Was he dreaming even now?

But then he saw the truth. The Eye of Belenus was still visible in the sky, but only as a glowing ring around a black orb. In the middle of the day, cursed darkness ruled the land.

Alexi wanted to cry out. Fear, anger, rage, and despair all fought for control of his heart. When Belenus closed his eye, it was a sign of his greatest displeasure.

The High Mother, perhaps more surprised even than Alexi, nonetheless reacted quickly. She dropped the sword as if her hand had been burned by it and lifted her staff over her head with two gnarled arms. Corona clattered onto the stone floor, ringing like a blacksmith's hammer, then lay still and silent. As the High Mother spoke another word of command in the holy tongue, the fiery glow atop her staff brightened and spread its illumination throughout the cathedral.

The effect calmed the crowd somewhat, but the darkness outside threatened to flood them with panic. To be sure, these were educated men and women. They were nobles and scholars, not commoners or peasants. In their own way, however, they were as superstitious as the serfs who toiled in the fields.

Apparently sensing that more effort on her part was needed, the High Mother began to chant. As she sang words of prayer and benediction, the members of the audience gradually joined in. As their voices grew, the panic and fear slowly receded. Amid this sudden darkness, the entire assemblage pleaded with their god for mercy and begged for his forgiveness. They knew that he was angry with them and prayed that the High Mother would see them through this time of fear and terror.

Alexi, for all his piety and devotion, did not join in these songs of worship. As soon as the darkness filled the cathedral, despair greater than he had ever known gripped his spirit. He closed his eyes, trying to deny the reality of the moment.

Tears formed and trickled slowly down his face. His throat tightened, making breathing difficult and speech impossible. Although he could hear the chanted prayers of his countrymen, he could not join them.

The young knight knew that the Darkening was an omen of the most terrible significance. Its occurrence at this particular moment could signify only one thing: Belenus had found him unworthy.

Why? Have I done something to incur your displeasure, my god? Alexi searched his memory. Finding no answer, he searched his heart. Is it my faith? Do you doubt my devotion?

His prayers received no response. Belenus had forsaken him. An emptiness more black and vast than the darkness covering the earth eclipsed Alexi's spirit.

In time, the prayers and songs of the people did their work. The Eye of Belenus began to open again, returning his gift of warmth and light to the terrified world below. An almost visible burden was lifted from the masses assembled for the Ascension of Alexi Shadowborn.

The anguished knight opened his eyes to see the light of Belenus returning. The radiance of the High Mother's staff poured across the gathered people, giving them hope and bolstering their faith. Where the light fell upon Alexi, however, it seemed pale and weak. He took no consolation in the blazing holy relic.

Alexi realized that he had fallen forward in supplication. When the Darkening began, he had been kneeling before the High Mother. Now, as it passed, he was leaning forward on both knees supporting himself with his outstretched hands. He started to rise back to his feet, but then saw a flash of silver on the cold stone before him.

There, where the High Mother had dropped it, rested the gleaming Corona. A shaft of light falling upon it from the magical staff reflected brightly upon the blade. So true was the reflection that Alexi almost believed that the sword itself sparkled with sunfire.

Was it not enough to own such a blade, even if he were not a member of the Circle? He tried to take solace in this thought, but it offered only fleeting consolation. Corona, glorious as it was, meant nothing in comparison to a place among the Knights of the Circle.

And perhaps he would have neither. It was said that the magical Corona could not be held by an unworthy knight. There were even tales in which the crusading Kateri Shadowborn had defeated enemies who had managed to snatch Corona from her hand, only to drop it when the pain and smell of searing flesh had proven too great for them.

Were these stories true? Alexi didn't know. If they were, it seemed likely that his own hands would now find the weapon excruciatingly hot to the touch.

Putting aside his fear and doubt, he reached out a hand toward the pommel. There was no trepidation in his manner. Either he would hold the sword or he would not.

To his relief, nothing happened. Indeed, the act of reclaiming his weapon seemed to draw him back from the abyss of despair. The touch of steel, surprisingly cool in his hand, restored some of his lost confidence. Here was hope, if nothing else, that all was not lost.

As he slid Corona back into its scabbard, Alexi drew in a deep breath. He rose and lifted his eyes to the High Mother.

Her prayers for solace and absolution ended, she brought the brass-tipped base of the cedar staff down and struck it loudly on the floor. The radiance atop it dimmed but did not fail. The Eye of Belenus was fully open again, although Alexi scarcely felt its warmth.

The High Mother looked him sharply in the eye. Her ancient gaze burned with fire, and the warrior knew that he could not have looked away even if he had wanted to. Alexi sensed that she was taking his measure. Coolly and calmly, she assessed him as a jeweler might a precious stone. All his virtues would be clear to her, he knew, and no fault undiscovered.

"Alexi Shadowborn," she said at last, "you have been found wanting."

Alexi bowed his head. He focused his gaze on one stone of the hard floor, bracing himself.

"Belenus has closed his eye to you," she pronounced. "I call upon you to renounce your petition to the station of paladin and privileges of the Circle."

Alexi tried to speak, but his throat seemed to collapse. He closed his eyes, summoned all the courage and energy he could muster, and forced out the words he knew he must say.

"I . . . renounce my petition."

For a moment, Alexi felt nothing. It seemed as if his spirit had been drawn out of his body. All the life, all the emotion, all the hope was lost. Only a shell remained.

"The holy scripture tells us to judge no man for deeds we do not know," said the High Mother. "Never has word reached me of any misdeed or act of impiety on your part. I sense a taint upon your spirit, knight, but I see no evil. What has stained your heart so, I cannot imagine.

"Go in peace, Alexi Shadowborn. Return to your home, but take care that the darkness within you does not grow. Evil is a seductive thing, and it seldom releases even the most tenuous of handholds."

Alexi turned as crisply as he could, trying to maintain a dignified bearing. He could feel the eyes of his countrymen upon him as he strode steadily back toward the cathedral entrance. He focused his gaze straight ahead, unable to meet even his parents' eyes.

Whispered questions drifted to his ears. What evil could the warrior have committed? What dark secrets did he harbor? He struggled to ignore their speculation. The citizens of Avonleigh would create their own answers soon enough. He would be judged guilty by the people whose lives he had sworn to defend.

Ferran appeared at his side. He said nothing, but quickly matched his stride to that of his older brother. Alexi could see tears running down Ferran's cheeks and burned with shame at having been disgraced in the eyes of the youth.

As the cathedral doors swung closed behind him, Alexi heard a sound that chilled him to the marrow. From deep within the temple came a powerful female voice. Tones that mixed youth and vitality with maturity and wisdom reached out to destroy what might be left of his spirit.

"Dasmaria Eveningstar," called the High Mother, "step forward. As the next in line for Ascension, the honor of paladinhood falls upon you."

FIVE

Alexi wanted nothing more than to get as far away from the cathedral as he could.

Before he had taken a dozen steps, he emitted a high, sharp whistle. In prompt response, a sleek black warhorse sprang forward. As Alexi mounted Pitch, he heard Ferran whistle for his own destrier, a blue roan named Midnight.

Alexi rode at a wild gallop, as if the wind rushing through his hair could cleanse his spirit of the taint that sullied it. Halfway to Shadowfast, however, he realized that driving his stallion until it dropped would not ease his despair. Relieving the proud steed of its disgraced rider, he dismounted and walked beside the animal.

The light wind of the morning had cooled and stiffened. Thick, bulbous clouds formed and rose into the sky. They looked ominous and foreboding to Alexi, as if they frowned upon the fallen paladin. So unworthy was he that the Eye of Belenus would not even see him home.

As he plodded toward Shadowfast, Alexi heard a rapid series of detonations in the distance. At first, the warrior thought it was the rumbling thunder of the coming storm. Then, however, he realized the truth: He heard the echoing reports of fireworks bursting above the cathedral. The Ascension was complete. The Circle had been forged anew, with Dasmaria in his place.

A bitter, staccato rain began to fall upon the knight, hammering his armor and stinging his flesh. In no time at all, Alexi felt as miserable on the outside as he did in his heart.

Questions of Why? and How? tumbled through his thoughts, but he had no more answers now than he did while standing before the High Mother. He knew only that he had been judged undeserving by his god.

Not until Ferran twisted his foot on a rock and crashed to the ground did Alexi snap back to the present. Since leaving the Ascension ceremony—Dasmaria's Ascension ceremony—he had paid no attention to his brother. Indeed, he had forgotten his squire followed faithfully behind him.

His heart now even heavier with remorse, Alexi ran to where Ferran had fallen and dropped to one knee beside him. The ankle was already swollen and discolored. Ferran's face flushed and contorted in pain. "I think it's sprained," he gasped.

"Worse," said Alexi calmly. "It's broken. Looks like you've gotten your share of my luck today."

"That's—ouch!—a squire's job," Ferran said as Alexi examined the injury more closely.

Midnight moved nearer to look down upon his prone master. He leaned forward and put his long, dark nose against Ferran's. The squire reached up to push the curious horse back, but not before Midnight showed his concern with a quick lick along the youth's cheek.

"Pah!" cried Ferran, "Get back, you stupid horse! I hate it when you do that! Who taught you that, anyway?"

Alexi smiled in spite of himself. "Aurora's turning your war-horse into a trick pony," he said, offering a silent word of thanks for the little imp's lessons. If anything could keep his younger brother's mind off his injury, it was a few drippy horse kisses. "I'm going to have to lift you into the saddle. I'll try to be careful, but it won't be pleasant."

Ferran nodded but said nothing. Alexi knew that the young squire had a high tolerance for pain, but that fact didn't make the prospect of moving him any better. Still, there was nothing else to do. Alexi leaned forward. He slid one arm under Ferran's knees and looped the other past the small of his back.

"Don't move him," came a distant voice. It was weak and dry, speaking at once of age and infirmity. For all its frailty, however, something in its timbre commanded respect. Alexi paused, turning his head toward the speaker.

Perhaps twelve yards down the road stood a robed figure. Alexi estimated his height at no more than five and a half feet, but couldn't begin to guess his weight. Although the stranger was completely covered in crimson robes, they seemed to hang so loosely that Alexi almost wondered if anyone truly hid within them. From his vantage point, kneeling beside the injured Ferran, Alexi's gaze fell beneath the traveler's overhanging cowl. He expected to see the wrinkled face of an elderly pilgrim. Instead, he saw only darkness and the faint sparkle of keen eyes.

"Who are you?" asked Alexi. He doubted the traveler posed a threat. Even if the frail figure proved to be a spellcaster, Alexi believed he could reach his sword before any magic could be woven against him.

"I am a stranger to these lands," responded the quietly

assured voice. "I am Lysander Greylocks, a servant of Brigit."

Alexi made a holy sign of respect at the mention of the moon goddess. Ferran did the same. While they had both sworn fealty to Belenus, the fiery master of the day, they respected his nocturnal counterpart and her haunting powers.

"Perhaps I can be of assistance to you," said the pilgrim, moving forward. The quickness of his gait caused Alexi to consider whether he had misjudged the stranger's vitality.

As the red-robed figure neared Pitch, the horse snorted, the sort of sound that Alexi associated with danger. Midnight also nickered his disapproval.

Alexi tensed, a disturbing thought entering his mind. How had the unexpected visitor drawn so close without the horses raising an alarm earlier? Pitch was one of the most highly trained war-horses in the Shadowlands, and Midnight was not far behind. Individually, either of them should have detected the approaching stranger. And yet the pilgrim had appeared before them as if from thin air.

The horses' concern for their wounded companion had probably distracted them. Not sensing any danger himself, Alexi allowed Lysander to kneel beside Ferran.

Lysander extended slender hands toward Ferran's unnaturally twisted ankle. What Alexi thought at first was deathly pale skin proved to be white satin gloves. Even through these, however, the bones of the old man's knuckles showed plainly. If the pilgrim was not already trouble by arthritis, Alexi felt certain that it would not be long before his hands began to ache.

Ferran's nervous gaze locked on Lysander's trembling fingers. If Alexi had learned anything about battlefield medicine, it was never to let a wounded man watch a healer tend to his injuries.

He called Ferran's name and lowered himself to the wet grass opposite Lysander. With his field plate on, the effort was not easy. "Little brother," Alexi said casually, forcing a light mood, "I've been meaning to ask you something."

"What?" asked Ferran, obviously a little confused by his brother's sudden desire for conversation. That was fine with Alexi—anything that kept Ferran from watching the delicate passes Lysander was making over the broken ankle.

"When are you going to announce your intentions?"

"My intentions?"

"About Dasmaria's squire—what's her name again?"

Ferran glared. "You know full well what her name is."

"Shandra, right?"

"Right," said Ferran, his attention now fully on his brother. "But what makes you think that I have 'intentions' to announce?"

Alexi smiled at the blush in his brother's cheeks. It appeared that Ferran was old enough to handle a sword and a bow, but the mysteries of the fairer sex would remain elusive for a few more years.

While Ferran was distracted, Lysander closed his eyes in concentration. Alexi watched from the corner of his eye as the old man prayed silently. He remembered his own experiences with practitioners of the healing arts. The pilgrim placed his hands on either side of the injury, pouring healing energy into the limb. Alexi imagined the warmth he knew would spread from those ancient fingers into the damaged tissues. Even as he watched, the bones began to knit. A minute later, as the wandering priest ended his entreaty to the moon goddess, Ferran's ankle was completely healed. Although the skin would remain discolored for a day or two, he had freed the squire from most of the injury's burden.

At that moment, Ferran's voice grabbed Alexi's attention. He realized that his mind had wandered.

"What was that?" Alexi asked.

"I said, 'When are you going to announce your intentions about Dasmaria?'"

A warm sensation crept up Alexi's neck and into his face. He had left himself wide open for that riposte. Could everyone see his feelings for Dasmaria?

His thoughts turned dark again. What chance did he have of winning—or retaining—the love of a woman who had witnessed his ultimate disgrace? Dasmaria was now a paladin. What use could she possibly have for someone whose failure had been proclaimed by Belenus himself?

"There's nothing to tell," he said brusquely.

A great clap of thunder ripped across the countryside, bringing rain pounding down upon the trio. Alexi rose to his feet, no small effort in his heavy shell of armor. Once he was standing again, he offered a hand to Ferran and pulled his younger brother to a standing position.

As Ferran tested his still-delicate ankle, Alexi turned to Lysander. "We are in your debt," he said formally. "If there is anything that—"

"I was at the Ascension ceremony," interrupted the stranger. His voice held neither judgment nor pity, but Alexi bristled at the statement.

"Then your help is even more appreciated," Alexi said. He knew that once word of his shame spread throughout the Great Kingdom, any act of kindness would be more than he could expect.

"Do not judge yourself too harshly," said the pilgrim. He folded his arms across his chest and tilted his cowled head to one side. Clearly he was taking Alexi's measure, just as the High Mother had done.

"I fail to see how this is any of your concern," said Ferran. Alexi motioned for his squire to be silent. While he appreciated his brother's support, he wanted to deal with the pilgrim himself.

"Perhaps it is not," said the monk with a shrug, "but I have been watching you for some time, Alexi Shadowborn. I have seen nothing that causes me to believe you unworthy of the honor denied you this day."

Alexi tensed. "Watching me? Why?"

" 'Tis not important now," said Lysander with a wave of dismissal. His robes grew heavy with rainwater. "What matters is that you now watch yourself closely."

Alexi shook his head. "I don't understand."

"You will, in time. Look within yourself, Alexi Shadowborn. Look into your heart, and look into your dreams. There you shall find the answers you seek."

A chill that had nothing to do with the cold rain ran up Alexi's spine. Something in the old man's words told Alexi that he knew of the knight's dreadful nocturnal visions. Alexi had never mentioned them to Ferran, his family, or even Dasmaria. Lysander had already admitted to watching Alexi. For how long? How many other secrets did this strange visitor know about him?

A sound off to his side caught Alexi's attention. Ferran stood not far away, listening to every word. He caught his younger brother's concerned gaze and decided he had heard enough of the pilgrim's cryptic musings. He turned around to demand some answers.

Lysander Greylocks was gone. And again the horses had been silent.

"Where—where did he go?" asked Ferran, moving with only a slight limp to stand beside Alexi.

"I don't know," said the warrior in a hushed voice. "But I think it's best to get you home. We can worry about the old man later."

As they rode, heaviness settled over Alexi's spirit again. Lysander's mysterious words and the High Mother's grave pronouncement echoed in his mind, leaving him as bewildered as ever. Mercifully, Ferran remained silent.

The rain continued to fall. By the time they reached the gates of Shadowfast, the shower had become a veritable gale. Fierce winds drove a torrent of water sideways into their faces. Lightning cracked the sky with traces of actinic blue, followed almost instantly by the cannon fire of thunder.

Alexi turned the care of his mount over to the grooms and pushed through the front gates. No other servants came forward to welcome him. Instead of the usual chatter and activity of the manor, the only sounds Alexi heard were the lonely echoes of his own footfalls. That suited him just fine. He wanted to be left alone.

He strode past paintings, statues, and tapestries that told the story of a family that, until today, had never known disgrace. When he reached his bedchamber, he bolted the heavy oak door behind him.

It took him half an hour to get out of his field plate without Ferran's help. Though he had no interest in drying and oiling the rain-slicked pile of metal, he was too disciplined a warrior to neglect the care of his armor. Surprisingly, the mindless physical labor helped soothe his raw emotions, though it could not keep dark thoughts at bay.

When he had completed the task, he looped his sword belt over the post at the head of his bed and went to sit next to the window. As the storm tried to smash its way through the glass, he again considered Lysander Greylocks's words. Was the pilgrim a gifted soothsayer or just a spooky old man?

Look into your heart, he had said. But Alexi's heart was pure. Wasn't it? His prayers in the chapel this morning had been earnest. The shadow that had passed through him at their completion had been nerves. Only nerves. Or perhaps a flash of prescience at what was about to transpire—nothing more.

Look into your dreams, Lysander had counseled as well. With a shudder, Alexi recalled the portentous nightmare he'd awoken to this morning. What ill omens would his dreams hold tonight?

SIX

A powerful booming jolted Alexi awake.

He looked around in drowsy confusion as the fading echoes of the distant concussions fell upon his ears. His disorientation overshadowed any curiosity about the noise that had wakened him.

He apparently lay in his bedroom, yet it seemed unfamiliar to him. The furniture appeared changed, the decor of the room different. On the wall where he had displayed the mace of an ogre he once defeated now hung the helmet of an eastern warrior. In the corner where he kept the delicate, ornate crossbow he had received for his thirteenth birthday now rested a gleaming glass sphere atop a cold silver tripod.

Warily taking stock of the inconsistencies, he noticed with relief that at least one item rested where it should. His sword belt remained hooked over the bedpost, right where he had hung it. Whatever else had changed, Corona was near at hand.

A strange mist hung about the room. The tenuous white haze drifted as if carried on subtle currents in the perfectly still air of the room, clinging to the objects it touched. The mist, whose origin Alexi could not determine, stifled Alexi's vision, draining away colors to leave everything pale and muted. The curtains, his blankets, the rugs on the hardwood floor, all were bleached to a lifeless gray. Looking at his own hands, he saw that the same was true of them. His flesh now had the white look of a man whose long-dead body had been bleached white from the sea.

Only when his mind adjusted to the filter of the mist did Alexi realize he had gotten out of his bed. He didn't remember rising, but he must have, for he now stood near the window. His eyes opened wide as he noticed a lithe woman stretched out in his bed.

The mists hampered recognition. At first Alexi took the figure to be his mother, Victoria Shadowborn. As the vapors parted slightly, however, he saw that he was mistaken.

To be sure, the woman resembled Lady Shadowborn. She was tall and angular, with elegant features. This woman was more athletic than the former archer, though, and showed the well-defined muscles of someone who had known melee combat.

Still, there was something familiar about her. With a gasp, Alexi realized that he had been both right and wrong.

The woman in the bed was not Victoria Shadowborn, the woman who had raised him from infancy. She was Kateri Shadowborn, the woman who had given birth to him.

That explained both the warrior's build and the resemblance to his adoptive mother. Alexi remembered seeing his real mother only in paintings and sketches. The face before him could certainly be the same oil-and-charcoal beauty he had admired so many times.

The booming returned, sending shivers through the

mists. Alexi leapt at the sudden noise, his hand going to the place on his hip where his sword usually rested. His fingers touched only empty air, however, and he remembered that the blade hung on the other side of the room.

The woman on the bed sat upright with the speed of an arrow in flight. Her hand moved so fast that Alexi barely saw it grab Corona's handle. He marveled at this woman's reflexes. Could he ever be her equal?

Kateri climbed out of bed and stepped soundlessly onto the mist-shrouded floor. With a sharp twist, she slipped the silver sword from its scabbard. A brief pulse of white light sprang from the blade as it tasted air. The flash reminded Alexi of sunlight hitting silvered glass.

Kateri moved to the bedroom door, snatching up a robe as she did so, and transferred the sword to her left hand. As she deftly looped the sash into a knot with her right hand, she spoke two words in the ancient, holy tongue of the church.

"Karnas, radamar."

Alexi knew the first word; it was the name "Corona" in the holy tongue. The second word, however, was one seldom spoken outside of holy services. It was the name given to the rays of sunlight that were said to beam from the eyes of Belenus himself. Holy and pure, it was said to be one of the elemental forces of the universe.

No sooner had Kateri Shadowborn spoken than the sword glowed with light. Even the smothering mists could not obstruct the vibrant golden rays it emitted. Amid the empty shades of gray, recesses of pure black, and drifting white vapors, it was a single sliver of sunlight, warm and reassuring.

Kateri swept out of the room, her way lit by the glow

of Corona. Alexi followed, his mouth dry with awe and wonder. His mother approached the top of the stairs and descended them smoothly.

A wave of foreboding washed over him, although he could not say whether it came from the strange mists or something more substantial. He wanted to call out, to let his mother know he was with her. But some power made speech impossible.

As the beautiful warrior reached the bottom of the stairway, another volley of booms filled the air. They echoed hollowly, perhaps distorted by the mists, but this time Alexi recognized the sound. Someone was pounding on the door to the manor, lifting and releasing a great knocker that hung on the other side.

Something about the scene troubled Alexi. He couldn't define the cause, but the same sense had warned him of many an ambush. He tried to shake off the feeling, attributing it to the strangeness of this place. Then he noticed that Kateri seemed unsettled as well.

Kateri came to a stop beside the door and turned up the wick on a lantern. A wane, yellow light tried and failed to illuminate the area. It spread outward but was smothered by the mists, becoming nothing more than an area of lighter gray. Contrasted with the fierce glow of the magical blade, the lantern was impotent against the darkness.

As Kateri reached to open the door, she made no motion to sheathe her sword. Indeed, she spoke to it again.

"Karnas, ramorte."

Instantly the glow died, extinguished by a holy word used to observe the setting of the sun. To look at the weapon now, no one would suspect the sword was any different than one carried by the common constabulary.

Kateri opened the door. The faint shaft of gray lantern light revealed a dark figure. He wore black robes and hid his face beneath a great hood. In his hand, the visitor held an ornate long sword. Alexi squinted, trying to get a better view of the stranger, but the effort proved futile. Everything about the visitor seemed black: his robes, the sword he carried, and the long shadow that stretched out behind him to fuse with the darkness beyond.

Kateri seemed to relax slightly. Her face held recognition, but anxiety as well. She stepped back from the door.

"What brings you here at this hour?" Her tone suggested that she greeted a friend. Perhaps Alexi had mistaken her feelings. After all, Kateri had been asleep when her visitor came calling. Perhaps she was merely weary, not wary.

"It could not be helped," came the thin response. So soft were the words of the dark-robed figure that Alexi barely heard them. Indeed, he seemed to know what the man had said without actually hearing him speak.

"We found this weapon in the ancient catacombs beneath Forenoon Abbey," the visitor continued. "When none of the brothers could identify it or read the inscription, the abbot directed me to bring it here. Surely the wisdom of the great Kateri Shadowborn can unravel the mysteries that confound us."

Kateri tilted her head to the side and regarded the black weapon with a curious eye. Alexi noted that the runes on the sword seemed even darker than the mysterious metal into which they had been inscribed. They were visible only because of their apparent invisibility. It was as if patches of nothingness were set into the midnight black blade. Try as he might, he could not focus his eyes on the letters.

Suddenly fire burst from the monk's blade.

A scintillating orange blaze sheathed the black weapon. The effect resembled the eclipse that had stripped Alexi of paladinhood. The monk raised the sword high, throwing a rippling pattern of black shadows across the misty entrance hall. Like the radiance of Corona, the glow pushed back the muting vapors.

Alexi knew in his gut that the monk's weapon was every bit as evil as his mother's blade was holy.

Kateri cried out in surprise. She stepped back, her eyes wide with wonder. This was a moment of betrayal. His mother had greeted an ally, but now faced a deadly assassin.

The monk brought his blade down, trailing curls of hellfire behind it. Alexi tried to rush forward but could not move. Just as something had compelled him to follow his mother earlier, now an invisible ward constrained him from aiding her. The knight tried to shout a warning, but no sound escaped his paralyzed throat.

Nonetheless, the sudden blow did not catch Kateri off guard. When the blazing blade fell, it cut only air. The trained warrior had fallen away from the stroke, dropped to the floor, and rolled smartly to the side. Completing its arc, the fiery metal bit deep into the entrance hall rug and threw out a shower of glowing embers.

By the time her attacker recovered from his errant blow, Kateri had kicked herself back to her feet. She brought up her own gleaming blade and whispered "*Karnas, radamar*" again. The silver sword unleashed a blinding glow. Beams of pure sunlight lanced through the mists, driving them back and battling the smoldering fire of the black blade.

The spectacle of dueling lights paled in comparison to the effect of Corona's radiance upon the monk. Wherever one of the amber shafts fell on the dark intruder, smoke roiled up and flame erupted. A shriek of agony tore through the air, but the burns did not slow the attacker. Howling in rage, he pointed the tip of his ebon blade at Kateri. The monk spoke a command in a language Alexi did not know, but which somehow offended his ears all the same.

With the utterance of that vulgar sound, a searing bolt of fire drove outward from the weapon. It splashed across the paladin, causing her to topple back and cry out in agony. The gleaming Corona fell from her hand as Kateri crashed to the floor. It struck the floor and fell dark.

As flames danced upon her robe, the smell of burning flesh and hair filled the room. Defiance burned in Kateri's eyes even as pain contorted her features. The sinister monk strode forward, raised high his weapon, and brought it down in a final deadly stroke.

Alexi and Kateri Shadowborn cried out as one.

SEVEN

The coming dawn threw a blanket of thick, gray light across the whole of the Shadowlands. Yesterday's storm had passed, leaving swollen streams, swampy puddles, and muddy roads in its wake. Dark green leaves hung limply from the trees, and tortured branches drooped weakly after brutal winds had torn at them all night long.

Alexi rose before anyone else, even the servants. He quickly donned a cotton shirt and buckskin pants, and slipped out of Shadowfast into the slick predawn air. He had no desire to meet his parents, siblings, or any of the household staff. In time, he would come to terms with the events of the last twenty-four hours and be able to face others again. Until then, however, he wanted no contact with anyone.

Beyond his shame at the Darkening, last night's dream left him in a troubled mood. He had often wondered about the exact circumstances of his mother's death, but heretofore he believed it had occurred in honorable battle. To see her die by a traitor's foul sword awakened feelings he never realized he had toward the mother he had never known.

The vision, combined with Lysander's cryptic words, had inspired this early morning trek. If his dreams indeed held the answers he sought, he knew where he must go to piece together the clues.

After traveling some distance down the hard-packed road that linked Shadowfast with the rest of the Shadowlands, Alexi came upon a trio of men. They were clad in the clothing of commoners, out and about on some early morning business. As he drew near, he saw that they were fishermen headed for the docks. No doubt they were eager to take advantage of the bountiful fishing that so often came with the dawn that followed a storm.

Their laughter and conversation vanished the instant Alexi came into sight. While none of them dared show any disrespect to a knight, they had obviously heard that Alexi Shadowborn was the cause of the Darkening. They had come upon the man whose deeds made even the radiant Belenus look away.

Alexi knew he would have to grow accustomed to such responses. Much time would have to pass before folk could look at him without thinking of the darkness that had fallen over their land. Words like "impure" and "unholy" would be forever linked to the name Alexi Shadowborn.

The fishermen lowered their eyes and made the appropriate signs of respect to a noble. Alexi greeted them in kind. As he passed the trio he heard, or believed that he heard, their whispered comments. Fear tinged their voices.

He turned off the path and into the forest. Rain-soaked trees showered him as he broke through the scrub bordering the road. Shaking off the chilling drizzle, he emerged into the dark of the wood. With the sun just sneaking over the horizon, the depths of the forest were still obscured with night.

At first Alexi pressed forward despite the poor visibility. After several yards, however, his foot caught on an unseen curl of a root and he toppled forward. A layer of leaves and loam broke his fall.

He got to his feet, brushed the clinging forest floor from his clothes, and sighed. It was too dark to continue. Even after giving his eyes a few minutes to adjust to the dim light, he realized it wouldn't be safe to travel for some time.

He mentally berated himself for forgetting to bring a light. Of course, the glow of the coming dawn had enabled him to see his way easily when he left the house, but it could not penetrate this shroud of trees. He ran a hand through his hair but stopped in midpass. Maybe he hadn't forgotten a light after all.

The elegant scrape of steel sliding free of a scabbard sounded crisply in the stillness of the dark wood. Alexi considered the blade carefully, noting that it looked unnaturally bright in these gloomy surroundings. He swallowed nervously, as if about to attempt a dangerous feat.

"Corona, radiance," he whispered.

Nothing happened.

A moment elapsed before the fullness of his disappointment registered. He knew that the images he had seen in the night were nothing more than dreams, but he had hoped for something more. He had hoped Corona would respond to his words as it had to Kateri Shadowborn's.

He closed his eyes, seeing again his mother as she spoke to the blade. And he remembered that she hadn't used the common language of the Great Kingdom but the sacred tongue of the mother church. He opened his eyes. Holding the sword at arm's length, blade high, he spoke again.

"*Karnas, radamar!*"

At once the blade flashed to life. Brilliant light poured out to illuminate the area as brightly as if Belenus had focused his gaze on this place and this place alone. Warmth and well-being coursed through Alexi's body, driving back the despair still haunting his heart. The purity of Corona's light made him feel as if he held a sliver of the sun itself in his hand.

He stared, enraptured, at the shining blade for several moments before his awe faded enough to return him to the present. He could still scarcely believe he held the very sword that Kateri Shadowborn had wielded during her crusades in the Heretical Wars, let alone that the legendary weapon indeed held great magic.

Such artifacts were not unheard of, to be sure. The magic of the High Mother's staff was widely known even before she had displayed its power during the Darkening to calm the masses. Alexi felt despair rise again at the memory, but forced his thoughts back to the radiant Corona. He had never dared hope to possess such a wonder.

With the light of Corona to guide him, Alexi had but a ten-minute walk to reach his destination. Now easily able to skirt roots and other hazards, he struck a quick pace.

As he stepped through the bushes that formed the edge of a wide clearing, the true glow of Belenus fell upon him. In its brightness, the light from Corona's blade seemed to dim, but he no longer needed the magical radiance to see. His mind flashed back to the dream, and he spoke again in the sacred tongue.

"*Karnas, ramorte,*" he commanded. The glow faded.

Once more the blade now looked like a common, if finely crafted, sword. He slipped the weapon into its scabbard.

With Corona resting on his hip, Alexi's attention returned to the objective of his chill, damp morning walk. Upon waking from his unrestful sleep, he had speculated that his dream might have been more than a simple nightmare. In ancient tales of the faith, those called upon to serve Belenus often received their instructions through nocturnal visions.

He scarcely dared believe that the very god who had forsaken him by day should whisper in his ear at night. He prayed Belenus would forgive his presumption. But Corona's light had fueled his hopes that his had been no mere dream. How else could he explain the fact that Kateri Shadowborn's magical words had proven efficacious, if the dream had not been sent by the merciful sun lord himself?

Alexi stopped short. Might some sinister power be toying with him? Taking advantage of his despair and shame? It seemed a distinct possibility. He dared not give the matter serious consideration, for even thoughts about the dark gods were both blasphemous and dangerous.

He stepped across a puddle and onto the first of five marble steps rising before his family's mausoleum. He moved nimbly up them and stopped before a heavy steel grate set into thick granite walls. The smooth stone glistened in the morning light as it hung on to the cold of the night and sheathed itself in a layer of dew. Here and there, where a bit of condensation became too heavy to hold itself up, a tiny stream rolled down the side of the great structure. Sunlight followed the trickle carefully, making it sparkle until it vanished into a seam or onto the ground around the tomb.

Alexi slipped his hand under his shirt and withdrew a leather cord from around his neck. A heavy iron key dangled from it. Like the great lock on the metal door, it bore the radiant solar disk of the Shadowborn family. Alexi slipped the key into the lock, giving it a sharp turn. The mechanism ground into action with a scrape, followed by a sharp report.

The door rolled open easily before him, spilling sunlight into this final resting place. As Alexi entered, the cold air of the sepulcher set upon him.

He experienced a sense of homecoming. Much time had passed since he last communed with the spirits of his family, but in his youth he used to spend countless hours here. Indeed, the grass outside still showed earth where he had worn it away practicing the basic movements of swordplay. Hour after hour he had drilled and rehearsed here, hoping to gain favor with those who had come before and, with a little luck, draw inspiration from the store of wisdom and valor interred in this stone fastness.

In recent years, however, Alexi had been unable to visit the crypt very often. When he became a knight, his role as a protector of the Shadowlands had called him away for long periods. Still, whenever he returned from his campaigns, he always found his way to this quiet shrine.

He wandered between the rows of vaults. Before passing each tomb, he stopped and whispered a prayer for the soul of the departed resting within it. When he first visited the crypt as a boy, he had depended upon the epitaphs decorating each headstone to tell him about the person inside. As the years passed, however, he had carefully studied the lives of all who slept in this place. Now he knew each one by heart.

Some of those who had gone before him Alexi revered above the others. Since the dawn of the Great Kingdom, when the Thirteen Provinces united under the banner of Belenus and his most holy church, a dozen members of the Shadowborn family had chosen to devote their lives to the faith.

All but one of them became members of the clergy. No fewer than three Shadowborns had held the title of bishop, entrusted with keeping the faith throughout the whole of the Shadowlands. One, the most revered Cassandra Shadowborn, had even risen to become the High Mother. Although she died shortly after assuming that blessed office, her time upon the Radiant Throne was marked by fairness and a resurgence of faith among the common folk.

Other ancestors had taken up arms and become knights. Justin and Catherine Shadowborn were two such noble warriors. They had spent their lives fighting for justice and the glory of the great kingdom.

And then there was his mother, Kateri Shadowborn, who had taken up both the mantle of faith and the arms of a warrior. As a paladin, she had devoted her life to serving Belenus and battling evil in all its many forms.

It was her tomb he sought today. When he reached it, he saw in his mind the face of the woman from his dream. He saw her youthful features, her golden hair, her agile form. How difficult to imagine that the vibrant paladin he had seen last night lay still and cold in the stone chamber before him.

He fell to one knee and bent his head low. "I come to seek your guidance, Mother," he said, trying to put into words the heaviness within his heart. "Belenus has closed his eye to me. He will not accept me into his Circle."

He swallowed in a futile attempt to clear the strange tightness from his throat. "I don't know how I offended him, Mother. And I don't know how to serve him, if not as one of his holy paladins."

"The dead seldom respond, I'm afraid."

With a start, Alexi whirled around.

Behind him stood Lysander Greylocks. Alexi hadn't even heard the pilgrim's entrance.

"I thought I was alone," Alexi said, his ire rising at the old man's intrusion into a very private and painful moment. Alexi had been too ashamed to face his own kin after the Darkening, yet here he was, forced to confront a stranger who knew his darkest shame. "What are you doing here? Watching me still?"

"In a manner of speaking."

Alexi rose, towering above the stooped figure. "Why? Does my fall from grace amuse you?"

"Not in the least." With a sigh, Lysander shuffled to a stone bench in the center of the mausoleum. He sat down, gathering the endless folds of his red robe around him. "You have not fallen so very far, Alexi Shadowborn. Recall that 'No man is so pure that he throws not a shadow when Belenus gazes upon him.' "

"A priest of Brigit quotes the *Libram of Belenus?*"

"I have spent much time among followers of Belenus," the pilgrim said.

"Spying on them, too?" Alexi bit back further sarcasm. He tried to peer beneath the cowl that still obscured the old man's face. "Who are you, really, Lysander Greylocks? And what do you want with me?"

The monk held up a staying hand. "One question at a time, Alexi Shadowborn." He let his hand drop back to his lap. "I am, as I told you yesterday, a servant of

Brigit and her church. Though I once came from the Southern Empire, I have long lived among the people of the Great Kingdom. Most cannot discern my accent anymore."

Alexi narrowed his eyes. The Southern Empire—a land of swarthy folk who worshiped strange gods—was the enemy who had battled the Great Kingdom in the Heretical Wars. "How came a heretic to worship the true gods?"

"I met Kateri Shadowborn."

Alexi gasped. "You knew my mother?"

The pilgrim nodded. "When I first met Kateri, I was a man tormented," he said. "She could have slain me or turned me away, but she did not. Her words and deeds soothed the evil in my heart."

Though Alexi had been prepared to disbelieve Lysander, the old man's voice held an echo of sincerity. "Her tender attention persuaded me to leave the land of my birth and come to live among the folk of the Great Kingdom," the pilgrim continued. "It was she who guided me to the worship of Brigit."

Alexi's anger ebbed. His mother had shown this man kindness; he would at least show him patience. "If you have such respect for my mother, why won't you leave her son in peace?"

"You came here seeking guidance, did you not? Perhaps I have some to offer."

"What counsel can you possibly give to one cursed by the Darkening?" The knight turned away, ashamed to let Lysander see the deep pain still reflected in his eyes.

"Was it a curse, Alexi, or merely a message?"

Alexi looked out past the door of the crypt. Outside, the light of Belenus warmed and dried the earth; the air within the sepulcher, in contrast, remained cold and damp. Alexi closed his eyes. How he longed to bask in the radiance of Belenus's favor!

"I have been rejected by the god I would have willingly served unto death," Alexi said. "That is, to me, the ultimate curse."

"Consider otherwise, my friend. I believe that in the fullness of time, you will see that Belenus has another plan for you."

Alexi turned to face Lysander again. "I don't understand."

"Do not the scriptures say that no man can fully comprehend the motives of the gods?" Lysander rose and rested a frail hand on Alexi's arm. "For now, you need understand only this: Your god has not deserted you. Belenus still needs Alexi Shadowborn as his champion—but not in his Circle. Your path lies a different way."

A chill that had nothing to do with the cold air ran up Alexi's spine. "How can you know that?"

"I know many things you do not, Alexi. Some of my wisdom is born of age, and some gained through despair even greater than that which you feel now. But my problems belong to the past and are best left there."

Alexi regarded the old man skeptically, but also felt a spark of hope flare within him. "If what you say is true, how do I find the path Belenus has chosen for me?"

"When my spirit was in turmoil so long ago, I searched for answers and found them in my heart." He gestured toward Alexi's chest. "Did not I tell you to do the same? What did you find?"

The only thing Alexi could feel in his heart at the moment was the vise of anguish yet gripping it. "That I still want, more than anything, to be a paladin."

"Then what stops you?"

Alexi glared at Lysander. The pilgrim had seen the Darkening. He knew the answer perfectly well. "Belenus forbids it!"

The old man shook his head. "Belenus denied you entrance into the Circle. If you truly have the heart of a paladin, can you not still use your warrior's training to serve your god by vanquishing his enemies?"

Alexi paused, searching the eyes that glowed from the darkness within Lysander's hood. "Who would he have me fight?"

"I think you know." The monk pulled his cowl even more firmly around his head. "As I told you yesterday, Alexi Shadowborn, search your dreams." With that, he turned and shuffled away.

Alexi sank onto the bench. Which dreams was he to search? The horrific images of ghoulish unlife? He could hardly believe that Belenus would make walking corpses the subjects of Alexi's lifework.

The nightmare of his being consumed by blackness? Alexi discarded the possibility. That prophecy had already come true with the Darkening.

The vision of his mother's death? He paused. After all, it was this most recent dream that had brought Alexi to the crypt today. In an abstract way, would he receive guidance from his mother after all?

He considered the events of the dream. Kateri had been murdered in the Southern Empire while doing the work of Belenus in the wake of the Heretical Wars. In that sense, she had died a martyr. And to Alexi's knowledge, her killer had never paid for his crime.

Was that the answer? Did Belenus seek justice for the slaying of his faithful champion?

If so, it was a quest no one could perform with as much determination as could Alexi. He would, after all, not be just a knight serving his god, but a son avenging his mother.

And as a member of the Circle, he never would have been permitted to do so. A paladin could not allow even the appearance of impure motives to tarnish his integrity. He would have been accused of seeking revenge for his own reasons, pursuing his own agenda instead of his god's. The quest would have been forbidden.

But as a mere knight—nay, one considered a rogue knight after the Darkening—he had the freedom to choose his own quests. If he wanted to avenge his mother's death, he could do so with impunity.

And if Belenus wanted him to, he would.

Was that, then, the reason for the Darkening—to enable Alexi to perform a holy quest that he otherwise could not have undertaken? If so, then his way indeed lay on a path other than the one traveled by the Knights of the Circle.

His path led due south.

EIGHT

He comes.

My agent has done his work well. The fool does not see that he makes only the choices I mandate. These pitiful creatures revel in their "free will." They take such pleasure in going where they wish and doing as they please. They live their transient lives without the faintest notion of how easily I can manipulate them. In life and death, they are but puppets for such as I, with the resolution and knowledge to master them.

He will seek to destroy me.

It will be amusing to watch him learn the nature of the power that calls him. He will think his power is growing, until he feels unstoppable. Then he will draw his sword, proclaim his pitiful faith, and challenge me. Seconds later, his spirit in tatters and his body broken, he will die. And in death, he will serve me even better than he did in life.

He doesn't know that I am a prisoner.

For so many years I have yearned to escape this place. I find it appalling that the spirit of a wretched mortal has contained me here, but soon that will no longer be a concern. The spirit of Kateri Shadowborn has grown strained to the breaking point as it strives to keep me contained within this prison. If that accursed trio of mortals had not trapped me, I would have swept her aside long ago and laughed at her final agony.

But I am twice chained.

Those mortals managed to seal me inside this metal shell. The fact that I have learned how to travel about in this form has made it no less a prison. It did not reduce my desire for revenge. I have destroyed the triad who brought me into this world, but not the woman who had once before driven me from it. How could I have known her power would transcend her worthless life? Her death should have freed me to travel her world and bend its pitiful inhabitants to my will. I should have been the master of this place. But somehow I became its prisoner.

And still she torments me.

Instead of roaming free to rule and destroy, I remain her prisoner. But the coming of this new warrior marks the beginning of the end for the spirit of that accursed woman. She has called many heroes to this land, hoping they would destroy me. One by one, the stinging insects came, and one by one I annihilated them. Each defeat saw her hold over me slacken. She has gradually come to accept that victory will never be hers. She knows that her champions are doomed even before they step into this realm.

When this boy dies, she will break.

He is her kin. The mortals place great importance in such things. When she sees one of her own line swept out of existence, the sight will undo her. Her despair will shatter the spiritual chains that hold me, and I will be free. Then her torment will begin. But why should I wait? Can her torture not begin now? I can make her suffer even before I shatter her hold over me.

"Kateri Shadowborn, I would speak with you."

Her attention is slow in coming, certainly evidence of her failing will. Her spirit wanders, and she takes longer now to compose herself. When our time together began, she was quick to respond to my calls—such a considerate jailer. Perhaps she felt less certain of her power then. Whatever the case, I see she has finally taken notice of my summons. Caution hides within her spirit. She fears that I will challenge her will and break free. I sense her gathering her energy to do battle with me. It is tempting, but the hour for that has not yet come. I will bide my time.

"Another champion travels this way."

I can hardly keep my laughter in check. She knows that no one has responded to her call. Indeed, I perceive that she no longer continues to summon warriors to her aid. It seems she has given up her foolish efforts to destroy me. Her confusion tastes sweet indeed, spiced with panic, fear, and apprehension. She demands to know more.

"His name is Shadowborn . . . Alexi Shadowborn."

For a fleeting second, the endless darkness that encircles me resounds with my laughter. I cannot contain myself while I watch the shock register on her weakening mind. But no sooner has my mirth filled the void than another sound smothers it. This sound I had almost given up all hope of hearing. I force myself to silence, basking in the shrill resonance that echoes only in this region of darkness and confinement.

Kateri Shadowborn is screaming.

NINE

Pitch snorted eagerly and pranced on the hard-packed dirt. Standing beside him, Alexi patted the stallion's neck. "Take it easy," he whispered in the horse's ear. "We'll leave in just a few minutes. As soon as Ferran gets here with—"

"Ferran is here!" called the squire as he led Midnight out of the stable. He drew open one of the steed's saddlebags and dropped the last of their provisions inside. "Ready to go?"

Alexi soberly watched his brother. "I wish you would reconsider, Ferran." Last night Alexi had announced not only his quest but his intention to complete it alone. Ferran, however, had insisted upon accompanying him.

"This again?" Ferran shook his head.

"I told you, this journey isn't like our other adventures," Alexi said. "I don't know who our enemy is, and more importantly, I don't know for certain whether we have Belenus's protection." He felt a sense of foreboding about the journey, but nothing he could clearly identify. This morning, he had awakened once again to his ghoulish nightmares. The creatures had swarmed around him, biting and clawing at him. And then he had been one of them, feeling their utter evil permeate his heart. He woke up clutching his chest, and an aura of unease had gripped him ever since.

"I wouldn't be much of a squire if I let you ride into this battle alone." He met Alexi's gaze. "Or much of a brother."

Alexi studied Ferran's face. It held the most serious expression he had ever seen. He thanked Belenus for giving him such a devoted brother, one whose loyalty had not faltered even momentarily in the wake of the Darkening. "All right, then," he conceded. "Thank you, Ferran."

They led their horses to the front of the estate.

As they reached the reflecting pool that spread out before Shadowfast, Lord Vincent and Lady Victoria emerged from the manor and strode toward them, followed by Aurora. The girl shadowed her parents until they were about ten yards from her brothers. At that point, she broke forward and raced toward Midnight. The horse bent down its head and licked the side of her face.

"Aw, Aurora!" Ferran pulled her away from his normally proud steed.

Lord and Lady Shadowborn joined them. The early morning light seemed to deepen the lines of concern evident in both their faces.

"Are you sure you don't want to give this quest more thought, Alexi?" Lord Vincent asked. "After more than fifteen years, surely a few days more won't make a difference."

"Nor will a delay affect my determination." Alexi shook his head. "Please understand, Father. As I told you last night, this is something I need to do."

"We do understand," Lady Victoria said. "And we will

pray to Belenus every morning for your safe return."

After hugging both her sons, Lady Victoria held out a bundle of black cloth to Ferran. He tilted his head inquisitively before reaching out to take it.

"The other night, we gave your brother a present," his mother said. "This morning, it's your turn."

Ferran undid the knotted golden cord encircling the black satin. As the strands fell away, the package unfolded, and the squire gasped to see a trio of silver-tipped, mahogany shafts inside.

"I can't accept these," he stammered. "These arrows were a gift to you, Mother."

"Actually they were a prize," said Lady Victoria with a smile. "His Highness, King Christopher, presented them to me after I was lucky enough to win a competition held in honor of his son's wedding."

"Luck had nothing to do with it," said Lord Vincent. "Your mother was the finest archer I'd ever seen."

"Ferran's better," said Aurora as she hugged the squire's leg. "He beats Mummy all the time."

"That's because your mother's much older now," said Lord Vincent. Then, as his wife shot him a stern gaze, he backtracked. "I, uh, don't mean that she's old, of course. She's just out of practice."

"No she's not," said Aurora innocently. "She practices almost every day."

Everyone chuckled, but the levity died quickly in the solemnity of parting. When the silence threatened to become oppressive, Alexi stepped forward and lifted his little sister in his arms for a hug. Then he turned to his mother.

"Hurry back," she said, her arms tight around her eldest son. At moments like this, it seemed impossible to Alexi that the woman who held him so tightly was not truly his mother.

"I will," Alexi assured her with a confident smile. Then he stepped back, slipped his foot into the stirrup, and took the saddle in a smooth vault. Pitch snorted contentedly at the familiar weight. After his own good-byes, Ferran followed suit and sprang onto Midnight's black leather saddle. Without further comment, the knight snapped Pitch's reins and the two horses set off.

Pitch needed no guidance down the familiar road. Their way lay through mostly forested terrain on the first leg of their journey, a fact that pleased Alexi, since they were unlikely to encounter many villagers. Already he had come to dread the reception they gave him since the Darkening.

They rode in silence. Alexi knew this was normally a time for lighthearted speculation about what might lie ahead, a chance for him and his brother to ease any trepidation about the dangers they might face. This time, however, Alexi couldn't even guess at the perils before them.

I ought to strike up a conversation with Ferran, Alexi thought, but he could contrive nothing that would ease his sense of dread. He knew Ferran probably sensed his distress, but the boy gave no indication that this wasn't the way every adventure started. And so the chirping of songbirds echoing among the trees was the only sound that accompanied the rhythmic hoofbeats.

Alexi noted that the leaves on many of the trees had begun turning color. Already Belenus had painted the treetops with his warm shades of red, orange, and gold as autumn asserted itself. What would the trees look like upon their return? Would heavy snow burden their branches? Would fragile buds grace their limbs? Would they wear the full crown of summer's glory?

Pitch's warning snort snapped Alexi's attention back to the road. He held up his hand, motioning Ferran to stop. At the crossroads some hundred yards ahead, where they would turn south onto the broad flagstone expanse of the King's Way, a dark mounted figure blocked their path.

Alexi leaned forward in his saddle and squinted to see the distant figure more clearly. As he did so, a chill wind blew past him and parted the branches of the forest canopy over the crossroads. For a brief second, a shaft of bland, filtered light fell upon all-too-familiar crimson robes.

"Lysander Greylocks," Alexi murmured, only half surprised to see the ancient pilgrim again.

"The man who healed my leg?" asked Ferran.

"The same." Alexi had kept to himself his second encounter with the old man at the crypt.

"What do you suppose he wants?"

What indeed? Alexi sighed, weary of Lysander's sudden appearances. "We might as well find out." He nudged Pitch forward. The war-horse snorted uneasily, apparently not caring for something about Greylocks.

"Good morning, Alexi Shadowborn," called Lysander as the brothers approached the crossroads.

"Good morning, Lysander Greylocks," said Alexi. "It seems our paths were destined to cross again."

"They may do more than cross," responded the old man. "If I am not mistaken, I believe that you ride south. As it happens, I am returning to my home in the southern provinces of the Great Kingdom. May I ride with you?"

Alexi knew that Lysander's company could prove beneficial to his mission. Not only was the pilgrim a skilled healer should misfortune befall them en route, but the man had known Kateri Shadowborn and might have more information to reveal. Yet there was still much Alexi didn't know about Lysander Greylocks. And as the scriptures of Belenus clearly stated, no enemy was more dangerous than the one sharing your campfire.

As Alexi considered the pilgrim's request, a small voice in his head told him to refuse: *The last thing you need is an old man dragging you down,* it warned.

"I'm afraid not," Alexi said. "While I'm grateful for the aid you've rendered me—us—in the past couple of days, we expect to confront danger. You'd be safer traveling alone."

"I understand," said Lysander. "But my request yet stands. As you have seen, I have healing powers that could prove useful if danger crosses our paths—"

No! The voice grew more insistent. *It's bad enough that you have your younger brother tagging along.*

Alexi blinked. Where had that sentiment come from? He had never considered Ferran's presence on the journey a liability; his reluctance to let the squire accompany him had stemmed from concern for his brother's safety—and the grief his parents would suffer if they lost two sons at once.

He shook his head to clear it, a gesture Lysander interpreted as a second refusal.

"I'm afraid you cannot refuse my request," said the old man in a stern voice. "You know as well as I that, according to the laws of this kingdom, a pilgrim is entitled to the protection of a knight who shares his destination."

Alexi was well aware of his obligation. "You cite a rule seldom invoked," he said, "but I am indeed bound to honor it. Very well, Greylocks. You have my protection as far as the southern provinces." In case the pilgrim had guessed his ultimate destination and intended to follow him farther, he added, "But once we reach the border of the Great Kingdom, my squire and I travel alone."

"As you wish."

Alexi snapped Pitch's reins. The horse clopped onto the King's Way and turned sharply to the south. Ferran and Midnight rode alongside. Lysander's rust-colored mare fell into step behind them.

"Alexi, why didn't you—"

"Shut up, Ferran." *Pesky kid.*

At Ferran's wounded look, contrition pricked Alexi. It wasn't like him to lose patience with his younger brother. "I'm sorry, Ferran," he said. "I seem to be in a foul temper this morning."

"It's okay."

Now the silence of the trip hung even more uncomfortably. Alexi wanted to tell Ferran of his concerns but did not care to speak of them when the pilgrim would hear. Even if he were willing to risk being overheard, Alexi wasn't sure he even knew what to say. The old man had done him no wrong. Indeed, he was more than partially responsible for the knight's current quest.

Why, then, had Alexi reacted so strongly to Lysander's request for protection? And why did Alexi suspect there was more to this old man than there seemed?

Apparently sensing that something more was amiss than Alexi's irritable mood, Ferran had shifted position in his saddle to make sure he could bring his bow into play easily. Alexi didn't think he need fear a physical attack from Lysander. After all, the pilgrim had opportunities to catch the knight in a more vulnerable state in earlier encounters. But Alexi did resolve to be watchful.

After several minutes, Lysander nudged his horse forward, pulling even with Alexi and Ferran. "I appreciate your hospitality," he said.

Alexi shrugged, casting a sidelong glance at his new companion. The fact that he still had not clearly seen the monk's face contributed to his unease. "As you said, I had no choice."

"Yes, you did," said Lysander. "You could have chosen to ignore the laws. As long as one retains free will, one has a choice. Just as this journey you undertake is your choice."

"You know our purpose, then?"

"I believe I do," said the pilgrim. "And I believe you have made the right choice. It is easier for a man to see the future if he puts the past to rest. Avenge Kateri Shadowborn's death, and you will face your own inner darkness as well."

At Lysander's words, the aura of disquiet hanging like a pall around Alexi's heart suddenly gripped him. For the second time since their initial meeting, Alexi sensed the pilgrim knew about his ghoulish nightmares. Was that the "inner darkness" he meant? Or did he merely refer to Alexi's despair following the Darkening?

"Alexi," Ferran whispered. "What's he talking about?"

Alexi cast their new companion a critical look. "Nothing, Ferran," he said. "Nothing at all."

TEN

With a loud pop, the campfire spat a shower of glowing embers into the blackness of the night. For a second, the sparks hung motionless, then a chill autumn breeze swept in and lifted them toward the sky. His hands clasped around his warm coffee mug, Alexi watched the little spots of light rise until they vanished into the night. Whether they faded out or became permanent fixtures of the heavens, he couldn't say.

He rose from his seat on a fallen log and lifted a pot from the fire. "More coffee?" he asked Lysander, filling his own mug. "It's a cold night." Unseasonably cold, he thought.

"No, thank you," came the rasping voice from beneath the red hood. "The chill doesn't seem natural, does it?"

Ferran stepped out of the darkness with a bundle of wood that he'd gathered from the forest around their campsite. "I thought the Borderwood was mostly elm and oak," he complained, "but this place is full of the sharpest, scratchiest pine I've ever seen."

Alexi started to answer, but the pilgrim spoke first. "The northern reaches of the Borderwood are full of pine," he said, "but as we travel farther south, they'll virtually disappear. By the time we pass into the southern provinces, you won't find anything but broadleafs."

With a crash, Ferran dropped his burden near the fire. This marked his fifth foraging expedition and finally brought their supply of wood to a level that should see them through the chilly night.

For a time, silence fell over the camp. The still darkness was punctuated only by the whoosh and snap of the fire. In the background, the hooting of owls and the sounds of other night creatures all blended to form a delicate, pleasant melody.

Alexi breathed in a deep lungful of sweet-smelling smoke and let it out in a long sigh. Under better circumstances, this would be a reasonably pleasant evening for camping, despite the chill. But tonight his thoughts were filled with his mother's murder and the steps he would need to take to identify and locate her killer once he reached the Southern Empire. The more he thought about what lay ahead, the more he realized he didn't know. Had he embarked on a hero's quest or a fool's errand?

Pitch snapped his head up and released an uneasy whinny. Alexi froze, noting that the sounds of the Borderwood had vanished. His eyes darted to Ferran, who was only a beat behind him in noticing the sudden descent of silence over their camp.

Lysander began to speak, but Alexi flashed a hand up to command silence. The pilgrim looked left and right. "What's wrong?" he whispered.

"Someone—or something—is moving toward our camp," responded Alexi. "Just keep looking into the fire and act as if nothing is wrong."

Lysander nodded almost imperceptibly.

Alexi rose and stretched in the dancing yellow light. He placed his hand on the hilt of his sword in a nonchalant fashion and slowly drew out the blade. "Ferran," he said casually, "fetch me a whetstone and some oil."

The squire hopped to his feet and loped over to horses. With as little fuss as he could manage, he picked up one of the saddlebags from the ground. Pulling it open, he drew out a buckskin pouch and brought it to Alexi.

Alexi accepted the package with a meaningful look at his brother, then dropped back to his seat beside the old man. He turned his sword over, allowing the firelight to trickle down its razor edge. As he began to hone the weapon, he looked up again and nodded at his squire. "It's time for you to get some sleep, little brother. We have a long ride ahead of us tomorrow."

Ferran offered a muttered protest, exactly as he might have on any other night, then gave in. He moved away from the campfire and vanished through the flap of his small tent.

Anyone watching the campsite would have mistaken the shuffling sounds inside the tent for the normal noises of a young man getting ready to retire for the night. Alexi, however, knew better. He didn't have to see what was going on to know his squire was drawing a string across the graceful curves of his yew-wood bow. In a few seconds, all was quiet in the tent. The knight smiled. He knew that a steel-tipped arrow was nocked and ready to greet anyone who might threaten them.

With a steady, tapering motion, Alexi drew Corona across the rough surface of the whetstone. At the conclusion of every fifth or sixth stroke, he lifted the blade to examine its edge. As he repeated this ritual, he whispered to Lysander.

"I'm going to get up and leave you in a moment," he said, fairly certain that the grinding of the whetstone covered his every word. "Remain by the fire. Whoever waits out there should continue to watch you. I'll move around behind our visitor and take him by surprise."

"You mean I am the bait?" murmured the old man. Though Alexi assumed he must be afraid, his voice betrayed no emotion.

"Exactly." He gave Corona's edge a final taste of the whetstone and rose again. Drawing a chamois from the pouch, he deftly wiped the blade down, then returned it to its sheath.

"I think I'll turn in now as well," Alexi said in a normal voice. "But first I have a little business to tend to in the woods."

"Too much coffee?" offered the old man.

Alexi chuckled in response and then walked calmly away from the fire. He carefully left his hand on Corona's hilt but made sure he didn't appear on his guard.

As the branches of spruce trees stung him, Alexi moved quickly. He brought Corona out of its scabbard and circled the camp. In less than a minute, he came upon the edge of the King's Way and knelt behind the row of scrub that lined it.

His eyes, still partially blinded from the glare of the campfire, saw no sign of an enemy. For a second, Alexi thought that perhaps there was no one to see. Still, Pitch was seldom wrong when he sensed danger, and Alexi could feel the horse's tension from across the camp. *Something* was out here. He just had to find it.

As his eyes adjusted to the meager light offered by the stars on this as yet moonless night, he heard a faint, staccato sound. Steady and rhythmic, it was a sound he knew well—hoofbeats on a stone road.

Then he saw the outline of the intruder. The poor light hampered his vision, but he could see and hear that the approaching rider was armored. Did another knight ride this way, or was the horseman a traveling mercenary? Alexi bet on the latter. And would this warrior prove friend or foe? The Borderwood harbored as many evil swordsmen as honest ones, the stories said.

His sword drawn, Alexi stepped from the brush directly into the center of the King's Way. The approaching horse did not rear up as he had hoped, showing it to be an animal of good training and solid nerve. That was a bad sign, for it meant the beast was used to surprises—perhaps even combat.

By now Ferran should have slipped away from the camp as well. If nothing had gone wrong, the squire would have his bow drawn and be ready to drop the rider at the first sign of hostility. The lack of moonlight would make for a difficult shot, however. Alexi decided to improve his brother's aim.

"*Karnas, radamar,*" he commanded.

At once the blazing light of day burst from Corona. The trees, which only seconds before had been towering patches of darkness against an equally black sky, now blazed colors nearly as bright as the sword. Below, the stones of the highway stretched before him like a gray ribbon, while above, the stars instantly faded out of existence. To his wonder, Alexi found that the sudden brilliance did not blind him or even force him to shield his eyes. Somehow Corona's magic protected his vision from the sudden luminescence.

The approaching horse, however, was not so lucky. While it had bravely withstood Alexi's sudden appearance on the road, the onset of Corona's brilliant light broke its nerve. Whinnying in terror, the golden beast reared up on its hind legs and kicked madly at the air before it.

The armored figure, equally unprepared for the burst of light, pitched from the saddle. After a less than graceful arc through the air, mail met stone with a loud crash. Either unconscious or stunned by the fall, the rider lay motionless on the highway. A circular shield clattered to the ground beside its owner.

Alexi moved quickly. He reached the fallen knight and, for the first time, saw the four-pointed star and nimbus on the shield.

"Dasmaria!"

For a moment, he was convinced the fall from the saddle had killed her. Her features were still and her eyes closed. As fear began to grip his heart, a low groan slipped from her lips.

Relief washed over him as he checked for broken bones. In a few minutes, as she regained consciousness, Alexi was certain that Dasmaria's injuries would be limited to bruises and a cut or two.

"Are you trying to kill me?" she asked finally, slowly sitting up. She glared at Alexi, anger gleaming in her dark eyes.

"You're lucky I didn't," said Alexi as he got to his feet. "Sneaking up on our camp like that."

"I was riding down the middle of the road!"

Alexi held out a hand to Dasmaria. She grasped him about the wrist and pulled herself to her feet. After a few uncertain steps and a couple of deep breaths to get her lungs working again, she released his arm.

He searched her face, not quite knowing what to say to her. The last time they had spoken, he was preparing to take his place in the Circle. Since then, the Darkening had elevated Dasmaria to paladinhood by shrouding him in shame.

She met his gaze, and he could see reflected in her eyes all the awkwardness he felt. Silence hung between them. Finally she broke off eye contact, focusing instead on the glowing sword.

"Fantastic," she said in a hushed voice. "Is that Corona?"

"It is." Alexi could not help but marvel at the way the pure light glowed on her olive skin and illuminated the depths of her dark eyes.

Dasmaria reached out her hand tentatively. With her fingertips less than an inch from the flat of the blade, she suddenly became still. The wonder in her face mixed with trepidation. Then, as a look of confidence spread over her features, she stretched out her fingers to touch the glowing steel.

"It's cool to the touch," she said, "just like normal steel. I've never seen anything like it."

"Nor have I," said Alexi. "Would you like to hold it?"

She nodded. With a snap of his wrist, Alexi spun the blade about and handed her the weapon. She took the falcon-shaped hilt in her hand and reverently lifted the sword.

In that instant, darkness crashed down upon them. For a second, Alexi panicked. Had some evil smothered the magic of his sword? But although the sudden darkness obscured his vision, he sensed no immediate peril looming in the brush.

"What happened?" asked Dasmaria, her voice tinged with disappointment.

"I'm not sure," Alexi said. "Perhaps you have to activate it again."

"How do I do that?"

Alexi told her the words that he had spoken to bring light to the weapon, and she repeated them. Darkness, however, continued to envelop the highway.

"That won't work," came a voice from the edge of the forest. Dasmaria bent low, ready to strike with the sword in her hand. Alexi, recognizing the gravelly voice, laid a calming hand on her arm.

"It's all right, Das," he said. "That's Lysander Greylocks, a pilgrim traveling with me."

"A friend of yours?" She kept her voice too low for the approaching figure to hear.

"I'm not sure about that," he said just as softly. "But he's been with Ferran and me since we left the Shadowlands."

Dasmaria handed Corona back to Alexi, who slipped it smoothly into his scabbard. He turned to face the pilgrim as Dasmaria reached out to take the reins of her still jittery war-horse.

"Why won't Corona light for Dasmaria?" Alexi asked.

"Because she is not the child of Kateri Shadowborn," said the old pilgrim. "Do you know so little of magic and arcane weapons as to believe that just anyone can call upon the powers of a noble blade like Corona?"

"I admit to ignorance in such matters," said Alexi defensively.

There was a momentary pause, then the old man bowed slightly from the waist. "Forgive me," he said solemnly, "I meant no disrespect."

Alexi's muttered response was lost as he knelt to recover Dasmaria's shield. He handed the heavy disc to its owner and gestured toward the sanctuary of the glowing campfire. "Come," he said. "Our camp lies just ahead. I think we even have some stew left from dinner."

When the trio came into the light of the blazing campfire, Ferran joined them. As Alexi had expected, his younger brother had also circled into the woods. Dasmaria acknowledged the returning squire with a smile and handed Ember's reins to him, then released the catches on her helmet and slipped it from her head. Her raven braid spilled out onto her shoulder as she cocked her head to one side and then the other. Alexi knew the gesture well—such headgear could get quite heavy after a day on the road.

He swallowed hard and took a deep breath. "I never congratulated you on your Ascension," he said. "I know you'll bring more than your share of honor to the order."

"Thank you," she said stiffly. "I—" she met his gaze— "I truly wish the day had gone differently, Alexi."

As if hoping that putting some physical distance between them would dissipate the awkwardness they both felt, Dasmaria walked over to her amber mare. Although not a match for Pitch, Ember was a fine, spirited animal. Dasmaria hooked her helmet onto her saddle. "Keep an eye on this for me," she said affectionately, offering her mount a private smile.

As he sat down on the fallen log, Alexi shook his head in contemplation. He had known Dasmaria for years, ridden beside her on quests, and stood back to back with her in pitched battle. Never in all that time had he seen her treat anyone with the tenderness that she showed Ember. Even Shandra, her able young squire, received only Dasmaria's usual reserved treatment.

What made this beautiful woman keep her distance from everyone around her? Alexi doubted that anyone knew her better than he did, but he had no answer for his own question. And now that the Darkening had created such tension between them, he feared he would never crack her shell.

She stepped away from the horse, her stilted motions clearly showing the stiffness of a long day in the saddle—and the sudden end that had come to that day. She reached beneath the yellow and red surcoat draped over her breastplate. After a few moments of effort, her fingers found and released the bindings holding her chausses on. With a slick sound, the chain mail leggings fell away to reveal the light brown buckskin beneath.

Dasmaria picked up the heavy chausses, folded them over, and stowed them in her saddlebag. Like Alexi, she chose to leave her metal breastplate on, and hence the chain mail hauberk that protected her arms. Both warriors had spent enough time in battle to feel a good deal safer with at least some armor on, even when there was no apparent danger.

With all that done, Dasmaria strode over to Alexi. "There's only one thing that feels better than taking armor off—" she said, beginning the punch line of a joke so old that neither of them needed to hear it to enjoy it.

"—and that's putting it on," finished Alexi. Despite the awkwardness, it felt good to have Dasmaria here. Her presence made the journey seem more like former ones, before the Darkening. "I haven't asked yet how you found us."

"I was concerned about you, so I went to Shadowfast this morning," she said. "Your parents told me that you had just left, and why. So I got my gear together and followed you."

"Where's Shandra?" Ferran asked.

"I left her behind," said Dasmaria. She turned to Alexi. "Just as you should have done with your squire." Her eyes held intensity. He had seen this expression in Dasmaria often, but usually just prior to battle. Something weighed heavily upon her.

"What do you mean?" Alexi asked.

Dasmaria glanced pointedly at Ferran.

Alexi was silent a moment. Then he rose and motioned Ferran away. "It's time you got some sleep."

Ferran looked as if he were considering a protest, then decided this was not the time to push his luck. Instead, he nodded obediently and slipped away.

Turning to offer similar advice to the old man, Alexi discovered that Lysander had gone. Clever man, he thought. The pilgrim must have gathered that this conversation was not for his ears. It was oft said that age begot wisdom.

He glanced back at Dasmaria. "You were saying?"

"You have no business embarking on this quest, Alexi."

"Why?" The muscles in his jaw tightened. One day a paladin, and already Dasmaria was judging him.

"Because the Darkening . . ." She stopped, her expression pained.

Now every muscle in his body tensed. "Go ahead and say it, Dasmaria. Because of the Darkening, you think I'm unworthy."

She shook her head. "That's not what I was going to say."

"What, then?"

"Alexi, the Darkening altered the whole course of your life. And just two days later, you ride off to take revenge on the whole Southern Empire? You're going to get yourself killed."

"You have so little faith in me?" he asked, her words twisting in his heart like barbs. Dasmaria was his closest friend, his staunchest ally. If she no longer believed in him, who would?

"I didn't say that. It's just that you're only—"

"Only a knight?" His wounded spirit now burned with anger. "Is that it, Dasmaria? I'm a mere knight, not a *paladin* like you?" His fists clenched at her audacity. Wasn't it enough that she had usurped his place in the Circle? Did she have to flaunt the fact?

"Only one man," she finished stiffly. "You're not being fair, Alexi."

He'd learned this week that a lot of things weren't fair, he wanted to retort. But deep down, he knew she was right. She did not deserve to be the recipient of his pent-up anger, nor the envy that had wormed its way into his heart. The Darkening and its subsequent events had not been her doing.

"I'm sorry, Das," he said. "I thought I was handling this better." He sat down on the fallen log and stared into the fire.

Dasmaria sat down beside him. "Alexi, if I could change—"

"Don't." He turned to face her. "Belenus chose you, Dasmaria. And if the honor could not be mine, I would have chosen you, too."

She was silent a moment, her expression serious. "Alexi," she said finally, "I felt no joy after the Ascension service, for I knew the despair in your heart. I am your friend. You know that, don't you?"

He nodded. Her words soothed away some of the shame he felt at his outburst.

"Then you know that I'm here only to offer my help."

"I appreciate that," he said, "but the Darkening is my own burden to bear. There's nothing you can do."

"Isn't there? I think talking you out of this suicidal quest is something."

Why could no one trust his judgment? The quest wasn't suicidal, and he didn't want to be talked out of it—not by his father, and not by Dasmaria. Alexi stood and held out a hand to her. "Walk with me," he said quietly.

She took his fair hand in her darker fingers and rose. "Where are we going?"

"Just down the road a bit," he responded. "Ferran's already heard an earful, no doubt. He doesn't need to hear any more."

She dropped his hand and walked beside him away from the camp. In a matter of seconds, the darkness had swallowed up the welcome light of the campfire. Brigit, however, had finally started her ascent in the night sky. They headed back toward the highway.

"Tell me why you think this quest is suicidal," Alexi said as their feet struck the stone.

"Because I don't believe you've thought it through," she said.

Her statement forced a wry smile from him. "So we're back to this argument again, are we? Alexi rushes in where Dasmaria fears to tread?"

"I'm serious, Alexi. Ever since the Ascension, I've been doing a lot of thinking about the Darkening. I don't believe it was a sign that you were unworthy."

"No?" He stopped, searching her expression in the moonlight. "Then what did it mean?"

"Alexi, I've fought alongside you for years," she said. "If you were unclean, I think I would have noticed. No, I believe that the Darkening was a warning from Belenus that joining the Circle was not the path for you. I believe he calls you to another service, perhaps something even more noble than being a paladin."

Her words echoed Lysander's so closely that a shiver ran through him. Surely both of them could not be wrong.

"I think you need to return to the Shadowlands and work with the High Mother to discover what this calling is," Dasmaria continued. "If you run away on this personal vendetta—"

"I am not running away from anything. And seeking justice for my mother is no mere vendetta."

Dasmaria stepped back. "Forgive me, Alexi. It's difficult for me to talk about this. Perhaps I chose my words poorly." Pausing, she reached out her hands and clasped them around his. The display of tenderness surprised him, but he said nothing. "I only want to help you find your way."

Alexi looked into her eyes. "I think I know my way," he said. "I believe Belenus showed it to me in a dream."

"A dream? Tell me about it."

He related the vision he'd had of his mother's final hour, the traitor who had come for her, the evil sword that had slain her. He told her also of his encounters with Lysander. "The dream couldn't have been pure fancy, Das," he said when he had finished, "for that's how I learned the words to light Corona."

"This Lysander . . . do you trust him?"

"I'm not sure," he said. "He's a holy man, and he healed Ferran's broken leg. But I find his sudden appearances a little spooky."

"And coincidental." Dasmaria sighed. "I shall have to give this matter more thought. Meanwhile, we'd best get back to camp. Matins come early. Besides, we've been gone a long time, and I don't know if either of us trusts that old man enough to leave him with Ferran."

"Don't worry," Alexi said. He had seen his squire in battle many times. "If anything had happened at our camp, we would have heard it."

She nodded and turned with him to retrace their

steps along the flagstone highway. Alexi felt a strange sense of relief at having confided in Dasmaria. While he had told Ferran and his parents the generalities of his dream, he could express only to Das all the emotions that had accompanied it.

During Alexi's recounting, Dasmaria had kept quiet. Now, as they stepped into the woods again, she finally voiced her opinion.

"I still think this quest may be ill-advised," she said. "But I also can tell that you're not going to turn back no matter what I say."

"You're right on the second count," said Alexi, "but I hope that you're wrong on the first."

"Me, too," she said softly. "Me, too."

With that, Dasmaria stopped walking. Alexi felt a tug on his shoulder as he started to take his next step. Only then did he realize they had been walking hand in hand. He turned to face her.

"Just to make sure I prove myself wrong," she almost whispered, "I think I'd better ride south with you for a time." Alexi blinked in surprise and started to respond, but she pressed a finger to his lips. "Don't say anything," she said, "or I'll have to invoke the same order of protection the old man did."

A smile touched his lips. "It will be my pleasure to act as guardian and protector for the honorable Dasmaria, Paladin of the Circle, as she rides through such dangerous country."

"Don't take the Borderwood so lightly," came the voice of Lysander, who seemed to materialize from the very darkness. Alexi, who started at the sudden arrival, noticed that Dasmaria had gone for her weapon the instant Greylocks spoke.

"Sneaking up on armed knights is a good way to get

yourself killed," she cautioned, hand still gripping the gilt sword at her side.

"I'll have to remember that," said the pilgrim, "or I might die while I'm still young."

The old man pressed past them. Lysander took several steps, then pointed at something on the ground with the steel-shod tip of his staff. "Here's another one," he said grimly. "Take a look at this, Alexi. Your horse is more clever than we are."

Alexi and Dasmaria moved to see what the bent figure had discovered. There, clearly visible in the soft soil of the forest, were several newly made footprints. Although they looked human, there was something slightly wrong about them.

"It wasn't the young lady's arrival that upset Pitch," rasped Lysander, his expression unreadable behind the folds of his red hood. "We've had other company tonight. Ghouls."

ELEVEN

Alexi drew in a lungful of thick, foul air and made a sour face. A trickle of sweat ran down from under his helmet, reminding him how miserably hot the weather had become this morning. The air had been so chilly when they broke camp at dawn that it seemed impossible for the temperature to have risen so high. Nevertheless, it had.

Swatting away a swarm of gnats and bloodflies, he reined Pitch to a halt and unrolled a map. Its edges curled in the humidity.

"This isn't right," he said, shaking his head. He turned to face his companions. "There's no swamp on the map."

"Forget the maps," growled Dasmaria as she, too, tried to chase away a relentless cloud of insects. "There isn't a swamp anywhere along the King's Way. I've traveled this road a dozen times since we moved from the southern provinces. Lysander, you must have done the same if you were born among the heretics."

Alexi looked to the old man's face, expecting to see some measure of disapproval at Dasmaria's tone. However, even the blistering heat had not caused him to draw back his crimson hood. Alexi and the others saw only an emotionless nod. "She is right, Alexi."

"Perhaps we're lost," said Ferran.

"That's impossible," Alexi snapped. "We haven't left the King's Way." He struggled to keep his irritation in check. None of them had gotten much sleep last night, since they had doubled up on watches because of the ghouls. Fortunately the creatures had not made a return appearance.

"Damn!" Alexi swatted at a bloodfly on his wrist. Already, his hands were covered with bites. Dasmaria raised a brow at his uncharacteristic oath but said nothing.

Alexi surveyed the situation. Behind them, the thick forest of the Borderwood spread out like a great living wall. Indeed, so sharp was the line of demarcation between forest and mire that Alexi and Pitch were clopping through stagnant water before Ferran, whose horse followed some thirty yards behind, had even left the cool shade of the trees.

The swamp stretched out from the edge of the forest on both sides of the King's Way. The murky gray and green water steamed under the intense sunlight. Tangles of trees, almost hidden beneath creepers and vines, rose like islands in the mire. Dark shapes, likely snakes or other predators, slithered through the water. Leaving the road to travel east or west was out of the question.

Ahead, the road south looked equally uninviting. Already half an inch of thick water spread across the road, cracks appeared in the flagstones, and outcroppings of dense, mosslike grasses threatened to trip the unwary traveler. Even the air seemed different in this place: It took an effort of will to breathe.

"Do we continue," asked Dasmaria, "or do we turn back?"

She already knew the answer, as did the others in the company. "Keep your weapons at hand, especially your bow, Ferran," Alexi said as he nudged Pitch forward. The other horses fell into step behind him. "We don't know what sort of creatures live in this cesspool."

They rode in silence most of the morning. The oppressive heat of the swamp and the sickly taste of the air made casual conversation too uncomfortable to be worth the effort. Besides, no one was in the mood for small talk. Occasionally someone would growl in irritation at a painful insect bite, but that was the extent of their dialogue.

Alexi noticed that the insects of the swamp seemed to ignore Lysander; no doubt the pests could not bite through the heavy robes he wore. He wondered if the protection was worth it; those heavy robes must be uncomfortably hot. Indeed, he and Dasmaria were already wearing less armor than they normally did when riding. Both had chosen to remove and store the chain mail that protected their legs and arms. The knights still wore their breastplates and helmets, although the latter were in place primarily to keep the sun off their faces.

As they continued on, the mists thickened and the temperature rose, as though Belenus had focused his searing gaze on the offensive swamp water to boil it away. The relentless splashing of hooves became an almost soporific melody.

They plodded on, the miles crawling past. A thick mist gradually rose out of the swamp. Instead of being cool and refreshing, however, the mist was cloying and thick, more like steam than fog. Could they have found their way into some volcanic region? Certainly none appeared on the map, but neither did the swamp.

With the Eye of Belenus obscured by the mist, Alexi found it difficult to judge the passage of time. Every minute of riding through this vile place blurred into the next. With visibility so low that he couldn't see more than fifteen feet ahead, he couldn't fix on landmarks and use them to estimate their pace.

Even if he could see, Alexi doubted anything of interest lay ahead. Vine-choked trees and sickly-looking swamp plants offered little in the way of scenery. They had entered a realm that seemed to consist wholly of muck and heat.

When Alexi guessed that sunset approached, he signaled a halt. The group had come upon a ridge of stone and earth that offered something of an island where they could camp. It was slick with algae and could only barely be considered dry land, but they needed a break, and it was time for the knights to offer sunset devotions to Belenus.

As Ferran did his best to gather wood for a cookfire, Dasmaria and Alexi prayed to the sun god. Somewhat to Alexi's surprise, Lysander joined in the holy rite. Even though he was a follower of Brigit, not Belenus, he had certainly studied their customs well. Alexi doubted he would be able to return the compliment in kind when the moon goddess made her way into the night sky.

By the time they concluded the service, Ferran had a small cookfire started. Alexi actually felt thankful the wood was too wet and scarce for a larger blaze. The last thing this place needed was more heat or thicker air, though he hoped the smoke would ward off some of the insects. And the light would help illuminate the area once night fell. The four of them would have to be every bit as watchful as they were last night, though with luck they had left the ghouls far behind.

As he sent Ferran to the saddlebags for provisions, he noticed Lysander kneeling by the water's edge. Curious, Alexi stepped closer to the pilgrim—and watched in horror as Lysander filled the last of their drinking skins with murky swamp water. He snatched the leather pouch out of the old man's hand, but one sniff told him he was too late. All their precious water was tainted with the muck.

"Are you mad?" demanded Alexi. "We don't know how much farther we have to ride through this place! That might have been our only clean water for the next day or even a week!"

Dasmaria and Ferran sprang to his side. "What happened?" asked the squire anxiously.

"He filled our waterskins in the swamp!"

"We can try boiling it," suggested Ferran.

"It won't taste any better," said Dasmaria, her revulsion evident.

Lysander shook his head. "No matter what you might think of me, I am not a fool," he said calmly. "And I am not out to poison you, either. Please place the skin you hold over there with the others."

Alexi replaced the stopper and reluctantly did as told. When he stood up, Lysander motioned for him to step back. The old man slowly opened his arms to the sky. Alexi noticed again how thin the pilgrim's arms were. The knight had seen mummified corpses with more life in them than this old man. It was a wonder he could match the pace of the younger riders.

In the ancient holy tongue, the same language that held such power over the magical Corona, Lysander chanted a prayer. For a man with a usually harsh and scratchy voice, the pilgrim's intonations sounded almost musical.

Alexi so thoroughly lost himself in Lysander's hypnotic prayers that before he realized it, the thick swamp air had swallowed the last of his words and the old man was reaching out to touch each of the waterskins. For a moment, the slate-gray sky seemed to slacken just enough to allow a trace of early evening moonlight to glint briefly on each of the skins.

The old man sighed, with either effort or satisfaction or both. He lifted one of the waterskins slowly, his arms shaking a bit with the effort. Turning unevenly, he handed his burden to Alexi. "Open it," he said softly, his voice rough again. "See what you think of the old fool now."

Alexi pulled the stopper and raised the plug to his nose, wrinkling his face in expectation. Then he glanced at Lysander in surprise. He put his lips to the spout and tilted his head back. Water drained into his mouth—not the hot, brackish fluid he'd expected, but cool, refreshing liquid that might have been freshly drawn from a mountain spring.

"Amazing," he said, wiping his mouth.

Dasmaria accepted the skin and took a tentative taste, her eyes widening in astonishment. Seconds later, Ferran did the same.

"I think the time has come for you to answer a few questions," Alexi said to Lysander. He turned to Ferran and instructed his squire to start making their evening meal. The boy looked disappointed to miss what promised to be a revealing exchange but did as he was told. Dasmaria moved to stand beside her fellow knight, presenting a unified front to the mysterious pilgrim.

"In the country of my birth," said Lysander, "we are

more polite in asking questions of our elders."

"I mean no disrespect," said Alexi, "but there are things I must know before we continue. Until now I was content to just keep an eye on you while we rode. But with this display, circumstances have changed."

"I understand," the pilgrim said. "You fear the powers I just used on your behalf."

Alexi's eyes narrowed. "I fear nothing," he said. "But I am responsible for the safety of the entire company. If you are more than you appear to be, I must know."

"Very well," said Lysander. "Ask me your questions. And you need not worry. I shall answer them truthfully."

Before Alexi could begin his interrogation, however, the horses began to nicker loudly. The knights whirled as one, their blades flashing into their hands. Alexi called out a terse command and Pitch fell silent. Similar instructions by Dasmaria and Ferran stilled their mounts, although the animals all continued to fidget. Ferran appeared at his brother's side, bow in hand and a slender shaft ready to fly.

"Everyone form a ring," ordered Alexi. "Put your backs to the fire and prepare for an attack."

The others followed his instructions, Lysander taking the position to Alexi's left. The old man held no weapon, but radiated a self-confidence that announced his familiarity with combat. Alexi couldn't imagine the pilgrim as anything more than a hindrance in battle, but the old man had surprised him once already today.

The swampy waters around the campsite suddenly seemed to explode. All around them, black shapes erupted from the mire. At first glance, they might have been crocodiles or other natural creatures of the swamp. But Alexi knew better. He had encountered these beasts before.

Ghouls.

Though he'd seen them often enough in his dreams, Alexi still found it difficult to look upon the ranks of the cannibalistic dead. Their dry flesh stretched so taut over their bones that it gave them a jagged, spiky appearance. Mouths open wide in howls of fury showed rows of needlelike teeth that Alexi knew could easily flay the flesh from a man's bones. Wicked claws on the ends of unnaturally long fingers groped for him and his companions. Even the wretched air of the swamp could not smother the stench that hung about the creatures.

Ferran cried out in terror at the sight of the hideous beasts. He tried to hold his bow steady, but the arrow trembled nonetheless. Alexi found no fault in his brother's fear, remembering very clearly his own terror when he first faced the undead monsters.

Like Alexi, Dasmaria had battled such creatures before, but even so, she recoiled in disgust as they sprang toward her. Only Lysander seemed unaffected by the hideous foes. Alexi added that to his list of questions to ask the supposedly reformed heretic.

He abandoned his thoughts quickly, however, as two ghouls leapt upon him. He brought Corona around swiftly. The blade caught one of the revolting creatures cleanly in the neck and instantly severed its head. Black ichor as thick as tar bubbled from the open wound as the ghoul's momentum carried it past Alexi. It splashed into the murky water behind the knight and was instantly sucked beneath the surface. The other creature, seeing its fellow so swiftly dispatched, halted a moment to assess its enemy with glistening black eyes.

Out of the corner of his eye, Alexi saw Ferran. The boy had fallen back, hoping to keep his bow in play. The young squire loosed a shaft that buried itself deep in the chest of an advancing ghoul. The creature staggered forward two more steps, then toppled. Before it hit the ground, Ferran had another shaft in place and took aim at a second creature.

Suddenly the ghoul before Alexi lunged forward. It slashed at him with black claws and hissed toxic breath in his face. Alexi flashed Corona through the air. It passed effortlessly through the ghoul's wrists, cleanly removing its gnarled hands from gangly arms. Putrid black ichor boiled out of the wounds, and a shriek of agony filled the air.

Beyond the creatures, Alexi saw Dasmaria working with her usual smooth efficiency. Her golden blade flashed cleanly with every stroke. Indeed, from where Alexi stood, Dasmaria seemed to battle the beasts with bolts of golden lightning. Two ghouls fell quickly before her dancing blade, but another pair promptly moved in to take their place.

Three more ghouls advanced toward him. This time, Alexi took the initiative. As the creatures licked their needlelike teeth, their raspy tongues salivating at the thought of the marrow in his bones, the knight sprang forward. Before the restless dead knew what was happening, Alexi had cleanly beheaded one and skewered a second.

The third tried to attack from behind, but Alexi whirled in time to fend it off. The creature swiped at him. Alexi quickly backed out of reach. He had to avoid those filthy talons and their paralytic toxin at all costs. Again he aimed his strikes at the ghoul's hands, severing the offensive claws. Once the creature lost its primary weapon, it was easy work to slay the beast.

Alexi spun around to see if any more ghouls advanced and found himself staring straight at the bent form of Lysander Greylocks. The mysterious pilgrim now held a heavy mace in his hand. It was short but dangerous-looking, with a haft just over twelve inches long and a golden ball for a weight. Clearly this was an item of his faith, for the head of the weapon was brightly polished and looked almost like the moon itself.

But Lysander did not depend upon the weapon for safety. Instead, the monk seemed to be keeping the ghouls at bay with his free hand. Twice the creatures rose to attack Lysander, and twice the pilgrim drove them back with nothing more than a silver crescent moon on a chain: the symbol of Brigit. Alexi knew that especially pious priests and paladins had such powers over the ranks of the undead, but he hadn't realized that Lysander might be counted among that number.

Unless, that is, this attack was an elaborate hoax, orchestrated by a man who could command the undead to do his bidding. Suspicion raced through Alexi's mind that perhaps the mysterious pilgrim was not actually driving the creatures away but commanding them to fall back until a later time.

Alexi, however, had no time to dwell on such thoughts. To his side, three more ghouls rose from the brackish water. At the same time, he heard a cry of pain behind him. He dared not turn his head to see what was happening, but the voice was Dasmaria's. One of the hideous creatures must have gotten past her whirling blade. Alexi shuddered to think of so profane a creature laying its twisted claws upon his companion.

But Alexi had his own problems. The three ghouls sprang at him, one of the beasts impaling itself on Corona in the process. Before a shocked Alexi could free the weapon, the other two creatures crashed headlong into him. Their putrid weight drove him back and, when two more of the beasts leapt upon him, bore him down to the ground.

The impact drove the air from his lungs and nearly sent Corona tumbling out of his hand. He thrashed about, trying in vain to free himself. Held fast to the lichen-covered rock upon which they had camped, Alexi found himself looking directly into the corpselike face of one of the ghouls. He gasped, retching at the smell of the creature's foul breath.

The ghoul leaned close, its black eyes glistening scant inches from Alexi's own. Its dry, leathery lips spread wide in a sadistic smile. Black saliva dribbled out of the fiend's mouth to splatter on Alexi's cheek as an almost serpentine tongue slipped out between them, stretching down to scrape across his face.

The powerful fingers of another ghoul tore off his helmet and grabbed fistfuls of hair. The monster forced back Alexi's head, straining his neck to the breaking point and exposing his throat. With a hissing laugh, the first ghoul opened its mouth wide and leaned forward.

Alexi tried to raise his sword, but his arm was pinned. If only he could distract—

Two words flashed into his mind. Although he could hardly even breathe with his head forced so far back, Alexi forced himself to speak. "*Karnas* . . ." he croaked.

The creature's teeth touched the delicate flesh of his throat. The sadistic beast moved slowly, enjoying every lingering second of this horrid *coup de grace*.

". . . *radamar*."

Brilliant shafts of pure, holy light flooded the twilight. The ghouls cried out in an agony so terrible that Alexi almost felt sympathy for them. The smell of burning flesh filled his nostrils.

Where golden light touched the exposed skin of the

living dead, coils of smoke twisted into the air. The undead flesh boiled, blackened, then smoldered away to expose the bone beneath. Free of the arms that had restrained him, Alexi forced his way clear of the smoking, shrieking corpses.

Corona's radiance was affecting all the ghouls in the same manner. Those who could still move shuffled away as quickly as they could into the outlying darkness. One of the ghouls, however, a creature taller and more powerfully built than its peers, hesitated for a second. Even as its skin blistered under the light of the holy sword, the malevolent creature fixed Alexi with a withering gaze of pure, unbridled hatred. Then, snarling like a rabid dog, it joined the rest in retreat.

Even as the beast turned away from him, Alexi saw that it bore a crimson mark on its forehead. Contrasting sharply with the sickly gray flesh, the tattoo was the same horned death's-head that Alexi had seen on the graveyard ghouls. What could the emblem mean?

He had no time to contemplate it. All at once, Alexi was seized by anguish and agony so great it brought him to his knees.

The scene around him dimmed until it finally faded into blackness. Pain seared his chest. He doubled over, scarcely able to move.

Images of death and undeath flashed before him. Crypts, coffins, graveyards, ghouls. Dark shapes conducting unholy rites in inhuman voices. An altar inscribed with a horned death's-head.

It was happening again. Just as when he had killed the ghouls in the cemetery, their existences somehow merged with his own. Only this time, it was worse. Much worse.

A malevolent force pressed upon his spirit, trying to

smother it. He focused all his energy on fending it off but could not. It found a crack in his defenses—a crack, Alexi somehow realized, left there by the first incident—and entered his heart like a shard of ice. Coldness beyond his ken seeped into his chest. From there, the malignancy attempted to spread throughout his being.

No! He had to contain it, had to keep it from dominating his will. He gripped Corona reflexively, but all his warrior's training could not help him in this battle.

Alexi convulsed. He knew he was losing the struggle. He could feel the negative energy battering for release, feel his own resistance failing. He couldn't hold out much longer.

In desperation, his spirit cried out. *Belenus, help me!*

And then it was over.

The sinister force left him. Belenus had answered his prayer.

Gasping for air, Alexi opened his eyes. He lay curled in a fetal position, Corona still clenched in his hand. The sword still glowed with Belenus's light, but the warmth could not dispel the cold that clung to his heart.

Trembling, he rose to his feet. He turned to see whether any of his companions had noticed his seizure. Lysander stood with his back to Alexi, watching the last of the few surviving ghouls vanish up the road and into the night. Alexi glanced around, trying to spot the others.

The sight of Dasmaria nearly made his heart stop.

"Dasmaria!" he cried.

She lay flat on her back, the lower half of her body under the foul water. A lengthy gash exposed the bone in her forearm. Blood poured from the wound to form a scarlet pool on the slick black rock.

Alexi extinguished his glowing sword and buried the

blade in its scabbard. In what seemed a single bound, he was beside the fallen warrior. Her dark features looked pale from loss of blood, and agony showed clearly on her face. Her eyes were wide open, and Alexi could clearly see the suffering in them.

Lysander joined him, kneeling beside the pair of warriors. "She can hear you," said the pilgrim, "but she can't respond. It's the doing of the ghouls. Their claws and fangs carry a toxin that paralyzes the muscles."

"I know," Alexi said. But it wasn't the paralysis that mattered right now. At the rate she was losing blood, Alexi knew Dasmaria would be dead in minutes.

He pressed his hands to the gash and felt the warm flow of blood wash over his fingers. He put all his strength into an effort to stanch the crimson torrent but knew at once that it was no good. This wound was too great for conventional healing.

"Lysander, can you heal her? Like you did Ferran?"

The pilgrim nodded. "I can try."

Alexi moved aside to make room for Lysander. The old man placed his withered hands on either side of the wound. He began to pray fervently, holy words in an ancient language calling upon the healing powers of Brigit to aid the fallen paladin.

As Lysander prayed, Alexi whispered words of his own. "You're going to be all right, Das," he said in her ear, recalling the terror he had endured while lying paralyzed and vulnerable. "Lysander is a skilled healer, and we're going to watch over you until you can move again."

Alexi could almost feel the warmth spread outward from Lysander's hands as he watched the unnatural sight of muscle and flesh knitting before his eyes. If only that same warmth could penetrate the knot of cold still within his chest.

Was this response a normal after-effect of fighting ghouls? Alexi pushed the thought from his mind. Right now Dasmaria had to be his chief concern.

Finally the flow of blood slowed and stopped. Lysander slumped back. Alexi took his place at Dasmaria's side and drew her limp body up in his arms.

"Alexi," said Lysander in a soft but urgent tone.

Cradling Dasmaria, the knight pulled her clear of the filthy water. Her even, smooth breathing indicated that the paralysis of the ghoul toxins was fading—no doubt the potent healing power of Brigit had helped to free her of that poison as well.

"Alexi," repeated the old man.

"Yes, Lysander?" He tore his gaze away from Dasmaria's face to look at the old man.

"Ferran is gone. The ghouls have taken him."

TWELVE

"Damn it, Lysander!"

Alexi was tempted to yank off the pilgrim's cowl so he could see Lysander's face. Yelling at a large red hood provided little release for his ire. "Why didn't you say something sooner?"

Lysander shrugged. "What could you have done sooner? Abandoned a wounded paladin to save a squire?"

"He's my brother!"

"In combat, he is your servant," he replied calmly, despite Alexi's agitation. "If you cannot keep that in perspective, you should get a new squire."

Rage flooded Alexi. He wanted to strike the callous old man. "What the hell kind of cleric are you?"

"A practical one. What kind of knight are you to curse at me thus?"

Alexi stormed off to collect his helm and other pieces of armor he'd removed when they made camp. He couldn't believe his brother was gone, taken away by those revolting creatures, and Lysander had allowed precious minutes to elapse before speaking a word. His gorge rose at the thought of Ferran being held by the ghouls. Was he dead, or had he been taken for some more sinister purpose?

"How long before Dasmaria can ride?" he barked, donning his chausses.

"Two or three hours yet," Lysander said. The pilgrim had returned to his patient's side. "She should be able to talk soon, though."

Alexi cursed under his breath. He hated leaving Das alone with the pilgrim, but had little choice. "Good. She can tell you what an idiot you are."

Once Alexi had put on the rest of his armor, he whistled for Pitch. "I'm going to pursue them south," he said. "Follow as soon as Dasmaria is able."

Without waiting for the old man's response, he mounted Pitch and galloped off. The stallion's hooves hammered on the broken flagstone road and threw sheets of water out with every step.

Hold on, Ferran, Alexi thought. I'm coming. The broken branches and disturbed plants along the side of the road marked the ghouls' trail and encouraged him. Surely he was moving far faster than the ghouls. No matter how swift the living dead might be, Pitch was more than their match.

The cold spot in his chest from the attack of the ghouls throbbed. He tried to ignore it, focusing his thoughts on Ferran. He would worry about himself only after his brother was out of danger—or avenged. He was going to slaughter the monsters, leave their rotting carcasses littering this whole vile swamp.

The icy ache grew with each breath, until finally Alexi gasped for air. He tried to rein in his thundering horse, but a barrage of foreign memories and sensations swept over him. Not again, he thought. Not now.

He grew dizzy, unable to tell where the real world

ended and the ghostly universe of the ghouls began. He seemed to be flying—or falling. And then he lay still in utter darkness.

As in the graveyard, Alexi sensed that he now experienced the memories of one of the ghouls that had fallen under his blade. The blackness receded to reveal stone walls lit by flickering candlelight. His heart ached in his chest yet seemed not to beat. He smelled burning incense, felt the presence of someone standing over him.

And then he heard the voice.

"Is it done?"

The moment he heard it, Alexi knew it to be the voice of evil incarnate. The booming tones held no hint of humanity, no echo of mercy. At first Alexi thought it came from the figure near him, but then realized his error. The voice belonged to a power that was everywhere and nowhere.

"It is," the man standing over Alexi responded. The minion's voice implied absolute obedience. "The abbey is ours. All of the monks are dead. They await only your attention, my master."

"There are no survivors?"

"None."

"And the traitor?"

"He is counted among the dead."

"Then the time has come for the dead to walk again."

At that instant, Alexi knew pain greater than he had ever before withstood. Agony swept through his limbs and fire burned within his chest. Muscles and tissue became infused with new and blasphemous energies. He tried to cry out but had no voice.

And then it was over.

Alexi opened his eyes and had to blink several times before the world came into focus. He lay on his back in the murky waters of the swamp. His right arm throbbed with pain. He must have fallen from the saddle during the spell.

He heard the drumming of hooves and tried to reach for his sword. Pain shot through his arm and shoulder. No doubt about it, he had broken his arm. Awkwardly he pulled Corona from its scabbard with his left hand as he rose unsteadily to his feet. He could fight left-handed if he had to, though not as skillfully.

Pitch, however, seemed less concerned about the approaching rider. As Lysander's horse came into view, Alexi resheathed his sword. He leaned on Pitch's flank for support while he waited for the pilgrim to reach him.

"I heard you clatter to the ground from the camp," Lysander said. "What happened?"

"Pitch got spooked and threw me," Alexi said, gripping his limp arm. Pitch nickered as if to protest the lie.

Lysander climbed down from his mount. "Are you injured?"

"I think my arm is broken," Alexi said. "Can you heal it?"

"I'm afraid not," Lysander answered. "My powers of healing are limited. Dasmaria's wounds were quite severe. I can set the bone for you, but I need to rest and meditate before I can heal the break."

Alexi shook his head and turned to mount Pitch. "Ferran can't wait that long."

"Alexi, you have no choice," the old man said. "I know you are angry with me right now, but consider this reasonably. You cannot take on a whole pack of ghouls by yourself with a broken arm." Lysander gestured up the road. "And while we stand here arguing, we leave Dasmaria unprotected in her vulnerable state."

"But Ferran—"

"You might have more time than you think. If the ghouls only wanted to kill the boy, they could have done so right here." He rested a frail hand on Alexi's good arm. "At the very least, come back to the camp, let me set your arm, and wait until Dasmaria can help you."

Alexi could not imagine sitting idle for hours while his brother remained in danger. But Lysander was right—he could not save Ferran by himself with a broken arm. Feeling as if he were admitting defeat, he swallowed hard and nodded. "All right."

He awkwardly climbed into Pitch's saddle and followed Lysander back to camp. The icy pain in his heart had subsided into a dull, cold ache, as if a chunk of ice the size of a peach pit lay embedded in his chest.

By the time the firelight came into view, the pain in his arm had begun to smother his anger at Lysander. If only the old man could heal him now, he wouldn't have to wait for Dasmaria's paralysis to wear off.

Dasmaria sat propped against a large rock, her arms still hanging limp at her sides. "Alexi, what happened?" she called as he entered camp. "Did you overtake them?"

"No." Alexi dismounted slowly, the uselessness of his arm affecting his sense of balance. He walked over to Dasmaria and lowered himself to the ground in front of her. "I slipped from the saddle," he admitted, softly enough that Lysander couldn't hear.

Dasmaria's brows shot up. "You what?" Despite her surprise, she kept her voice down to the level of his. "But, Alexi, you're an excellent—"

"There was more to it." He paused. "Das, I have to ask you something. When you fight ghouls—afterward, do you ever have . . . visions?"

She frowned. "What kind of visions?"

Foreboding flooded him. If she had to ask, she had probably never experienced them, which meant that what was happening to him wasn't normal. "Glimpses of the creature's life—or death." He swallowed. "Or undeath."

She regarded him closely. "No, Alexi. Nothing like that. But you do?"

He hesitated, not sure whether he wanted to divulge the details. The Darkening had cast enough doubts on his character without admitting that he also channeled the thoughts of the undead. But if he couldn't confide in Dasmaria, to whom could he turn to help him make sense of the experiences?

Alexi nodded. "The first time it happened was just over a week ago."

She studied him closely, concern evident in her features. "And it happened again tonight? While you were riding just now?"

"Yes." He considered telling her about the earlier incident in the camp—the one that left the coldness in his chest—but somehow he didn't want to reveal that secret even to Dasmaria.

Lysander shuffled over with a straight piece of wood and some strips of cloth. "Ready for me to set that arm?"

Alexi nodded. At Dasmaria's quizzical expression, he explained that Lysander could not heal him right away. "But regardless, as soon as you're able, we go after Ferran."

The pilgrim removed Alexi's gauntlets, elbow and shoulder pieces, and brassard. He then pressed his fingers along Alexi's upper arm to determine the exact location of the break.

Alexi sucked in his breath. "There—that's it."

Lysander placed the length of wood along the arm. "I heard you telling Dasmaria about having visions of the ghouls," he said as he tied the splint above and below the fracture.

Alexi jerked his head up and stared at Lysander. How had the old man heard them? They had taken care to speak softly, specifically to prevent him from listening.

"If you are of a mind to tell me as well about the visions," Lysander continued, "perhaps we can use the information to figure out where the ghouls have taken your brother."

Alexi wasn't of a mind to share anything with the old man after he had shown so little concern for Ferran earlier. Yet the knight would do anything to help his brother. Could they trust Lysander? He turned to Dasmaria.

She understood the unspoken question. "If we pursue the ghouls with your arm broken, we need every advantage we can gain," she said.

Alexi knew she was right. He couldn't withhold information that might help Ferran. He turned back to Lysander. "In the vision, I was lying in a room with stone walls. It was very dark, but some candles were lit. I smelled incense."

"Were you alone?" Lysander asked. As Alexi spoke, the pilgrim created a sling for Alexi's forearm to take pressure off the broken bone.

"No. Someone was in the room with me, but I couldn't see him," Alexi said. "He was talking to someone, or some*thing*—a deep, ominous voice that echoed off the walls."

"What were they saying?" Dasmaria asked. She turned her head slightly to face him better, a sign that the ghoul toxin was loosening its hold on the muscles of her upper body.

"They spoke of an abbey—I think they had just conquered it." Alexi frowned, trying to recall the conversation exactly. "They said all of the monks were dead, and that they awaited the master's attention." He turned to Lysander. "That's all I remember."

"I don't see that it will help us very much," said Dasmaria.

His ministrations finished, Lysander sat back. "On the contrary, my dear lady, Alexi's information could prove very useful." He glanced at Alexi. "I believe it holds clues to both your brother's whereabouts and your larger quest."

"This vision relates to my mother? How?" Alexi leaned forward, intrigued. What connection could a pack of ghouls have to his mother's crusades?

"In the final months of the Heretical Wars," said Lysander, "Kateri Shadowborn often spoke with a monk whose counsel proved invaluable to her. Once the wars ended, agents of the defeated Southern Empire made their way into the Great Kingdom. They went to Forenoon Abbey, the monastery where that monk served, and assassinated him and his brothers."

"Is that the abbey in my vision?" asked Alexi.

"I believe so," said Lysander. "If, as you say, the dead monks were 'awaiting their master,' it's possible that the unfortunate holy men were not allowed to rest in peace. The ghouls who attacked us tonight may well have been the undead remnants of the murdered monks of Forenoon Abbey."

Alexi shuddered. What an awful eternal existence for men who had devoted their lives to serving their god. "If your speculations prove true, what have they done with my brother?"

"They are probably carrying young Ferran back to

their lair—the abbey itself."

"And you know where that is?" asked Dasmaria. Alexi thought he detected a trace of skepticism in her voice.

"I believe I do."

"Then we ride there as soon as possible," Alexi said.

Lysander shook his head. "Reaching the abbey is not that simple." He picked up a long stick and poked at the sputtering remains of the cookfire Ferran had started.

"Why? Does the abbey lie across a sea? Atop a mountain?" Alexi waved his hand in dismissal. "Whatever the terrain, we can handle it."

The old pilgrim sighed. "Alexi, you do not understand." The rekindled flames cast an eerie glow on Lysander's crimson hood, obscuring his face even more deeply in shadow. "Since its destruction, the abbey lies in another world altogether."

THIRTEEN

Alexi and Dasmaria exchanged glances.

"What do you mean, 'another world altogether'?" Dasmaria asked.

"The land in which we now stand borders a strange, dark land not found on any map," said Lysander.

As the old man spoke, he again poked at the cookfire. Each time the embers flared, however, the thick, wet air choked them down again. He tossed more kindling into the tentative blaze. It sat there as the flames lapped at it, apparently refusing to burn.

Alexi frowned, trying to comprehend Lysander's meaning. "What can you tell us about it?"

"I have tried to learn its history and origins—no small challenge, for the local populace oddly has little interest in such topics," Lysander said. "Based on my findings, I believe that this realm is of an artificial nature. In fact, evidence suggests that the creation of this place is tied directly to the death of Kateri Shadowborn."

Alexi frowned. "How so?" Though his mother had carved a place for herself in history during her short life, he found it hard to believe that her influence could have been as profound as Lysander intimated.

"The land first came into being fifteen years ago," Lysander said. "At that time, it consisted of nothing more than Shadowborn Manor and its grounds."

"Shadowborn Manor?" asked Dasmaria.

"Kateri's home. During her time in the south, Kateri Shadowborn commissioned the construction of a chateau similar to Shadowfast. She intended to live out her life there when she retired from her career as a paladin. It is my understanding that Shadowborn Manor was very similar to your own home, Alexi."

"Almost identical," Alexi murmured, remembering his dream. "I have seen it in a vision."

"The one that inspired this quest?" asked Dasmaria. Alexi nodded.

"What exists beyond the estate, I cannot say," continued Lysander. "I have found references in certain ancient texts to a realm of nightmares ruled by dark powers. I believe there is a connection, but nothing upon which I would care to expound without more research."

He paused, getting up to retrieve one of the waterskins. "In the years that followed the creation of this land, it has grown like a living thing," he said over his shoulder as he ambled toward their supplies. "What began as a small domain centered around the estate has gradually expanded. It is now an island of sorts some twenty-five miles across."

"An island?" interrupted Dasmaria. "Surrounded by what sea?" Slowly she lifted one arm and flexed it.

Alexi was encouraged by this evidence of her recovery. "How does it feel?" he asked, nodding at the arm.

"It tingles sharply, like it's been asleep." She tried to lift her sword arm but could not yet do so.

Lysander returned with the waterskin. He also carried some nuts and dried fruit, which he handed to Alexi. "Here. Eat while you have a chance. We will need energy to fight the ghouls."

Anxious to ride after Ferran, Alexi felt guilty about calmly having a meal while his brother remained in danger. But he knew Lysander was right. It would be a while before Dasmaria regained full mobility; they should at least use the time to replenish their strength. He took the offered provisions and helped Dasmaria eat the meager supper.

He noticed that Lysander was not partaking of their light meal. "Aren't you going to eat?"

"I am not hungry," Lysander answered.

Alexi found the old man's lack of appetite curious but was too intrigued by his story to give the matter much thought.

"As I was saying," continued Lysander, "no sea, but a swamp surrounds the land. If you ride away in any direction from Shadowborn Manor, which lies in the center of the island, you will encounter the morass that we traveled through to get here. Ride back into that expanse of heat, mists, and stagnant water and you will emerge elsewhere. In some cases, the road will lead you back to your home, the Great Kingdom."

"And in other cases?" Alexi asked.

"I do not know. Others—persons whose veracity I have no reason to doubt—have told me they emerged elsewhere. My travels, however, have taken me only back to Avonleigh. Whenever I try to leave this dark domain, I emerge in your realm. When I desire to return here, any road that I take leads me to this place. I cannot say how or why that is the case, it just is."

"Do you labor under some sort of curse?" Alexi regarded the hooded figure. That might explain why Lysander never allowed anyone to see his face. Perhaps he was disfigured in some way, or found the full exposure of light on his eyes painful. Alexi had heard of similar curses—even seen them in force—during his travels.

"I can think of no better way to put it."

Dasmaria shook her head. "This is absurd!" she said harshly. "How old is this swamp, then? Ten years? Five?"

"I should call the latter a more accurate estimate," Lysander said.

She swept her arm to indicate the drooping trees and lichen-covered rocks that surrounded their campsite. "Have you looked around? Trees like this don't grow to maturity in half a decade. Sure, plant life probably grows fast with all this heat and moisture, but these trees can't be less than twenty years old."

"Curious, is it not?" said Lysander.

Alexi rose to his feet, unable to sit still any longer. He rolled his neck to relieve the stiffness already forming from the sling. "Even if we accept what you've said, none of it explains exactly *how* my mother's death created such a place."

"Or why you've lured us here," added Dasmaria coldly.

"I have not lured you anywhere, my dear lady," said Lysander. "Alexi freely chose to undertake this quest, just as you chose to join him. And he, not I, has led our party the whole way." He looked up at Alexi. "As for your question, I do not know exactly why your mother's death triggered the formation of this place, but I suspect it may be related to a highly dangerous mission she performed during the wars."

"Tell me about this mission," Alexi said.

"It is a rather long story."

"Unfortunately we have plenty of time." Alexi nodded at Dasmaria. "If she gets up and walks away in the middle of it, you can finish as we ride after Ferran."

Lysander pressed his emaciated hands together, giving him an aspect of prayer or contemplation. He seemed to be making a considerable effort to search his memory and order his thoughts. "You are both familiar, I assume, with the causes of the Heretical Wars?" he asked.

"Of course," Dasmaria said. "The Southern Empire moved against our southern provinces, threatening to annex some of the Great Kingdom's most holy places."

"Do you know why?"

"Because the people of the Southern Empire also claimed those lands in the name of their gods," said Alexi.

"That is indeed what most people believe." The old man nodded beneath his voluminous red robes. "But as I shall relate, it is not entirely accurate.

"In the years before the Heretical Wars, our nation was ruled by the peace-loving Muhdar ab Sang, the Grand Caliph. He was renowned for his wisdom and piety. His was a just and benevolent rule during which our people prospered. It was said that his dedication to our gods was so great that their avatars visited him in times of crisis. In those days, although people your age seldom know this, our two nations were at peace."

"If he was such a wise man," Dasmaria asked, "why did he lead your nation into war with ours?"

"He did not," said the pilgrim.

Dasmaria's face flushed with anger at Lysander's denial.

Alexi knew this was a delicate subject to bring up in her presence—her family, like his, had its ties to those bloody days. She leaned forward to glare at Lysander. "Do you mean to say our armies were the aggressors? I hope you don't expect us to believe that! Everyone knows about the raids on Letour and Sanschay. Your peace-loving caliph had thousands of innocents put to the sword when his armies attacked those cities. Do you dare defend his actions?"

"Curb your anger, Dasmaria," Lysander said, raising his hand. "I make no effort to deny the guilt and responsibility of my nation for the Heretical Wars."

Alexi moved behind her and placed his hand on her shoulder, a gesture that seemed to calm her for the moment. "Continue," she said tersely.

"One night, when the Grand Caliph was praying for guidance in his dealings with the north, a sinister presence came to him. Believing this dark creature to be an aspect of his god, Muhdar embraced him and accepted his counsel. Had he but recognized the malevolent nature of his visitor, he would have rejected the fiend at once. Instead, he unwittingly caused a war that would cost both our nations dearly."

"You're saying that Muhdar ab Sang, a man we have been taught to revile, was simply the pawn of some diabolic spirit?" asked Alexi.

"That is exactly what I am saying, young man," said Lysander. "In our language, the creature who called on our Caliph was known as Lussimor. In your tongue, his name would be Ebonbane. I advise you to remember that name, Alexi Shadowborn, for it is one with which you of all people should be familiar. Remember it, and abhor it."

The cold stone in Alexi's chest grew icier. He shuddered, trying to shake off the chill that passed through him.

"Lussimor drove the blessed Muhdar to madness and corruption," Lysander continued. "Our leader became cruel and violent. All the good he had done in his life was undone in the span of six short months. To ordinary citizens of the Southern Empire, the transformation of our leader was difficult to see. They were told that the crumbling changes in their daily lives were the fault of the Great Kingdom. But those who served in the palace could not mistake what was happening. One by one, as the truth dawned on them, they were slain and replaced with men who would follow the orders of the corrupted caliph without question.

"The most important of these new servants were the Ahltrian, a group of explorers and adventurers. They reported directly to the caliph, answering only to him and acting on his wishes without pause. It was the Ahltrian who oversaw the destruction of Letour and Sanschay."

"You seem to know an awful lot about the inner workings of Muhdar's government," observed Dasmaria.

Lysander paused. "I, too, fell under the sway of that terrible creature," he finally said. "I was a member of the Ahltrian. Unlike my brothers, however, I discovered the truth. I saw that our caliph's will had been stripped from him."

"But you were not killed," said Alexi. Restless, he left Dasmaria's side and paced around the fire.

"The dark one, Ebonbane, saw a use in me," Lysander said.

The pain in Alexi's heart once again flared. He stuck his hand beneath his breastplate and massaged his chest, but the effort did little to ease his discomfort.

"The fiend dominated my will as he had my leader's," the pilgrim continued. "I became his puppet in the Ahltrian, making certain that no others learned what I had learned. To my eternal torment, I did things so terrible that I have vowed to speak of them only in my prayers, when I ask almighty Brigit for forgiveness."

Again the old man paused in his tale. It seemed that this admission had taken something out of him. Alexi studied Dasmaria. Her expression indicated that she didn't place much credence in the old man's words.

Alexi, on the other hand, believed the tale was largely true. He felt the anguish in Lysander's words, and for some reason, it touched him deeply. Perhaps he had done this tortured man a great disservice by doubting his motivations.

"And it was while under the influence of this fiend that you met my mother," Alexi said, recalling his conversation with Lysander in the crypt.

"Yes. I was commanded to attack a fortification overlooking the port city of Hammerlin. A company of knights was quartered there, and Ebonbane wished them destroyed. I carried out my mission—Brigit forgive me—and almost to a man, I exterminated those poor cavaliers.

"Those we did not kill were taken prisoner. Our intent was to bring them back to the caliph for interrogation. While these knights were in captivity, I ordered many terrible things to be done to them. I wanted to break their spirit. In those days, I did not understand the depths of the human heart and the resilience of a knight's spirit. One of the warriors, Kateri Shadowborn, refused to surrender her spirit to us. She led a handful of her kindred in a daring escape."

Alexi felt a surge of pride toward the mother he had never known. He prayed to Belenus that his spirit would prove as strong as he faced the challenges that lay ahead.

"When I returned to the caliph without captives, I was tortured. I was not killed, however, and so fared better than Kateri and her companions would have in the end."

The old man seemed to tremble with the grief of his memories. Alexi wondered if Lysander would suffer in the afterlife for his misdeeds. He seemed to be living in purgatory already.

Alexi knew that he should feel some degree of anger or indignation toward the former heretic. After all, here was a man who freely admitted that he had killed hundreds—thousands?—of Alexi's countrymen and tortured his kin. For all that, however, the knight felt only pity.

Dasmaria, on the other hand, fairly trembled with rage. Her fists were clenched and the muscles of her jaw pulled tight. She would require time before she could forgive Lysander's misdeeds—if, indeed, she ever did.

"Some two years later, the tables were turned on me," Lysander said. "While we rode through the Sined Pass, a company of knights charged forward to attack us. Although we outnumbered them, they conducted a masterful offense. In the end, I found myself a captive of the very woman who had once been my prisoner. I expected to be tortured and killed. Such retribution seemed no less than I deserved for my past cruelty, and it would certainly have been her fate if the situation had been reversed."

"No paladin of Belenus would mistreat a prisoner!" hissed Dasmaria through clenched teeth.

"I did not know such things in those days, Dasmaria." Lysander looked at her, but she turned her head away. He then addressed Alexi. "Kateri Shadowborn seemed to sense that I was possessed by an evil presence. Instead of repaying my treatment of her in kind, she took steps to drive the evil from my body. With the aid of her god, a power which seemed at the time strange and alien to me, she freed me from the diabolical grip of Ebonbane. I was my own man again."

The ache in Alexi's chest flared sharply once more. He gasped, then coughed to cover his reaction.

"My gratitude to Kateri Shadowborn was and is unending," said Lysander. "She repaid hatred and malice with compassion and sympathy. She returned to me a life that had been stolen away by the darkest of evils. But while her kindness buoyed my spirit, despair gripped the depths of my soul. The memory of the things I had done while under the fiend's influence almost drove me to suicide."

"But you acted under the domination of another," said Alexi.

"In judging someone else, I would feel as you do," said Lysander. "But as the scriptures tell us, it is easier to forgive another than one's self."

Alexi glanced at Dasmaria, but he could not see her face. She bent her head down as she focused on massaging feeling back into her legs. As he watched, the thought struck Alexi that he wouldn't mind helping her with that task.

He kept his hands to himself, however, and returned his attention to Lysander. "What kept you from taking your life?"

"Your mother," he said. "Once again she proved my salvation. She conducted me to the doors of a monastery and placed me in the custody of the abbot. Under his care, my spirit was mended. I renounced my soldier's ways and embraced a life of penitence.

"For a time, I lived among the monks and learned their rituals and scriptures. I believe they hoped I would join them in their worship of Belenus. Indeed, I very nearly did. I found, however, that it was the moon goddess who called me to her service."

"Did you ever see my mother again?"

Lysander nodded. "From time to time, Kateri Shadowborn returned to visit me. Those days were the highlights of my existence." His voice softened. "Kateri was a beautiful woman, and I was not so old then that her charms were lost on me.

"During her visits, I would do what I could to aid her military efforts. Often she would come with questions about the dark fiend and his plans. My years of intimate contact with the evil spirit enabled me to provide her with sound counsel. Armed with my advice, Kateri Shadowborn eventually confronted the dread Ebonbane, driving him out of our world and back into his own."

As Lysander spoke of Kateri's victory, the iciness in Alexi's chest subsided once more into a dull presence. Perhaps it was merely the tale's dramatic tension that had caused the increased ache. "And the caliph?" he asked.

"With the defeat of his master, Muhdar was returned to himself," Lysander said. "He could not bear the knowledge of his sinister deeds, however. Within a fortnight, he was dead, slain by his own hand."

"Assuming all this is true," Dasmaria said, her attention still focused on her legs, "how does it explain the mysterious domain you told us about?"

Lysander rose to his feet. "Unfortunately I have no solid answer for you. But I believe that Kateri's battle with Ebonbane left its imprint on her spirit. One cannot face pure evil without being changed by the experience for all time—even beyond death. Sometimes I wonder if her spirit is yet locked in some eternal struggle with his, for when I enter this land, I sense his presence. Though it may be that I but feel an echo of his former hold on me." The old man's voice sounded more ancient and frail than Alexi had ever heard it. "Regardless, I have come to think of the mysterious domain as Ebonbane's realm. Though the local populace call the island Shadowborn Manor, after the estate, I feel his influence more strongly than I do your mother's."

Lysander picked up the waterskin and provisions pack and carried them to the horses. He then started securing their other supplies to the mounts.

Alexi stepped over to Dasmaria, who had grown still and sat staring at the dying remains of the cookfire. Her features still held the rigid set of anger. "Das?" he said. "Are you all right?"

She nodded. "It's just that—" She fixed her gaze on Lysander. "It was very hard for me to listen to him."

"I know."

Sadness replaced the rancor in her eyes. "When I think of how many of my kin died in the holocaust at Sanschay, how my parents escaped so narrowly. And to learn that he oversaw it . . ."

"I know, Das." Her candor both surprised and touched him. Dasmaria normally kept her emotions bottled up so tight that no one could see them. That she trusted him with her feelings he took as a sign that they were indeed growing closer.

She glanced up at him. "How can you forgive Lysander so easily?"

Alexi sighed. "My mother was a victim of his crimes, and she forgave him. Brigit has forgiven him, too. If she hadn't, his healing prayers would go unanswered. If the sainted Kateri Shadowborn and the moon goddess can find it in their hearts to absolve Lysander, it is not my place to hold a grudge. Nor yours."

Her eyes narrowed. "How can you say that to me?"

"Das, have you forgotten you're a paladin now? If Kateri, a fellow Knight of the Circle, forgave Lysander, he has been pardoned by the rest of the Circle as well. You are bound to honor her decision."

She looked back at Lysander. "I had no idea my first challenge as a paladin would be such a difficult one."

"Belenus will help you."

She nodded absently. A moment later, she shifted her position and glanced at Alexi. "I think I'm ready to try standing."

"Thank the gods," he said. "I didn't want to rush you, but I don't think I can bear much more of a delay in going after Ferran."

He held out his hand to her. She took his wrist, and he pulled her to her feet. She wobbled, grabbing his shoulders to keep from falling. He slipped his arm around her for support. "Steady now. Got your balance?" He met her gaze.

She nodded but didn't let go of his shoulders. Her dark eyes regarded him as if seeing him for the first time. Alexi's heart stilled. Ever so slowly, he bent forward and touched his lips to hers.

He fully expected her to pull away. She didn't. Instead, she returned the kiss, leaning into him, sliding her hands down his shoulders.

"Ouch!"

"Your arm!" She glanced at the injured limb. "I'm sorry, Alexi. I forgot."

"It's okay, Das." He caught her gaze again and smiled. "Eventually we'll get this right."

She tentatively touched the splint. "Did I disturb it?

Here, let me redo the ties."

Lysander approached. "You can do a great deal more, now that your paralysis has worn off. As a paladin, your touch has the power to heal. You can mend Alexi's arm."

At Lysander's words, jealousy crept into Alexi's heart. Had the Darkening not occurred, he—not Dasmaria—could perform the laying on of hands ritual. The icy core in his chest reached out to freeze his whole heart. Alexi stiffened, the closeness he had just felt with Dasmaria gone.

Dasmaria was still for a moment. "I . . . I don't know if I can," she said. "I've never tried to—"

"Do you doubt the power of your god?" asked Lysander.

"Of course not!"

"Then recall that Belenus, not you, will heal Alexi. Your hands but serve as an extension of Belenus's own, just as Brigit guides mine."

Dasmaria looked to Alexi, but he held his face impassive. If Ferran didn't need his aid so badly, he'd have told Dasmaria to keep her damned gift.

"I'll try," she said.

"Excellent," Lysander said. "I will guide you. First, place your hands on Alexi's arm, one on either side of the broken bone."

Dasmaria did as told, then closed her eyes and pursed her lips. Alexi knew that she had studied the word of healing; it was a verse of scripture anyone who hoped to become a member of the Circle was expected to study and memorize. Though he had committed it to memory, for Alexi it would never be more than a mere prayer for health and recovery. But for Dasmaria and others specially blessed, it was a magical invocation of great power.

Dasmaria recited the holy words. The almost musical verse, rhythmic cadence, and warm tones of her voice began at once to soothe Alexi's pain. As she continued, a feeling of warmth grew where her hands touched his arm. The sting of pain subsided as a tugging, crawling sensation indicated that his bone was knitting itself together.

Dasmaria's prayer also soothed his envious heart. The icy grip on his chest lost hold, freeing him to appreciate his friend's new talent instead of begrudging her the gift he had been denied. Alexi regarded Dasmaria's face. Her features seemed softened, as if the act of healing were drawing away the sometimes hard edge of her personality. As he watched her lips form the ancient words, he knew that the Circle would be well served by its newest member.

And he knew as well that his feelings for her ran deeper than he had ever imagined. When they had sorted through the mysteries of his past and avenged his mother's death, perhaps then Dasmaria would be ready to sort through her feelings for him. He had already seen one treasure, the Rite of Ascension, slip through his fingers. He would not allow himself to lose another.

Dasmaria finished the ritual and opened her eyes. She met his gaze. "Better?" she asked softly.

He thought not of his arm but of the ugly feelings of envy she had washed from his heart. "Completely," he answered.

"Then let us be off," said Lysander.

Alexi yanked off the sling and splint, replacing them with the armor pieces Lysander had removed. Dasmaria, too, donned her gear for battle.

As they mounted their steeds, Alexi became aware of

the icy sensation returning in his chest. He glanced around the swampy terrain, toward the site where he had battled the ghouls. There was something about this unknown land that clawed not only at his heart but at the edges of his mind. Was it, as Lysander speculated, the presence of Ebonbane? Or merely his own self-doubt in the wake of the Darkening?

He addressed Lysander. "The monastery you sought shelter in—was that Forenoon Abbey, the place you think the ghouls are taking my brother?"

"It is," he said solemnly.

"So you can lead us there?"

"Yes. The abbey is about two days' journey from here. The road is not a good one."

Alexi nodded grimly. "Then we'd best get started." He glanced at Dasmaria, whose countenance reflected his own determination, then back at Lysander.

"Let's go slay some ghouls."

FOURTEEN

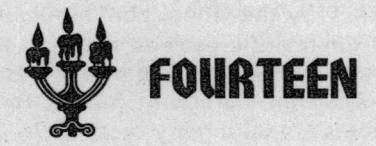

He calls himself "the Ghoul Lord."

A laughably grandiose title. At best, he commands a legion of the dead, one hundred rotting corpses. They are nothing more than feral beasts who hunger for the flesh of their living kin. Is the lord of such creatures any more significant than the minions he rules? I think not.

He exists only at my will.

With gray skin stretched across grotesque features, he is as revolting to humans—his own kind, at one time—as he is to me. In life, he was a wizard. To be sure, he was powerful for his kind—a mighty sorcerer of considerable magical potency. By my reckoning, of course, he was an amateur who understood nothing of the powers he wielded. His energies were those of a mere spawnling. That he and his trifling friends could summon and contain me at all was a matter of trickery and deceit, not arcane knowledge or mystic skill.

Now he is no more than an extension of myself.

I make his senses my own. With just a moment's concentration, I see what he sees, hear what he hears, know what he knows. I can observe the disintegrating stone walls of the crumbling monastery and smell the lingering remains of the incense that once burned there. I can even feel the offensive taint of goodness, a residue from the time when the place was sacred to light and life. Now it is mine, a shrine to darkness and death.

The boy is brought in.

He was taken by the Ghoul Lord's minions. The fact that such insignificant creatures captured him tells me all I need to know about this one's power. He is nothing. They have bound his hands behind his back with leather straps. How such pitiful strips can restrain anyone, I cannot imagine, but they appear to be doing their work.

The Ghoul Lord bids him to advance.

The boy does not respond. He is a proud whelp, and a brave one. He trembles in the presence of so many enemies but conceals it well. How much more he would shiver if he knew his real enemy was not the Ghoul Lord but me. Could he even survive the knowledge of his foe's true nature? At last the ghouls force him forward with a sharp blow to the back. To his credit, the child staggers without falling.

The boy vows to see the Ghoul Lord destroyed.

It is a hollow threat, of course. The child's power falls far short of his captor's. The Ghoul Lord knows this and laughs openly at the whelp. He motions to his minions, who land another blow upon the boy. This time it drives him to his knees. I wonder how much abuse his frail form can endure. He was clearly wounded in his capture. If the Ghoul Lord kills him, the boy will be of no use to me. The Ghoul Lord and all his wretched servants will follow him into damnation.

The Ghoul Lord makes his offer.

He tells the child that no one wishes him any harm. He assures him that he will be free to leave this place after their parley. The youngster scoffs, but I see hope light up his weak face. His is an emotional spirit, with feelings not easily hidden.

The softness of his heart will prove his undoing.

The Ghoul Lord presses on. He explains how the child can purchase his life simply by betraying the elder Shadowborn. A single arrow loosed in the darkness of night, and it is done. What could be simpler? As expected, the whelp refuses. He repeats his vow to see the Ghoul Lord destroyed and struggles to break his feeble bonds. This reaction pleases me, for I know what the Ghoul Lord will do now.

A call goes out for the Vapir.

When she was alive, the Vapir was a creature of faith and devotion. She served a dark and sinister god. Had she known how little she meant to him, I wonder how faithfully she would have served. I suspect it would have mattered little. Like all mortals, she considered herself far more important than she ever could be.

The Vapir strides proudly into the chamber.

Such arrogance. She imagines herself more powerful than the Ghoul Lord. In truth, they are mere mites—fleas infesting a tiny corner of my universe. She moves with determination toward the pitiful youth while the Ghoul Lord assumes a position of authority. Their posturing is laughable.

Two ghouls grab the boy.

They haul him to his feet and drag him across the stone floor to the long-unused altar. Once this monastery was sacred to the god whom this boy would one day serve. In a vulgar physical display, one of the ghouls bites through the cords securing the boy's arms. With strength far beyond that of the child, the ghouls throw their prisoner onto the altar. Lifting iron manacles into place, they secure the young Shadowborn to the stone slab.

The Vapir advances.

She moves with a fluid motion, like the predator she has become. Her fingers trace themselves along the boy's face. Unlike the Ghoul Lord, her appearance has not greatly changed from what it was in life—with a single exception. All the color has drained from her skin, leaving it the hue of bone. In her own way, she proves as offensive to her former kind as the desiccated Ghoul Lord. The boy's shudder of revulsion at the sight of her says as much. She bends low over him. After pausing to lick her pallid lips with a translucent tongue, she presses them against his.

The boy screams.

It is a delight to hear the pure tones of his terror. Even before she begins her work, the Vapir wears down his resistance. It seems that she is not without promise in the science of inspiring fear. I must make note of this talent. It might be interesting to change my perspective, to share the Vapir's experience instead of the Ghoul Lord's.

The boy's outburst suddenly dies.

He has felt the intangible touch of the Vapir's mind. Her presence gradually flows into his own spirit. The boy thrashes back and forth, as if this physical resistance could hamper the Vapir's mental caress. A sudden paroxysm of pain rips through his body. He arches his back spasmodically. His eyes roll back in his head. For a split second, his entire body is rigid. Then, just as quickly, he collapses again.

I can resist no longer.

In an instant, I have abandoned my contact with the Ghoul Lord and become one with the Vapir. Her power courses along invisible conduits that trace unseen paths through the air between her and the boy. His thoughts are panicked and chaotic. No one has ever violated him so thoroughly before. He begins to weep. It is delightfully pitiful.

Then the Vapir begins her work.

She starts by sending out calming patterns. Like the rhythmic music of the spheres, her power rolls across his mind. Gradually she contains his horror, controls it. He tries several times to resist her, but his will is nothing compared to the power of the Vapir. In the end, the boy becomes little more than an extension of my creature. Another extension of myself.

Now she looks into his heart.

Within every being lurks something dark. No doubt the boy harbors secrets as well. Is it fear—perhaps there is something upon which he cannot bear to look? Could it be doubt—a feeling that his faith is nothing more than a sham? Perhaps it is desire—a heart impure and tainted with lust. No. It is none of those things.

His weakness is envy.

The boy longs for the things that belong to his brother. He knows that, as the second son, he will always follow in the steps of the elder Shadowborn. Always, he fears, he will be known as the younger brother of Alexi Shadowborn. It is the child's greatest regret that he must be the squire and not the knight. The Vapir seeks to magnify this longing, turning this innocent rivalry into covetous resentment. But I think that will not be enough to serve my needs.

I force the Vapir aside and send a thought into the boy's mind.

It is one that he knows, but which he at first refuses to accept. I step aside, allowing the Vapir to regain contact. She repeats the thought. It is the truth, there is no denying that. In time, he will accept it. In time, it will dominate him. In time, it will destroy him. I can hear it echoing back and forth in his mind.

Alexi Shadowborn is not your brother.

How amusing to see the conflict in the boy's heart. He knows it to be true. He knows that he and the older Shadowborn lad are the spawn of different women. But he has always lived his life as if this were not the case. He wants to know that the prestige of his line will fall to him, not to his so-called brother. At the same time, though, he refuses to embrace anything the Vapir tells him. His resistance will gain him nothing. For good or evil, the truth is an insidious thing. It will eat away at him until he finally accepts it—especially with the Vapir's help.

The Vapir abandons him.

Quickly withdrawing her mental contact, she leaves the boy as shocked by her departure as he was by her arrival. As he regains control of his body again, he screams. For several minutes, he howls in panic and terror, breaking off his cries only long enough to gasp for air. I draw back from my minions as the Ghoul Lord orders the sobbing child dragged away and imprisoned.

My laughter echoes through my infernal home.

FIFTEEN

Nearly a day of hard riding brought Alexi and his companions to the edge of a broad, black river. What remained of the road vanished into the languid water and did not appear to continue into the forest on the far side.

Alexi wrinkled his nose at the smell wafting from the turbid water. It was an unnatural odor, born not of living matter, yet neither of decay. No, the scent seemed to be the very essence of the darkest emotions endured between birth and death—chaos, despair, anguish, grief. He tried not to breathe too deeply, afraid that to inhale the air was to invite those feelings to take hold of his spirit. And his spirit was already weighed down by the cold stone still chilling his heart.

He dismounted to have a closer look. A few seconds passed with only the sound of buzzing insects and croaking amphibians hanging in the air before Dasmaria and Lysander followed his lead. Dasmaria stepped to Alexi's side.

"I don't like the looks of that river," she said. He nodded in agreement.

"You are wise to exercise caution," said Lysander.

Dasmaria stiffened at his voice. She had spoken little to the old man since leaving camp, though the hard pace of their journey had limited any conversation.

"Does it contain predators?" Alexi tried to see into languid ribbon of water. He could only imagine what terrors might hide in that oily darkness. Sickly strands of water grasses swayed slowly in the shallows. Toward the center, occasional large shapes seemed to appear just beneath the surface. More than once, Alexi thought he saw large tentacles or fins emerge, but they disappeared so quickly that he wasn't sure he had really seen them.

"After a fashion," acknowledged the pilgrim. "The river has guardians, but they are not mere creatures of flesh and blood. This waterway marks the border of Ebonbane's domain."

Alexi felt a sinister shadow pass through him, like a spider creeping down his spine. He sensed someone, or something, watching him from the ghostly, moss-covered trees on the far riverbank. His wary glances, however, revealed nothing.

"On this side of the river," Lysander continued, "we are in a region that is neither under the dark one's sway nor free of his influence. On the other side, however . . ." He let his voice trail off.

Dasmaria stepped to the river's edge and looked down into its depths. Kneeling, she stretched tentative fingers toward the water.

"Don't allow that river to touch your flesh," cautioned Lysander. "I believe that the water boils up from the depths of the Abyss itself. Touching it could well prove fatal."

Dasmaria snatched back her hand. "How are we to cross it, then?"

"The way across this river is not a pleasant one," Lysander said in a heavy, serious voice.

Alexi gazed across the watery expanse. His brother was on the other side of that boundary, and nothing was going to keep him from crossing it. He looked into the blackness beneath Lysander's hood. "What must we do?"

Lysander said nothing. Instead, he walked to the edge of the river and reached into one of the many folds in his red robes. After a few seconds, he drew out a slender white flute. It was wrapped in a black cloth and had yellowed slightly with age.

"We must wait another few minutes," said Lysander. "We cannot cross the river until the sun has set."

At first Alexi thought the flute was made of ivory. Closer scrutiny, however, revealed that it had been fashioned from bone—bone that looked too human for his liking. Dasmaria stepped toward the pilgrim. Something in her manner told Alexi that she had noticed the same thing.

"Is that what it appears to be?" she demanded.

"I am sorry to say that it is," responded the pilgrim solemnly.

"That's blasphemous!" she cried. "What kind of monster are you?" Her hand moved to the hilt of her sword, threatening to bring the deadly weapon into play. Alexi stepped forward, ready to interpose himself if necessary. Lysander held up one hand and Dasmaria stopped short. His fingers were spread in a gesture of truce.

"Perhaps I am a monster," said Lysander. "Certainly I have committed monstrous acts in the past. History will judge me, as it judges us all. In this particular case, however, I believe you do not fully understand our situation." His voice remained calm and composed, as if he hadn't even noticed that the paladin stood ready to strike him down. "I had nothing to do with the creation of this object. I employ it now only because there is no other way by which we may cross this barrier."

"There is always another way." She turned to Alexi. "We cannot allow him to use that vile instrument."

Alexi gazed at the flute. Though at first the pipe had filled him with revulsion, the same cold presence that chilled his heart cooled his reaction to the object. Perhaps using it was not so wrong—if they did so for a good reason. "Let Lysander do what he must," he said.

Dasmaria stared at him with incredulous eyes. "Alexi, as a servant of Belenus, surely you can't countenance—"

"Belenus be hanged! I'm not his servant—at least, not in any way that matters. You're the only paladin here." Resentment gnawed at his gut as the icy core in his heart expanded to fill his chest. How dare she appoint herself the moral conscience of the party?

He saw the shock on her face at being spoken to in such a manner, at his having taken Belenus's name in vain. Somewhere in the back of his mind, he knew that he was not acting like himself. Was it the gloomy atmosphere or merely fear for his brother that had taken such hold of him?

"I'm sorry, Das," he said, the chill in his chest receding. "Concern for Ferran clouds my mind."

She searched his face for a long moment. "I understand," she said finally. "Now, what of the flute?"

"I believe the good of our cause outweighs the evil of the instrument's construction," Alexi said. "When our work is done, we can destroy the thing."

Dasmaria hesitated for a moment, indecision obvious on her face. Then, without a word of either protest or assent, she released her sword and stepped back.

"The sun has set," proclaimed Lysander. Alexi couldn't say how he knew this, for the vapors and shadows that surrounded them seemed unchanged.

Lysander lifted the flute into the darkness beneath his hood. The old man began to play, and Alexi's breath caught in his throat. The flute produced low and somber music, unlike any he had heard before.

As the heavy music rolled through the air, darkness came on quickly. The faint residual rays of the departed sun were smothered by mournful notes that reminded Alexi of nothing so much as the groaning of a remorseful spirit. The shadows around them grew darker, the outlines of the trees more ghostly, the currents of the river more still.

The changes around them did not escape Dasmaria's notice. She stepped closer to Alexi, her hand hovering near the hilt of her sword. Pitch and Ember shuffled nervously, snorting as they tasted the darkening air. Lysander's horse seemed unaffected. Alexi found it hard to believe that the animal was so well trained that the macabre music and brooding atmosphere had no effect on him.

A thick blanket of fog rose out of the river. It ascended as an unnatural mass of slowly churning vapors, the sort of effect Alexi had seen only in his nightmares. It swayed and rolled to the haunting music of Lysander's flute, mirroring the notes in coiling tendrils of fog.

A dark shape stirred within the vapors.

Alexi fought back the urge to unsheathe Corona and bring its radiance into being. He had decided to trust Lysander's judgment and didn't want to jeopardize the pilgrim's efforts. And yet the idea of some unknown creature, summoned by so offensive a magical item, cried out to the warrior for action. If he had any doubt about the nature of this place, it had long since fled. This mysterious land into which they had traveled was one of darkness and evil. He had no place here—or so he prayed.

The fading twilight had passed into full night now. The speed with which darkness had fallen would have alarmed Alexi anywhere else. Here, however, it seemed no less natural than anything else he had witnessed.

The dark shape drifted forward, gliding smoothly across the surface of the fog-shrouded river. Alexi heard the gentle sound of rippling water and knew that a boat was being slowly poled toward them. Beside him, Dasmaria gasped. Alexi lifted his gaze toward the boatman and could not help but do the same.

The boatman was a gaunt figure, standing over six feet in height and draped in the tattered remnants of sackcloth and a funeral shroud. The torn, moldering remains of a hooded robe were fastened around his neck. Beneath the hood, Alexi could see the stranger's face, at least what there was of it. He found himself looking into the empty sockets of an ancient, yellowed skull. Pinpoints of crimson light burned where eyes should have been. Jagged teeth, anchored in a crooked jaw, formed the mirthless smile of the dead.

As the boatman bent forward to plant his long, slender pole in the riverbed, Alexi realized Lysander had stopped playing. The haunting melody of the flute was gone, although the mood of despair and doom that it created still hung heavily in the air.

"Lysander," whispered Alexi, his voice dry.

"Silence, my boy," answered the pilgrim. His hands moved again into the shadowy folds of his robes. Alexi split his attention between the slowly approaching skeleton and the old man, watching to see what Lysander would do now. With the flute wrapped in its black cloth and returned to whatever pocket had held it, the pilgrim drew out a small canvas pouch. He loosened the tie about it and slipped slender, bony fingers inside. Alexi could not help but notice that the old man's hands had little more flesh on them than those of the looming mariner.

"Take these," murmured Lysander, drawing something out of the pouch. Alexi held out his hand and felt two coins pressed into his palm. Reluctantly, Dasmaria did the same. "One is for you," whispered Lysander, "the other is for your mount." He paused a moment, then handed Alexi a third coin. "For Ferran's horse."

Alexi regarded the cold metal discs in his hand. At first glance, they looked very much like the crowns used throughout Avonleigh. Instead of being minted from gleaming silver, however, they were cast from some black alloy. A shudder went through him as he remembered the black metal of the sword he had seen used against his mother.

As he looked up, the ferryman poled his boat to the river's edge. Alexi wondered that the craft was able to stay afloat. Like its master, the ramshackle boat was in sorry shape. Although its wooden framework seemed sturdy enough, the leather hides stretched around those timbers looked worn and tattered. Why the entire boat didn't fill with water, Alexi could not imagine.

"Now do as I do, and *only* as I do, and all will be well." Lysander stepped boldly forward. The skeletal mariner held out his sepulchral hand, palm up, but made no sound. With slow movements, Lysander held the two coins up for the boatman to see. The red glow of his eyes sparkled on the metal discs. Then the pilgrim gently deposited the coins in the outstretched palm. Bony fingers curled to make a fist. After a second, the hand opened again with no sign of the coins.

His offering apparently accepted, Lysander took the reins of his mount. He strode forward, with the horse following close behind, and moved carefully to the punt's stern. Catching Alexi's eye, the old man nodded.

Alexi moved forward. He clicked his tongue and Pitch trotted after him. Midnight, seeming to sense that this signal was meant for him as well, followed. The boatman held out his hand, fixing Alexi with his chilling gaze. The knight swallowed. He held out his three coins, fanning them so that the boatman could make an easy count. After a few seconds, he deftly turned his hand over and dropped the black coins into the mariner's bony palm. Once again the coins vanished into his fist.

Foreboding flashed through Alexi. The mysterious ache in his chest, already stronger than when they had left camp, had grown since they arrived on the riverbank. Now, as he stood facing the boatman, the iciness flared. Was Alexi somehow attuned to the sinister forces surrounding Ebonbane's realm? If so, what would happen once he actually crossed into it?

Lysander cleared his throat, and Alexi realized that he was delaying. He tugged for Pitch to follow and, with Midnight moving close behind, made his way onto the boat. When he turned to look back at the shore, he saw that Dasmaria had already stepped forward.

With the same self-assured confidence that had always impressed him, she flashed the coins upward. Allowing them to linger only for a moment, she brought her hand down sharply and snapped them into the bony palm. Even as the mariner made his customary fist, she led Ember onto the pitching boat.

The boatman paused a moment, as if he were waiting for another fare to arrive. Then, seeing no sign of another patron, he turned and stepped almost gingerly onto the boat. Planting the slender pole against the shore, he leaned heavily, and the boat lurched into the river.

As the shore fell slowly away, thick coils of vapor rose up to engulf them. The coolness of the vapors surprised Alexi. He had expected them to be warm and heavy and sickly, like the mists in the swamp. These, however, felt vibrant, almost alive. That thought sent a shudder through him.

As they crossed, Alexi felt a frostiness settle in his heart. Where once a chill the size of a stone had been, now a snowball-sized chunk of ice occupied his chest. What was happening to him? He tamped down his fear. He could not panic. Ferran needed him.

The boat landed against the far shore before Alexi even realized it was drawing near. Lysander, now standing closest to the shore, climbed out to stand on the firm soil of the riverbank. Alexi moved to follow, with Pitch and Midnight in tow. He hoped his companions didn't notice his haste to exit the brooding craft.

Once Dasmaria had joined them, Alexi turned to look back at the river. The swirling vapors had largely dissipated, taking with them any sign of the macabre ferry or its unnatural master. The dark night enveloped the swamp on the other side of the river as well.

Lysander spoke in a low tone, his voice filled with grim solemnity. "We have entered the domain of Ebonbane," he said. "From now on, be aware that every move you make may be your last.

"Death surrounds us. Let us be sure that it does not also overwhelm us."

SIXTEEN

Once off the eerie ferryboat, Alexi pushed his companions to continue as far as they could into the darkened forest. He itched to overtake the ghouls, to rescue his brother from their filthy clutches. He could not rest until he had ascertained Ferran's fate.

But before they had traveled very far into the forest, both Dasmaria and Lysander declared that further progress was impossible until morning. The road on this side of the river was rough and broken, resembling a dry streambed as much as anything else. Even though the moon made a wan effort to shed pale light over the place, travel remained nothing short of dangerous. To continue farther, they argued, meant risking a horse with a broken leg.

Alexi drew Corona from its scabbard and weighed the weapon in his hand. Two simple words would make it blaze with light, illuminating the whole of the forest around them. As he began to speak, however, Lysander cut him off.

"Better we should make camp and wait for sunrise than let everything in the surrounding forest know where we are," the old man said. Dasmaria nodded her agreement.

"By the face of Belenus, do neither of you care that every minute lost is another minute Ferran remains in danger?" Alexi exclaimed.

Dasmaria seemed taken aback by his oath. "We do share your concern, Alexi. But we're no good to Ferran dead."

"Damn it all," Alexi swore under his breath. At every turn, it seemed that he was forced to concede more time to the ghouls. Pressing his lips tightly together, he drove Corona sharply into its scabbard and reined Pitch to a halt.

Alexi dismounted and allowed his gaze to drift over the brooding forest around them. The trees were tangled and knotted, with branches that seemed to strain hungrily toward them. The skinny limbs looked like the withered remnants of the very ghouls they pursued. As a slow breeze slipped through the trees, leaves rustled and branches swayed. Owls called into the darkness, seeming to challenge their presence.

The moonlight fell upon them with a dim, pearly radiance. Most of it was blocked by the forest canopy or swallowed up by the endless darkness between the trees. Here and there, however, a slender shaft of pale light reached the floor of the forest. At each such point, an eerie radiance seemed to spread outward, as if the moonbeam caused the forest floor to glow on its own.

Out of the corner of his eye, Alexi thought he saw something moving through one of these radiant patches. When he looked more closely, however, he saw nothing.

He swore again. This whole realm got under his skin, sending prickles of unease racing along his spine. The place also seemed to amplify the pain in his chest, which licked at his heart like cold flames. The chill had seeped into his bones, almost making him regret leaving the heat of the swamp.

"Do we dare risk a small fire?" he asked. Not only would he appreciate the warmth, but also the opportunity to cook over it. He had eaten his fill of cold rations in the last few days. If they had to stop, they might as well indulge in a decent meal.

"We shall not need a fire," said Lysander. He reached into the folds of his cloak and drew forth a small black pouch, identical to the one from which he had produced the black coins. He stretched narrow fingers into the bag, emerging with a faintly glowing blue stone perhaps an inch in diameter and almost perfectly round. The stone threw off about as much light as a small oil lamp.

Lysander placed the stone upon the remains of a shattered tree that had fallen in some forgotten storm. It did an adequate job of illuminating the area around them, but did little to warm Alexi. And he knew that he wasn't going to be cooking over it.

In the increased light, Alexi again surveyed the area. Years of training for battle left him unhappy with their choice of a campsite. The woods were thick enough to prevent them from seeing approaching enemies, but not overgrown enough to prevent foes from sneaking up on them. Still, in the hour or so since they had left the river behind, he had seen no better place. The horses would provide warning if something drew too near.

Despite his misgivings about their location, Alexi removed his armor. He noticed that several yards away, Dasmaria did the same. After the heat of the swamp and their full day of riding, Alexi's skin itched and his cramped muscles needed stretching. As soon as he had a chance to work the kinks out of his back and neck, he would put some of it back on. He didn't want to pass the whole night in this place completely defenseless. Even now he kept his sword at his side.

Dasmaria approached him. "Alexi, we missed sunset devotions because of the river crossing," she said. "Hadn't we better offer our prayers to Belenus now?"

The last thing Alexi felt like doing at the moment was praying. He had too much nervous energy, too great a restlessness to continue their pursuit of the ghouls. "You go ahead, Das. I have other things I need to do."

Her eyebrows arched in question. Sunset devotions were an important ritual for paladins of Belenus and should be missed only in the most extreme circumstances.

But then, he wasn't a paladin, was he?

Alexi ignored the disappointment in Dasmaria's face and opened one of his saddlebags. He withdrew his whetstone and walked toward the light of Lysander's glowing sphere. As he unsheathed his sword and sat down, the old man regarded him askance.

"Did you not just sharpen your sword two nights ago?" Lysander inquired. The question drew Dasmaria's attention as well.

His tone rankled Alexi. Of all people, the pilgrim—who had just used a flute fashioned from a human femur to summon Belenus-knew-what to ferry them across the river—dared question his battle preparations?

"I want my blade sharp enough to split a hair," he said. Apparently satisfied, or at least discouraged from pursuing the matter further, Lysander turned to join Dasmaria in her devotions.

"So that when we fight the ghouls tomorrow, I can

slice their vile heads clean off their shoulders," Alexi continued, drawing his blade over the sharpening stone. "And then gut their rotting entrails right out of their repulsive corpses."

Dasmaria regarded him in shock, her lips forming a round **O**. She stepped toward him, searching his face. "Alexi, you sound as if you intend to revel in the slaying."

He met her gaze evenly. "I do." He hoped to massacre the beasts.

"You know that's against the church's teachings. Belenus instructs us to kill only out of necessity and to take no pleasure in the act."

"Belenus never had a brother kidnapped by ghouls," he said. Alexi knew he spoke blasphemously, but he didn't care. Only revenge could thaw the chill in his heart.

At that moment, Pitch let out a sharp snort and pranced nervously. The animal's nostrils flared, trying to draw in a scent. The stallion's black ears thrust into the air, as if attempting to sort out a single sound from the nocturnal buzz of the forest. Ember echoed Pitch's every action.

"Kill that light," Alexi said softly to Lysander. He cursed himself for having removed his armor so soon, but there was no help for it now. Corona already in hand, Alexi saw that Dasmaria had drawn her sword as well. The pilgrim scooped up the radiant sphere and dropped it into the black pouch. The pale light vanished at once, leaving only the dim glow of the moon to illuminate the area.

Or so it seemed at first.

Then Alexi saw a faintly shimmering figure advance from the depths of the forest. It moved forward slowly, shedding a faint green light as it came. The edges of the figure were soft and indistinct, like something seen in a dream. Long white hair trailed away in billowing tresses that blew endlessly in a delicate breeze that Alexi could not feel.

"A ghost," whispered Dasmaria. Her voice was marked as much by wonder as fear, something that Alexi understood instantly. In the presence of the ghouls, he had felt little more than revulsion. This apparition, however, seemed strangely beautiful. Its features were those of a lovely young woman. Softened by transformation into an ethereal creature and accented by the glow that surrounded her, she was indeed entrancing.

"More than one," said Lysander.

Alexi looked away from the first ghost and saw that several more of the spectral creatures were emerging from the depths of the forest. Each was a frail thing of gossamer, light, and indistinct edges. Some were male, others female, but each was a beautiful and splendid sight to behold. Could anything so wondrous be deadly? It seemed impossible, but Alexi knew better than that.

The spirits, accompanied by glowing orbs that floated in the air, formed a ring around Alexi and his companions. The horses snorted and shuffled in fear. Pitch and Ember, experienced as they were from many battles, seemed less panicked than Midnight. Lysander's mount appeared unconcerned by the circle of spirits. What horrors had the pilgrim's travels carried him through to allow the beast to take the presence of these supernatural creatures so lightly?

More colored lights moved forward from the tangled trees. They swooped forward, shimmering orbs of scintillating hues bobbing in the air. With the delicate movements of dancers, they whirled around the apparitions and then raced above the travelers. Alexi ducked instinctively, although the closest sphere didn't come within a yard of his head. Dasmaria struck at one with her sword as it shot past, but either her hand proved too slow or her blade did not affect the radiant sphere.

A baleful wailing drifted in the air. It began as a faint moaning, like the echoes of distant thunder, then swelled to become a deafening cacophony. Alexi tried not to listen to the overwhelming chorus of lamentations and shrieks, but it was impossible to ignore.

When he could bear it no longer, Alexi swept Corona into the air and allowed the multicolored wash of spectral light to play upon its gleaming blade for a moment.

"Karnas, radamar!"

For a fraction of a second, Alexi feared that the power of this ghostly horde had proven too great for Corona. But then the blade's radiance spread forth, driving back the spectral glow. Alexi sensed a resistance to the magic of Kateri Shadowborn's holy sword. While Corona's light managed to keep the supernatural denizens of this wood at bay, it appeared to do them no harm. He had apparently created a barrier through which they could not pass. But beyond that region, which was no more than thirty feet across, the incorporeal undead held sway. This was their land, and Alexi Shadowborn was nothing more than an intruder.

"Corona doesn't appear to have done much," he murmured.

"On the contrary," said Lysander. Like Dasmaria, he had taken up a position with his back to the center of their campsite. The triangle formed by the three companions made it possible for them to watch the whole of the ghostly assemblage but required them to speak to each other's backs. "You have bought us time. Corona is a powerful weapon. Any lesser enchantment would have done nothing in this place. Were it not for the pure light of your sword, we would even now be as they."

Alexi shivered at the terrible thought of becoming a ghost. He could accept the idea of death; as a warrior, he had by necessity come to terms with it long ago. But the idea of roaming the earth eternally, denied the blessings of the afterlife and ultimate union with Belenus, was unacceptable. Should it appear that they were about to perish in this forest of the undead, he would see to it that his own blade ended their lives. If he had it within his power, he, Dasmaria, and Lysander would never be condemned to such a fate.

But the matter could not be allowed to end so. If it did, his beloved brother Ferran had no one to save him from life as a revolting ghoul. Compared to the endless tortured existence of a ravenous walking corpse, the spectral half-life of a ghost seemed almost peaceful.

Lysander stepped forward, as if attempting to enter the long shadow thrown by Corona's glow. He spoke in the almost musical dialect of the ancient language. Alexi knew at once that he was casting a spell. He could feel Dasmaria tense as the same thought occurred to her.

For nearly a minute, Lysander pronounced powerful words, gripping his mace before him. Alexi could feel magical energies gather in the air around them. As the pilgrim finished his incantation with a final harsh exclamation and a sudden gesture, those same powers were spent. What effect they were supposed to have had Alexi could not say. To him, nothing appeared changed.

"You!" commanded Lysander, addressing the woman whose spirit they had first seen. "Who are you?"

To his surprise, Alexi saw the beautiful spirit's mouth open. Her delicate voice was almost impossible to hear. With great effort, however, he discerned her words.

"I . . . am . . . Cassaldra." Her words hissed like wet firewood. The contempt in her voice was almost more audible than the words themselves. Clearly, she answered Lysander under the compulsion of his spell.

"Cassaldra." Lysander nodded, then gestured widely at their surroundings. "What is this place?"

"Our home," she answered. Her words came faster this time, as if she grew more accustomed to speaking. "Among the living, it is called the Phantasmal Forest."

Alexi looked around. Even without the unliving host of radiant spirits that surrounded them, the name was appropriate. Between the dark shadows and the gnarled trees that cast them, even an unimaginative observer would assume this place haunted.

"The domain in which we stand, that bordered by the black river," Lysander said. "Who rules it?"

"Ebonbane."

At that, a terrible howling broke from the unholy denizens of the Phantasmal Forest. The tortured screams of dying men, the keening of mourning women, and the wretched lamentations of the damned all combined to hammer Alexi's spirit. Within him, his heart nearly froze solid at the confirmation of their worst suspicions.

"Why do you serve Ebonbane?" demanded Lysander, shouting into the fury. "What power does that fiend have over you?"

Cassaldra's voice rose clear and sharp above the tempest. "We do not serve the evil one," she proclaimed. "We are his victims. One by one we fell to the sinister creatures that dwell in Forenoon Abbey. Our bodies have satisfied their hunger, but our spirits were not theirs to consume."

The howling showed no sign of abating, even when Lysander lowered his mace to the ground. "Then we have a common enemy," he proclaimed. "We ride to Forenoon Abbey to battle the ghouls and save the brother of this warrior beside me." The old man gestured at Alexi.

For a moment, the pilgrim's words appeared to have passed unheeded. Then the moaning and howling slackened. Cassaldra made an effort to step forward, but the light of Corona kept her from doing so. Having failed at that, she assessed Lysander carefully, appearing to take his measure with her scintillating eyes.

"If this be true," she said quietly, "you have no enemies here."

"It is true," Lysander said. Alexi marveled at his composure. Here, standing face to face with dozens of spectral creatures, he was as calm as he had been at any time in their acquaintance.

"What proof have you of your intentions?" As the ghost spoke, the glow surrounding her seemed to flare brighter.

The spirit's question gave Lysander pause. Alexi knew what he was thinking. Should this gathering of the restless dead choose to oppose them, even if the ghosts did not directly attack, they would make it almost impossible for the trio to continue. If the spiritual army turned their supernatural power upon the party, their quest would come to an inglorious end.

But if Cassaldra could be convinced that Lysander spoke the truth. . . .

"*Karnas, ramorte!*"

The blazing sphere of light thrown off by Corona failed instantly at the warrior's command. In its wake, the shimmering blue-green radiance of the ghostly assemblage washed over the party and their mounts. It was an uneven glow with no warmth to it. Indeed, it seemed to chill Alexi's flesh where it fell.

Dasmaria whirled to face him. Her wide eyes regarded him with incredulous alarm. "Are you mad? You have stripped us of our only protection!"

"I have shown them we mean them no harm," he said. But even as he spoke, Alexi knew Dasmaria was right: If the spirits chose to strike now, they might well overwhelm the party before he could rekindle the holy blaze.

Cassaldra drifted forward, moving toward Lysander without appearing to take a step. The gossamer tendrils of mist surrounding her trailed behind like the train of long dress. Blue light twinkled in her cold, emotionless eyes.

When she reached a point directly before Lysander, the delicate spirit stopped. Her left arm rose stiffly, a slender finger reaching toward the pilgrim. Alexi tensed, fearing that the spirit was about to attack.

Cassaldra's fingers shimmered just shy of the old man's face. Alexi realized that he held his breath. He tried to lick his lips but found his mouth suddenly dry. His grip on Corona tightened.

"No lie has been spoken," proclaimed the ghostly woman.

Her voice carried through the forest like a cold wind, sending a tremor through Alexi even as it promised a sliver of hope. "You shall have one day to prove yourselves," she continued. "If tomorrow's sunset finds you still within the bounds of the Phantasmal Forest, you will become as we."

Alexi let out a long breath. He moved to Lysander's side, keeping Corona in hand. "We shall not disappoint you," Alexi said.

A whispered voice issued from beneath the crimson hood. "She will not acknowledge you, Alexi. It is the spell of Brigit that commands her to speak. As the hand of that power, I alone can communicate with her."

Alexi nodded. "Can you ask her about the abbey?"

Lysander turned to Cassaldra. "Will this road bring us to the ruins where the ghouls have made their lair?"

"It will. The Phantasmal Forest encircles that mournful place."

"When our work is done there," Lysander said, "we would ride on to challenge the master of this place."

"You intend to face Ebonbane?"

"We do."

"Then your fate is sealed. You will join us."

As these words escaped her lips, Cassaldra's image grew indistinct. One by one, the whole of the company faded from sight. Cassaldra was the last to vanish, and Alexi thought that he saw a single tear on her alabaster cheek. Was that for us, he wondered, or herself?

"Your bravery does you credit," Dasmaria said to Lysander. She seemed to have softened her attitude toward the old man since earlier in the evening.

"Kind words," said Lysander. "I am, however, quite unworthy of them." Withdrawing his glowing stone from its pouch to illuminate the camp once again, he turned to face the two warriors. "You see, these woods hold no menace to me. Cassaldra's host could do me no harm."

"What do you mean?" asked Alexi.

Lysander was still for a moment. "I believe the time has come for you to know something more about me."

The pilgrim's withered hands reached upward. His bony fingers took hold of the crimson hood and drew it slowly back, allowing the blue light of his magical orb to flow across it. Even under that peculiar glow it was obvious that the old man's flesh bore an unnatural pallor. Unnatural, Alexi realized, for a living thing.

But Lysander was no living thing. He was a corpse.

SEVENTEEN

Lysander's skin drew tightly across the bones of his face, rendering him every bit as sepulchral-looking as the boatman who had brought them into this realm. His eyes bore the same sinister glow that Alexi had seen in those of the ghouls. The old man's throat was a mass of knotted tissues; the few patches of hair that remained on his withered scalp were tattered and white.

At a flash of movement in the corner of his eye, Alexi brought Corona around in a perfect arc to intercept Dasmaria's sword with a loud *clang!* Had he not done so, Lysander's decapitated body would now lie on the broken road.

"Let him speak, Das!"

"Have you lost your senses? He is in league with our enemies!"

"You don't know that."

The two warriors stood still for a moment, their eyes locked. Then, without a word, Dasmaria lowered her blade. She did not, however, return it to its scabbard.

Throughout this exchange, Lysander did not move. Alexi turned to him, trying his best not to stare—or recoil. This was the being whom he had allowed to share his campfire? From whom he had accepted counsel in the crypt? Who had touched Dasmaria and Ferran with his shriveled hands to heal them?

At this final thought, a fraction of Alexi's horror abated. Lysander had aided them in times of crisis. And he had just prevented the ghosts from attacking his companions, even though the spirits held no threat to him personally. He at least deserved a chance to explain himself.

"Tell us how it is that you walk the earth," Alexi said tightly.

"I shall." He shuffled over to the fallen tree and sat down, gesturing for the two warriors to do the same. Alexi leaned on the far end of the tree, reluctant to get too close. Dasmaria remained standing even farther away.

"I exist because of circumstances surrounding the death of Kateri Shadowborn. In order to tell you my own story, I must tell you also of Kateri's final days."

Alexi's thoughts turned to the dream he'd had of his mother's death. Could Lysander shed some light on the events he had witnessed? He motioned for the pilgrim to continue.

"A year or so after I had entered the monastery, Kateri Shadowborn led the armies of the Great Kingdom to victory in the Heretical Wars. The day of their triumph was greeted with celebrations throughout the Thirteen Provinces. On that same day, Kateri decided that she had seen enough warfare. She announced to the king and the High Mother her intention to retire her sword.

"Kateri's enemies, however, did not retire. Instead of accepting their defeat with grace, they plotted revenge. In the aftermath of the wars, several elite members of the Ahltrian sought each other out. They called themselves the Dark Triad, for they believed they were the only three survivors of that sinister order."

"They did not know of you?" Alexi asked.

"No. I suppose that even if they had, they would not have considered me a survivor. After all, I was living in a monastery under an assumed name and practicing a different faith. And as a friend of Kateri Shadowborn's, I was hardly amenable to what they had in mind. You see, they wanted to call the fiend Ebonbane back into our world."

Alexi shuddered, a chill starting in his heart and sweeping through him. "Surely they realized his evil?"

"That is precisely what appealed to the Dark Triad. They intended to command that horrible creature to obey them," Lysander said. "Such foolishness was short-lived, however. As soon as Ebonbane appeared, he devoured their lives and left them as I—unliving creatures. He forced them to obey his every command.

"Having punished the Dark Triad for their folly, Ebonbane cast his gaze about the world in search of the woman who had defeated his armies and driven him from the world of men. With his baleful vision, he saw not only the lady in her retirement, but also me in my hermitage.

"The wicked being made his way to the forest around Forenoon Abbey and commanded the Dark Triad to bring me before him. When the corrupted creatures came to the abbey, my brothers attempted to hide me, to protect me. It was a foolish mistake. The triad slaughtered them all, killing them in terrible and painful ways. As they dragged me away from the monastery, I could hear the agonizing screams of my brothers." Lysander's long, bony fingers clenched tightly in the folds of his robe. "Words cannot express the misery I felt that night. Suffice it to say that their screams still echo in my ears."

Alexi said nothing, but he knew exactly what the pilgrim meant. He had felt the ghouls' deaths in the depths of his soul. Their screams, their agony, the fear that they felt in the last second before death—all were indelibly pressed upon his memory. The difference, Alexi supposed, was that he felt no remorse for the deaths of those fell things. They were nothing more than rabid beasts and deserved to die. But Lysander remembered them as the monks of Forenoon Abbey, innocent servants of Belenus who were attacked and slain in the name of evil.

"I, too, was killed. My horrified spirit watched as Ebonbane took control of my body. I—he—traveled to Shadowborn Manor. In the dead of night, in the guise of a friend, he arrived at the home of the woman who had saved not only my life, but my soul as well."

Uneasy comprehension washed over Alexi. "It was *you*," he said as images from his dream rushed before his eyes. "You were the monk who came to my mother's door with that black-bladed sword. You killed her with it."

Lysander met Alexi's accusing glare. "Aye," he said quietly. Then he lowered his gaze to the ground. "It was my body, but not my spirit."

Alexi stood up and turned his back on Lysander, unable to look at the old man. Nausea roiled his stomach. The whole while he had journeyed to avenge his mother's death, the murderer had ridden at his side.

The icy void in his heart filled with blackness. His hand itched to unsheath Corona and run the holy blade right through Lysander's traitorous heart, then end his own foolish existence. Dark thoughts flooded his mind—vengeful, violent thoughts. He had seen the killer in his dream. How could he not have realized the old man's guilt from the start? *Belenus, when you closed your eye to me, did I become blind, too?*

The supplication no sooner flashed through his head than a passage from the holy scriptures followed it: *Only the gods can see into a man's soul.* Alexi recalled what he had said to Dasmaria just last night, that Brigit had forgiven Lysander's sins. She had seen into his soul and found him worthy of her gifts. It was Ebonbane, not Lysander, who had truly killed his mother. The fiend was the rightful target of Alexi's vengeance.

He turned back to Lysander. "What happened after the murder?"

The pilgrim's gaze remained lowered. "Ebonbane guided my body back to the monastery. He returned my spirit to my dead flesh and filled my dry bones with an animating force, then had me interred. Of all the monks who had lived at Forenoon Abbey before the coming of the Dark Triad, only I was given a grave to rest in. It seemed to amuse the fiend to leave me in a place where I could watch the tragedy that had been wrought in my name as it unfolded. For years I lay in my grave, unable to act but keenly aware of what the abbey had become."

"And that was?"

Lysander finally met Alexi's gaze. "The triad turned it into a stronghold of evil. For a decade and a half, I lay in the earth. Every day of that imprisonment was pure torture. Every night, as the sun fell below the horizon, I watched men who had been good and just in life move out into the world in search of innocents to feast upon.

"As they gorged themselves on innocent flesh, I

prayed to almighty Brigit. I begged her to give me the strength to rise from my grave to avenge the death of Kateri Shadowborn and all my brothers at Forenoon Abbey. About the time you became a knight, Brigit answered my prayers.

"While you gained combat experience, I gained as much knowledge as I could about Ebonbane and his realm. It was my hope that together we could avenge your mother's death. I knew if ever there was an ally whose steel I could count on in this crusade, it would be the son of Kateri Shadowborn."

Alexi regarded him for a long moment. Though the cold fury in his heart urged him to exact revenge on the emaciated old man, cold reason acknowledged that Lysander had merely been a weapon in the hand of a much stronger foe. Only with his help could Alexi bring Kateri Shadowborn's real killer to justice.

Was this, then, the plan Belenus had for Alexi? To drive Ebonbane from the world, as his mother had before him? If so, the sun god had indeed chosen a different path for him to follow, and an unusual ally to accompany him.

"Ebonbane will pay for his crimes," Alexi said.

As the words left his mouth, a searing pain shot through him, as if a stake of ice had been driven into his heart. He winced and turned away, drawing on every shred of his warrior's discipline to prevent his face from revealing his agony.

"I thank you," Lysander said. Alexi heard him draw his cowl back over his head. "And I apologize for making you look so long upon my decrepit form. I forget my own appearance sometimes."

Thankful that the pilgrim mistook the cause of his distressed expression, Alexi merely nodded. The pain in his chest ebbed to a dull ache, though each beat of his heart magnified it.

He opened his eyes to see Dasmaria turn on her heel and stride away without a word. She headed toward the edge of their campsite, beyond the reach of Lysander's glowing stone.

Alexi followed her into the shadows. She looked somehow smaller to him as the darkness enveloped her, but then he realized it was because he rarely saw her without armor. Normally she wore at least a breastplate while in camp, but she hadn't yet donned it since their incident with the ghosts.

Despite the lack of armament, she didn't look defenseless. Dasmaria held herself with a warrior's confidence, her strength evident in every movement. At the moment, contempt was also evident in the firm set of her jaw and her ramrod posture. Was she disgusted with Lysander or with him?

He touched her shoulder. "Das?"

She shrugged off his hand. "How can you join forces with him, Alexi?" She did not face him, but rather stared into the dark forest. "Knowing what he is and what he did?"

He sighed, bringing his hand up to his own chest and trying to massage away the pain. "Lysander isn't the real enemy. But he can help me defeat the creature who is."

At last she turned toward him. "How do you know he isn't just manipulating you?" She tried to search his eyes in the pale moonlight. "Alexi, the Darkening left you terribly uncertain about yourself and your relationship to Belenus. Lysander could be merely taking advantage of that to serve his own ends."

He shook his head. "I admit the possibility exists. But

deep inside, I don't think so."

At her skeptical look, he motioned for her to sit down with him. He dropped onto the long grass and rested his forearms on his bent knees. Reluctantly she, too, sat down.

"Ebonbane has to be stopped, Dasmaria. As a paladin, surely you realize that. If I don't do it, someone else must." Absently he rubbed his chest again. The cold ache receded, replaced by a heat that slowly coursed through his veins. "But I can feel Ebonbane, sense his influence in this land. I believe that through my mother, I have some sort of connection to the fiend, that only I can banish him. But I can't do it alone, Das. Lysander has critical information. Just as my mother needed his aid, I do, too."

She glanced toward Lysander, who seemed to be praying or meditating as he rested on the fallen log. "But even with Lysander's help, Ebonbane defeated your mother in the end by using her own ally against her." She turned back to Alexi. "If the famous Kateri Shadowborn could not prevail against the fiend, what makes you think you'll fare any better?"

He studied her face. The moonlight softened her features, bathing her in a glow almost as enchanting as that of the ghosts. "I hope I have an advantage she did not."

"And what is that?"

"You. Tell me you'll help me, Das. With you at my side, I know we'll succeed." He grew warmer, his blood seeming almost on fire. His heart beat in an odd rhythm.

"You know I'm not going to abandon you now." She sighed heavily, the strain of the past two days evident in her tired voice. "Of course I'll help."

Her pledge brought a smile to the corners of his mouth. "Good. We make a great team, you and I." He paused, then leaned toward her. "In more ways than one."

He gently touched his lips to hers. When she responded favorably, he deepened the kiss and slid his arms around her, pulling her body close to his. He reveled in the feel of her curves against the hard planes of his chest, unobstructed by the armor usually between them.

The close contact sent a current of desire through him. His pulse roared in his ears, its heat dizzying. He wanted Dasmaria, wanted to possess her, wanted to claim her as his own. Right now.

She broke off the kiss. "Alexi—"

He captured her lips again and pushed her to the ground, conscious only of the fire in his blood. As he kissed her hungrily, he brought his hand up to cup her breast.

"Alexi, no—"

Ignoring her muffled protests, he bore down on her with his full weight.

"No!" She pushed him off of her and rolled away, coming to her knees in a defensive position. Trying to catch her breath, she held her hand out as if to keep him from advancing again. "I'm not ready for this."

The burning sensation still coursed through him, blackness enveloping his heart. "Come on, Das," he said bitterly. "Just how long am I supposed to wait for you to make up your mind?"

She stared at him with bewildered eyes. "A few days ago you said to take all the time I needed."

"Things are different now." His gaze drifted to her swollen lips. He could still taste them, still feel their softness against his own. A spark of anger ignited within him. Dasmaria was nothing but a tease—one minute kissing him, the next minute pushing him away. He was a fool not to have realized it sooner.

"No, Alexi—*you're* different." She lowered her hand but kept her distance. "You're changing, Alexi."

He rose to his feet. "You don't know what in the name of Belenus you're talking about."

"No?" She rose and came to stand in front of him. "How about what you just said, to begin with? You never cursed before. Now you take Belenus's name in vain at the slightest provocation. You skipped tonight's sunset devotions without a thought of—"

"You're the paladin, Dasmaria, not I." He tried to walk away, but she grabbed his shoulder and made him face her.

"You've started taking pleasure in killing. You turned a blind eye to Lysander's vile flute, and now you intend to ally with him—a walking corpse! These things aren't like you, Alexi."

"Maybe you don't know me as well as you think you do."

She gazed fiercely into his eyes. "The Alexi Shadowborn I know would never try to force himself on a woman."

"Well, if you spot one around here, tell me."

She looked at him as if he'd struck her. Then she shook her head in confusion, sadness clouding her features. "What has gotten into you, Alexi?"

With a final look of disgust, she strode away.

EIGHTEEN

Alexi watched Dasmaria walk to her armor and don her breastplate. Was she protecting herself from the ghosts, or from him?

Once she was out of proximity, the fire in Alexi's veins subsided, leaving only the cold, empty void in his heart that had become all too familiar. He could think more clearly again, see more clearly again.

And when he looked inside, he did not like what he saw.

What had gotten into him, indeed? Whatever this icy darkness was inside him, it was growing. And the larger it grew, the more it affected his actions. It clouded his judgment. It set his nerves on edge.

It was taking control.

What had begun as brief bursts of temper had progressed to unforgivable conduct toward his closest friend. He shuddered as he thought of what he had said to her, what he had done. The memory filled him with shame.

"Das, I'm sorry," he whispered into the night.

The dark force in his heart scared him. How could he fight it if he didn't know what it was? Yet some small part of him did know, though he scarcely dared admit the truth even to himself: Evil itself had gained a foothold within him. The knowledge chilled him to the marrow. As the High Mother had told him on the day of the Darkening, evil seldom released its grip on a man's heart.

But fight it he would, with every breath he took. Perhaps a victory tomorrow at Forenoon Abbey would break its hold over him. Or perhaps, he thought as despair swept through him, fighting so many ghouls would forever seal his fate.

His gaze again settled on Dasmaria. She sat alone, apparently lost in thought—thoughts, no doubt, about how horribly he had just treated her. Even if he managed to exorcise the evil from his heart, had he destroyed any chance of happiness with her? Was there a friendship left to salvage? He prayed to Belenus that there was.

So ashamed that he could barely hold his head up, he approached her to apologize. She didn't look up when he reached her side.

"Das?"

She kept her face impassive and her gaze fixed solidly on the ground. "Alexi, please leave me alone," she said quietly. "I can't speak to you right now."

He couldn't tell whether she was furious, disgusted, or deeply hurt. A wave of regret and sorrow washed over him for making her feel any of those things. "Das, I'm—"

"Not now. Maybe tomorrow, but not now."

As much as he wanted to beg her forgiveness, he remained silent. He would respect her request, as he wished to Belenus he had done earlier. He left her and went to sit beside Lysander.

"If it is any consolation to you," said the old man,

"Dasmaria is not speaking to me either." Sighing deeply, Lysander gazed into the woods surrounding them. "I believe it is Ebonbane's influence. He seeks to conquer us by dividing us."

* * * * *

They passed the night in safety if not in peace. Through the long hours of darkness, as the grim face of the moon drifted slowly through the heavens, the howls of the damned filled the air. Their moans seemed to echo the despair in Alexi's own heart.

He got little sleep. Throughout his shift of guard duty, a litany of concerns occupied his thoughts: how to apologize to Dasmaria, how to rescue his brother from the ghouls, how to battle the growing evil within him. After he woke Lysander and bedded down, the same thoughts kept him awake long into the pilgrim's shift. And once he finally drifted off, he awoke twice with the sensation that he was being watched by one of the ghosts in the woods. When he opened his eyes, however, only the dim glow of Lysander's magical light greeted him.

The din of the tortured spirits ceased just before dawn. As the Eye of Belenus peeked over the horizon, the trio broke camp hurriedly. Once more Alexi tried to apologize to Dasmaria, but the firm set of her jaw was more than enough to discourage the attempt.

They rode mostly in uncomfortable silence. The terrain proved only slightly less difficult to negotiate in the daylight than it had been at night. The bramble-covered road buckled with protruding tree roots as it twisted along.

About the time the sun reached its zenith, they arrived at a clearing in the forest. Dasmaria drew rein and slipped off her horse. She stretched the kinks out her muscles, a fluid process that reminded Alexi of a cat getting up from a nap in the sun. "We need to take a break," she said tersely. "My muscles are knotted, and I think we could all use something to eat."

"Fifteen minutes," said Lysander, "no more."

Both of the warriors turned to look at the old man. He had spoken with a tone of authority, one he had probably cultivated during his service in the Heretical Wars.

"Forgive me," he said when he saw their eyes upon him. "I simply mean that we must press on if we are to arrive at the abbey before sundown. At our current pace, we will cut it close, and I, for one, would prefer to encounter the ghouls during their vulnerable daylight hours. If we must wait until morning and spend another night in this forest, we will be at the mercy of the spirits, and I daresay their mercy would be a precious commodity indeed."

"You're right," said Dasmaria. It took Alexi several seconds to realize that Dasmaria had not only spoken to Lysander, but she had also agreed with him. If she was beginning to soften toward their unliving companion, perhaps before long she would be ready to hear Alexi's apology.

They spent a few minutes moving around and working muscles that had been too long dormant. After stretching, they each took a handful of dried rations, returned to the leather saddles, and started on the road again.

For Alexi, the ride seemed to last forever. Dasmaria's anger, though well deserved, distressed him almost as much as the constant iciness that sat like a glacier in his chest. But of even greater concern was the knowledge that his brother waited at the end of this twisting road—a brother he had no idea whether he would be rescuing or burying. Or whether there would be anything left of Ferran to bury.

At last the dark silhouette of Forenoon Abbey rose against the waning colors of the sky. The monastery showed little sign of occupation. A few sections of the walls had crumbled, but the structure otherwise appeared intact, with two exceptions—both apparently signs that some evil presence now resided in this once holy temple.

The first alteration could have been wrought by nothing more than repeated storms and the passing of years, although Alexi suspected otherwise. Every single stained-glass window that had adorned the stout brick walls was broken. Shards of glass, like rows of fangs lining the inside of stone maws, glittered in the dying light of the day.

The second indication, however, was more obviously the result of blasphemous intent. High atop the monastery's bell tower, where Alexi knew the solar disk of Belenus should have gleamed, there was nothing. If any part of the abbey had been built to weather storm and disaster, it was that golden pinnacle. It had not fallen under the weight of the years—it had been pulled down. And Alexi knew what manner of creature had done it.

Lysander called a halt. "The ghouls are still there," he said with disgust. "I can feel their presence."

"And Ferran?" Alexi asked.

"I cannot tell," replied the pilgrim. "The ghouls were once my spiritual brothers, but I have no special rapport with Ferran. There is, of course, no obvious sign of his presence."

Already dusky shadows enveloped the abbey. "We have arrived later than I had planned," said the pilgrim.

"We should move quickly if we hope to find Ferran before the sun sets."

They kicked their horses into motion to close the remaining distance, but in this gloomy land under Ebonbane's power, the sun left the sky faster than it did in the Great Kingdom. Just as they reached the stone walls, the Eye of Belenus dipped below the horizon.

They dismounted and prepared to enter the abbey. In that instant, however, a dark shape sprang from the brush. A dozen others followed, surging out of the darkness from all sides. Ghouls—all of them bearing the hideous death's-head tattoo on their foreheads.

As the night stalkers charged, Pitch reared up and let out an alarmed whinny. He kicked out with his powerful forelegs and crushed the forehead of a ghoul. Where his fierce hooves had struck the undead creature, leather flesh tore away and blackened ooze seeped out. Splinters of bone tore through the membrane around the wound, showing clearly that the skull had splintered. The ghoul toppled backward, crashed to the ground, and lay still.

Alexi brought Corona flashing out of its scabbard, impaling one of the slavering ghouls almost immediately. But even as he pulled his sword out of the creature and kicked its dying body aside, another appeared to menace him. A step to one side and a lateral sweep of gleaming steel felled the vile beast.

Not far from where the body of the second ghoul had fallen, Alexi saw Lysander raise his arms high over his head. In the ancient language of the scriptures, he called upon the power of Brigit through prayers unknown to Alexi's ears. With a final cry of fervor, he snapped his right arm down and swept the left one forward to point at a trio of looming ghouls. Speaking the name of his goddess, the pilgrim closed his hand into a fist. A jet of flame sprang forth.

The flame grew to a length of some three feet until it looked like the blade of a sword. Lysander drove forward, sweeping his blazing weapon from side to side. With each blow, a ghoul fell backward and cried out in pain. A second blow invariably slew the wounded creature. Lysander fought with such fury that his cowl slid off. One of the ghouls, trying to claw him from behind, tore the heavy fabric with its steel-sharp talons. The hood slipped to the ground, forgotten.

Two more creatures pounced on Alexi. He kicked one away as he hacked off the arm of the other. The injured ghoul cried out, black ooze gushing from the wound. With another blow, Alexi put the beast out of its misery, then set to work on its fellow. The second ghoul proved more dexterous than the first, dodging three of Alexi's passes before finally falling to the fourth.

From the corner of his eye, Alexi saw Dasmaria drive into a mass of ghouls—no fewer than half a dozen—and set to work with her golden sword. The dancing blade looked as much like lightning as cold steel in the hands of its skilled wielder. Two ghouls fell before they even knew they were under attack. A third raised his talons to strike, only to find a sword buried in its chest. Its mouth fell open, and a howl of agony split the night.

The fourth ghoul, forced to dodge around the falling body of its companion, found itself suddenly facing Dasmaria's unprotected back. Its talons lashed out, ripping through leather leggings and the flesh beneath.

Dasmaria cried out. Alexi tried to get to her, but another ghoul charged forward, blocking his way. As he cleaved the beast in half, he saw Dasmaria over its shoulder. She tried to shift the weight from her wounded leg but was forced to lean away from another attacker. The injured limb buckled and she fell.

"Das!" he shouted. An instant later, she was buried under the clawing bodies of a dozen ghouls. Alexi felt his blood run cold as he saw the faces and hands of the terrible creatures smeared with red. Unnaturally long tongues ran over jagged teeth, and Alexi felt the urge to vomit.

But he had no time to mourn. With one of their prey down, the ghouls were emboldened. They drove forward like a surging tide, apparently assured of their success.

Four more ghouls surrounded Alexi. As he thrust at the closest one, he knew he and Lysander needed a new strategy before they, too, were overwhelmed. Then, in a flash, the answer came to him.

"*Karnas, radamar!*"

As the warm rays of Belenus spilled forth from Corona, Alexi felt nothing but despair. Why—why hadn't he thought to invoke the sword's power sooner? In the heat of battle, he had fallen back on his old battle tactics, the ones ingrained in him from countless skirmishes and hours of training with an ordinary weapon. Too late, he had recalled the magic at his command.

Too late for Dasmaria, but not for the rest of them. The unexpected flash of radiance took the ghouls unawares. One of the creatures was caught in midleap by the sudden flare of bright light. A lance of radiance pierced its chest, burning the monster like kindling in a hearth. Cries of pain tore into the night as the unholy creatures felt the sting of purity.

The screams were music to Alexi's ears. "Die, you filthy beasts!" he shouted. The chill in his heart swelled, sending a surge of ice water coursing through his veins. Darkness filled his body and soul.

He looked around, reveling in the spectacle before him. He would have his revenge on the foul creatures who had taken first his brother, then Dasmaria. But as he gazed with twisted pleasure on the agony around him, a horrible sight met his eyes.

Lysander was down, clutching at his head in a futile attempt to shield it from Corona's burning aura. Alexi realized that during previous battles, the ancient man had been careful to keep his back to the scintillating blade. Now, without his shielding hood, the light was as deadly to him as it was to the undead attackers. In seconds, the pilgrim would be dust.

As the three war-horses fought on, hammering away at those ghouls who were not instantly slain by the holy light, Alexi rushed toward Lysander. Midway, he commanded Corona into darkness. At once the night descended again. Alexi knelt at the old man's side.

"Lysander! Can you hear me?"

"I . . . hear," whispered the pilgrim. Agony tainted his words, forcing him to speak through clenched teeth. His eyes were tightly shut and his body trembled. "Rekindle the flame!"

"I cannot," said Alexi. "You'll be destroyed!"

"You must," ordered Lysander, "or we will be overrun!"

Alexi knew Lysander was right. The woods around them were alive with dark shapes flitting through the moonlight. Here and there, a pale red eye flashed in the undergrowth and a slavering hiss broke the air. No matter what the cost, he must light the holy blade and drive this ravenous enemy back.

Alexi stood and raised the gleaming blade aloft. A cold wind rose from nowhere and blew past him, carrying on it the stench of rotting corpses and the fetid breath of the cannibals surrounding him. *"Karnas—"*

Before he could complete the holy command, a ghoul crashed down upon his back. He fell forward, the obscene creature raking its talons down both his cheeks. The force of the impact drove the air from his lungs and loosened his grip on Corona. When he tried to draw in his breath, he found the creature's stink overwhelming.

More ghouls raced forward and pressed his face into the damp soil. Foul talons clutched at his arms, and he was jerked hard around. Corona spun out of his fingers and landed with a thump on the earth. The sky was gone, blotted out by the horrible faces of things long dead.

But he did not lose hope. As one of the ghouls licked at the trickles of blood that ran down his cheek, Alexi called once more to his blade.

But no sounds issued from his mouth.

He tried to scream but could not. The toxin of the ghouls' claws had paralyzed him once more. It was all he could do to breathe. He had no way to save himself.

Or Lysander.

Or Ferran.

NINETEEN

The knight has fallen.

My minions, pathetic though they are, have proven too much for him. He has been taken by the ghouls and is even now being carried into the ruined monastery. The Ghoul Lord hungers for his flesh, but Alexi Shadowborn is not his. It angers him, but that is of no importance to me. They have feasted upon the corpse of the paladin, but the others are mine—the knight, the boy, and the traitor. Their demises will be more terrible than even the Ghoul Lord can imagine.

The knight's despair is delightfully tactile.

I can feel it radiate from him. He does not know whether his brother still lives or not. He has hurt the woman he loves and seen her destroyed by the most pitiful of my underlings. He has learned that the man who travels with him is no more living than the creatures who have defeated him. By the time he is brought before me, his spirit will be broken. And with his ultimate defeat, Kateri Shadowborn's spirit will also break.

But there is something more.

His mind is not on the death of his companion, the fate of his brother, or even the almost certain doom that awaits him. No, he is wracked with images drawn from the minds of those who fell before him in combat. He feels their pain and relives the sensations that surrounded their destruction.

He has discovered the seed of darkness within him.

He struggles with it, yet he does not understand it. Little does he know that if he did, his power would be greatly magnified. But he denies the darkness instead of embracing the power it promises him.

Is he that foolish?

I do not think so. I believe that he must know in his heart what the truth is, where this power comes from. And yet he lacks the many senses that are mine to command. I have overestimated him. His intelligence is but a fraction of my own; his perceptions are dim at best. He does not know the truth.

But that is a situation I can remedy.

I reach out. A touch of my power, and the darkness stirs. It is exactly as I expected. While the warrior still suffers the agony of those he so recently slew, I have given the shadows that torment him a power they have not had before. It will be most amusing to watch the young warrior torn apart by that which abides within him.

I think I shall keep this from Kateri Shadowborn for now.

TWENTY

Ferran was alive.

It was more than Alexi had reason to hope.

Indeed, he considered the fact that the ghouls had not devoured either Lysander or himself something of a wonder. That the three of them were now prisoners in the bottom of a deep, black pit seemed secondary. To find that their efforts had not been in vain was an incredible stroke of good fortune.

And the fact that Dasmaria had fallen was an unthinkable nightmare.

She had died as she had lived: bravely, honorably, and fighting for the cause of righteousness. As a warrior, she had been prepared for such a fate. Yet that knowledge could not assuage Alexi's grief. Not only had he lost a friend, but the Circle had lost a paladin who had only just begun her career as a champion of the cause of right. What she might have accomplished, the world would now never know.

That their last words had been spoken in anger, he could not bear to contemplate. He would carry that burden with him to his own grave.

But Alexi knew he must force these thoughts from his

mind and concentrate on the situation at hand. If he allowed grief and guilt to overwhelm him, Dasmaria's death would have been for naught. He would grieve later, when this dreadful quest was concluded—if he were still alive to do so.

He turned his attention to Ferran, once again the recipient of Lysander's curative arts. Alexi could see the boy only by the pale light of several phosphorescent lichen patches.

"How is he?" he asked Lysander.

"Your brother has been badly used." Lysander lifted his eyes from Ferran's dirty, battered body. "I have exhausted my healing spells, and still he is not fully revived. He will wake soon, but it will be some time before he is truly himself again."

Assuming the ghouls didn't kill them all in the very near future. Alexi tried to battle the despair seeping into his heart. If nothing else, he would have the chance to say a last farewell to his beloved younger brother.

"How are you faring?" asked Lysander, rising slowly to his feet.

"As well as might be expected." It was true enough, he supposed. His body had thrown off the paralytic effects of the ghoul poisons. He could move freely again, if somewhat stiffly, although the lacerations on his face would take a long time to heal. And even when they did, he would likely wear terrible scars for the rest of his days. Even magical healing could not fully erase such evil wounds.

"What about you?" Alexi asked.

"I am well enough, though I will not soon forget the sting of Corona's fire. The greatest trial of my curse is that I may no longer allow the holy light of day to fall upon my pale skin."

"Alexi?" came a faint voice from the other side of the pit. It was the first sound Ferran had made since he and Lysander were tossed in here. Alexi hastened to the boy's side and took his brother's hand. He adjusted the bundle of clothing they had placed behind Ferran's head to make the boy more comfortable.

"Lie still," Alexi said softly.

"Where . . . where are we?" asked Ferran. "How did you get me away from . . . from . . ."

Alexi pressed a finger to his brother's lips. Poor Ferran had been so traumatized by their captors that he couldn't bring himself to identify them. Alexi had nearly as much difficultly saying what he had to.

"We haven't gotten you away, Ferran." Alexi stroked a lock of the boy's matted hair away from his eyes. "Lysander and I have been taken as well."

At the mention of the pilgrim, Ferran rolled his eyes to gaze upon Lysander. He stood several feet away, almost completely cloaked in shadows. As he stepped forward, the boy saw his face and cried out in terror.

"Forgive me," gasped the pilgrim. He threw the new, makeshift hood he had constructed over his head to shield his disturbing countenance from the boy. "I lowered my cowl to pray. I forgot to replace it."

Alexi motioned for Lysander to be silent. As the monk fell back into the darkness, Alexi clutched Ferran to him. The boy trembled and shook as sobs of fear and loathing wracked his body. Though Lysander could heal his brother's physical wounds, the mental scars would fade only with the passage of time. Whatever the ghouls had done to his brother, Alexi vowed, they and their master would pay. Somehow, before this was all over, justice would be served.

It was several minutes before his soothing words

calmed Ferran. When at last the boy fell still, Alexi lowered him back to the floor and tried to explain all that had happened since the battle in the swamp. He began with the closing seconds of the skirmish in which Ferran was taken and the flight afterward. He recounted the happenings in the Phantasmal Forest and, much as it pained him to do so, told the gruesome tale of Dasmaria's death. The weakened boy listened, though he seemed barely able to remain conscious.

"Alexi," said Ferran, "they tried . . . to turn me against you. . . . They told me things . . . I remember the pain . . . I tried not to listen. . . ."

Alexi held his brother tightly. Ferran's eyes had gone wide with fear, and sweat beaded on his forehead. Gradually, as Alexi rocked him gently in his arms, the boy's eyes closed. Except for shallow, anxious breathing, he lay still.

"He's asleep," said Alexi.

"Perhaps that's best," said Lysander.

Alexi nodded. But from the trembling spasms that soon shook the squire's body, he knew Ferran's slumber was not a peaceful one. The knight could only imagine what terrors filled his brother's dreams. Knowing how the depths of his own soul were haunted by dark shapes and phantasmal ghouls, perhaps he did not have to imagine at all.

Alexi rose and turned toward Lysander. The monk had moved to the far side of the pit and knelt. His whispered prayers echoed shallowly in the darkness. Lysander was reciting the predawn prayers with which the followers of Brigit bade farewell to their goddess.

Alexi had no idea what time of day it was. Was Lysander guessing, or did the dead have some innate ability to sense the rising and setting of the sun? Considering its fatal effect upon them, the idea might not be too farfetched.

He knelt beside the monk and bowed his head. Drawing in a deep breath, he joined his voice to the pilgrim's. Though it was not a prayer that Alexi was thoroughly familiar with, the words of faith chased away some of the darkness within him.

After the devotions, Lysander placed his hand on Alexi's shoulder. "You should get some rest," he said. "It is certainly after sunrise now, and I doubt the ghouls will return to deal with us until after sunset."

Alexi nodded. "What about you?"

"The pleasure of sleep is denied me," he said, "though I made a pretense of it on our journey to disguise my true nature as long as possible. Still, I shall make good use of the next few hours. Through contemplation, prayer, and meditation, I will refresh my spellcasting abilities. If the blessed Brigit permits me, I may be able to further heal Ferran before the ghouls return. Perhaps we can give my former brothers a surprise or two."

Alexi nodded and stretched out beside his brother. He remembered nights—nights that seemed not so long ago—when Ferran had begged to sleep in his older brother's room. Once in a while Alexi had granted his younger sibling permission to do so. On those evenings, they had shared stories, secrets, and dreams. It was little wonder that as Ferran grew older, he had elected to follow in his older brother's footsteps when it came time to choose a career.

Though Alexi tried get comfortable, he was as tired and sore as he had ever been in his life. Every muscle seemed to complain even when not called upon to do anything. And when he did move, the residual toxins of his ghoul attackers made every gesture awkward. He closed his eyes with a shallow sigh.

And before long, ghouls surrounded him.

He cried out, grabbing for his sword and biting off a curse when he realized that he no longer had his weapon. The creatures leered at him, their horrific faces illuminated by the pale glow of lichen as they circled. Had he been armed, Alexi would have said that they were looking for a chance to strike. The truth of the matter, however, was that they were toying with him.

When he looked for Lysander and Ferran, his heart jerked to a stop.

Both of his companions had risen and stood with the ranks of the undead. Lysander was uncowled, his eyes burning like fiery coals. In his gaunt hands, he clutched the grip of his deadly mace. Like his eyes, the pilgrim's weapon now seemed to be wreathed in a ruddy glow.

Far more terrible than this, however, was the sight of Ferran. His brother was not as he had appeared a few minutes before. Instead, he had become every bit as gaunt and skeletal as Lysander. And in his hands, the squire held a bright silver blade: Corona.

Alexi knew that to wait for the coming attack was to invite death. Setting his jaw firmly, he lunged forward and threw his shoulder at Ferran. If he could get his hands on Corona, the tide of battle would turn. It wouldn't matter how many of the revolting creatures opposed him; the warrior could at least hold his own.

Ferran must have expected the attack, however. Just before Alexi reached him, the restless corpse of his brother slipped nimbly aside. The knight crashed to the stone floor, gasping for breath. He rolled over and saw the ranks of the undead looming over him.

"Alexi Shadowborn," called Lysander. "The time has come!"

He cried out.

And then his eyes flew open. He was awake again.

Alexi sat up, trying to catch his breath. The nightmares were growing stronger and more vivid. The familiar pain in his chest had returned, more terrible and icy than ever. With it, he could almost hear mocking laughter inside him.

The coldness began to spread. He shut his eyes tightly, imagining a small box inside his chest, surrounding the malevolent presence. With every ounce of will he could muster, he concentrated on trapping the coldness within the cell. He had to contain it, had to keep it from overwhelming him.

When he felt he had the force under control, he opened his eyes once more. He heard no sound of the ghouls returning yet, but the moment could not be long in coming. And he could imagine only too easily what the creatures had in store for their three captives.

He rubbed his eyes. His mouth tasted worse than the fetid air in the pit smelled, and his joints had grown even more stiff during his fitful nap. "How's Ferran?" he asked Lysander.

"I think he'll pull through," said a soft, youthful voice.

Relief washed over Alexi as he saw his younger brother standing beside the monk. He rose hurriedly and swept Ferran up in a powerful embrace.

"Be careful with him," said Lysander. "I've only just gotten his ribs to knit. If you crack one, you'll have to heal it."

Alexi lowered his brother gingerly, as if the boy were a delicate porcelain figure that must be treated with extreme care. He prayed to Belenus that, whatever horrible fate might befall himself, somehow his brother would escape to safety. No sooner had he finished the silent supplication than scraping sounds above heralded the approach of their captors.

"Have you got a plan?" Ferran asked.

"I'm sure I do," Alexi said grimly. "I just haven't thought of it yet."

With a sudden crash of steel on stone, their jailers threw aside the metal grate covering the top of the pit. At almost the same instant, a wooden ladder was jabbed down, narrowly missing Alexi's head. The trio looked at each other in silence. Finally the knight, after glancing once more at Ferran, stepped in front of his companions.

Alexi put his foot on the ladder and started upward. The wood was old, and each rung bowed under his weight. When he neared the top, clawed hands seized him and tossed him roughly aside to clear the ladder for Ferran and Lysander.

A dozen ghoulish guards led the three companions away from the pit and through a series of dark corridors. Every so often one of the creatures would poke at the captives in the same way farmers herded their cattle to the slaughterhouse.

Looking about him, the knight surmised that this level had once held a wine cellar. As they stumbled through the darkness, he caught faint impressions of row upon row of racks, all filled with dusty bottles. If it hadn't all gone to vinegar, he imagined one could find some vintner's prizes here. From the smell of rotting meat that filled the area, Alexi dared not guess what the ghouls used the rooms for now.

Twice during the transit, Alexi attempted to speak. Each time, however, he got no further than the first word before a hissing voice ordered him to be silent. The second time, a sharp talon threatened his throat. After that, no one dared make a sound.

Alexi used the time to take a good look at his captors. While he hated the sight of these vile creatures, there was something riveting about them. From the speed with which they moved and the sinister fire in their eyes, it was hard to believe they were not alive. Still, their pallor and the leathery texture of their flesh spoke of nothing but the grave.

And then there was the stench.

Alexi had ridden through battlefields where a hundred bodies lay rotting in the sun. Even that rank odor had been nothing compared to the stink of these creatures. He observed, however, that Lysander and Ferran did not appear bothered by the smell. At first this worried Alexi, but then he realized that Ferran must have grown used to the smell during his captivity, and Lysander, one of the walking dead himself, probably didn't even notice it.

The group abruptly came to a broad flight of stone stairs. The steps rose no more than five feet to a pair of wide cathedral doors. Torches burned unevenly in sconces at the top, throwing rippling shadows around the darkened hall. Two of the ghouls moved ahead of the others, ascending the steps and pushing open the great portal. Before he could get a clear look through the opening, Alexi was grabbed, dragged up the steps, and thrust through the door.

Stumbling, he managed not to fall. The less agile Lysander crashed to the floor beside him. Alexi moved to help his friend up, but a sharp blow to his back stopped him in his tracks. He sank down on one knee, flashes of light obscuring his vision, but he refused to fall. By the time his eyesight cleared, Alexi saw that

Lysander had gotten back to his feet.

When the three captives had been led away from the pit, Alexi hadn't understood why the ghouls hadn't bound them in some fashion. However, as they were prodded forward, the reason became clear to him.

The room before Alexi and his comrades, the monastery's minster, crawled with ghouls. Even unbound, who could hope to escape such an unholy host?

Like all churches sacred to Belenus, this minster was a vast chamber capped by a gilded dome set atop stout stone walls. Openings in the wall showed where a dozen stained-glass windows had once celebrated the hours of the day. Shards of colored glass still hung in the window frames, all that remained of those traditional decorations. Like the temple back in Avonleigh, this cathedral featured concentric rings of pews, all facing the central altar.

Based on Lysander's estimation of the number of monks cloistered here when Ebonbane defiled the abbey, Alexi had expected to find perhaps twoscore ghouls hiding in the monastery. However, more than thrice that number now waited in the minster. Clearly the ghoul population had increased. Perhaps this was a reflection of the growing power of their master, Ebonbane. The fiend had grown stronger through the years, managing to defeat the woman who had once driven him from the world. Apparently he had continued to amass power and influence after her demise.

The creatures formed a great mass of dark bodies pressed one upon another until Alexi had difficulty distinguishing where one ended and the next began. In the flickering, uneven light of the half-dozen torches scattered around the minster, their eyes glowed yellow and green. He felt as if he were being cast into a chamber filled with gluttonous rats.

All of the ghouls shared the crimson death's-head mark on their foreheads that Alexi had first seen in the Brimstadt graveyard back in Avonleigh—the night his nightmares had started. Had Ebonbane sent his minions there? Did he seek to expand his domain to encompass all the people and places Kateri Shadowborn had ever held dear?

Alexi wished he had Corona. With the radiance of the holy blade, he could sweep this host of evil out of existence in a second, instantly incinerating them all with the fire of Belenus.

But he had lost his blade outside the abbey when they were taken. What would become of it now, he could not imagine. He took some consolation in the fact that it was a holy weapon. Even if he could not wield it against the ghouls, they would at least be unable to turn its power upon him.

Musings about his sword evaporated as he saw Ferran trembling. Alexi wished he could comfort his brother. From all appearances, Ferran had almost certainly endured his torture here in this defiled chamber. No doubt the same fate now awaited him as well.

As the trio neared the center of the room, the mass of undead parted to reveal a crude throne set upon the dais. A thick shadow hung over the area, preventing Alexi from seeing who or what rested upon that seat. Two glaring yellow-green eyes stared out from the darkness, watching the three companions with a predatory hunger.

When Alexi reached the edge of the dais, a pair of taloned hands grabbed his arm. He halted no more than a dozen feet from the dark throne and the mysterious master of this place. A pair of torches were brought forward and secured to the side of the throne. In their dancing amber light, Alexi saw a creature more revolting even than the ghouls.

It leaned forward in the throne, much as a scholar might while considering a tricky problem. Although the thing could once have been human, it had now become the embodiment of the grave. Gaunt and skeletal, its flesh was a sickly gray, with mottled patches of green and black. The eyes had sunken deep into their sockets beneath the few wisps of white hair that managed to cling to this long-dead thing.

A crimson death's-head adorned its forehead. But unlike the tattoos the other ghouls displayed, this mark appeared to have been branded with an iron of supernaturally intense heat. The skull icon was seared into the creature's withered flesh, its edges still black.

At the sight, the iciness in Alexi's chest surged. He struggled to contain it, forcing it back into the imaginary cell he had fashioned with his will.

"I am the master of this place," proclaimed the obscene creature. He hissed out the words between stiletto teeth, punctuating them with a slender, rasplike tongue that tasted the air like a serpent's.

Alexi said nothing, although he suspected that some response was expected of him. After a few seconds of defiant silence, a blow to the back of his head knocked him to his knees. He dragged himself to his feet, blinking to chase away the spots in his vision.

When his vision cleared, he locked his eyes with those of the creature and resumed his impertinent silence. He expected to be struck again, but this time the vile thing on the throne raised a hand to halt the ghoulish guard.

"So you are Alexi Shadowborn." The leering creature

rose to its feet and stepped toward Alexi. Its gangly limbs looked weak and frail, but based on his experience with the other ghouls, Alexi suspected otherwise. He tilted his head to the side, assessing the knight with a curious eye. "Long ago I had a name as well. I left it behind with the frailty of life. Now I am known simply as the Ghoul Lord."

Alexi tensed as the self-proclaimed Ghoul Lord stepped forward and peered into Ferran's eyes. The squire cringed but held his ground. Alexi took pride in his brother's bravery; the boy had been through much, yet still managed to present a show of courage.

The Ghoul Lord's leathery fingers reached out. A single talon slid down Ferran's cheek. It did not break the skin, but left a white scratch behind.

"You are looking well, young man," said the creature. "I appear to have underestimated your stamina."

The Ghoul Lord's head once more tilted to the side, this time fixing Lysander with his predatory gaze. The edges of his mouth turned up in what Alexi assumed was a smile, although it looked more like the baring of a jackal's teeth.

"Or perhaps," he said slowly, "it is our brother whose power I neglected to consider. Is this the case, Lysander? Have you still some measure of your clerical ability? Does your precious moon goddess still grant her pitiful blessings to her dead follower?"

Ferran turned his head to cast a wary gaze at Lysander. Apparently the boy was still uncomfortable with the thought that he had been traveling in the company of an undead creature. Alexi couldn't guess how much of that trepidation was simply normal human reaction and how much was a product of his recent torment at the hands of the ghouls.

"You are no brother of mine," said Lysander calmly. "Your master is a creature of darkness and evil. I and my companions serve the powers of light. Their might is something that your kind cannot understand."

"I see that your years in the grave have not taught you respect for Ebonbane. Perhaps the time has come for you to return there."

At that, a pair of ghouls moved forward to grab Lysander's arms. Reflexes took over, and Alexi moved to aid his companion. Before he had taken a step, however, another brace of the revolting creatures grabbed the knight and held him in their iron grip. While Alexi struggled to break free, Lysander was forced to his knees.

The Ghoul Lord began to draw a dark-bladed scimitar from a scabbard he wore, but then halted. For a second, eight inches of razor-edged blade shone in the uneven torchlight before he drove the weapon back into its scabbard. Again the revolting mockery of a smile played over his face.

"I believe it will be the hand of Alexi Shadowborn that ends your life," the Ghoul Lord said smugly. Then, in a loud voice, he called out a single word.

"Vapir!"

Again Alexi tried to break free, but the ghouls who held him remained as strong as ever. He looked to his brother. From the terrified expression on Ferran's pale face, the boy apparently knew what was coming.

Seconds later, the sea of ghouls parted to allow a slender woman to advance. From a distance, she resembled in some ways Lady Victoria. She stood nearly as tall as Alexi, with long, slender limbs and hair like a sleek, flowing cascade of gold. She moved with the grace and elegance of a natural athlete. But the similarity ended there.

At first Alexi thought the Vapir was a living woman. As she came closer, however, her skin appeared pale, almost translucent. Beneath it, he could see her muscles, tissues, and veins pulsing with sickening rhythm. With every step, she became more horrible to behold. If he had been asked to choose, Alexi would have been hard pressed to say which creature revolted him more: the Ghoul Lord or the Vapir.

She slid through the shadows and torchlight with the rolling stride of a harlot. Without a word, she moved to the Ghoul Lord's empty throne and draped herself over it. Seated, she looked down at Alexi and his companions with a sultry fire in her eyes, assuming a pose that might have appeared seductive in a living woman. In this creature, however, it turned Alexi's stomach.

But Alexi's disgust transformed to fear when he looked at Ferran. His brother seemed on the verge of collapse. All traces of color had drained from his face, and perspiration ran freely down his brow. There could be no doubt that this creature was responsible for his torture. Despite her frail appearance, there must be more to this unearthly woman than met Alexi's eye. He swallowed hard and tried to steel himself for whatever might happen next.

"My dear," said the Ghoul Lord, "the time has come for our friend Lysander to die . . . again."

At these words, a cruel smile crossed the Vapir's face. Alexi couldn't help but think of her as a deadly spider about to savor the taste of her helpless prey.

"It is my desire that Alexi Shadowborn see to this matter," hissed the Ghoul Lord. Slurping, jeering laughter rippled through the assembled undead. Anything that so amused his captors, Alexi knew, could not bode well for him.

In the next instant, the Vapir's mind slammed into his own, hammering his will. The assault was as unexpected as it was terrible. The knight clutched at the sides of his head. The spasms of pain that wracked his body granted him strength enough to break the grip of the ghouls, but left him helpless to take advantage of his freedom. He fell to his knees as wave after wave of vile images flooded his mind.

He saw in an instant all the dark deeds this woman had done, both before and after her death. In many ways, the impressions were like those that he received after running a ghoul through with his holy sword. But there was something more terrible about these visions: they were relished and treasured.

He saw lovers slain in blissful sleep.

He saw innocents cut down like wheat before the farmer's merciless scythe.

He saw children put to the sword while their helpless mothers watched.

The horrible mosaic threatened to overwhelm his spirit. An ordinary man could not have resisted the power of the monster's mind, or even have survived the initial assault. But this was not the first time that Alexi had seen such things. His own mind was so frequently assailed by dark and evil visions that he was able to steel himself against the worst of their effects.

The barrage worsened. Alexi tried to block out the ugly images by focusing his thoughts. He was a knight, he told himself, very nearly a paladin. He believed in the innate superiority of good over evil, light over darkness, truth over deception. As the impressions and thoughts of darkness bombarded him, he called upon the only defense the ghouls had not been able to strip from him: his faith. While the onslaught of evil threatened to overwhelm him, he prayed to Belenus to bolster his resolve and fortify his spirit.

The clash of good and evil seemed to go on within him for hours, but Alexi knew that only a few minutes had passed. At first he merely held his own. But then, as his prayer and willpower rallied, he began to drive back the profane images. With words of salvation on his lips, he forced the Vapir to withdraw her violating presence from his mind.

Alexi gasped for breath. Heaving and shaking, he drew in lungful after lungful of foul air. His senses seemed to be failing him, growing fainter with every passing second as his heart struggled to beat out a frantic pace within his breast. He had fallen forward during the onslaught. Although still on his knees, his weight now rested on his hands.

Worse, the pain in his chest had returned. The mental effort required to keep the Vapir at bay had exhausted his willpower. The imaginary cell within him splintered, allowing the malevolent presence to seep out like ice water. He fought to maintain control, to force the darkness back into its cell and hold it there.

For a moment, the whole of the temple fell dark and silent. The Vapir lay upon the throne, her eyes wide and face drained. She gazed with surprise at the knight.

"You are an impressive man, Alexi Shadowborn," hissed the Ghoul Lord. "Never before have I seen a mortal fend off the advances of the Vapir. Either her powers are weakening or your faith is strong."

"I daresay," remarked the Vapir languidly, "that the knight might even be strong enough to resist the will of our master." Clearly shaken by her efforts, she made every effort to appear unruffled. Loose tendrils of hair had fallen forward over her eyes, and she swept them back with fluid strokes.

"Indeed," said the Ghoul Lord with a sinister laugh, "it is fortunate that the traitor Lysander is not so powerful. He has done the master's bidding before and will be more easily controlled. I will not be cheated of my amusements." At that, he nodded at the Vapir, and she allowed a cruel smile to paint the edges of her thin, translucent lips.

Alexi gathered enough strength to lift his head. Still barely able to breathe, he saw Lysander's head snap back suddenly. For the faintest fraction of a second, the monk struggled to throw off the will of the Vapir. The pilgrim's eyes opened wide and his jaw clenched in pain. Then the emaciated body sagged. Lysander's resistance had been overwhelmed. Despair filled Alexi's heart at the thought of the tortured man being once more in the grip of evil.

"It is done," said the Vapir. "He is mine."

She flipped her wrist, as if breaking the pilgrim's spirit were a thing easily done. Her eyes had taken on a red glow with the delight of domination. She ran a translucent tongue along bone-white lips in a sultry gesture that made Alexi want to vomit. "I can control the child as well," she said with a sadistic grin.

The Ghoul Lord laughed slowly. He nodded, and the Vapir languidly stretched out her slender arm to point a skeletal finger at Ferran. The youth threw his arms out in a futile gesture of defiance, but with no other sign of resistance, Alexi saw his brother's eyes go blank. Like the Vapir's, they were now rimmed with red fire.

That was too much for Alexi.

The floodgates within him broke, allowing the cold waves he'd tried so hard to contain to crash over his heart and wash through him. He knew then, beyond a doubt, what the force was that had taken root inside him. It was anger. It was rage. It was hate.

Strength poured back into him. With a vengeance, the knight sprang forward. Before the ghouls could grab him, Alexi had thrown himself onto the Ghoul Lord. They crashed to the ground. Alexi pinned the creature and skillfully withdrew the black scimitar at the Ghoul Lord's waist.

As the fell master of the monastery fixed him with a withering gaze, the knight brought the blade sweeping toward the Ghoul Lord's neck, intending to decapitate the beast with a single stroke.

Then everything went black.

TWENTY-ONE

Alexi snapped awake.

The foul odor of Forenoon Abbey, more effective than smelling salts, assailed his nostrils. Retching, he hung his head between his knees and spat twice before he realized that the effort did nothing to drive the vile taste from his mouth.

As the memory of where he was flooded over him, he fought back the nausea and raised his head. His eyes met a sight as blasphemous as it was horrifying.

While he'd been unconscious, apparently thwarted in his attack on the Ghoul Lord, the ghouls had all taken seats in the temple pews, as if preparing for a worship service. Their eyes burned like hot coals in the dim torchlight, like malevolent stars speckling a black night sky.

Alexi found himself seated in a front pew. On one side of him sat the wretched Ghoul Lord. His tongue flicked back and forth like the tail of a cat between needlelike teeth. On his other side sat the repugnant Vapir. She leaned close to Alexi, coiling her arms around him and periodically running her bony fingers along his cheeks. The touch of her cold flesh made him cringe.

Within him, the darkness the two denizens had unleashed still quaked. Though it had subsided to a whisper of its earlier roar, Alexi could yet feel the iciness chilling his heart. But now he welcomed its presence. He would marshal the rage, not try to subdue it. He would await his chance, then use it to destroy the foul creatures at his sides.

He turned his attention to the center of the profane spectacle before him. Upon the dais normally reserved for the priestess and her deacons, Ferran and Lysander waited. They stood back to back, upright and motionless, still apparently under the spell of the dreadful Vapir. The fact that she could dominate both of them while still managing to pay such unwanted attention to Alexi spoke volumes about the scope of her powers.

Each of them held a weapon. Lysander had wrapped his mummified fingers around the heavy golden mace that he had wielded during the battles in the mire and the Phantasmal Forest. It seemed to give off nearly as much light as the torches, though Alexi knew—or believed—the weapon did not hold magic.

Turning his attention to Ferran, Alexi gasped. His brother held Corona! Here at last, presented to him as if by the hand of Belenus himself, was the key to their salvation.

Alexi tried to spring to his feet, but slender, bone-white hands caught him at once and drove him back onto the hard wooden pew. He never would have believed the Vapir capable of such strength. He made a painful landing, but it did not stop him from calling out the words he had never expected to say again:

"*Karnas, radamar!*"

Nothing happened.

Alexi required several seconds to realize that his

sword had failed him. No light sprang forth from the holy weapon to burn and destroy the undead.

His hope deflated. He remembered handing the glowing weapon to Dasmaria in the Borderwood. The instant that her hand enfolded the grip, Corona's radiance had faltered. Until Alexi held the hilt, Corona could not respond to him.

"Disappointed?" the Vapir whispered. Her breath broke over him like a wave of stagnant water as she scraped her dry tongue along his ear. A shiver of revulsion passed down his spine. Alexi found the Vapir's overt sensuality more threatening than her attempts at mental domination. Her mere touch violated him. He tried to pull his face away from her, but found himself held tightly against her abhorrent form.

Revulsion gave way to rancor as the darkness seethed within him. Somehow he would exact his revenge on the Vapir and her ghoulish consort. They would come to a violent end, and he would take pleasure in bringing them to it. With every pulse of his heart, icy rage traveled through him. He would bide his time. And then he would act.

"I think the time has come for our entertainment to commence," said the Ghoul Lord. He rose to his feet and waved an arm at Alexi's companions. "Which one of them will die first?"

At the resultant cheers from the crowd of ghouls, Lysander and Ferran spun to face each other. Both dropped into a defensive crouch and circled clockwise. Alexi wanted to look away, but he could not. No otherworldly power held his gaze on the combatants; he simply could not bear to tear his gaze from the macabre duel.

Ferran's combat training appeared only slightly diminished by the Vapir's mental domination. He hung back, waiting for Lysander to strike. When the monk's gleaming mace swept low in an attempt to strike beneath the squire's guard, Ferran was ready. He leapt into the air, allowing the mace to pass beneath his feet. As he landed, he plunged Corona into Lysander's shoulder.

Under other circumstances, Alexi would have taken pride in Ferran's skill. His blow would clearly leave Lysander's arm useless, gaining Ferran a critical advantage. But a victory in this contest would be hollow indeed.

The ghoulish spectators hissed and cried out their enjoyment of the entertainment. Alexi tried to take advantage of the commotion to break the Vapir's grip, but in vain. She proved as strong as any knight he had ever battled, forcing him back into his seat with hands that roamed too freely. Alexi swallowed bile at her touch.

Again she breathed into his ear. "Be still, my precious one. The fun has scarcely begun, though your brother seems to have the upper hand. Of course, once he dispatches our old comrade, an even more dramatic fate awaits him."

Alexi longed to learn what the Vapir meant, but he didn't want to give her the satisfaction of asking. The hate within him simmered. The moment he got his hands on Corona, he would make her its first victim. He could hardly wait to see the vampyre go up in holy flames.

She ran her bony fingers along his jaw and neck. His flesh crawled wherever her foul touch strayed. "I wonder," she purred, unable to resist provoking him further despite his refusal to take her bait, "what happens to a sacred sword when one throws himself upon it?"

Rage nearly choked him. These fiends intended to execute his friends in the most heinous of ways. And in the process, they also hoped to defile Corona, robbing the blade of its divine power by employing it as an instrument of evil. First Ferran would slay a priest of Brigit with the sword, then use it to commit suicide. Such profane abuse would almost certainly render Corona corrupt in the Eye of Belenus.

Cold hatred flooded his veins and filled his mind with thoughts of retribution. No doubt the fiends intended to slay him, too—probably with his own sword. Let them. Before they delivered the killing stroke, he would destroy as many of them as possible. If Corona would no longer respond to him, he would use his bare hands if necessary. He would crush the Ghoul Lord's skull and break the Vapir's body with his fists.

The sound of metal on stone shattered Alexi's violent reverie. Lysander had managed to land a glancing blow on Ferran's leg. The squire had fallen, striking Corona's blade against the cold stone floor. It rang sharply, releasing a shower of sparks.

Lysander raised the mace above his head. The fire of chaos and destruction burned in his eyes, as it did in those of the Vapir and the Ghoul Lord. Both of his captors leaned forward, their features showing their hunger for the imminent moment of death. As the monk brought his weapon down, the Vapir's embrace tightened. Her fingernails cut into Alexi's flesh, causing rivulets of blood to flow from the jagged punctures.

But Ferran wasn't prepared to die just yet.

In the instant before the mace crushed the boy's skull, Ferran rolled quickly to the side. A great impact rang through the temple as the weapon crashed into the stone floor. The squire sprang to his feet as Lysander recovered from the momentum of the blow. In a second, the two men faced each other again, just as they had at the start of the duel.

The Vapir purred like an obscene cat. Alexi jerked as her tongue flicked over the wounds her excitement had opened in his arm. Nausea threatened to overcome him as she loosened her grip to lap at the blood that trickled from his veins.

He glanced at the Ghoul Lord. The duel completely occupied the diabolical master's attention. With the Vapir momentarily distracted by the taste of his blood, Alexi saw his chance.

He sprang forward, throwing off the Vapir's grip.

In three long strides, he reached Ferran and Lysander. Even in that short space of time, Alexi sensed the tide of events turning against him. Throughout the minster, ghouls poured from the darkness. In seconds they would overwhelm him again.

He lunged at Ferran, hoping to wrench Corona from his brother's hands. But the Vapir must have sensed Alexi's intent. Still under her control, Ferran whirled to face his brother. Alexi knew the undead temptress would order the squire to strike him down.

Even in his weakened condition, Ferran struggled against her command. The youth's features knotted in defiance. In his heart, he balked at attacking his brother. Yet despite this mental resistance, the young squire's limbs obeyed his undead mistress.

That momentary struggle, however, was enough.

Nearly blinded by fury for his captors, Alexi crashed into Ferran and brought the two of them tumbling to the ground. Rough stone tore at his cheek as the knight cracked his head against the floor. For a moment, he didn't know where he was. His ears rang, and a shower of flickering stars tore his vision apart.

Then the ghouls were upon him.

Even as his hands grabbed frantically for the hilt of

his holy sword, the ghouls yanked him in what felt like six different directions at once. The choking stench of the undead fell upon him from all sides. Torchlight glinted off sinister black eyes and trickled along the gleaming edges of upraised talons.

Hatred coursed through Alexi. He must not let these foul beings triumph. With a final, desperate grasp, his fingers instinctively closed around Corona's hilt. A wicked smile came to the knight's lips as he shouted the last words these ghouls would ever hear.

"*Karnas, radamar!*"

The minster remained dark. Corona shed no light.

No! Alexi's mind screamed.

His very spirit blazing with wrath, he slashed at the nearest ghouls, slicing off heads and limbs before the creatures knew what had hit them. Black ichor spurted onto the defiled altar as screams filled the air. Darkness surged through him like lightning ripping the sky.

Yet even as he cut a swath through the sea of bodies around him, Alexi felt a feather-light caress touch his raging heart. He'd experienced the sensation only once before in his life, when he'd believed that Belenus called him to become a paladin.

It was a moment of grace.

The touch lasted just a fraction of a second, but in that moment, the eternal light of Belenus enabled him to see clearly.

The evil inside him had taken over. He had to resist it, contain it, control it. Or be damned.

He parried the ghouls' swipes and blows, barely keeping their paralytic talons at bay as he fought the real battle raging inside himself. With a prayer to Belenus and every scrap of will and faith he could muster, he forced the burgeoning hatred within him back into its imaginary cell. He nearly collapsed with the effort of fighting on two fronts—one a struggle to defend his body, the other a war to save his soul.

Trembling as he strained to maintain his tenuous hold over the evil, he once again called out to Corona.

With an almost audible surge, light filled the befouled temple. Like hot water poured into a basin, the sun-bright rays splashed against the walls and rolled across the remnants of the gilded dome.

The cries of dying ghouls sounded at once terrible and beautiful. The smell of their burning flesh filled the air, choking him even as Corona's radiance promised life and hope and justice, the ultimate triumph of good over all that is evil and dark.

Not far from Alexi, Ferran was shaking his head, as if trying to clear it. He had gotten to his knees, but had not fully recovered from the effects of the Vapir's will. She no longer commanded Ferran and Lysander, but it would take some time before . . .

Lysander!

Alexi whirled about, still holding the flaring Corona high above his head. A dozen feet away, Lysander lay crumpled on the floor. He had managed to throw his arms over his face, buying himself a few more seconds of existence, but he seemed doomed.

Alexi knew he should quench the blade to save the life of this holy man. But if he did so, the rest of the ghouls would swarm over him and Ferran. The knight had sacrificed men in battle before, but he had never been forced to stand by and watch a friend die like this.

Then a shadow fell over the tormented monk. Ferran had risen to his feet and staggered to his brother's side. Alexi began to shout out a command, then saw that no words were needed. Ferran moved at once to protect the monk whose healing magic had done so much for him.

As his brother fell upon the agonized figure of the pilgrim, Alexi turned away and swept Corona back and forth. He waded forward through the dying bodies of those already long dead. Where the glow of the magical blade had not yet done its work, Alexi struck with the cutting edge of justice.

He reached the pew where the Ghoul Lord sat. Clearly the holy light had caught the foul master of Forenoon Abbey unawares. Exposed to the full brilliance of Belenus's wrathful gaze, he had been annihilated almost instantly. Little remained of the creature now. Alexi could identify the body only by the raiments that had marked the unholy creature.

The Vapir, however, was another matter.

There was no sign of the foul seductress. How could she have escaped? Alexi frantically searched the minster for her. Perhaps she had managed somehow to avoid the sword's radiance. Or was it possible that Corona's blaze had no effect upon her? Alexi clenched his jaw. Even if that were true, he was willing to bet the blade itself could still take its toll on her obscene flesh.

As he ran through the stone halls of the ruined abbey, the brilliant glow of the holy sword threw harsh shadows in every direction. With each racing step, they jerked and danced madly. Each corner seemed to promise new dangers, but Alexi knew he had little to fear while Corona burned in his hand—unless other horrors like the Vapir hid somewhere in these halls.

Alexi caught sight of his quarry's pale garments billowing behind her as she darted up a twisting flight of stairs. He pursued, though the slender corridor left little room for his muscular frame. The Vapir wasn't far ahead, he knew, for her sepulchral scent hung in the air. Soon his sword would taste her blood as her obscene lips had tasted his.

At the top of the stairs, Alexi caught a fleeting glimpse of the creature as she vanished through a narrow door. Even as he reached it, the portal swung closed and Alexi heard a catch fall into place. He wasted no time trying the latch, instead hurling himself directly at the wooden barrier like a ram. With a sound of creaking, rending hinges, the door exploded inward. Alexi stumbled through the debris, hacking it out of his way with the sliver of sunlight in his hand.

As he lifted his head and looked around the room, Alexi saw his prey waiting for him. She crouched on the floor like a lynx about to leap upon a helpless deer. Her eyes flashed as the light of Belenus fell across her features. Every harsh line of her cruel face was sharply exaggerated by the unwavering glow of Alexi's sword.

And she was smiling.

That grin confirmed Alexi's worst fears. The fiendish Vapir was immune to the purifying fire of sunlight. Was her evil greater than Corona's good? Perhaps this land of madness made the dark things of the world more powerful than those of the light. If that was so, then what chance did he or any creature of goodness have to prevail?

The knight brought his weapon up to defend himself, wary that the crouching thing might hurl herself at him. He checked his forward momentum and locked his eyes with those of the Vapir. At this, the wounds in his arms throbbed painfully. He felt the overwhelming evil of her spirit pressing down upon him, but he forced it aside. His faith was stronger now than it had been in many days.

Invoking the grace of Belenus, Alexi swept his fiery

weapon in a perfect arc that would end with the blade buried deep in the Vapir's breast. By the time he reached her, however, the vile woman was gone. His blade struck only the cold stone of the floor.

The Vapir's terrible laugh echoed through the room from behind him, ringing sharply off the walls like pealing of a sinister bell. As he whirled about to attack her again, she held out a transfixing finger and emitted a hiss that seemed to freeze his heart.

"You are too slow, Alexi Shadowborn," taunted the Vapir. "Your blade will never catch me."

"It shall not rest until it does."

He lunged forward. The tip of the sword tasted only empty air, however, for the creature had swept to the side with a swift, phantasmal motion. The sight of muscle and tendon working beneath translucent flesh distracted him, but Alexi tried to focus on his attack.

Spinning around to protect his back from an unexpected attack, the knight saw the Vapir had leapt to the windowsill. Ironically, this particular stained-glass window, depicting the triumph of Belenus over the dark prince of the dead, remained intact. The harsh light of Alexi's sword made the stained glass behind the Vapir glimmer. Her eyes burned hotly, and her mouth hung open to allow her dancing tongue to taste the stale air.

For a moment, the two faced each other in silence. Outside, a cold wind moaned in darkness and rattled the glowing facets of the window. Then suddenly the Vapir laughed again, and Alexi lunged at her.

With a backward flip, the profane woman plunged through the window. Her weight, slight though it was, shattered the stained glass and filled the darkness beyond with a hail of sparkling shards. The glow of the sword spilled out of the window as Alexi reached it. The

Vapir plunged downward thirty feet in the brilliant shaft of light. All around her, a tumble of dancing colors filled the night.

She struck the ground smoothly and rolled across rocky, broken soil. Splinters of stained glass fell like multicolored snow around her. Without hesitation, she sprang to her feet and raced away from the abbey. She moved with the swiftness of a wolf, in great sweeping strides that made him doubt his own eyes.

Tasting the fresh, chill air, Alexi desperately considered his next step. If he abandoned his pursuit, the creature would be loose in the world. At best, she would carry news of the events at Forenoon Abbey to her dark master.

To continue the chase, however, Alexi must spring from the window, perhaps breaking a leg in the attempt, and abandon Ferran and Lysander. When he had left them in the minster, they were alive but weak and in need of care. There was no guarantee they would survive without his aid.

Then, from out of the darkness, a flash of racing blackness broke into sight, moving with a swiftness that Alexi could scarcely credit. A loud whinny cut the night air. Pitch. The war-horse must have smelled the blood of its master on the fleeing monster.

With a surge of furious speed, Pitch overtook the Vapir. Owls and bats and other animals of the night cried out in unison as the thundering hooves of the rearing war-horse crushed the Vapir's ribs. She cried out in the darkness, a sound of terror and sorrow that echoed in the depths of Alexi's mind. The Vapir lashed out at the horse with diabolical fury. But even her frantic efforts to claw the stallion could not slow Pitch's attacks. Again and again, the great horse rose into the air and brought its hooves crashing down on the fallen creature. By the time the unholy light in her eyes had faded away into final stillness, the slender body was broken almost beyond recognition.

As the last inhabitant of Forenoon Abbey fell, a change swept across the vast expanse of the Phantasmal Forest. Fiery glows of spectral forms appeared throughout the tangled trees. Echoing howls, as spectral and unnatural as they were joyous and celebratory, filled the night air.

Alexi closed his eyes and offered a silent prayer of thanks to Belenus. This night had seen a critical victory in the struggle against Ebonbane, but they would need still more help from the sun god to complete their quest. His prayer complete, he turned away from the window.

And was knocked to the floor.

A torrent of grief, despair, and sorrow assaulted his spirit, rocking his body with its intensity. He experienced the anguish of holy men enslaved by evil and forced to commit heinous acts. He felt the self-loathing their cursed existence inspired and the agony of their tormented souls.

When he thought he could bear no more, the evil of the Ghoul Lord himself battered his heart. He saw the destruction of Letour and Sanschay, the torture of innocents in the holocaust, the persecution of those who would not bend to Ebonbane's will. He saw the summoning of Ebonbane himself and his triumphant return to the world. And he felt Ebonbane wither the Dark Triad's wizard into an animated husk.

He writhed on the floor as the onslaught threatened to rend him asunder. Wave after wave of malice and wickedness crashed over him, until he feared the evil would consume him. Finally, as he experienced the pain of the Ghoul Lord's final moments of undeath, Corona's radiance ended his torment.

Alexi lay trembling for nearly a quarter of an hour before he could rise to his knees. This time the barrage of evil had almost been too great for him to survive. Indeed, had he, not Pitch, delivered the Vapir's final blow, the onslaught would surely have killed him.

As he stood, his heart knew great heaviness. For the darkness he carried within was stronger than ever.

TWENTY-TWO

I am impressed.

The child of Kateri Shadowborn has brought down the Ghoul Lord and forced the destruction of the Vapir. His determination is far greater than I had conceived. He has proven himself a worthy opponent.

It was the same with his mother.

When we faced each other, she had the power to resist my will. Her faith gave her a strength that even I could not break. I would not have believed that mere mortals could have such resilience.

It is her will that contains me even now.

So long as her spirit remains unbroken, I shall remain her prisoner. But her time draws to a close. With her spawn journeying ever closer, the moment of my ultimate victory looms near.

His demise will shatter the shackles that hold me.

Once Alexi Shadowborn is within my power, he will die. He will die slowly. He will die painfully. But he will die. And his mother will watch his demise. No matter how strong her faith, this will be more than it can withstand. With her spirit broken, I will be free.

And when I am free, this world will burn.

TWENTY-THREE

The wall rose out of the forest so suddenly that the riders almost ran into it before they realized it was there. One moment Alexi, Ferran, and Lysander were riding along the hard-beaten forest road, and the next moment the highway came to a sudden halt. Without warning, and for no apparent reason, a stone wall abruptly blocked their path.

When the company had come to a stop, Alexi dropped out of the saddle. He strode to the edge of the wall to better examine it.

The barrier stood in striking contrast to the crumbling monastery where they had passed the preceding night. At its best, the walls of Forenoon Abbey were never so precisely crafted. This wall's construction was almost seamless. Smooth, even bricks, all perfectly aligned, were held in place with an absolute minimum of expertly trimmed mortar. Any mason would have regarded the barricade as artistry.

In fact, the precision seemed almost too fine. Like a trail that seemed too easy to follow, it made Alexi uneasy and suspicious. A single word came to his mind: *trap*. Was the wall an illusion? It certainly looked solid.

Was it a magical construct? Something told him it was.

Ferran dropped to the ground beside his brother and let out a sigh as he turned his head first one way, then the other. The wall extended out of sight to the left and right, with no sign of a gate or other entrance. Were it any lower, they might have simply scaled it. But at twenty or more feet in height, it posed a formidable barrier.

"We'll have to ride around it," said Lysander. "With luck, we will discover a gate."

"You didn't know this was here?" asked Alexi. He had begun to think of Lysander as an inexhaustible font of knowledge. The thought that so pronounced a hindrance might be unknown to him unnerved the knight more than a little.

"I did not," answered Lysander. "We are very near to the manor now. Though I have traveled in the mysterious land surrounding Shadowborn Manor, I have not been to the estate itself since the night Kateri Shadowborn died."

With a nod of acceptance, Alexi put the matter out of his mind. Taking the reins of his horse, he turned to his right and led the way off the road and into the underbrush. Ferran, leading Midnight, followed about ten feet behind. Lysander brought up the rear, although he chose to remain in the saddle as his lighter horse followed the others. Ember, now riderless, followed along, keeping company with Pitch.

They followed along the wall, skirting dense patches of thorns and jagged weeds that seemed to scratch at them intentionally. The brambles were thick here. Alexi also noted the absence of birds and other animal life. Although he said nothing to the others, these observations disturbed him. Back at the road, the forest had appeared normal enough. The farther away from the path they traveled, however, the more menacing their surroundings grew.

After fifteen minutes, they determined that the wall wasn't straight, as it had appeared when they first came upon it. Instead, it curved away from them imperceptibly. Given enough time, it would describe a complete circle, leading them right back to the road.

Half an hour passed. Alexi wondered if they were going to find a gate at all. The forest had become quite feral, and he was beginning to feel that some dark presence watched their every step.

Was this twisted place still a part of the Phantasmal Forest? Most likely it was. Alexi began to worry about their safety. Darkness couldn't be more than a few hours away, and he had no wish to test the hospitality of the spirits a second time.

When three-quarters of an hour had passed, Alexi was ready to give up hope. They must be almost back to the road, he knew, and yet they had seen no sign of a gate or portal. He released a disgusted sigh.

"I think there must have been a hidden entrance back near the road." Ferran swatted a swarm of gnats away from his face. No sooner had he made this gesture than they returned again. Despite the cool air here, the annoying creatures were as common as they had been in the swamp.

Alexi nodded. Ferran's hunch seemed logical enough. Yet did logic carry any weight in this place? Even if a secret entrance did exist, he doubted they could find it in all that length of wall.

Then, as quickly as they had come upon the wall in the first place, they reached the road once more. An hour wasted, and they were right back where they had begun.

Ferran looked at him and shrugged. So casual a gesture brought a wry smile to the knight's face. It mattered little, Alexi supposed, how hard it was to get past the wall. They had certainly overcome more challenging problems than this one. He was reminded of the scriptural verse in which Belenus told the Great Prophet to listen well to the words of children and madmen. He would not be the first knight to learn a lesson from his squire.

"All right, Ferran," he said. "Go ahead and search for that secret entrance."

The boy stepped over to the wall, stopping about six feet away to study it. Alexi could see no imperfections in the barrier; judging from Ferran's furrowed brow, neither could his brother. Frowning, Ferran moved closer to the wall.

"Is your squire skilled in such matters?" asked Lysander.

"Not that I'm aware of."

Suddenly Ferran cried out. Alexi darted to his brother's side. Lysander arrived only a second behind the warrior, his supernatural speed surprising Alexi once again.

Alexi gasped. At first he thought Ferran's hands had been cleanly cut from his wrists. But then he saw the truth. The boy's hands had sunk into the wall, as if he had buried them in sand at the beach. Around them, the seamlessly stacked surface of bricks spread out evenly.

"I—I reached out to touch the wall," Ferran said, "but it wasn't there. Before I knew what was happening, I'd stuck my hands inside it. When I tried to pull them out, they wouldn't budge!"

"An illusion?" muttered Alexi.

"No," Lysander responded. "An illusion is nothing

more than a construct of light, not unlike a rainbow or ray of sunshine. Ferran could not be bound by it. This is something else. I have never encountered its like before."

For nearly a minute, no one spoke. At last, however, a smile spread across Alexi's face. "I think I have it. Try pushing your hands in a little farther."

Ferran turned wide eyes upon him. "Why? That'll only make things worse!"

"First of all," said Alexi, "things can't get any worse. You're already stuck. If you sink your arms in up to the elbows, you won't be any more or less trapped, right?"

Ferran nodded, but still did not do as he had been told.

"The only other way that I can see to free you," said Alexi, "is to cut off your hands. While Lysander might be able to keep you from bleeding to death after we did that, I doubt he could grow you a new pair of hands."

Ferran glanced expectantly at the withered man. With a gentle shrug, the old man admitted that Alexi was right.

Swallowing hard, Ferran eased his arms inward. As expected, he met with no resistance. And just as predictably, they could not be withdrawn again.

"I think the only way you're going to get out of this is to press on through the wall," Alexi decided.

Ferran's eyes widened.

"I think you are correct," said Lysander.

Without another word, Ferran nodded. He closed his eyes, drew in a deep breath, and stepped forward. The wall seemed to flow around him like water, but no ripple marked his passage into the seemingly solid barrier.

"I have to go after him," said Alexi.

"Of course," said Lysander, "but I'm coming with you."

Alexi considered ordering the old man to stay behind. After all, there was no need risking both their lives. On the other hand, they had no idea what waited beyond the wall. Ultimately the knight nodded in agreement.

Alexi grabbed the reins of Pitch and Midnight. He took two steps toward the wall and, with a sleek clang of steel, brought out his sword. Drawing in a sharp breath, he spoke the ancient command words to bring the magic weapon to life.

The blade at once sheathed itself in a brilliant radiance. With the war-horses in hand, Alexi threw himself at the bricks. Half of him expected to hit and bounce off, but as he struck the wall, he experienced a tingling sensation, then found himself surrounded by a cool, ruddy darkness.

He was inside the wall.

After blinking several times, he realized the deep red haze that surrounded him wasn't going to clear. He turned his head to the left and then slowly to the right but could see nothing else around him. He could still feel the reins of the horses in his hand, but he couldn't see them. Indeed, his vision didn't even extend all the way to his own wrists. It was like walking through an incredibly thick red fog.

Then suddenly the knight became aware that he couldn't breathe. Panic gripped him for a second, but he forced himself to remain calm. He surged forward as quickly as he could, holding the reins tightly. The dark redness around him seemed to grow thicker as his lungs demanded air.

For a second, he considered releasing the horses. He didn't know if that would gain him any speed or not, but some instinct told him to do it. Reason overcame emotion, though, and he tightened his grip. Leaving the beasts to die, entombed within this semicorporeal wall, was unthinkable.

Just when it seemed that he could last no longer, daylight spilled onto his body. The horses emerged from the wall a few seconds later. As soon as they did, the knight collapsed. He gasped in great lungfuls of air, only half noticing that Ferran stood safe beside him.

When Alexi caught his breath, he forced himself back to his feet. He smiled at his brother and was about to speak when something occurred to him. Lysander hadn't emerged from the wall yet.

Alexi released the horses and threw himself at the stone wall. As he had expected, it was solid on this side. Whoever—or whatever—had built this magical barrier did so to keep things in, not out. But was it a cage or a trap? Had he and his companions just stepped into a snare from which there was no escape?

"Lysander!" cried Alexi. He pounded his hands on the wall, as if hoping to crack it open and free the pilgrim. For fifteen or thirty seconds, his futile assault continued. Then, realizing that he could do nothing, he allowed his hands to fall to his side.

"There's no way out," said Ferran. "I even tried climbing it. Something about it makes it impossible to get a grip on the bricks. I haven't tried a ladder or anything, but I'd bet that won't work either."

Alexi looked up into his brother's eyes. "You can't breathe in there," he said with false composure.

"You don't have to tell me," said the squire. "I was in worse shape than you were when I finally got out."

"If Lysander doesn't get out soon . . ." began Alexi. He turned to face the featureless wall, but saw only the perfectly smooth stone pattern staring back at him. He gripped his magical sword in steely fingers, but even the great weapon could do nothing for him now.

He felt powerless—as he had during the Darkening, as he had when he the ghouls had taken his brother, as he had when he watched Dasmaria die.

If Lysander was trapped forever, it would be a loss to both the quest and Alexi personally. There was so much he wanted to know about the old man and so much that Lysander could tell him about Kateri Shadowborn. The pilgrim was a link to Alexi's past unlike any he had found before.

After an eternal minute had passed, he turned away from the wall. This ill-fated quest of his had claimed another friend.

"We've lost him," he said to his brother in a lifeless monotone.

"Lost whom?" Lysander's sandpaper voice emerged from the wall just a moment before he did. His slender mare trotted out beside Ember, their reins held loosely in the old man's hand. "I'm sorry if I caused you any concern. It took me a few minutes to persuade Dasmaria's horse to follow me."

"But there's no air in there," gasped Alexi. "I thought you were dead."

"I am," said the monk. "I suppose the horses might have noticed the lack of air, but I never did."

Alexi started to say more, to laugh at his own folly, but then saw that the old man no longer paid any attention to him. Instead, his eyes focused on something behind them. Alexi turned around, ready to defend himself, but there was no need.

Lysander was staring at Shadowborn Manor.

Alexi's mouth fell open as his sword dropped low in his hand. While his concern for Lysander was at the forefront, he had taken no notice of the grounds beyond the wall. The place was very much like the home he had grown up in, a sprawling estate built atop a shallow crest with a single bell tower rising from its center. The brilliant sun shone down upon it, gleaming on the whitewashed walls and giving the place a radiance of its own. Where light struck the flawlessly cast windows of the upper floor, it flashed like a brilliant beacon in the perfect azure sky.

A grassy lawn surrounded the place, spreading out to touch the edges of the mysterious wall. A broad cobblestone road ran away from the brick barrier behind them to a carriage house near the front of the manor. To Alexi, the place looked like an island floating in the midst of a great emerald sea of faintly rippling grass.

Alexi could see nothing to stop him from riding right up to the front door of the manor and marching inside. Evil had never been so accommodating.

Lysander seemed to sense his thoughts. He nodded solemnly and stepped closer to Alexi. "I do not think approaching the manor or even getting inside will be our problem. The evil we face is content to wait for us to come to it. After all, Ebonbane knows we must come, for if we turn away now, our entire journey will have been in vain."

Alexi thought about that for a second. It wasn't the way he would have planned to do things, but there was truth in Lysander's words. Ebonbane certainly knew the threesome had arrived and would be waiting for them. There was no way around it: They would have to ride up to the manor house. Alexi felt like a fly compelled to hurl himself directly into the heart of a spider's web. It was suicide, but what other choice did he have?

A sound of whispered words in the holy tongue fell upon Alexi's ears. He turned and saw Lysander offering a prayer for guidance and good fortune in the battle that loomed before them. The knight sank his blade back into its scabbard and reached out to take the old man's frail hand in his. Ferran joined them, completing a circle. As one, they repeated the appeal for blessings that had traveled before the armies of the Great Kingdom for untold years. Even here, where everything felt wrong, the words held comfort.

When they finished their communal worship, the circle remained intact for a few moments longer. In silence, each of the travelers offered his own private prayers. It was a solemn time that all warriors of faith went through before battle.

At last they unclasped hands and broke the circle. Alexi turned to face the manor house. With no further word, he hopped nimbly into the saddle. Ferran and Lysander mounted their steeds as well, and the three faced their destination.

With a ring of steel, Alexi drew his sword and held it aloft. The Eye of Belenus focused on it, gleaming like fire against the brilliant blue sky.

"Onward!" he cried, his words resounding over the rolling grass like a clap of thunder.

TWENTY-FOUR

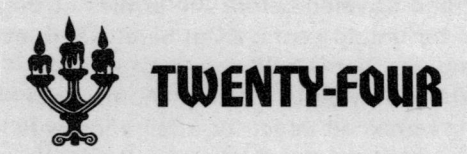

Alexi spurred Pitch toward Shadowborn Manor. Lysander and Ferran followed closely behind.

As if the entire grounds knew that visitors had arrived, a strange transformation took place. Pitch hadn't charged more than a dozen yards before dark clouds boiled into the sky. So swift was their onset that the Alexi suspected the hand of Ebonbane.

Inside, he fought to quell the malicious presence that threatened to rise up at any moment. Since absorbing the energies of the Ghoul Lord and its minions, containing the icy fury within him had become a constant struggle. At present he could keep the force subdued without the effort requiring his entire concentration; he only hoped that when he at last faced Ebonbane, he could continue to exert enough subconscious control to focus on defeating the fiend.

With every forward stride of the horses, the sky grew darker. Soon an oily rain began to fall upon the riders. Cold and slick, it smelled of corruption and decay. With the downpour came lightning, leaping from cloud to cloud in resplendent lattices. Claps of thunder, booming like the reports of an army's bombards, pounded down upon them.

When they had crossed half the distance to the manor, Alexi saw that the sky was not the only entity responding to their approach. The land itself had begun to change. What had once been a neatly manicured lawn of curling green grass was rapidly becoming a tangle of thorns and spines. The cobblestone road upon which the horses' hooves clattered broke apart as jagged shoots emerged to slow their charge. Before long, the road had become so treacherous that Alexi was forced to give rein rather than risk injury to the horses.

Before their eyes, the manor itself transformed. Whitewashed walls grew gray with age. Cracks ran like a thousand spiderwebs across the surface, spilling onto the once gleaming windows. No longer was Shadowborn Manor the elegant home of a lady knight, but an abode of darkness well suited to the fiend they expected to find within the crumbling structure.

Some twenty yards from the looming archway at the front of the house, Alexi motioned the riders to a halt. He dropped from his saddle, Corona still in hand. As the others gathered around him, he moved forward. Ferran nocked an arrow in his bow, while Lysander held his gleaming mace at the ready.

As they reached the front of the manor, the rain pounded so hard that it stung their exposed flesh. The air grew bitterly cold and thick with the smell of rotting meat. The atmosphere was enough to challenge even Alexi's nerve; he couldn't imagine how his relatively untested squire must feel. But then, considering all that Ferran had been through recently, it was hardly fair to call him untested anymore.

"Do we knock?" asked Lysander as they came to a halt before the manor's ornate double doors. Alexi couldn't tell if he was joking or not, but didn't bother to answer. Instead, he met his brother's gaze. Ferran raised his bow and drew back the arrow.

With a mighty kick at the door, Alexi burst inside. Weathered hinges gave out with a series of sharp snaps, and the portal fell inward. It landed with a crash that was promptly smothered by a tremendous clap of thunder.

Alexi's sword flashed with the blue glow of lightning, but he faced no menace within the chamber. For the faintest second, the knight had the impression that his weapon felt disappointed. Did Corona itself hope to face the murderer of Kateri Shadowborn?

Instead of meeting armed resistance, Alexi found himself standing in the center of a comfortable parlor. The well-appointed room displayed both the prosperity and refinement of his mother. Time and Ebonbane's evil influence, however, had ravaged the chamber and its trappings. Where his feet touched the ornate rug, they crushed it into powder, leaving marks like footprints in new-fallen snow. A plush sofa and its matching chairs had fallen apart where they stood, collapsed under the weight of the air above them. Something seemed to have aged everything unnaturally. Instead of only a decade and a half, millenia appeared to have passed.

Alexi circled slowly, his sword at the ready. He expected to be attacked at any moment, although he had no idea what manner of enemy he would be called upon to face. Twice, brilliant flashes of lightning flooded the room with an actinic blue light, but no danger presented itself.

Relaxing only slightly, he motioned for Ferran and Lysander to join him.

The instant the pilgrim stepped into the house, a movement flashed at the edge of Alexi's vision. He spun, prepared to strike if necessary.

A beautiful woman moved gracefully into the room, descending a long flight of stairs. The tall, slender figure wore a white dressing gown. Her long blond hair formed a nimbus around her porcelain face. Every movement of the athletic woman spoke of a warrior's grace and readiness. She said not a word to the three visitors, apparently thinking nothing of finding intruders in her home.

As she reached the bottom of the stairs, Alexi saw that he had been mistaken. He beheld not a beautiful woman, but the image of a beautiful woman. As she moved into the room, a steady glow filled it. The light spread outward from the blade of her sword, which could be none other than Corona.

"Mother?" he murmured.

"Kateri," whispered Lysander, recognizing the woman at the same instant. The monk made a sign of protection with his hand as he moved forward. "Is it truly you?" His shallow voice held awe and reverence.

Alexi didn't know how to respond to the spectre. If the figure was indeed the ghost of Kateri Shadowborn, she surely would not harm her own son. But if the apparition were some trick of Ebonbane's, the spirit could prove far more dangerous than any mortal foe.

He risked a look away from the creature to check on Ferran. The squire had not lowered his bow. Indeed, he had the gleaming arrow aimed directly at the phantasm. Should a battle ensue, Ferran would certainly score the first hit.

Lysander stood directly before the ghost now. Alexi stayed back, ready to respond quickly if something went wrong. The pilgrim was the only one in their company who knew Kateri Shadowborn. It was best to let him speak for them all.

Curiously, however, the spirit did not stop to talk. Indeed, she paid Lysander no heed at all, proceeding instead past him and toward the door. With a start, Alexi noticed that the door he had burst through hung undamaged from its hinges once again.

As the ghostly woman neared the door, two sharp booms of thunder filled the air, although Alexi had seen no lightning a moment earlier. Lysander turned to follow the passing spirit, his hooded head cocked to one side in curiosity. In a voice that Alexi seemed to feel rather than hear, Kateri whispered the words that would darken Corona.

At once the light from her weapon vanished, plunging the entryway and parlor into darkness. Lysander's robes rippled softly. In a moment, he had withdrawn his glowing stone. He held it in his palm, spreading a faint glow across the chamber. Alexi nodded his approval but immediately returned his attention to the apparition.

As the ghost of Kateri Shadowborn reached for the latch, Alexi sensed that he had watched her do so before. The scene seemed much like his dream. Sudden realization burst upon him.

"Ferran! Cover the doorway!"

Without pause, the squire moved his aim from the apparition to the portal before her. At that instant, she drew back the door to reveal a black-robed figure.

Lysander gasped.

The visitor was also transparent, as much a spectre as Kateri herself. Heavy robes obscured his shape, and a great hood hid his face. He held in his hands an ornate long sword, its black blade covered with glowing red runes.

The appearance of the monk confirmed Alexi's suspicions. He was seeing the events of his dream unfold.

No, more than that: He was witnessing firsthand his mother's murder.

Kateri stepped back from the door, clearly recognizing her visitor. She seemed to relax but remain wary, just as Alexi had seen before. "What brings you here at this hour?" Her voice was faint, hard to hear.

"It could not be helped."

Sorrow crept into Alexi's heart as he recognized the voice—it was indeed Lysander's. Though Lysander had revealed the truth the night they camped in the Phantasmal Forest, actually witnessing the possessed monk's treachery was another matter entirely. Alexi's gaze darted to the old man, who looked suddenly helpless. Like Alexi, he had recognized the scene and seemed uncertain what to do.

"We found this weapon in the ancient catacombs beneath Forenoon Abbey," said the apparition in the doorway. "When none of the brothers could identify it or read the inscription, the abbot directed me to bring it here. Surely the wisdom of the great Kateri Shadowborn can unravel the mysteries that confound us."

Only then did Ferran appear to recognize the woman before him. He met his brother's eyes in a questioning gaze, and Alexi nodded curtly. To the boy's credit, Alexi noted, his bow did not tremble in the slightest. He wished he could say the same for his own sword hand.

Then, before Alexi even saw what was happening, fire burst forth from the dark blade. The phantasmal monk raised the blade above his head, casting dancing shadows across the entrance hall. Kateri's ghost cried out in alarm.

Alexi remembered this point in his dream vividly. At this moment, he had tried to rush forward and defend Kateri Shadowborn. His entire body, however, had seemed frozen in place. Now, with the same events unfolding before him again, he hesitated. Whether he was held in place by fear, apprehension, or disbelief, he could not say.

Ferran, on the other hand, seemed unrestrained. His bow snapped tautly, and a gleaming arrow sailed forward to pierce the apparition holding the blazing sword. The boy could not have released a more perfect shot. The feathered shaft struck its target squarely in the chest.

A cheer almost burst from Alexi's lips. But then he saw that, instead of instantly felling its target, the arrow had passed through the ghost as if the figure were nothing more than a thing of vapor. With a dull thump, it buried itself in the archway outside the portal.

At the same second, however, the real Lysander clutched at his chest and staggered forward. He released a wheezing gasp, then fell facedown to the floor. His mace and glowing marble clattered to the dusty carpet beside him.

Even as Lysander crashed to the ground, his spectral twin brought the black blade down, leaving a trail of crimson fire in the air behind it. The air was thick with the choking smell of brimstone. Kateri dropped backward and rolled out of the blade's path. The fiery metal bit deep into the floor, throwing a shower of glowing embers into the air.

Alexi darted around the phantasmal figures in an effort to reach his fallen comrade. Though he ducked and dodged, the spirits took no notice of him.

Back on her feet, Kateri brought the duplicate Corona between her and the ghostly monk. Using its point to hold back her attacker, she whispered words Alexi could not hear but knew very well. The phantasmal blade shed a paler version of the real sword's brilliant glow.

Alexi knew only too well the effect those beams would have on the fallen Lysander. If the crumpled pilgrim were not already dead, the holy rays might finish him off. As he reached his friend, however, he saw that the phantasmal shafts threatened Lysander no more than the material arrow had his ghostly counterpart.

The spectral monk screeched in pain, sending ripples of gooseflesh along Alexi's arms and legs. He pointed his evil weapon at Kateri and spoke his foul word of command.

Crimson fire erupted from the blade, searing Kateri and knocking her down.

At the same time, pain shot through Alexi's chest. The iciness he'd managed to contain at the abbey ripped through him as the monk uttered his profane words. Splinters of ice coursed through Alexi's veins, forcing him to his knees.

As the ghostly murderer lifted his blade to deliver Kateri's killing stroke, Alexi clutched his breast.

For the second time, Alexi and Kateri Shadowborn cried out as one.

TWENTY-FIVE

An instant later, as the ringing of Alexi's cry still hung in the air, the phantasms vanished.

A sudden blue light blazed outside, seeming to freeze the moment in time, before a deep, drumming thunder rolled in behind it. Booming laughter seemed to echo in the heavy crescendo of the storm.

The knight winced, his face contorted as he struggled to subdue the evil burgeoning within him. Inch by inch, he forced the cold hate and rage back into the place inside himself that he had carved out to contain it. All the while, an urgent voice tugged at the edge of his mind.

When the tide had ebbed, he realized Ferran was calling his name. He opened his eyes and turned to his brother. Ferran knelt beside Lysander. Alexi had all but forgotten that one of his comrades had fallen. After a few deep, fortifying breaths to steady himself, he hastened to the pilgrim.

Ferran frowned as his brother approached. "Are you all right?" he asked Alexi.

Alexi realized he still held his hand to his chest. "Fine," he said, dropping his arm. "But I can't say the same for our friend."

Lysander lay limp, so slight that his body seemed nothing more than a pile of cloth. Alexi drew back the seemingly endless layers of fabric to find the desiccated flesh beneath. Ferran, still unused to the fact that they traveled with a living corpse, turned his head away.

"You can't choose your allies in this world, Ferran." Alexi placed a reassuring hand on his brother's shoulder. "You need to learn that if you aspire to wear the armor of a knight in a few years."

Ferran forced himself to return his gaze to Lysander. Though he seemed to understand his brother's counsel, he evidently had difficulty accepting it. Still, Alexi knew the squire would not allow himself to disappoint his brother and mentor. Alexi regarded Ferran with pride. The boy would make a fine knight.

Directing his attention back to their injured companion, Alexi saw no sign of a wound on Lysander's unmoving body. Whatever force had harmed him, it was not a physical one.

"I hit the spirit square in the heart." Ferran sounded apologetic.

Alexi nodded. "And it was an excellent shot. Would have dropped any normal foe in his tracks." He glanced to his brother. "There is no blame here."

"Can you do anything for him?"

Alexi drew in a deep breath and exhaled slowly, lacking an immediate answer for his brother. Lysander had no visible wound for him to tend, and yet seemed in mortal peril. Was the wound spiritual? Had Ferran's shaft somehow impaled his soul? If so, Alexi had no idea what he could he do to treat such an injury. Probably nothing.

But giving in to despair would do Lysander no good.

Alexi could still sense some animation in the frail, withered body. He would not give up hope until he had at least tried something.

He closed his eyes and began to pray. Ferran added his own voice to the supplication. After a minute of prayer, however, a chill crept into Alexi's heart. His words felt hollow and offered him no comfort.

"Is he dead?" asked Ferran in the quiet, reverent voice one normally reserved for a funeral.

"I can't tell."

As if to prove he was still with them, Lysander moved slightly. He opened his eyes, clearly straining at the effort, and pursed his lips. Alexi took the old man's hand, trying to comfort him with a firm grip. He put on a stoic face, the one he had used in the past when saying farewell to a mortally wounded companion. "Lie still," he said.

Lysander murmured something. Alexi could see urgency in his face, visible even though his animating force dwindled rapidly.

Alexi bent forward, trying to discern the wounded man's words. At first, he thought that the injured Lysander had slipped into a delirium and was speaking in his native language, that of the Southern Empire.

No . . . the word sounded more like the sacred tongue of the gods. The old monk must be praying, trying to find peace in his final minutes. Lysander muttered the word again. This time, with his ear pressed almost to the pilgrim's lips, Alexi understood him.

"*Lache*," said the fading man. His tone was one of entreaty, as if demanding the one thing he wanted most but knew would be denied him.

Alexi closed his eyes and squeezed Lysander's hand, already grieving the passing of his friend. Not only had the monk known Alexi's mother, he had also led a remarkable life in his own right. Now, before Alexi could fully come to know Lysander, the old man was leaving him.

The pilgrim closed his eyes, released a withering sigh, and lay still.

Ferran put his hand on Alexi's shoulder. The touch was comforting, even in this abysmal land.

"What did he say?" asked the squire. "I couldn't make it out."

"It was in the ancient tongue," answered Alexi softly. "It means 'Life.'"

As the word left his lips, a glint flashed in the corner of his eye. He turned his head to see Corona, lying beside him where he had set the weapon down to minister to Lysander. The blade caught the blue light of the monk's glowing stone and winked again.

Alexi received a sudden spark of inspiration. He sprang to his feet, almost knocking Ferran to the ground as he grasped the gleaming artifact and held it aloft. "*Karnas, lache!*"

A warm emerald glow spread out from the blade. Where it fell upon Alexi, it felt soothing and healing. He brought the shimmering weapon down, touching the flat to the old man's brow. As soon as steel contacted flesh, the glow ran off the blade like water. It rippled over the monk's body and then seemed to soak into his skin.

Lysander's eyes opened slowly, glowing clear and bright in flesh that looked warmer than Alexi had ever seen it before. If he didn't know the terrible truth of the matter, he might even have said the monk was alive again.

Alexi sheathed his sword and, with help from Ferran, lifted the pilgrim to his feet. After a moment of silence, the old man spoke.

"A most timely use of an ancient power."

"It wouldn't have been so close," said Alexi, "if you had told me about that ability earlier."

"That blade was a gift to Kateri Shadowborn from the lords of the east," said the pilgrim. "No one in the world can match their skill in the creation of weapons, magical or otherwise."

"Does Corona have more powers?" Ferran's eyes were wide with amazement.

"If it does, I have not witnessed them. Alexi will have to discover any further abilities for himself." Lysander, by all evidence fully restored, gathered his mace and glowing stone from the floor.

Alexi decided he would explore the sword's potential at some future time. Right now he felt the need to press on. Somewhere within the walls of this house he would find the evil that had brought them so far from home.

"Which way do we go?" asked Ferran. He had nocked another arrow and held his bow loosely. To an untrained observer, the squire might have looked unprepared for a surprise encounter. Alexi, however, knew how quickly the boy could take aim and fire. Lysander's recent brush with oblivion offered more than ample proof.

Alexi looked to Lysander for an answer to Ferran's question. The old man, his hood still thrown back, wrinkled up his mummified face in thought. Evidently he didn't have the solution Alexi sought, so the knight turned without waiting for a response and led the way forward.

The cool blue radiance of Lysander's marble lit their way. The shimmering light did little to brighten their spirits, however. The magical aura seemed somehow unnatural, reminding them of the spectral nature of their enemies.

They stepped cautiously through a parlor that

seemed nothing short of ancient. In its prime, the place must have been an elegant sitting room where Kateri entertained visitors. Alexi reached out to touch a low table, only to have it collapse under the faint pressure of contact. Clouds of dust rolled into the air, making the two living members of the party cough and choke.

Leaving behind that crumbling chamber, they came into a long gallery. Masterfully rendered portraits, encrusted with dust and lashed to the walls with thick cobwebs, hung evenly on both sides. As Alexi and Ferran stood ready to protect him, Lysander moved near one of the paintings and dragged a withered finger across the bottom of the frame. A thick layer of grime curled away from the brass plaque, revealing fine lettering beneath it.

" 'Sir Redmond Shadowborn,' " read the monk as he glanced at the picture above it. The face seemed familiar to Alexi, having many of the features shared by his mother and Lady Victoria.

"Mother's brother," said Ferran softly.

"Half-brother," corrected Alexi. "He died several years before I was born. She used his bow when she won those three mahogany arrows you're carrying."

As they ambled down the gallery, Lysander paused to read the name on each painting. Alexi could place most of the figures in his family tree, although a few of them required guesswork.

At the end of the hall, a single painting hung between two candle sconces. Above it, a skylight allowed a shaft of sickly gray light to fall upon the portrait. Lysander stopped when he came to this last piece of art. He needed no bronze plaque to tell him who it depicted.

"Kateri."

Alexi stood beside the old man. The wafting blue light of Lysander's magical orb spread a cool glow over the painting, flattening the colors into shades of gray. The result was disturbingly similar to the bleaching effect of the mists Alexi remembered from his nightmare vision of this place.

A stroke of lightning flickered through the skylight, accompanied by an instant reverberation of thunder that sounded like a giant had slapped his mighty hand upon the roof. In the wake of that tremendous discharge, the metal frame of the window glowed with a blue radiance startlingly similar to that of the monk's supernatural light.

Alexi noticed that the same aura had sprung into existence along the edges of Kateri Shadowborn's portrait. It traced the edges of the ornate frame, hissing and spitting out tiny streamers of brilliant blue sparks. The radiance gave the painting an eerie, ghostly look.

And then the arcane image appeared to move.

"Alexi," sounded a ghostly voice.

The warrior's heart nearly stopped. He recognized the voice from his dream and the phantasmal encounter of an hour or so earlier. He glanced to the side and saw by Lysander's slow nod that he knew it as well.

"My son, listen closely," the voice continued. "I have not much time."

Alexi reached out his hand to the portrait. The glow faded from it, and with it the voice grew fainter. As his trembling fingers neared the azure radiance, the delicate voice spoke again.

"Our enemy is powerful—a spirit of absolute evil. I have contained him here for many years by force of will and faith in the almighty Belenus. But after so long, so much exposure to his overwhelming corruption, I fear that I cannot hold him for much longer." The image in the painting softened into a smile but grew fainter. "You alone can challenge him, Alexi. You are a Shadowborn. And you are more than that."

At that instant, Alexi's fingers touched the outer edges of the magical radiance. The glow suddenly vanished. He yanked his hand back as if burned.

In horror, he saw the colors of the painting start to run. The pigments trickled like molasses, rolling across the frame and dribbling down the wall. Where they struck the wooden floor, they spattered and pooled. As the myriad colors melded together, they changed to blood.

Alexi jumped back. Fear covered Ferran's face. The boy had been through more on this one quest than in the whole of his short life previous to now. Alexi wanted more than anything to protect his brother from the trials still to come.

Lysander seemed less affected by the destruction of the painting. As one who could himself work magic, perhaps the effect was less impressive.

With a meaningful glance at Alexi, Lysander fingered his crimson sleeve. The robe appeared almost black in the blue glow of the light spreading across the hallway. Alexi realized the monk's intimation: How could the paint have taken on the color of blood in this dim light when his robes had not? Surely this spectacle was nothing more than a trick of the mind brought on by the fiend Ebonbane.

At a gasp from Ferran, Alexi turned his attention back to the pool on the floor. It had begun to run, leaving slender tracings across the wooden planks. The dribbles of paint formed letters, Alexi realized. And the letters made words—evil words that announced the presence that surrounded them.

> *Darkness fills the shadows,*
> *Drowning out the light,*
> *Step up to the gallows,*
> *Embrace the endless night.*

Even as he finished reading the sinister verse, the letters blurred and the ominous message shifted. Alexi blinked. The vision was gone.

The painting hung on the wall as it had when they entered the gallery. The enchanting image of Kateri Shadowborn was restored, and the floor retained no trace of blood or pigment or letters.

They all looked at each other, no one bold enough to break the heavy silence. Alexi forced a look of confidence onto his face and turned away from the portrait. He stood thinking for a moment, then addressed Lysander.

"Was that Kateri's voice?"

"I believe so."

Alexi nodded. "Do you think the first part of that . . . message . . . was truly from my mother?"

"Quite possibly. Ebonbane is not one to offer words of encouragement."

Alexi looked to Ferran, who indicated his agreement with a nod. "She said that you were a Shadowborn and more," Ferran said. "What did she mean by that?"

Alexi shook his head. "I don't know." His gaze turned to Lysander. "You've provided some unexpected answers in the past. Have you any clue?"

Lysander coughed and bent his head. When he glanced back up, he found both brothers' eyes upon him. He released a heavy sigh. "How much do you know about your father?"

"Only that, like my mother, he was a soldier in the Heretical Wars," Alexi said.

Lysander stared into his eyes for a long moment. "I can tell you more if you wish. But I warn you, it won't be easy to hear."

After a statement like that, how could Alexi not ask to hear the details? He bade the old man continue.

"Your father was a soldier in the armies of the Southern Empire," said the pilgrim.

Every fiber of Alexi's spirit demanded that he challenge these words. "My mother fell in love with a heretic?" The thought that he, a Shadowborn and a knight, could be the bastard son of a heretic shook his self-identity to the core. Yet he knew Lysander would not lie to him about such a thing.

"No," Lysander said quietly. "He was not her lover but her enemy." He lowered his head. "After the attack on Hammerlin, when Kateri was taken prisoner, one of her captors forced himself upon her. Battered and wounded, she was too weak to resist him."

Alexi felt as if he'd been punched in the stomach. "My mother was raped?" He turned his face away, not wanting to let even Ferran witness the troubled expressions playing across his countenance.

"Yes. After she escaped and returned to the Great Kingdom, she gave birth to her assailant's child. You."

Lysander cleared his throat before continuing. "Knowing she was needed in the south and that her life would never enable her to raise a child properly, Kateri asked her sister to care for you. Victoria and Vincent Shadowborn vowed to raise you as their own and never reveal the circumstances of your conception."

A barrage of emotions swept through Alexi. The hate

within him welled up at the unknown assailant who had violated his mother. As he struggled to keep the rage in check, an even more terrible realization flashed into his mind: On the last night of Dasmaria's life, he had nearly committed the same abhorrent act.

He trembled with self-loathing. Conceived in violence, was he destined to inflict it upon others? Was the evil inside him derived not from Ebonbane's influence or from the psychic energies of the fell creatures he had slain, but from his father's seed?

He saw in his mind the image of Dasmaria's face, and grief wracked him. He had never had an opportunity to beg her forgiveness. Or to tell her what she truly meant to him.

That the darkness inside himself had driven him to behave in such an abominable manner toward her could never palliate his actions. Yet somehow Dasmaria had known, even before he himself realized it, that some other force had influenced him. After his unpardonable conduct, she had not immediately walked away from him. Rather, as his friend, she had tried to reach out to him.

And his mother . . . how had she responded to her attacker? Had she granted him the same forgiveness she showed Lysander after the crimes he had committed under Ebonbane's domination?

At that thought, Alexi glanced sharply at the monk. Their eyes met. And Lysander's revealed more than the old man meant to.

"Alexi?" Ferran called softly.

Alexi tore his gaze away from Lysander and turned to Ferran.

"I want you to know that this changes nothing," Ferran said. "Whoever your father was, you are a Shadowborn. You are my brother. I've always looked up to you, and I still do."

With that, the squire extended his hand. Alexi clasped it, feeling warmth spread through his heart. "I hope you'll always feel that way."

"I know I will," said the squire.

Alexi released his brother's arm and faced Lysander. "There's more to the story, isn't there?"

Reluctantly Lysander met his gaze. "Yes."

"What do you mean?" asked Ferran.

"Lysander is my father," said Alexi calmly, never taking his eyes off the old man. "Aren't you?"

The pilgrim paused. Then nodded.

Booming laughter erupted in the hall. Crushing in its malevolence, almost a physical presence, it rebounded off the walls of the gallery and smothered the group from all sides.

Alexi knew, beyond a doubt, that they heard the voice of evil itself.

Evil and death.

TWENTY-SIX

Darkness welled up within Alexi. The booming laughter, raining down from all sides, struck a chord inside, releasing a host of black emotions that swept through him. Despair tried its best to smother his heart, but defiance rose to the surface.

"Show yourself!" he cried. "Show yourself, you coward!"

If Ebonbane heard the knight's words, he gave no indication of it. In time the laughter faded away, leaving a brooding silence that not even the thunder dared violate.

Then, with a loud snap, a series of locks unfastened. At the far end of the gallery, a door swung open. The darkness beyond seemed to pour forth from the portal and into the gallery, soaking up the light around them. A flash of lightning, oddly lacking the booming report they had come to take for granted, showed them that beyond the door lay a large kitchen.

Sword in hand, the knight started to move forward. Lysander, however, stayed him with a hand on his upper arm. "It's a trap," the old man whispered.

"Of course it is," Alexi said. "What better way to find the enemy?"

Ferran stepped close. His jaw was set and his bow bent in anticipation. Lysander gazed at the two brothers, seeming to measure their determination. Realizing he'd been overruled, the old man nodded and headed toward the open door.

Alexi moved smoothly in front of the pilgrim in the manner of an experienced campaigner. None could doubt that a battle lay ahead, and the knight's place was in the front rank. Ferran took up the rear.

The trio moved into the kitchen without incident, forming a triangle near the center of the room. Alexi took stock of the place, uncertain what he was looking for but sensing that they were nearer now to the evil than they had ever been before. This place held something—a presence no more visible than the air itself, but as tangible as a chilling bank of fog.

The stove—a huge cast-iron affair, cold, black, and brooding—first caught Alexi's eye. Beside it stood a plain wooden worktable, its surface coated with the dust from years of disuse. On the other side of the stove, a long, low rack held a variety of cookware. Pots and pans of every description, all woven together by an intricate lattice of cobwebs, rested upon it in neat stacks.

Alexi barely had time to notice the rack of cutlery above the pots and pans before the whole room was plunged into darkness. The glow of Lysander's marble died. Not even the unnatural lightning that had flashed continuously since they had entered the house lit the windows anymore. Alexi had never experienced more complete darkness.

Recovering his wits, the knight invoked Corona's radiance. Knowing what the holy rays could do to Lysander, he did his best to hold the blade so his body would shield the monk.

But it didn't matter.

No light emerged from the sword. Whatever force commanded the darkness in this room proved greater than the magic of the sword. The mere thought chilled Alexi's blood. Might the evil of this place be magnified in some way? And was good doomed to fail in the face of so overwhelming an evil?

"Perhaps only magical illumination is affected," said Lysander, as if reading his thoughts. The idea sounded very much like wishful thinking.

In the darkness, Alexi heard Ferran shuffling. "I think I glimpsed an oil lamp over here as we walked in," the squire said.

If Lysander's hypothesis proved correct—if the darkness smothered only supernatural glows—Ferran would soon have a light going. If not . . . Alexi decided not to consider that possibility for the time being.

Ferran indeed managed to restore light to the room. It spread out, orange and amber, like the faint glow of a sunrise on a hazy autumn morning. And the instant that it did, Alexi and his companions saw their peril.

Every knife and cleaver in the kitchen hung suspended in the air.

The blades hovered motionless, menacing in their potential if not in their action. "Backs together!" Alexi ordered.

With a roar of thunder, lightning once again returned to the dark sky outside. The bright blue glare stung Alexi's eyes, but he did not wince or blink. Instead, he moved into position in the tight wedge, his eyes wide open and alert.

As if signaled by the lightning, the blades at once hurled themselves forward.

Alexi's sword flashed upward, neatly deflecting a

large carving knife. With a ring of metal on metal, the utensil tumbled end over end to bury its point in the wall, where it trembled violently, whether from the reverberations of the impact or from trying to work itself free, Alexi could not say.

At the same second, a pair of thin boning knives ricocheted off his breastplate. He muttered a word of thanks for the snug metal cuirass, the only armor that he had decided to wear into the house. To be sure, his heavier plate would have offered him greater protection, but it would have slowed him down considerably. On the battlefield, that exchange was fair enough. Indoors, however, where movement would be restricted already, he opted for only the breastplate.

As quickly as one hazard was eliminated, another assaulted him. As he deflected and danced between the flying blades, he cast a quick glance at Ferran.

The archer had been forced to cast aside his bow after firing a quick shot to divert a large meat cleaver. Now he protected himself as best he could with the slender blade he carried. He swept the weapon, more a saber or cutlass than a sword, to and fro in an effort to parry the attacks of half a dozen dancing knives. Blood streamed from deep cuts on the boy's forehead and cheeks. Alexi feared they would soon be the least of his wounds.

The knight cried out in agony. Looking down, he saw a long flensing knife buried in his thigh, which now throbbed with excruciating pain. Blood began to pool on the floor beneath him.

He choked off his cry and threw an arm across his face in time to deflect a small dinner knife that had designs on his throat. How much longer could they hold off this onslaught?

Jerking his head as a steel skewer whooshed past his ear, Alexi saw that Lysander fared better than either warrior, wielding his mace with impossible swiftness. His inhuman skill reminded the knight of the ghouls at Forenoon Abbey, creatures to whom Lysander was as much kin as he was to Alexi.

Amid the clanging of steel on steel and the thunking of blades into the wooden walls, the orange light of the oil lamp glowed brightly. Suddenly it flared. Alexi whirled, barely deflecting a spinning carving knife, and saw that Ferran had lost his balance in an effort to avoid the attack of some deadly utensil. In his fall, he had knocked the lamp off the edge of the hard wooden table. It shattered, throwing its reservoir of oil across half the kitchen.

Wherever that blazing liquid fell, roaring fire instantly sprang to life. The timber of this sinister place was dry with age and burned like kindling. Within seconds, flames engulfed half the room and the air filled with choking gray smoke.

Alexi sprang to his brother's side. He managed to thrust an arm across the boy's face in time to intercept a rusted knife. It glanced off the knight's wrist, opening a long, jagged gash. With Alexi shielding him, Ferran grabbed at his bow, which had become endangered by the dancing flames.

Faster than seemed possible, the blaze spread throughout most of the kitchen. Wherever the flames touched, they instantly adhered and spread. Bits of fiery debris broke loose from the ceiling, raining down to help the spread of the flames. Alexi realized that he was doing more choking than breathing.

Lysander appeared beside the brothers. The smoke was so thick that Alexi didn't even see him until the man was upon him. His red robe hung awkwardly on his body, pinned here and there by knives that had buried themselves in the monk's flesh. Had Lysander been a living man, he would have been slain by these skillfully placed wounds. Exactly how much the walking corpse was suffering, Alexi could not guess.

The pilgrim gathered the two brothers in his arms, as if to protect them from the swarm of blades and sea of flames. A short prayer passed Lysander's lips, though Alexi could not hear the words over the roaring blaze and thunking knives. A hollow ringing sounded, almost below the range of his hearing. Then a shimmering yellow globe formed in the air around the three. Against the dancing flames, it seemed almost invisible.

The instant the bubble sprang into being, a pair of heavy knives struck its surface and bounced off. In seconds, a dozen blades—some bright and gleaming, others dull and brown with rust—were cutting, carving, and chopping ferociously at the almost unseen barrier that encased the little group.

For all the protection Lysander's spell granted them, it did nothing to shield them from the flames. Heat seared Alexi's flesh, and polluted air clawed at his lungs.

"We don't have long," Lysander shouted above the churning fire. "This spell will hold back the blades for a few minutes at most."

Ferran coughed. "What about the fire?"

At that instant, the room itself answered the squire's question. The floor beneath them tilted suddenly with a loud crack. The aged house, its floors every bit as brittle and dry as the kitchen walls, was beginning to collapse.

The floor crumbled. A shower of blazing sparks swirled into the air to mingle with their startled cries.

The darkness beneath the decrepit manor spread out beneath them.

Then it seemed the maw of the flaming abyss itself opened to swallow them alive.

TWENTY-SEVEN

Alexi lifted himself to his feet. The impact of landing had knocked the breath out of him, but he recovered quickly. He leaned against a block of cold stone, drawing in ragged breaths as glowing embers and flaming debris fluttered down like the ash of an erupting volcano or the falling of infernal snow.

After a few seconds, he sensed something seriously wrong about the atmosphere of the room. Or rather, something seriously right. The feeling of dread and oppression that had hung over him since the moment he passed through the brick wall had somehow lifted.

Surveying the chamber, Alexi understood why. He stood in a chapel—a chapel dedicated to the worship of the all-seeing Belenus. In fact, at the moment, he leaned on the granite altar. This must have been the place where Kateri Shadowborn had celebrated her morning and evening devotions. The chamber had become so infused with the faith and piety of his mother that even the overwhelming evil of Ebonbane could not darken it.

Alexi found it curious that the chapel lay hidden beneath the kitchen instead of standing open to the sun.

Perhaps it had been a secret chapel, protected from potential vandals among Kateri's hostile neighbors in the Southern Empire. Or perhaps Ebonbane's corrupting influence had twisted the original floor plan of Shadowborn Manor, shunting the sanctuary into the lowest level of the house.

Scanning the room, Alexi saw that Lysander and Ferran had not weathered the fall well. Both lay unmoving on the ground. He hastened to Lysander. Flickering debris had fallen across the monk, smoldering the old man's crimson robes. Alexi swept aside the flaming cinders, then dashed to his brother. No flames had lit upon the younger Shadowborn, but a dark bruise stained Ferran's forehead. Still, the boy clearly showed signs of life. Just as he was about to revive his brother, a strange feeling crept over Alexi.

Someone else was in the temple with them.

He slipped his hand to the hilt of his sword, only to discover that it was not in its scabbard. The weapon had been in his hand when the floor opened beneath them; the fall must have knocked it from his grip. Unarmed, he turned to face the intruder.

And knew he had no need of a weapon.

Not ten feet away from him, still and radiant before the altar of Belenus, stood his mother. Her white robe rippled in an unseen breeze, and her golden hair danced as if she were afloat in a pool of water. She looked shimmery and transparent, as she had when Alexi had seen her in the entry hall. But something was different about her now, something that made his heart hammer in his chest.

Kateri Shadowborn gazed directly at him.

There was no doubt about it. This encounter wasn't like the re-creation in the foyer, where she had been little more than an image of the past. Nor was it akin to their brush in the gallery or the vision he had seen in his dream. Here, where the power of her faith shone strongest, their meeting would be different.

"Mother?" He said the word tentatively, unsure whether he wanted the phantasm to answer or not.

"Yes, Alexi."

The spirit's voice was warm and comforting, everything a child could hope for. Yet it also conveyed a strength and determination unmatched in Alexi's experience. No—not quite unmatched. Dasmaria had spoken with similar confidence and assurance.

"I—I hardly know what to say," he fumbled. He had so much he wanted to ask her, yet now he stood in such awe that he couldn't pull his thoughts together.

"Do not be afraid," she said. "Your heritage is only beginning to dawn upon you. Do not expect to embrace the whole of your past and future in the span of a single fortnight."

"It's all true, then? Everything Lysander has told me?"

The spirit made no answer. Instead, she drifted forward like morning mist across the surface of a reflecting pool. He reached out a hand and allowed the spectral image to pass between his fingers. It felt cold and frail, a draft of winter air trapped beneath the burning structure above. Alexi shivered.

The phantom came to a halt beside the body of Lysander, looking down upon the pilgrim with concern. The expression on her face spoke of more, but Alexi had difficulty finding words for it. If she were facing a man who had been only her enemy, her response would have been easier to comprehend. As a fellow warrior, Alexi could understand respect for a worthy adversary.

But Lysander was no mere enemy.

The man whose body Kateri Shadowborn stood over had been her captor, her rapist, and ultimately her murderer. Even if she had somehow forgiven him for his earlier sins against her, as Lysander had suggested, could she feel anything but hatred for him after he slew her? Though Alexi had been able to absolve the old man of his deeds, years and circumstances had provided Alexi some distance from the events. Kateri was no dispassionate outsider. Yet she looked with sweet compassion at the man who now lay on the floor at her feet.

"Will he recover?" she asked.

"I think so."

A faint smile showed on the spectre's face as she knelt down beside the red-robed man. Her delicate fingers stretched out to touch his cheek, but stopped short. Alexi could see the disappointment in Kateri's face. Her incorporeal fingers could never alight on Lysander's physical form.

"He has suffered much," she said softly, "in his life and beyond."

Alexi shook his head in wonder. "I must confess, your compassion surprises me."

"I feel no animosity toward Lysander Greylocks," she said, still gazing at the old man. "The wrongs he did me were not of his own volition. Though he never had the nerve to ask, I forgave him long ago."

After a moment of silence, Kateri reluctantly stood again and returned her gaze to Alexi. "But we have not much time. You and I must speak."

Alexi glanced at the hole in the ceiling, where the fire still raged in the kitchen. In the amazement of conversing with his mother, he had nearly forgotten about the inferno above.

"We're safe here for the moment," Kateri said. "Ebonbane has never been able to enter this holy place."

"Yet he has trapped you in it?" Alexi struggled to understand why his mother's spirit was here and not enjoying the eternal embrace of Belenus. "Does he hold you here?"

"Ebonbane does not hold me, Alexi. Rather, I hold him. At the moment I was slain, my faith in Belenus was so strong that it enabled my spirit to dominate that of the fiend." She looked deeply into Alexi's eyes, her expression weary. "Since that day, I have bent my every energy toward containing Ebonbane. He has remained a prisoner in this place, held here against his will. But he has not taken his captivity easily. He rages against me, seeking to batter my will and escape.

"For many years, I have prayed for a champion to come to relieve me of this burden so that my spirit may rest. I hoped someone would find a way to destroy the fiend who now dominates Shadowborn Manor. Over the years, Belenus has seen fit to direct half a dozen champions here, each a Knight of the Circle. To a one, they fell before Ebonbane."

Alexi almost gasped at this thought. A dozen paladins, the greatest holy warriors of Avonleigh, had preceded him here. If they had all been slain, how could he hope to triumph? And yet his mother had called him here . . . hadn't she?

"Did you summon me as you did the others?" he asked. "Did you send me the dream that beckoned me to this place?"

"I sent for no one," corrected the spirit. "I prayed, and Belenus saw fit to reward me. But even if I had summoned those champions, I would not have called for you—not yet."

"Why not? Because of the Darkening?" A pang of despair stabbed him. Did even his own mother find him unworthy?

"Yes, Alexi, but not in the sense that you believe. It is true that Belenus closed his eye because of what he saw in your heart. But he barred you from the Circle to call you to an even higher service."

Alexi drew his brows together. "What do you mean?"

"My son, once in a very great while, a unique type of paladin is born, a holy knight who does not merely fight creatures of darkness but actually absorbs their evil to keep it from spilling out into the rest of the world."

Alexi inhaled sharply. The ghoulish visions, the icy hatred he struggled to contain within him—he had known that evil resided within him. Did this explain how and why? Even as she spoke, he sensed the darkness in his heart responding to her words, recognizing and acknowledging their truth.

"You believe," he said slowly, "that I am such a warrior?"

She gestured toward his heart. "Do you not know it to be true? My son, though you are not a member of the Circle, you are indeed a paladin, one of the most rare and noble order—what some call a 'lodestone' paladin."

Alexi nearly trembled with the joy that touched his heart. All that had happened had transpired as Belenus wished. He saw now that his god had not forsaken him. Even in the darkest of times, when Dasmaria had died or when he had been forced to wound Lysander with Corona's radiance, he had been serving the Radiant One. A sense of peace that he had not known in weeks washed over him.

He noted, however, that Kateri seemed to struggle as she spoke. He could read in his mother's eyes the anguish Ebonbane caused her even as they talked. Each minute the fiend was attempting to destroy her. She must have spent every hour of the many years since her death in absolute torment.

"I always believed that you would succeed against Ebonbane where the others had failed," his mother continued. "But I hoped, before you had to face such a great and terrible evil, you would have more time and experience to understand your calling and the heavy tax it will place on your spirit."

Alexi frowned, trying to comprehend her words. "If you didn't send for me, then how did I come to journey here?"

"Your reputation preceded you." The corners of her mouth turned up in a wry but pained smile. "When word went out of your imminent Ascension into the Circle, Ebonbane became aware of your existence. He knew at once who you were and understood your importance to me. It was he who called you here through the vision of my death."

Alexi shuddered. How many of his other nocturnal visions had been planted by Ebonbane? The evil he had absorbed from the ghouls gave the fiend a handhold on his very spirit. "If he knew that you believed I would one day destroy him, why did he summon me?"

"Ebonbane called you here to destroy you." She shook her head sadly. "I am weakening, Alexi. With each hero who came and fell, my strength diminished. You have always been my last hope. If you fall, Ebonbane knows that he will triumph."

At that instant, a sudden groaning sounded from above. What remained of the ceiling bulged and strained. Wooden planks split as jets of fire forced their way between them. In rapid succession, a score of timbers pulled loose from their joints.

Alexi quickly glanced at his mother. Kateri's image was fading fast. He reached toward her in a futile gesture. With a final, pleading look, she flickered, then was gone.

Fire and broken timbers showered down. Alexi threw his body across Ferran's unmoving form to shield his brother. He wished he could do the same for Lysander, but he was only one man. He prayed that the old pilgrim would survive.

Savage blows and searing flames fell upon Alexi's back. He clenched his muscles, trying to block out the agony. The disintegrating timbers cracked. Suddenly the heavy iron stove above broke through the buckling floor. It smashed upon the granite altar, metal striking stone with a sound like a great ringing bell.

The altar shattered. Stone fragments flew into the air, battering Alexi as if they had been hurled by a dozen slings. One glanced off his forehead, leaving him wincing and momentarily dazed.

In that instant, a spiritual shock wave swept through the chapel. The aura of peace and comfort that had set this place apart from the rest of Ebonbane's sinister domain vanished in the space of a heartbeat. In its place, a hot wind of absolute evil swept through the defiled chapel. The sanctuary was penetrated. Kateri Shadowborn's last refuge was no more.

Beneath the almost crushing weight of evil, Alexi gasped for breath, then wished he had not. Soot and dust scratched bitterly in his throat as burning smoke seared his lungs. He coughed and retched, half from the tainted air and half from the sickening malevolence that filled it.

The rain of fire had halted—at least for the time being.

The majority of the manor still stood above them, although it was being greedily devoured by the macabre flames. How much longer the place would stand Alexi could not say, but time was running out.

He pushed himself away from Ferran, who was beginning to stir, and stumbled toward Lysander. The evil in the air had become a physical burden that threatened to drag him down before he could even reach the pilgrim's still form.

Several timbers had fallen across the old man. Taking careful hold of the uppermost beam, Alexi flung it aside. The blackened wood seared his flesh, but his body was already so covered with burns and bruises that one more seemed inconsequential.

In less than a minute, he had cleared the heaviest debris from Lysander's body. He knelt down beside the frail figure, unable to tell whether animation lingered in the withered remains of the old man. Lysander still seemed to have a presence about him, a sense of life or its equivalent.

Alexi ran his hands down the old man's limbs, checking them for broken bones. As he had hoped, he detected no major wounds. He let out a sigh of relief as he considered how best to bring Lysander back to his senses. In that instant, the withered face twitched, and the narrow eyes opened.

And Alexi cried out in alarm.

Lysander's eyes burned with blistering red. The same flash of evil that Alexi had seen in the face of the ghouls and their terrible masters now gleamed in the countenance of his companion—his father.

Before Alexi could react, the abruptly animated ghoul lunged at him. Slender fingers, tipped with suddenly dangerous-looking nails, tore into his cheek. The edges of the parallel wounds stung as if someone had thrown salt into them.

The force of the blow threw the knight back. He crashed to the fragment-strewn floor, scattering burning debris everywhere. As the ghoulish pilgrim charged toward him, Alexi struggled to his feet. A dreadful heaviness seemed to fall upon him.

With horror, he realized that Lysander's fingertips carried the paralytic toxin of the ghouls. At least, though the blow had been powerful, the cuts were not deep. He might yet have a chance to defend himself.

He grabbed sluggishly for his sword. As his fingers touched the scabbard, he remembered with a sickening dread that Corona wasn't there. His eyes darted, looking for the blade, but saw no sign of it. With the ghoul bearing down upon him, Alexi realized that his only hope of salvation lay buried somewhere beneath a blanket of glowing, smoking, burning debris.

He turned to Lysander. "Father, don't do this!" he cried, hoping to touch some part of the man he knew was trapped in the shell of a ghoul's body.

In a voice of pure evil, Lysander's twisted countenance expelled a gust of putrid laughter. The beastly sound, at once terrifying and familiar, nearly stopped Alexi's heart. It was the same laughter the trio had heard in the gallery not an hour ago.

It was the laughter of Ebonbane.

With a strength that defied his emaciated frame, Lysander hefted a great slab of broken granite into the air. It must have weighed some twenty stone, easily twice the weight of the man lifting it. As the booming laughter continued, Alexi glimpsed movement behind the ghoul.

Ferran had risen to his feet. Somehow he had also

managed to recover his bow. Ferran's eyes met those of his brother, but they held no recognition. The boy must still be throwing off the effects of the fall and barrage of falling timbers. If he could come to his senses in time . . .

But there seemed little chance of that.

The possessed Lysander hurled the stone slab at Alexi. The knight rolled swiftly to the side, and the great block of granite shattered where he had just stood.

"Lysander! You can fight this!" Though he shouted words of encouragement, Alexi feared there was little hope of the pilgrim's throwing off the yoke of his old master. His will had been worn down by far too many years filled with far too much suffering.

The possessed pilgrim stepped slowly forward, his eyes burning and his rapidly elongating claws rending the air. A sinister smile curled on his withered face, revealing jagged teeth.

"You have come a long way to die," boomed a cold, sinister voice.

Alexi trembled with both rage and dread. He had never spoken to anything so absolutely evil, and hearing the words come from his trusted comrade chilled him to the marrow. The icy, sinister presence in his heart hammered at his chest, threatening to break free. Alexi forced it into submission but doubted he could contain it very long while facing Ebonbane's recaptured minion.

Then a source of hope caught his vision. Ferran had slipped an arrow into his bow. It was a dark shaft, not one of his normal missiles, but one of the three mahogany arrows Lady Shadowborn had given him. It glowed warmly in the light of the raging fire above.

Ferran blinked twice, as if trying to clear the morning haze from his eyes, then raised the bow and drew it back. The weapon betrayed the faintest hint of a tremor, evidence, no doubt, that the squire was suffering from the effects of the long journey and its many cataclysms.

Then Alexi gasped.

Ferran, eyes shining with that hated red gleam, aimed the arrow not at the approaching ghoul, but straight at his brother.

TWENTY-EIGHT

The knight's terror fills me with delight.

The color drains from his face as he tries to whip the corpse that was Lysander Greylocks into dominance. What a fool he is. The traitor monk is a relic of my past. Like the Ghoul Lord and the Vapir, he is mine to command. His meager spirit seeks to drive me out, but it is powerless against my superior will.

The gleam of hope fades from the knight's eyes.

It was his mistake to assume that his mouse of a brother might take me unawares. Although I am still somewhat restrained in the shattered chapel, this domain is mine to command. I see everything here—the smoke that fills the ruined chamber hides nothing from me. The younger Shadowborn has never been a threat.

And yet something unusual abides here.

In the time that it takes for the knight's heart to beat three times, I explore the whole of the chapel in detail. Since the day I was first imprisoned in this house, I have longed to see this sanctuary of light destroyed. With her chapel corrupted, the spirit of Kateri Shadowborn at last begins to fail. The death of her son will be, to her, the end of all things. Her will shall buckle, and the woman who has opposed me for so long shall be mine to consume.

Yet there is something about that arrow....

The weapon that whelp holds is unusual. I look more closely at it, uncertain what to make of it. Then I discover the source of my discomfort. The shaft is no mere physical object. It is not the cold matter of the universe. There is a warmth to it, a light. It is a holy thing, filled with the magic of another power. And I sense something more. It is a weapon of light, and I am a creature of darkness.

But I easily evade the danger.

The boy, having been beaten and broken by the Vapir, is easily dominated by me. It is a simple trick to touch his mind and turn him against the knight. I merely repeat, time and again, one thought: *You stand always in your brother's shadow.*

The litany resonates within the boy's heart. He tries to drive out my influence, but it is impossible. I am his master now, just as I am Lysander's. I can sense the times in his past when the young boy looked with envy upon his sibling. On the surface, these moments are nothing, merely the common feelings any such creature has for one placed above himself. But the slightest pressure of my will augments them. A normal sibling rivalry becomes a burning envy. He sees that he has lived the whole of his life eclipsed by another. He is reminded that Alexi Shadowborn is not actually his brother. His so-called sibling is an outsider. An enemy. A thief.

The whelp draws back his arrow, the missile aimed directly at his brother.

The knight's face betrays his confusion. He tries to understand what is happening. He had expected his beloved brother to use the weapon against my puppet, but now he sees the truth. If he has any faith left in his wretched god, this will certainly shatter it.

The knight stands alone.

One by one he has seen his allies fail him. The woman who rode with him, the spirit of his mother, the shell of his mentor, and now his own brother—all fallen, sacrificed to save him or turned against him.

And yet he does not falter.

His eyes cast about the room, looking for some weapon to use against my minion. Any number of tools could serve him in this moment of crisis, but he rejects them. One and all, they would bring grave harm to his companions, possibly even kill them. His belief that Lysander Greylocks can yet be rescued from my power will not allow him to strike down the ghoul. Once again the weakness of good and light proves its own undoing.

His courage is remarkable, however.

His spirit is stronger than that of his companions. He was able to drive out the influence of the Vapir. Among these pitiful creatures of flesh and blood, his is a fire that burns unequaled. No—not entirely unequaled. His mother, Kateri Shadowborn, once had such radiance. But her light is gone now. And soon his shall falter as well.

The time has come to put an end to these games.

I summon the energies of darkness into the body of the monk. He raises his hands above his head to gather the negative essence of unlife. A sphere of midnight black radiance coalesces between his outstretched hands. The knight sees what is happening, and fear darkens his countenance. His eyes widen in terror. The moment of his death is at hand. Even now, the last essences of his mother fade from this ruin. I shall soon be free to leave this place, unfettered by her accursed faith in a power of light and hope. His failure will complete my triumph. His death will mark the end of all that he knows.

But I sense another presence.

It is a bright and radiant creature whose power startles me. Is it another such as myself? No, nothing that grand. It is merely the woman, Kateri Shadowborn. Her spirit, on the verge of annihilation, has somehow regrouped its energies. An impressive effort, but one she cannot long sustain. Without the sanctuary of her temple, her power evaporates with each passing second. She must know that she cannot harm me.

I know what she plans.

She will attempt to break my hold on the monk to save the life of the knight. It is a desperate plan, one with no chance of success. She will channel all her energy, all that remains of her essence, into breaking my control over the monk. She will not prevail. Still, the wisdom of my experience has taught me not to underestimate her.

I release the child.

As I free the boy's pitiful will, my hold over the ghoul becomes absolute. No power in this realm can break my grip, not even the will of the woman who has been my captor for so long. I cannot help but laugh again at her paltry effort.

But I am glad she is here to witness the death of her son.

TWENTY-NINE

The heat of the inferno sweeping through the manor house seared Alexi's eyes as he glanced back and forth between Ferran and Lysander. Yet the physical pain was nothing compared to the despair that threatened to overwhelm him. His two trusted comrades stood poised to kill him, and he faced them utterly defenseless.

Lysander towered above him with his arms held high. Between the outstretched fingers of his emaciated hands glowed a perfect sphere of absolute darkness. The ruddy light from above silhouetted both man and magic. The sphere was cold and infinitely evil, clearly the manifestation of death itself. Lysander threw back his head, filling the ruined chapel with maniacal laughter.

Through the haze of black smoke, Ferran held his bow steady, its deadly missile aimed directly at his brother. Anger showed in his features, an anger obviously directed at Alexi.

Clearly Ebonbane held absolute sway here. The fiend had turned brother against brother, father against son.

Even as this thought came into Alexi's mind, a change came over the chapel. For the faintest fraction of a second, the heat of the fire vanished, leaving a cool, comforting presence in its wake.

Alexi sensed at once the spirit of Kateri Shadowborn. But just as quickly as it had manifested itself, the lingering traces of his mother vanished. The heat fell upon him again in all its deadly intensity.

He saw, however, that he was not the only one who had felt this spiritual touch. Ferran's face, a second ago masked in cruel hatred, now appeared at peace. The squire blinked, looking at Alexi as if he did not fully recognize him.

Then, in a single smooth motion, Ferran swung the bow away from Alexi and fired. The mahogany shaft flashed for a second in the firelight, leaving a ripple in the smoke-filled air behind it, and buried itself in Lysander's skull.

The roaring laughter instantly changed to a howl of rage and pain that threatened to tear the room apart. Lysander's dominated form whirled away from Alexi. Its withering gaze fell upon Ferran. With an inhuman cry, it released the orb of blackness. The deadly sphere landed on the boy, crackling with the supernatural energy of nonexistence.

At the same second, a cool breeze blew across the chapel. A flash of metal caught Alexi's eye, revealing Corona's blade protruding from beneath a pile of soot at the far side of the room. The knight lunged for it. Somehow Kateri Shadowborn had bought him a few seconds' respite and returned his weapon to him. He might not survive the next few minutes, but he would not allow her effort to be wasted.

Behind him, Alexi heard his brother howl out in pain. He couldn't help but turn to look at Ferran. The instant he did so, he wished he hadn't.

The boy had crumpled to the ground, his body seething in an aura of cold darkness. For a second, Alexi saw his brother's skeleton clearly visible through his skin. As his face struck the floor, the aura vanished with a sudden snap.

Ferran lay still.

Too still.

"Alexi . . ." came an almost unheard voice.

The warrior turned his head and saw that Lysander had fallen to one knee. The wound he had suffered from the enchanted arrow would have killed a living man, but Lysander had survived it—at least for the moment.

"Father," said Alexi, feeling some measure of meaning in the word for the first time. "You're free of Ebonbane—"

"Only for a short time, I fear," came the barely audible response. "His concentration has been momentarily broken. The instant he wishes me to obey him again, I shall be forced to do so. He has merely been distracted for a moment."

"There must be some way to prevent him from regaining control." Although Alexi said the words confidently, he feared they were nothing more than idle hopes.

"Listen to me," said the old man urgently, staggering to his feet. "There are times when the only way to triumph is to yield."

Alexi frowned. "I don't understand."

"I yield to you, my son," said Lysander. "Already I can feel Ebonbane's presence bearing down upon me again. You must take up your sword and strike first."

"No!" Shocked, Alexi shook his head, his eyes wide with horror at Lysander's suggestion. "You're my father. I can't—"

"You must." Lysander clutched Alexi's arm, his face a mixture of despair and pleading. "I submit to you, Alexi Shadowborn, not to the fiend who has dominated me for all those years."

"Lysander, I—"

A faint red glow began to rim the pilgrim's eyes. "Now, Alexi! I can feel Ebonbane taking control. You have no more time. Strike me down that I may triumph over my true enemy!"

Alexi hesitated. But the red glow grew stronger, and the light of recognition in his father's eyes became dimmer. With grim purpose, he drew Corona from the flames in which it rested. The hot steel burned his flesh, as if he had just drawn it from the heart of a furnace. But the pain was nothing to him.

He turned back to face the man who had given him life, preparing to repay that debt with death. He knew the truth of Lysander's words, knew that there was no other option. His eyes met the sunken orbs of his father and saw in them a last flash of approval and pride. Then Lysander lowered his head.

Lifting the silvered edge of Corona high, the paladin commended his father's spirit into the eternal light of Belenus.

The blade fell with a flash, instantly and neatly severing Lysander's head. The body crashed to the floor, throwing out a cloud of ash and smoldering coals. The head landed a yard away, halting with its open eyes looking up at Alexi. The paladin could have sworn that he heard Lysander's voice in the very air around him: *Thank you, my son.*

Mechanically, the act having drained every ounce of feeling from him, Alexi wiped the ghoulish ichor from his blade. Though emptiness echoed within him, somehow his eyes still shed tears. The drops, however, instantly evaporated in the heat of the fire.

Alexi knelt down beside his brother, fearing the worst but grateful to see the gradual, if uneven, rising and falling of Ferran's chest. He bowed his head in a silent prayer of thanks.

A scant second later, the manor house above groaned loudly, and the snapping of timbers rose to a dreadful staccato. One after another, the supporting timbers of the house gave way under the weight they bore. With each failure, a new shower of flaming debris dropped like falling stars upon Alexi.

He quickly scooped his brother into his arms. Shifting the uneven burden over his shoulder, he eyed the looming blaze. Little time remained for escape.

He darted toward the rounded bulk of the iron stove. One great step brought him to the top of the metal shell. It shifted under his weight, but Alexi kept his balance. He grabbed at the edge of the hole in the ceiling and drew himself and Ferran up with one arm.

He levered Ferran's body onto what little remained of the kitchen floor, vaguely wondering whether the dancing knives would be waiting to flay them alive. However, the beam that ran across the center of the kitchen commanded his immediate attention. The dangerously bowed support bore much of the weight of the floors above. It couldn't remain intact for much longer. The flames had devoured it almost to the point of collapse.

As he hauled himself up, Alexi noted with some relief that the knives had lost their enchantment. They stuck embedded in the walls or lay scattered about what remained of the floor.

He lifted Ferran into his arms again just as the timber

above buckled. The entire weight of the manor shifted overhead, rumbling like the crashing of surf.

Alexi negotiated two delicate steps around the edges of the kitchen, where a thin lip of flooring still stood, and reached a window. Sparing no time to look out through the glass, he threw himself backward through it, trying as best he could to shield Ferran's helpless form from the jagged shards.

With a roar like that of a dying dragon, the great house folded in upon itself. Alexi and Ferran hit the ground, the knight only vaguely aware of the frigid rain pounding down upon him. He rose to his feet, slipping in the mud, then dragged himself and his brother away from the inferno.

When he had put a dozen yards between himself and the blazing Shadowborn Manor, Alexi collapsed to the ground, his unconscious squire beside him. He turned to look back upon the house and saw only a wall of dancing flames licking into the stormy darkness of the night sky. The flames must be spurred on by the power of Ebonbane, he thought. Any lesser blaze would at least acknowledge the cascades of rain falling from the dark sky.

The rain poured down on him in rolling sheets, biting the countless burns and lacerations that covered his skin. For the first time, he became aware that his clothes had been reduced to little more than rags draped over his body, held in place here and there by a buckle or button. His breastplate, uncomfortably hot even after being quenched by the frigid rain, bit painfully into sensitive skin. His whole body ached, and his heart wept with the memory of his fallen comrades.

A great pyre rose around the blackened skeleton of the once sturdy manor. Curls of smoke wafted upward from the blaze, forming a dark gray sheet upon which amber and crimson light played. In every ripple and curl of the cloud, Alexi imagined his enemies hiding, imagined death waiting for him.

Something moved within the fire.

Alexi climbed to his feet and raised his sword. Instinctively he moved to stand in front of Ferran, vowing to protect his younger brother to the last.

A shape slowly emerged from the flames. It was more or less human, moving with an easy, graceful stride. As it reached the edge of the inferno, Alexi saw that the silhouetted figure was armed. A long-bladed sword swayed slightly back and forth with each step forward. The weapon resembled a snake swaying from side to side just before it struck.

The creature had a decidedly feminine bearing, one of delicate curves and lithe movement. Strange, Alexi thought. He had always assumed Ebonbane was male.

When the black shape stepped out of the flames, Alexi gasped. The slender figure was not a thing of flesh and blood, but a living construct of darkness itself. It had eyes of licking flame, burning against its ebon form like glowing coals.

Yet, dreadful as this spirit of midnight was, its weapon horrified Alexi more. He recognized the menacing black blade the figure carried: He had twice seen it used to kill Kateri Shadowborn.

Alexi moved protectively closer to his brother's prone body. If in Kateri's hands Corona had not triumphed over the sinister sword, did he and Ferran stand a chance?

As the dark figure continued to stride toward him, its features grew more defined, as if it were still coalescing out of the infinite night. He inhaled sharply. The creature had taken on shockingly, achingly familiar features.

Dasmaria moved toward him.

Despite the onyx cast of her features and the smoldering glow of her eyes, the likeness was unmistakable. Alexi had no doubt that this woman, this animated patch of darkness, was, in form at least, Dasmaria Eveningstar.

His jaw tightened. This was blasphemous! Dasmaria had died in battle as a warrior should. To see the noble paladin's image adorning this creature of unquestionable evil caused a surge of anger to well up within him. Shouting in rage, he sprang forward, righteous fury granting him strength.

"Alexi?" said the figure. The instant he heard his name on Dasmaria's lips, his resolution wavered. The dark thing spoke in the same clear, strong voice he knew so well. Could he be wrong? Could the phantom indeed somehow be the spirit of his fallen comrade?

No. It was impossible.

But dare he strike without knowing for certain?

The woman made no move to defend herself with the dark sword. Instead of attacking, Alexi assumed a defensive position, ready to strike the instant his suspicions proved correct.

"I saw you die nearly a day's ride from this place." His voice carried the hard edge of disbelief. "How can you be here now?"

"I was sleeping in a place of light and warmth," the dark figure said softly. "I don't know where I was. And then someone spoke my name. It was a voice I didn't know. It called for me to come to this place, to leave the lights behind and step into a place of darkness. I didn't want to obey it, but I found I could not resist."

"Throw down the sword," said Alexi.

The shade looked down at her hand, apparently startled to see the sinister weapon it held. The real Dasmaria would have reacted much the same way upon discovering that her own golden blade had been replaced by this macabre weapon.

She shook her head helplessly. "I—I can't."

Alexi bit his lip. He knew this must be a trick, yet he felt the warmth of Dasmaria's spirit in every word she spoke. Had he not seen the ghost of his mother just a short time ago? If that spirit could appear before him, why not this one?

He raked his gaze over the dark shape before him. Even cast in darkness, Dasmaria's figure stood proud and splendid. Her finely chiseled features reflected the elegance that had been hers in life.

Alexi's heart pounded. He wanted to reach his arms out to her, to embrace her and tell her all the things he had not found the courage to say in life. He wanted to say he was sorry for the way they had parted. He wanted to say that he loved her.

But this figure could not really be Dasmaria. Whatever the dark creature was, Alexi knew Ebonbane was behind it. And Alexi also knew—or prayed he knew—that Ebonbane could not so easily command the spirit of a paladin. When she died, the all-seeing Eye of Belenus would watch over her. The sun god's power would protect her. Alexi could not believe that any force of evil might overcome the holy strength of Belenus.

Indeed, the evil Ebonbane had been commanded to enter this world by three mere mortals. As he stared at the shadowy visage, Alexi remembered Lysander's description of those events. A triad of agents who served Ebonbane during the Heretical Wars had called the evil spirit back into the world after Kateri had driven him out.

These same agents had become powerful minions of the fiend, continuing to serve Ebonbane after their deaths. The Ghoul Lord had been one member of the triad; he believed the Vapir had been another. But where was the third? At a throaty laugh from the shadowy figure, Alexi knew.

The third stood before him now in the shape of his beloved Dasmaria.

Somehow aware that its disguise had failed it, the creature hissed like a serpent. Alexi jumped back as the black blade suddenly became crowned with a rolling sheath of fire. A violent boom of thunder split the darkness as the rain slackened slightly.

The iciness in Alexi's heart swelled and ached. The darkness and evil he'd fought down earlier screamed for release. He clenched his jaw, struggling to keep the hate and rage within from spilling out. He had to contain it. He had to maintain control. If he didn't, Ebonbane would surely triumph.

The false Dasmaria lunged toward Alexi in an attempt to skewer him with the blazing weapon. A quick vault carried him out of harm's way. The shadow's follow-through left her exposed to a quick strike, but Alexi couldn't bring himself to attack. Lingering doubts still held him back. What if he were wrong? What if this was indeed the spirit of Dasmaria, forced into submission by the demon Ebonbane?

In that instant's hesitation, the dark woman recovered and moved toward him again.

The flaming sword swept toward Alexi's neck, but he brought Corona into play just in time to block the attack. Metal rang on metal as the holy weapon deflected the blazing sword. Alexi staggered back under the impact. His feet slipped in the mud, almost bringing him down.

The cold fury within him seeped throughout his chest now, trying to winnow its way into his very spirit. He fought it back, trying to force it into its imaginary cell even as he prepared for the next pass from the ghostly warrior.

Another sweeping stroke of fire and steel split open Alexi's breastplate. Though the blow left him uninjured, it caused him to slip in the mud again. He flailed his arms, trying to regain his balance, but the effort proved futile. Before he knew what was happening, he found himself flat on his back.

Dasmaria stood over him, raising the flaming weapon high for a final deadly stroke. Alexi experienced a sense of familiarity, then realized that he had seen a similar image in the death of Kateri Shadowborn. The fiery black sword, standing out brightly against the darkness like a pillar of fire, was the last thing that his mother had seen before she died. And he was about to meet the same fate.

As he stared at the diabolical weapon, the blackness within him leapt as if in answer to a summons. And in that moment, he knew another truth.

The dark creature that he had come here to face, the wicked Ebonbane, was not a thing of flesh and blood like the minions who served him. Neither was it a spirit, drifting from place to place like the tragic ghosts of the Phantasmal Forest.

It was the sword.

He could see the image of a malevolent face in the flames surrounding the blade. A painful wave of horror shot through his body, tightening his heart and paralyzing his thoughts. He knew beyond a doubt that he was in the presence of Ebonbane.

He rolled aside as the blade fell. Its flames hissed out

in a cloud of steam as the weapon tasted not the knight's flesh, but the soupy mud where he had lain only a second before.

By the time his enemy had pulled the evil blade free of the earth, Alexi had regained his footing. He brought up Corona, aiming the point not at his attacker, but at the weapon she held. If he could destroy that thing, surely Dasmaria's spirit would be released.

"Karnas, radamar!"

At once the glow from Dasmaria's sword faded in the brilliant light of the noonday sun. In contrast to the holy light of Belenus, the ruddy fire of the inferno seemed a mere flicker.

Alexi had expected the glow to lance through Dasmaria as it had Lysander. He was both relieved and alarmed to see it did not—relieved because it might have spared the woman he loved suffering and pain, but alarmed to find that this shape of darkness proved more powerful than he had expected.

His grip tightened on Corona's hilt. He had no choice but to fight the phantom, even if it was Dasmaria's enslaved spirit. "Dasmaria," he said in a trembling voice, "I love you."

Even if the warrior was not the paladin's spirit after all, he knew that his words would somehow reach Dasmaria. If Belenus never answered another of Alexi's prayers, the sun lord would make sure of that.

But the words had an unexpected effect on Alexi himself. They eased the grip of darkness on his heart, subduing the evil enough to allow Alexi full concentration as he faced his opponent.

The dark figure turned toward him, holding the deadly sword at the ready once more. A cruel smile spread across her face, and Alexi knew at once that he had been correct: This dark phantom was not Dasmaria.

"Dasmaria, I love you!" the malevolent thing cackled in mockery.

Alexi sprang forward, calling out the holy name of his god in the language of the faith. Using every ounce of his strength, he brought his magical weapon around in a brilliant arc. He could see the dark creature about to counter, raising her black blade to block the onrushing steel.

He prayed Corona would not fail him.

The two weapons met with a thunderclap that drowned out the sound of the storm. A great burst of pure white light, tinged with a rolling halo of rippling red fire, spread out from the point of impact. The shock of the blast knocked Alexi off his feet and tossed him through the air. He landed with a splash in the slick mud, sliding several yards before smashing against the base of a gnarled tree.

It took a few seconds for Alexi to come to his senses. When he did, a sickening horror raced through him.

At first he thought he had lost his hand, for he felt no sensation other than a burning tingle below the elbow of his sword arm. The smell of burnt flesh and hair, a product of the expanding ring of light and fire, did nothing to ease his fears. Shaking his head to clear it, he pulled himself to a sitting position and looked down with trepidation.

The sight of his hand—whole—at the end of his arm offered him no relief. For while his numb fingers held fast to the hawk-shaped hilt of Corona, only six inches of the blade remained. The silver weapon, so steeped in the magic of the east and the faith of the west, was gone, destroyed in the striking of one last great blow against the darkest of all evils.

As soon as the sight of the shattered weapon registered in his mind, Alexi glanced frantically about. The shadowy, stormy landscape offered no sign of the spectral Dasmaria. Apparently the blast had torn her apart as it had Corona.

But what of Ebonbane?

Had the fiery light of Corona swept the fiendish thing out of existence? Alexi had never put more into a blow than he had in his final strike with his mother's weapon.

He was about to sigh in relief when a dancing trident of lightning cast a wild blue light across the scene. The blazing ruin that had been Shadowborn Manor, the rain that pelted him like gravel, and the body of his wounded squire—all were frozen in his mind's eye as if instantly rendered by an artist's brush.

A deep roar seemed to tear the sky apart. Forcing himself to his feet, Alexi caught sight of a faint glow. At first he thought it was nothing more than the glint of light from the dying manor house on the slick surface of a muddy pool. Looking closer, however, he saw a sliver of black steel, glowing a deep, hot red, lying on the ground. Sweeping his vision across the immediate terrain, Alexi saw that the muddy surface was littered with dozens of these fragments—clearly the final remnants of the dire Ebonbane.

It was over.

He breathed a low expression of relief. In the distance, at the edge of the tangled and twisted lawn, he could see that the brick wall surrounding the manor had crumbled as well. Like the iron shell of the sword, that, too, had apparently been a prison for Ebonbane. The fact that it now lay in ruins seemed to signal that all was right again.

Or was it?

Alexi tilted his head to the side, sensing a slight movement near the bits of darkly radiant metal. He tried to focus, certain it was merely a trick of the light. The inconsistent gleam of the burning house made it difficult to see even the glowing fragments.

Another flash of lightning showed him the truth.

Slender coils of darkness rose from each of the metal shards. They looked like smoke, but they seemed unaffected by the drenching rain. Their color was unnatural. These traces were more—or perhaps less—than they at first appeared. They were darkness, pure and simple, just like the black emptiness that had made up the body of Dasmaria's shade.

And they were rolling together, forming a brooding shape that loomed above Alexi.

The shape of evil itself.

THIRTY

Alexi looked around frantically for a weapon. He had a dagger on his belt, but he wore that more as a tool than anything else. Against an enemy like Ebonbane, it could do nothing. But what choice did he have? He drew it and gripped the leather hilt in his left hand. As an off-hand weapon, used in conjunction with some other armament, it could at least be used to parry.

Seeing nothing else that looked promising, Alexi grabbed up a long splinter of burning wood, a fragment of the dying manor house, and weighed it in his hand. It was heavy and would make a good bludgeon. Perhaps the blazing fire at its end would prove of some value against an enemy made of darkness.

The coils of blackness finally finished winding themselves together.

Alexi found himself breathless in awe as he took in the enemy before him. At least fifteen feet tall, the thing was humanoid, but very powerfully built. The creature reminded Alexi of the savage giants who lived in the crags of the Nordlands. Batlike wings stretched out from the fiend's back, flapping against the hot light of the fire in much the same way that a hunting cat swishes its tail. Long talons curled out from the fingers, looking more like hooks than claws. Alexi shuddered as he considered what those terrible members might do to living flesh.

All of this was forgotten when he looked upon the creature's face. It was round and fat, but marred with malevolence. Twin horns curled up from the temples, like those of a ram but with long, tapering points at their end. The demon's eyes seemed like windows of darkness within the blackness of its face.

The entire creature was sheathed in flame, just as the black sword had been moments ago. So much for the hope that his burning club might have some effect upon the fiend.

Alexi knew that he stood now before Ebonbane, a creature that had no place in the world of mankind. And against this beast, he held only a small silver-bladed dagger and a wooden cudgel.

"You have served me well." The fiend's voice reverberated in the night, causing the ground to tremble and drowning out the violence of the storm. If Alexi thought the laughter he had heard before seemed smothering, the voice of the shadowy fiend itself proved an order of magnitude much worse.

"I serve only Belenus!"

"Indeed." Ebonbane chuckled. "Perhaps you do not realize all that you have done for me. You and your companions have destroyed Kateri Shadowborn's accursed temple, weakening her to the point where I may now annihilate the last vestiges of her spirit. For that alone, I should thank you."

Silent, Alexi burned with hatred and doubt. Was it true? Had his actions led to the final destruction of Kateri Shadowborn's spirit, denying her the peace of the

Eternal Dawn? And had he also condemned Dasmaria to the same oblivion? He prayed it was not so, yet he feared it was.

The darkness within him simmered, nearly bubbling to the surface. He struggled to contain it, as his mother must have fought to contain Ebonbane all these years. Her memory granted him renewed spiritual strength—just enough to keep the rage from overpowering him.

"But that was not all you did for me, Alexi Shadowborn. No, indeed. It was your hand that shattered the cursed shell in which I had been imprisoned. Because of you, knight, I am free to leave this place and travel the world of man. The human race must be made to pay for my inconvenience, for the time I was forced to spend in this prison."

So saying, Ebonbane twisted his mouth into a wicked smile. He looked down upon Alexi, his features lit by flickers of flame. The fiend seemed to ponder the nature of the insignificant shape that stood defiantly before him.

"I wonder, Alexi Shadowborn, if your pitiful intellect can imagine the scale of my wrath. Your great Heretical War was to me nothing more than a moment's entertainment, engineered for my own amusement. To you, it was a holocaust—to me, a passing distraction. Now I have an interest in your race that I did not hold then. When I have satisfied my thirst for vengeance, I promise you will see the whole of your world reduced to ashes."

Alexi tamped down the hate that threatened to boil over and consume him. "My mother and father brought you down before. There are others like them. Our world is rich in heroes. You will fail, Ebonbane!"

"Yes, of course I will," mocked the dark fiend. "As my fire consumes each nation of your world, you can repeat those words once more. Perhaps they will bring you some small measure of comfort."

The towering dark shape that was Ebonbane began to move. Alexi jumped back, bringing his feeble weapons up to defend himself. But the monster didn't attack. Instead, the giant went down on one knee and bent forward to look directly into Alexi's eyes, an action at once condescending and terrifying. The scale of the obscene creature was utterly impossible to comprehend.

"You appear to be laboring under a misconception." Ebonbane spoke in a conspiratorial whisper that echoed in the eternal night. "You say that your mother and father were the ones who brought my diversions temporarily to an end. I think, perhaps, you do not understand all that transpired in those times."

The evil presence within Alexi leapt toward the demon like a child to its parent. In that instant, even before Ebonbane spoke again, Alexi realized the horrifying truth. He stood still, frozen with fear, fighting the urge to retch. The Darkening, his summons to this place, the dark nocturnal visions—suddenly all made terrible sense.

"Lysander Greylocks was nothing more than a puppet at the time of your conception." A sinister gleam lit the creature's midnight eyes. "He is not your father. The seed was mine."

Hearing the words somehow made the truth worse than merely knowing it in his heart. The darkness within Alexi rallied at the fiend's words, rising up to clutch at his heart. Despair swept through his spirit as the full scope of the nightmare became clear to him.

Hate and rage surged and spilled out. Alexi shouted in fury and lunged forward. Throwing the blazing cudgel aside, he gripped the gleaming dagger tightly in both hands. With vengeance burning in his eyes, he leapt forward with the name of Belenus on his lips.

The silver blade struck Ebonbane but failed to penetrate. Instead, the dirk bent and snapped under the force of the blow. The fiend lashed out with an arm, swatting Alexi away as it might an annoying insect.

The knight flew through the air, crashing down on the roof of a long-unused shed. The force of the impact shattered the decrepit building. With a crash of rotten timber and splintering panels, the entire structure folded around Alexi.

Pain wracked the warrior. It took all his strength to lift his head and take stock of his wounds. When he finally did so, however, his spirits sank still lower.

His right arm was bent and bloody, probably broken. A jagged splinter of wood had pierced the soft flesh of his forearm. Even if he survived this battle, Alexi might never wield a sword again.

Stabbing pains in his chest indicated that he had broken at least one rib. A similar agony told him that his left ankle was also shattered. He might be able to walk on it, but only with a great deal of pain.

For all this, however, Alexi was surprised to find that he felt no fear. Quite the opposite—he was relieved, for the confusion of the last few weeks had finally left him. He fully understood the darkness within him now, understood the Darkening. The spawn of a fiend could never have a spirit pure enough to join the Circle.

But perhaps his faith would yet prove strong enough to vanquish his sire from the world.

Lysander, Dasmaria, his mother—all had said that his path lay elsewhere. As the spawn of evil, was he the only one who could truly contain it? If not, he would die trying.

"You ought to be more careful, boy," mocked Ebonbane. "Your mortal form is fragile. It was very nearly destroyed."

Alexi hobbled away from the ruined shed. "How lucky for me that I did not cheat you of your chance to kill me in some more glorious fashion."

As he spoke, Alexi realized that his mouth was filled with blood. He spat it out and noted the loss of at least two teeth.

"Not at all, little one," said Ebonbane, his voice thick with derision. "You are not going to die. You are going to live on, as Lysander Greylocks did. I promised that you would see your world in flames, Alexi Shadowborn. Ebonbane is nothing if not a creature of his word."

The enormity of the threat fell upon Alexi with an almost physical concussion. He had been prepared to die. Death in combat was something he had long expected. No warrior ever rode into battle without understanding that he might not ride out of it again. That was part of the profession.

To live on, however, transformed into a creature of darkness, was something he had never considered. Even when he was battling the ghouls at Forenoon Abbey, the warrior had never considered that he himself might become as they.

At that instant, the dark force of Ebonbane's will descended upon Alexi. He cried out in agony as wave upon wave of black, unspeakably evil thoughts battered him in a spiritual assault.

He saw the southern cities of Letour and Sanschay in flames and knew that the same fate awaited the whole of his world.

He relived the torture of his brother and knew that

the youth would die here and now, never to become a paladin in his own right.

He felt every moment of the torment that his mother had experienced in this land, fighting to keep the evil of Ebonbane in check.

But worst of all, he saw the moment of his own conception.

Blood and filth and horrible laughter, he saw it all. It was more terrible than anything he could have imagined. Rage mixed with revulsion, and he cried out in despair.

But then he saw something in the memory of that most reprehensible deed. Kateri Shadowborn did not weep. She did not scream. She did not rage against her attackers.

She prayed.

Even in that dark prison, far from her home and any hope of rescue, she had not given up her faith.

And then another memory came into his mind. This one was not Ebonbane's, but his own. He remembered looking down upon the body of Lysander as the fires of Shadowborn Manor blazed around them, as the old man told him that sometimes the only way to triumph is to yield.

When he had told Ebonbane that Kateri and Lysander had halted his evil once before, the fiend had laughed at him. Alexi knew now that he had spoken true, even if the dark thing did not believe him.

Ebonbane had shown him the misery and suffering that his monstrous power had caused. At the same time, however, he had unwittingly revealed the valor of his victims. Dasmaria had given herself willingly to save him from death. Lysander had endured decades of unlife to one day bring Alexi to this place. And Kateri

Shadowborn had used the power of her faith to trap Ebonbane for many long years.

The fiend was not all-powerful, no matter how much he might believe himself to be. Ebonbane had his weaknesses, and he had inadvertently shown them all to Alexi. From scenes of despair, Alexi drew only inspiration. He felt the warmth of Belenus in his heart, knowing the glory of faith and the ultimate power of good.

And then he gave himself over to evil.

THIRTY-ONE

The crushing power of Ebonbane's will overpowered Alexi. The knight sank to his knees with the weight of the hatred, rage, and malevolence that buffeted him. He could sense the fiend's spirit trying to force his own out of his body, to seize control.

He tried to rally his defenses, seeking solace in prayer and the power of faith. But the barrage hit Alexi on two fronts: Ebonbane's will assaulted him from without, while the darkness he carried in his heart threatened to consume him from within.

The fiend hammered away at him, never relenting in the torrent of evil thoughts. Time and time again, just when Alexi thought he would be able to drive the incredible darkness out of his mind, the attack would renew itself. Indeed, with every second, his enemy seemed to grow stronger and more determined.

Animated by a will not his own, Alexi's left hand clawed at his face, nails digging into flesh and opening the deep, bloody gouges Lysander's talons had left across his features. His right hand, still numb, twitched spasmodically. The dagger it had once held now lay on the ground at his feet. His pulse hammered in his temples.

Ebonbane was winning. Alexi sensed his own spirit being pushed out, inch by inch, as the fiend's power invaded. He was about to die. He closed his eyes, hoping to gather more strength by eliminating the sight of the monstrous abomination.

Alexi's will was broken. His spirit clung to his body with only the most tenuous of holds. Every bit of his determination had been spent, yet still the onslaught continued. The fiend need only exert the faintest additional pressure and the knight would be destroyed.

Suddenly the assault was over.

No. Not over. Alexi could still feel the looming evil of Ebonbane driving itself into his spirit. But much of its force was gone. He opened his eyes and saw at once the reason for this momentary respite.

Ebonbane was under attack.

The air around the fiend glowed with spirits. They swooped and dove, lashing out at him with spectral fists as they passed. Rage and confusion showed on the creature's diabolical features, but Alexi knew exactly what was happening.

The souls of the Phantasmal Forest, long-suffering and vengeful, had appeared to attack their tormentor. Whether they had been kept out of this place by the power of Ebonbane or the mystical barrier that appeared to Alexi as an ordinary wall, the warrior couldn't say.

The dark giant slashed at the ghosts with his claws. The great, leathery wings flapped as if the fiend were having trouble finding his balance. He roared with a primal rage that struck a cord of instinctual fear somewhere in Alexi's heart.

Once Ebonbane overcame his initial surprise, he proved himself more than equal to the challenge presented by the spirits. As his blows found their mark, wicked black talons rent the ghosts as if they were made of paper. Torn apart, the phantoms howled a final shriek of anguish before fading into nothingness.

If Alexi were going to take advantage of this distraction, he would have to act fast. He rolled to the side, desperate to find any weapon that might prove effective against the fiend. The remnants of Corona lay scattered about, but none of them offered any use.

He shifted his gaze elsewhere, wincing as pain shot from his ribs. A sympathetic pain throbbed in his right arm, making the bloody fingers of his hand twitch spasmodically. The only weapon he could spot was the slender sword his brother wore.

Alexi dragged himself over to his brother's still form. He could see life in the boy yet, but whether that was a blessing or not he couldn't say. If Ferran were left to the mercy of Ebonbane, his fate would be terrible indeed.

He reached for the blade, his hand trembling with pain and fatigue. Why he should expect this weapon to fare any better than the broken dagger, he could not imagine.

Then he saw the mahogany shafts.

With renewed energy, he grabbed the silver-tipped arrows. The squire's bow had been left behind in the blazing manor, but perhaps their shafts could yet work their magic.

He turned around with struggling steps and drove himself toward the frantic demon. Ebonbane had nearly destroyed the last of the spirits. In a matter of seconds, Alexi would again face the dark behemoth alone.

Each step forward was sheer agony. His ribs felt as if he had been seared by a branding iron. He couldn't feel the arrow in his right hand because of the injuries that limb had sustained. In his head, visions of nightmarish torment mixed with flashes of pain and death to create a mental cacophony.

Alexi reached Ebonbane as the fiend was about to destroy the last of his ghostly foes. The knight noticed with regret that the spirit was none other than Cassaldra, the ghost who had granted them safe passage through the Phantasmal Forest. As her shimmering body was torn in half by the fiend, her gaze met Alexi's. Something in her eyes pleaded with him—her last hope for vengeance.

Without the pretense of a battle cry, Alexi sprang upon the fiend. He landed on the hulking creature's back, forcing the wings apart and locking his legs tightly onto the obsidian body. He raised the twin arrows high and called out the name of his god, then drove the gleaming tips between the shoulder blades of the seemingly unstoppable beast. Alexi half expected them to shatter as the knife had.

Instead, a brilliant burst of light erupted from the demon where the shafts pierced his body. The warm, comforting glow could only be the holy sunlight of Belenus.

Ebonbane howled in pain and spun around. Alexi lost his hold and found himself slammed away by buffeting wings and flailing arms. He splashed hard in the muddy dirt and slid across it, very nearly ending up inside the still-blazing ruins. As he tried to regain his feet, he saw that the arrows had broken off in his hands. They were useless now.

But perhaps they had already done their work.

Alexi had to shake his head several times to clear his vision. The creature was on his knees, muscular arms and leathery wings lashing wildly about. The shafts had broken off, but the arrowheads were embedded in the fiend's back. Beams of light shone out behind the creature, showing where the glow of truth was consuming its darkness. Scant seconds later, as the tortured screams of its inhuman pain rang in the knight's ears, Ebonbane pitched forward and fell facedown into the mud. The monster tore and clawed at his wounds, but could not ease his torment.

The glow spread outward from the wounds. A hissing sound that reminded Alexi of wet wood in a campfire filled the air. It grew louder as the glow consumed more and more of the fiend's dark body. A final cry of pain was followed by a brilliant flash of light. And then . . .

Nothing.

Silence.

The body of the fiend was gone, consumed by the holy radiance of Belenus. Alexi silently hoped that the dead would feel their sacrifice had been worth it.

He closed his eyes and listened to the silence.

Only gradually did he become aware that the air was not, indeed, actually quiet. Flames still crackled, although they had nearly finished consuming the last timbers of Shadowborn Manor. Rain splashed in puddles and clapped against wood and rock.

He lay back and let the cool rain fall upon him. In a minute, he would get up and tend to his brother. His own wounds still ached, though, and he needed a moment's rest. He closed his eyes, letting out a long breath.

Almost at once, visions of torment and anguish flooded him. The darkness of Ebonbane swept in, merging with his own spirit. Every evil the fiend ever committed invaded Alexi's being. He saw death. He saw destruction. He saw despair.

As had happened when he defeated the Ghoul Lord

and other vile creatures, tremors wracked him as he absorbed Ebonbane's essence of evil. Had he resisted, as he did previously, the sheer magnitude of Ebonbane's malevolence would have killed him. This time, however, Alexi did not reject the experience. He embraced it, drawing the villain into him as he might inhale the scent of smoke from a campfire.

The evil of the fiend, far worse than any he had ever encountered, threatened to drive him mad. But he knew now that containing this great evil was his future. The circumstances of his birth, his training to become a paladin, the Darkening, his journey here—everything in his life had unfolded according to Belenus' plan and come together to prepare him for this noble calling. Just as Kateri Shadowborn had served Belenus even in death, so her son must continue that service in life.

At last the barrage ended. Alexi tried to inhale deeply, despite the crushing weight in his chest. The battle was won. But his own struggle was just beginning.

THIRTY-TWO

The voice of evil screamed in Alexi's head.

It demanded freedom.

It demanded obedience.

It demanded despair.

In time, the knight told himself, he would be able to ignore the spirit locked inside his body. In his heart, however, he knew the truth. There was no way to shut out the screaming torrent of blasphemy that clawed always at his thoughts.

He satisfied himself that Ferran would be all right. The boy was still unconscious, but he would come to his senses shortly. Alexi intended to send him home immediately, to get his brother out of this evil place.

Moving about was excruciatingly painful. He had the use of only one leg and arm, and every movement of his torso sent sheets of fire up his spine. As every surge of agony wracked his body, the dark thing within him threatened to overwhelm him. How had Kateri Shadowborn managed to contain that evil for so many years? How would he?

He knew he could never go home.

Somehow the thought didn't upset him. One by one,

his friends had been called upon to make sacrifices in the name of righteousness. Now it was his turn. And his loss hardly equaled those of his friends, who had given up their lives to help light triumph over darkness.

He understood his destiny now. He must renounce his status, his heritage, and all that he had lived for in order to protect the world from a terrible storm of darkness. Belenus had asked an enormous sacrifice of him, and he understood now—more than he ever could have as a Knight of the Circle—what it truly meant to serve as his god's champion.

He called for Pitch. They had left their mounts near the front of the manor, some distance away, but the black steed appeared almost at once. Midnight and Ember trotted along a minute or so later. Lysander's mount was nowhere to be seen. Indeed, it had vanished without a trace. Perhaps it had followed the spirit of its master into oblivion.

Alexi struggled to lift the unconscious Ferran onto Pitch's back. It took some time, and a less cooperative beast would have made the task impossible. Like all war-horses, however, Pitch had been trained to carry a wounded rider home from battle. Just as he had finally seated his brother securely in the saddle, Ferran lifted his head and moaned. The sound held both pain and confusion.

"Stay quiet, Ferran," Alexi murmured. "Everything is all right."

The groggy youth opened his eyes, his face lighting up at the sight of his brother. The familiar sight caused a lump to rise in Alexi's throat, and the warrior blinked back tears. "Alexi . . ." Ferran rasped. "Ebonbane . . ."

Alexi laid a fond hand on his brother's muddy hair.

"He's gone, Ferran. He won't bother our family, or anyone else, again."

"I knew you could do it." His heavy eyes fell closed again as the youth rested his head against Pitch's strong neck.

Alexi bent forward to whisper softly in his brother's ear. "Tell Mother and Father I'm all right. I've just got to be gone for a while."

Ferran's eyes clouded. "Aren't you coming home?" he murmured.

Alexi shook his head. Within him he felt the churning force of evil. "No, Ferran. I can never go home."

"What will you do?"

"Perhaps . . . " Alexi stared unseeing at the dark landscape around him. "Perhaps here especially they need paladins of the light. A Circle . . . " he stepped back and stroked the nose of his beloved horse.

"Take good care of him." He winced as he inadvertently put too much weight on his broken ankle. "If anyone can get him home, you can." So saying, he slapped the stallion on the hindquarters. The black destrier broke into a measured trot.

"Get him home safely, Pitch," Alexi whispered. "It's the last thing I'll ever ask of you."

He stood motionless, watching solemnly as the ebon charger, followed by Dasmaria's proud steed, carried his brother away. A few minutes of careful trotting brought the horses and rider to the cobblestone road. Looking back, Pitch let out a loud whinny—a last farewell, Alexi knew.

Then they were gone, swallowed up by the shadows.

THIRTY-THREE

I am imprisoned.

Instead of being stripped away, my chains have been reforged. This wretch's will is every bit as strong as his mother's. No. It is stronger. He combines the vitality of his spirit with the energy of life itself. I feel weighed down by a burden beyond my experience.

But there is more.

His faith is the equal of any I have encountered. But I have destroyed mortals who were as pious before, destroyed them easily and commanded them to do that which I willed. How can it be that this boy manages to resist me? He has been wounded and battered. His allies have fallen. He is alone, struggling to learn his way around this dark land my evil created, and should be nothing more than despair incarnate.

My fury is unmatched.

I assail him with all my power. I throw images at his mind of things from realms he cannot comprehend. These tactics should have reduced him to madness by now. But they have not. His faith is too strong. The strength of his spirit continues to defy me.

How many creatures have I dominated?

The number is beyond measure. No mortal has ever resisted me, let alone dominated me. This is unprecedented. It cannot happen. Yet it does.

The truth is slow in coming to me.

It seems impossible, but there can be no other explanation. His piety and vitality are indeed formidable things. But it is not these alone that enable him to resist my power. He has a strength unknown among his kind because they are not truly his kin. Inside him resides a darkness that marks him as my own progeny. If he were a mere mortal, he would be lost. But he is more than that, and it is I who made him so. I don't know whether I should scream in rage or laugh at the irony of it.

Yet there is still hope.

The woman grew weak with the passing of the years. She held out longer than I had expected, true, but I defeated her in the end. The same will happen to Alexi Shadowborn. Eventually, his spirit will grow weak and he will falter. He may last longer than she did, but he will grow frail with the passing years. His mortal form will succumb, no matter how much vitality his unholy heritage might grant him. When that happens, victory will be mine.

It is only a matter of time. . . .

Ravenloft BOOKS

Spectre of the Black Rose

James Lowder

In this chilling sequel to the best-selling Knight of the Black Rose, factions vie for control of Sithicus as Lord Soth—Darklord and former Knight of Solamnia—fights to keep his reign from crumbling. Even as he struggles to defeat his enemies, rumour reaches him that the White Rose haunts the land. Has Kitiara finally returned to Soth, or is this another spectre from the Death Knight's tragic past?

Available in paperback, February 1999

RAVENLOFT® and the TSR logo are registered trademarks owned by TSR, Inc. ©1998 TSR, Inc. All Rights Reserved. TSR is a subsidiary of Wizards of the Coast.

Ravenloft GAMES

If you enjoyed this book, you'll love these games:

The Shadow Rift
William, W. Connors, Cindi Rice, and John Ratelitf
At the center of Ravenloft lies a gigantic, mist-filled pit, thousands of feet deep. Below is the realm of the shadow elves who raid the surrounding domains and steal peoples' shadows, leaving their owners in a zombielike state. If there are heroes brave enough to enter the Rift, they'll find the raids are just the tip of an evil iceberg.
(1163, ISBN 0-7869-1200-6)

Champions of the Mists
William W. Connors
They're far and few between, and they don't often live long, but the Ravenloft® campaign setting has its heroes. This supplement provides full stats and background descriptions so these luminaries can enter a campaign and interact with player characters. Included is a collection of player character kits, especially designed for roleplaying in a realm of terror.
(9559, ISBN 0-7869-0765-7)

Vecna Reborn
Monte Cook
The darklords of Ravenloft are powerful and evil, but now the Demiplane has ensnared one of the most infamous villains known to the AD&D® game: the lich Vecna! Inability to depart the Land of the Mists is quite irritating to the demigod, but he's got a plan.
(9582, ISBN 0-7869-1201-4)

Children of the Night: Werebeasts
William W. Connors
This next installment in the popular Children of the Night series features 13 character vignettes and short adventures, each of them focused upon a different lycanthrope.
(9583, ISBN 0-7869-1202-2)

RAVENLOFT® and the TSR logo are registered trademarks owned by TSR, Inc.
©1998 TSR, Inc. All Rights Reserved. TSR is a subsidiary of Wizsards of the Coast.

"Laura, what di[d you do?]"

The tone of Brando[n's voice gave her no] choice. She reached inside her purse and withdrew a matchbook.

His spirits sank when he saw Classic Escort Agency printed on it. "Where did you find this?" he asked.

"In Joan's coat pocket."

"She smoked?"

"No."

"Then why would she want a matchbook?"

"Maybe she handed them out to strangers she met." Her eyes glistened as she fumbled for a tissue.

Brandon looked at her carefully before he spoke again. "Are you sure you want to go through with this? You might not like what you find."

"I have no choice." she answered firmly. "I have to know the truth."

He didn't have the heart to tell her that truth is not always kind....

ABOUT THE AUTHOR

No Easy Answers is Joyce Porter's first solo Intrigue. Before that she and her daughter wrote under the pseudonym Deborah Joyce and have four Superromances and one Intrigue to their credit. Joyce says that her favorite books to read and write are Intrigues. "They give the reader a chance to get more involved," she says. "And from a writing point of view, they're a real challenge." Joyce, who lives with her husband in Houston, Texas, is currently juggling her busy schedule so she can write another Intrigue.

Books by Deborah Joyce

HARLEQUIN SUPERROMANCE
61–A QUESTING HEART
108–A DREAM TO SHARE
125–NEVER LOOK BACK
142–SILVER HORIZONS

HARLEQUIN INTRIGUE
37–A MATTER OF TIME

Don't miss any of our special offers. Write to us at the following address for information on our newest releases.

Harlequin Reader Service
901 Fuhrmann Blvd., P.O. Box 1397, Buffalo, NY 14240
Canadian address: P.O. Box 603,
Fort Erie, Ont. L2A 5X3

NO EASY ANSWERS
JOYCE PORTER

Harlequin Books

TORONTO • NEW YORK • LONDON
AMSTERDAM • PARIS • SYDNEY • HAMBURG
STOCKHOLM • ATHENS • TOKYO • MILAN

To Jennifer Cansler,
who is not only talented
and beautiful but a loyal friend
with a bright future.

All references to the Dallas Police Department are wholly imaginary and bear no resemblance to any one living or dead.

Harlequin Intrigue edition published May 1987

ISBN 0-373-22066-9

Copyright © 1987 Joyce Porter. All rights reserved.
Philippine copyright 1987. Australian copyright 1987.
Except for use in any review, the reproduction or utilization of this work in whole or in part in any form by any electronic, mechanical or other means, now known or hereafter invented, including xerography, photocopying and recording, or in any information storage or retrieval system, is forbidden without the permission of the publisher, Harlequin Enterprises Limited, 225 Duncan Mill Road, Don Mills, Ontario, Canada M3B 3K9, or Harlequin Books, P.O. Box 958, North Sydney, Australia 2060.

All the characters in this book have no existence outside the imagination of the author and have no relation whatsoever to anyone bearing the same name or names. They are not even distantly inspired by any individual known or unknown to the author, and all incidents are pure invention.

The Harlequin trademark, consisting of the words, HARLEQUIN INTRIGUE with or without the portrayal of a Harlequin, are trademarks of Harlequin Enterprises Limited; the portrayal of a Harlequin is registered in the United States Patent and Trademark Office and in the Canada Trade Marks Office.

Printed in Canada

Prologue

Always there had been three. Now there were two. Laura Gibson heard the words, but couldn't believe them. "Not Joanie," she whispered into the phone. A chill night wind blew through her open bedroom window, but it was warm compared to the icicles forming inside her. "How did it happen, Diane? A car accident?"

Diane Hastings hesitated, then spoke rapidly. "The Connors don't know the details yet. You're not all alone, are you?"

In the background Laura could hear a baby softly crying. Somehow the whimpering of Diane's daughter, so far away, made the news even more terrible. Laura forced her numb lips to form an answer. "Yes, I'm alone; my roommate's skiing in Colorado. How are Joan's parents?"

"In shock. Mrs. Connor is worried about Joan's dad. His blood pressure's been skyrocketing lately."

Tears misted Laura's eyes as she thought of the Connors. She knew Joan's parents almost as well as her own, perhaps better in some ways. For her last two years in high school, Laura had lived with them while her parents had been in Saudi Arabia with her father's oil company. Nearly a year had passed since she'd visited with the Connors, she realized guiltily.

Joan had been their only child, the center of their life. Laura couldn't imagine how they'd handle this tragedy. "Was Joan driving, or was she a passenger?"

Wasn't there an old saying about trouble always coming in threes? Laura thought. Yesterday's news had seemed bad enough. When Laura's supervisor had told her that the Houston electronics firm where she worked was on its last legs and would be folding soon, Laura had been devastated. Today's news made that seem unimportant. One of her best friends was dead. Please, no more bad news, she prayed.

"It wasn't a car accident," Diane answered, choosing her words carefully. "Perhaps it's best if I wait until morning to tell you what little I know. I shouldn't have phoned you this time of night, but when I heard the news I had to talk to you. The three of us were always so close, and now, with Joan gone..."

As Diane talked, Laura slid from the bed, groped around on the floor for her thongs, then reached for a robe. "It's all right, Diane. If you hadn't called immediately I would never have forgiven you." Brushing several strands of her tangled auburn hair out of her eyes, she added, "I'll catch the first available flight to Dallas."

"Are you sure you can get away from work?"

"For..." Laura stopped, choking back the thought of Joan's funeral. Joan should have had years of life ahead of her, years during which Laura and she could visit and talk and laugh and hug. Now it was too late. There'd be no more annual reunions for the three of them. Last summer, thinking that they had all the time in the world, they'd let themselves be caught up in the trivial business of daily life and had canceled their yearly meeting. "My job is about to end here," Laura told Diane. "I'm definitely coming."

"Then get a reservation and call me right back to let me know when you'll arrive. I'll meet you at the airport."

"I'd appreciate that. My parents are out of town. Diane, tell me now what happened to Joan. I need to know. I'm fully awake, and if you don't tell me I'll spend the rest of the night wondering about it."

There was a long pause.

Laura's heart beat was deafening in the silence. When Diane finally spoke, her voice was so low Laura had to strain to hear. "Laura, the police told the Connors that they think Joan was murdered."

Murdered? Impossible! Laura clutched the phone with such force that her fingers ached. *People you know, people like Joan, aren't murdered!* "How? Where? By whom? I can't believe it."

In the background the infant's cries grew shrill and insistent. "I don't have the answers," Diane said. "Perhaps it's all just a terrible mistake. The police have been known to identify the wrong person. Laura, please come quickly. I need you."

"I'll be there, Diane. *Nothing* can keep me away," Laura vowed.

Chapter One

At a quarter to two in the afternoon, Laura arrived at the Dallas police headquarters. She found a parking space and made her way toward the large building. As she walked, she realized she was nervous; in all her twenty-six years, she'd never been inside a police station—not even this one in her own hometown.

The front door was heavy, and she put her weight determinedly against it and pushed. She could think of a dozen places she'd rather be, including some that were decidedly unpleasant, but she had no choice. It had become clear these last few days that if she and the Connors wanted the details surrounding Joan's murder, they couldn't simply wait passively and patiently for the police to get in touch.

Once the heavy door had rumbled shut behind her, Laura paused to take in the scene before her. *Not very dramatic,* Laura thought. But then, what had she expected? Reassured by the ordinariness of it all, Laura headed towards the reception booth. A trim woman with long dark hair threw her a quick glance before turning her attention to a man speaking rapid-fire Spanish.

Laura waited while the man was directed on his way and the receptionist signaled her with a smile. "I'd like to speak with the officer in charge of the Connor case," Laura said.

"Burglary? Traffic? Homicide? Rape?" The receptionist rattled off the departments as if they were ice-cream flavors.

"Homicide." A week after Joan's funeral, the word still seemed foreign to Laura. Her mind refused to process the idea that Joan had been murdered. But the part that was totally impossible to accept was the official police version of the crime.

"I'll check that department," the woman said. After a brief murmured conversation on the telephone, she turned back to Laura. "Have a seat over there. Someone will be out to talk with you in a few minutes."

Laura selected a seat, then glanced in her purse to make certain she had the letter from Joan's father authorizing her to make inquiries concerning Joan's death on behalf of the family. Mr. Connor had made several unsuccessful attempts to learn more than the sketchy details the police were willing to share immediately after the crime. Each time, he had been told that the case was under investigation, that as soon as anything definite was known the family would be informed.

Laura was less patient about being kept in the dark that way. While she fully understood that the police had to keep certain details confidential until they had gathered enough evidence to make an arrest, she couldn't understand why they had been so ready to accept what few details had surfaced—including the preposterous ones. Their insistence that Joan had been working for an escort service the night of her death was rubbish.

Not Joan! While she was outgoing with her friends, under it all she had always been a little shy. Laura and Diane used to tease her about how long Joan took to feel at ease with a new acquaintance. No one, including the police, would ever be able to convince Laura that Joan had willingly gone out on a date with two total strangers and had ended up being murdered in a downtown hotel room.

Who were these men? Why couldn't the police locate them? And why should they want to murder Joan? There were just too many unanswered questions, and they haunted Laura.

Restless now, she reached for the tattered magazine on the table beside her and thumbed through it aimlessly, trying in vain to divert her thoughts from the unsolvable puzzle of Joan's last night.

When the magazine failed to hold her interest, she looked around the room. The receptionist's booth blocked out the middle section of what she could see, but on either side of it people were at work. On her left three policemen, one policewoman and a man, either a civilian or an off-duty officer, were gathered around a long gray metal table and were engaged in animated conversation.

It was the man who caught Laura's attention. He was dressed in a natural-toned fisherman's knit sweater that had the comfortable look that comes only from countless washings. His tan cord pants were equally well-worn, and fit his lean body superbly.

Taller than the others, he appeared to be the focus of their attention. Laura could see why; she found it difficult to keep from staring at him herself. His tousled, glossy brown hair swept down over his high forehead, and his casual manner of brushing his forelock back while he talked was hypnotic. His strong features offset one another in a way that set her pulse throbbing, as it always did when she met a man she knew she could like.

The group parted to admit another woman in a blue uniform. Laura watched as the woman set a large white bakery box on the table, opened the lid, and lifted out a pink-and-white birthday cake. Within minutes, candles were inserted and lit. A short, muscular blond man was shoved forward, and he leaned over, his face red, and puffed out the candles.

The man Laura had been admiring gave his blond friend a comradely hug and said something that made him laugh. Laura felt her throat tighten as she remembered the last birthday she had celebrated with Joan several years before. *How could I have let things slide like that?* Laura thought. She reached for a tissue to dab away the moisture gathering on her eyelashes. When she looked up, she met the direct, disconcerting gaze from the tall man's gray-blue eyes as he studied her from across the room. Uncomfortable, Laura turned her head and stared at a calendar on the wall.

After a few moments, a man's voice startled her. "Did you want to see me? I'm from Homicide."

Laura glanced up and saw that a thin, older man was standing beside her chair. "Yes," she said, standing. She held out her hand. "I'm Laura Gibson."

The man shook her hand with a solemn formality that reminded Laura of the funeral directors she had encountered during the past week. "I'm Captain Quill," he said. "How can I help you?"

Surely he didn't expect her to discuss it here? "I'm a close friend of Joan Connor's family. Mr. Connor isn't well, so he's asked me to make inquiries about his daughter's case with you on the family's behalf. Could we go somewhere private?"

"What would you like to know, Miss Gibson?"

Laura stared at the man with a mutinous expression, but he met her stare with an equally determined look. "We feel that you're overlooking some important information in the case. Joan's murder was not what you seem to think," she said.

His smile seemed forced. "Families always feel we're not moving fast enough in a tragedy such as this. Let me assure you, we're not ignoring any leads. Do you have any new information about what Miss Connor was doing on the night of her death?"

"Well, no." Laura made the admission reluctantly. "It's just that we feel you should be treating this case as kidnapping and murder."

"Kidnapping?" He repeated the word as if he'd never heard it before.

"Yes, we're certain Joan would never have gone to that hotel room voluntarily." Still irritated that she was being forced to have this discussion in the open reception area, Laura glanced around pointedly. To her left she met the unnerving gaze of the tall man once more, and she turned back to Captain Quill. "Can we go to your office to discuss this?"

"I have another appointment in a few minutes."

"Then I'll make an appointment," she said, her tone slightly desperate. "When will you be available?"

He shrugged. "The department's policy is to limit discussions about a case unless new evidence has been found."

"Would it help if the family engaged an attorney?"

"We'd only tell the attorney the same thing we've already told Mr. Connor. Miss Gibson, I suggest you go home now and let me get back to work on your friend's case. Give the receptionist your address and phone number, and we'll call you if there are any new developments."

Laura saw that the receptionist was watching her, her pencil poised. Laura quickly recited her parents' address and phone number, adding, "Captain Quill, do you want me to tell the Connors that you refused to make an appointment with me?"

His eyes narrowed. "I'd rather you said I gave you some good advice. It's difficult to lose a close friend. You must accept that there's nothing you can do to help find her killers. The police are trained in these matters."

"Citizens have the right to information," Laura returned angrily. She turned to the receptionist. "I'd like to make an appointment to see the police chief."

"You'll have to go through Public Relations," the woman said, pointing behind her. "I'd suggest you call first. The chief's out of town right now."

Totally frustrated, Laura turned back in time to see the police captain walking away from her. She reached for her purse on the chair where she'd laid it, and started for the exit.

Just as she reached the heavy doors, the tall man she had been admiring earlier stepped away from his friends and moved toward her. "Ms Gibson," he said, "I couldn't help overhearing some of your conversation. I'm Brandon Powell, a private investigator. Is there anything I can do to help?"

"Help?" All the pent-up frustration and rage she was feeling exploded into that one word. "What can you do to help? You're one of *them*." Her hand made a sweeping indictment of the entire assemblage. "This smells like a setup to me. First, the police are uncooperative with the family. Then a private investigator, who is obviously on very friendly terms with the police, conveniently steps forward and offers to take the case. What kind of fool do you take me for, Mr. Powell?"

As she pushed past him and hurried for the exit again, she heard gales of laughter erupt from the group around the table.

BRANDON POWELL IGNORED the derisive laughter from his friends. As far as he was concerned, the angry young woman had every reason to be suspicious. It was easy to see why she had misconstrued the situation. He smiled wryly, thinking how far off the mark her accusations were. The last thing he had needed was another case. Would-be clients were already clamoring for his services.

No, he had only wanted to ease her way through a bad moment. When he'd caught her watching their birthday celebration a few minutes later, he'd almost drowned in the depths of the sadness in those luminous green eyes. And his interest had grown as he'd noted the shoulder-length auburn hair spilling around that perfectly oval face.

Quill's bureaucratic attitude had been a part of it, too. Powell remembered only too vividly being dressed down by the by-the-book captain for spending too much of the department's time with crime victims' families. But, dammit, that was part of a policeman's job, Brandon had always countered. Finally, he had given up, leaving the police force so that he could work alone and do things his way.

He turned toward the group, who were still smiling at him. "Anyone know what case she was here about?" he asked.

The blond policeman who had been celebrating his birthday answered, "I heard her mention the name 'Connor.' Didn't you read about that one in the paper, Brand? A female Dr.-Jekyll-and-Ms-Hyde. By day, the victim was a sedate little schoolteacher. By night, she was moonlighting for an escort service."

"That one," Brandon said tersely. He'd read the story, all right. The woman had been brutally murdered. "I heard Ms Gibson mention kidnapping, Winn. Any chance of that?" Winn Johnston had been his partner during his last two years on the force. He was like Brandon in some ways; he, too, had a maverick streak. Unlike Brandon, though, he'd elected to remain a detective in the homicide department. Brandon seldom had time to spend with him these days, but he appreciated the way Winn was always willing to share information on his cases.

"Nothing to the kidnapping theory," Winn was saying. "You know how families are. They have a hard time accepting the raw truth. The case appears to be fairly cut-and-dried from what I've heard. The Connor woman ran into some weirdos."

"Who?" Brandon asked. "Or is it just a case of rounding up the usual suspects?"

"It's not my case, but everyone in Homicide has attended a couple of briefings about it. I've heard the men were probably from out of town. They used false ID's." Winn came over and clapped a hand on his former partner's shoulder. "You don't want to get involved in this one. It's the kind you always hated. And you may as well admit it. For once, Quill is right. That woman's going to have to put her friend's death behind her. She'll end up with nightmares if she hears all the gory details."

Brandon smiled briefly and gave his friend an affirmative nod. Winn was right, but that didn't erase from his memory the vulnerable line of the woman's shoulders as she'd sat watching the birthday celebration. He was grateful, though, that she hadn't taken him up on his offer of help. Only a fool would volunteer to get involved in a case this tragic.

BY THE TIME LAURA had reached her mother's small gray compact car in the parking lot behind the police station, her anger had cooled. As she slipped into the driver's seat, she tried to recall exactly what she'd said to the attractive man. He was probably only being polite!

What right did she have to dump her fury at the entire police force on his head? Usually she was fairly level-headed and reasonable, but the events of the past week or so had left her short fused and ready to explode without warning.

What was his name? Brandon. Brandon Powell, he'd said. She couldn't deny that something about him had attracted her, diverting her thoughts momentarily from the somber ones that had dogged her for days now. There was a certain compelling energy about him that had quickened her heartbeat at the first sight of him.

He'd probably been aware of her response and had thought she'd be flattered by his attention. Was he really a private investigator, or was that just a line? Laura grew warm recalling his friends' laughter at her outburst.

Disgusted with her reaction, she shifted her thoughts back to the dilemma facing her. It was obvious that she had some tough decisions to make, and at the moment she felt as limp as a rag. She certainly wasn't ready to face the Connors' questioning looks. Mrs. Connor had confided in her only the evening before that she was concerned about the state of Mr. Connor's health. His doctor had warned that if he got too agitated, his blood pressure could soar out of control.

In an effort to offer Mrs. Connor some support, Laura had promised to go to the police, to try to convince them that Joan could not have been working for an escort agency and to persuade them to search from some solid leads. How could she tell the Connors she couldn't even get a polite hearing from the homicide department? They were depending on her.

Still at loose ends, Laura started the car and headed out of the police lot, deciding to take the long route to her parents' condo. Her dad had retired the summer before, and he and Laura's mother were spending several months in Europe. When Laura had contacted them with the news of Joan's death, they had urged her to stay as long as necessary in their Dallas condo. Her mother's car was at her disposal, and she had their blessing to take on the task of clearing Joan's name.

The phone was ringing when Laura arrived. "Did you find out anything from the police?" Diane Hastings asked. Diane was counting on Laura, too. With two small children underfoot all the time, she couldn't do much herself to track down the answers to the questions that haunted them all.

"Nothing. They wouldn't even discuss the case."

"Maybe they don't know anything."

"Why not? What are they *doing*, Diane? You know what I think? I think that because they're convinced Joan was working for that escort agency they're not even attempting to solve the case. They don't care what happened to Joan. The captain that I spoke to looked like the kind who would say, 'Well, what can a woman expect if she makes dates with strangers?'"

"I know. It makes me furious," Diane said. "What are you going to do now?"

"That's the problem. I don't know what to do. I've already called my boss in Houston and told him I won't be back for the last few weeks before the company closes. My severance check is large enough that I can afford to take the time to help the Connors before I look for another job. But I don't know if I'm going to be able to get anywhere. I feel so helpless in the face of all that bureaucratic indifference."

"Maybe you should just leave it alone," Diane said slowly. "I've been thinking about what happened to Joan."

Laura could imagine the frown on Diane's face that always accompanied that tone of voice. Diane, with her short, curly black hair and large brown eyes, had always been the thinker of the trio, the perfect foil to Joan's blond, wholesome looks, and Laura's own vivid, dramatic appearance. "Thinking what?"

"I wouldn't want the Connors to know about this, but there *was* something different about Joan the last few months."

"What?" Laura demanded. "You haven't mentioned any of this to me before."

"That's because I'm not sure how to describe it. Look, Laura, I find it as unbelievable as you do that Joan would have dated strangers, but she was different lately. You know how she always loved to entertain close friends?"

"Yes."

"The last time I went by her house, she didn't even want me to come in."

"Diane, you must have imagined that. Tell me what happened."

"I was in Joan's neighborhood a few Saturdays ago, so naturally I stopped by for a chat. I rang the doorbell, but no one answered. Just as I turned to leave, Joan opened the door. She invited me in but I got the impression she barely recognized me at first. She seemed to be somewhere else, to be so absorbed in something that everything else was shut out. Nothing about her was normal. She didn't even offer me any tea."

Laura couldn't suppress a laugh. "That's all that happened? Maybe she was out of tea."

"Laura, it was more than that. I asked for a drink of water. When Joan went to get it, I followed her into the kitchen. When she opened the refrigerator to get some ice, it was almost empty."

"Maybe she was on a diet, or was eating out a lot. I think your imagination has been working overtime since Joan's death."

"I knew I couldn't explain what bothered me. Joan just didn't seem herself. She appeared relieved when I said I couldn't stay long."

For a moment, Laura couldn't think of a reply. It was totally out of character for Joan not to urge her friends to stay longer. Everyone joked about taking sleeping bags to Joan's afternoon get-togethers and luggage to her dinner parties. Then it dawned on Laura that there just might be a logical explanation. "There's another possibility. She may have been entertaining a guest and you'd interrupted her."

"That was my first thought, so I started teasing her about a new man in her life. She got upset and told me to quit imagining things."

"No wonder," Laura said with feeling. "Since you got married, you've been constantly pressuring Joan and myself to join your happy state. Now that I think about it, I don't think that could be why Joan wasn't too eager to talk to you that day. The Connors say she hadn't mentioned dating anyone special since her fiancé died last year. They *did* say she had been terribly busy and preoccupied lately."

Laura paused as her conversation with Diane replayed in her mind. Then she sighed and continued in a new tone of voice. "Diane, do you realize what we're doing? We're beginning to construct a theory on the basis of a few insignificant events, and it's the same one the police came up with. We both know Joan wasn't working for an escort service. There has to be some perfectly logical explanation why she was behaving oddly. The last time I talked to her on the phone, she mentioned how well her writing was coming. She didn't say what she was working on, but I imagine it was that collection of poems she'd hoped to get published. Maybe she was so wrapped up in that and the writing classes she taught that she didn't have time for people to drop by without calling first."

"You're right," Diane said. Her tone lacked its usual conviction.

After a few minutes of mutual assurances, the phone called ended, but Laura found it impossible to dismiss Diane's worries. As she struggled to find an explanation for Joan's unusual treatment of Diane, she was reminded that she still had to go to Joan's house. She'd been putting off the visit, dreading the memories it would stir up and the emptiness she'd find there.

When she'd offered her help, the Connors had asked her to arrange to have Joan's things packed and stored in a warehouse until they were emotionally ready to deal with them. They had asked her to contact a realtor to see about putting Joan's house up for sale. Selling the house seemed so final. But it was necessary. It didn't make sense not to roll up her sleeves and get started now.

THE SUN GLINTED off the roof of Laura's mother's car in the parking lot at the rear of her parents' condo as Laura headed for it fifteen minutes later. For the first day of spring it was unusually warm, and the wool-blend suit she wore was heavier than she needed. Only ten days earlier, on the day of Joan's funeral, a few snowflakes had fallen. Fickle Dallas weather. As the old saying went, if you don't like the weather today, stick around, because it'll be different tomorrow.

Everything about this place is unpredictable, Laura thought as she got in the car. A flood of memories washed over Laura as she drove the familiar route to Joan's house. It was in one of Dallas's older neighborhoods, where there was nothing resembling the mammoth mansions shown on the TV drama that used the city's name.

Although Laura had loved living in Houston these last five years, she missed Dallas. Big D, as it was known locally, sat stubbornly on a barren prairie as though abandoned there. With no natural resources or dramatic scenery to nourish it, it had flourished seemingly through strength of will to become a bustling, dynamic city of steel-and-glass buildings headquartering oil and insurance companies.

Joan's small, two-story house was indistinguishable from its neighbors. Laura remembered that Joan had chosen it for its homey charm and for the climbing roses that grew on the white picket fence surrounding it. Although she had said it gobbled up entirely too much of her modest teacher's paycheck, she'd always insisted it was worth every dollar.

Today, the rosebushes were bare, showing only angry thorns on their thin branches, Laura noted as she pulled up in front of the house and stopped. The only sign of life were the tiny green leaves just beginning to show on the ash tree that claimed the small front yard.

As Laura started up the front walk, she noticed two women chatting in front of a house down the street. She wondered if they and the other neighbors believed the lurid accounts of Joan's supposed double life that the newspapers had run and if the police had even bothered to question any of them.

One woman glanced up and gave Laura a curious look. Before Laura could respond, the woman turned and waved at someone across the street. Laura looked in the direction of the wave and saw the postman. She was struck by the fact that Joan's death seemed to have made no difference to the daily routine of the neighborhood.

The key Mr. Connor had given Laura fit easily in the lock. She took a deep breath, pushed open the door and stepped inside. The slate-tiled entry was cool; the silence was deafening. She paused, trying to analyze how she felt. She'd expected a momentous reaction, but instead felt a measure of comfort as she looked around the familiar surroundings that Joan had loved so dearly. Slowly, silently, almost reverently, she walked into the living room and looked around.

Everything looked exactly as she remembered. The couch and matching chair were covered in a rose chintz. A pine coffee table sat in front of them, and Laura noticed the antique rolltop desk that she had found at an auction. She remembered calling Joan to see if she wanted to buy it. A colonial floor lamp was switched on, and Laura automatically went over and clicked it off.

The pine table in the dining room held piles of books. Joan was an avid reader, and usually had several going at the same time. Laura walked over and glanced at the titles: literary classics, mainly; probably being reviewed for lesson plans for Joan's classes. The very normalcy of the scene made Laura's chest ache.

Remembering Diane's concerns, Laura went straight for the refrigerator when she reached the kitchen. Joan had always loved to cook and to eat. Slightly plump, she had talked constantly about going on a diet, but Diane and

Laura had known it was just talk. Food was too much a part of Joan's life.

The refrigerator was stark in its emptiness, holding only a six-pack of imported beer and a hunk of bright yellow cheese wrapped in clear plastic wrap. Joan hated beer, Laura thought. She said it tickled her nose. The freezer compartment was jammed with TV dinners. On further inspection, there was no sign of the vegetables and fruits Joan usually kept on hand for the gourmet recipes she prepared.

Confused, Laura turned to the kitchen cabinets and systematically opened the doors. A few unopened boxes and cans of staple items were positioned neatly, but it was obvious that no serious cooking had been done for a while. Had the Connors sent someone over to throw out opened packages without telling her? Laura wondered. No, that didn't make sense. She had been put in charge of handling all those details, and they certainly would have mentioned it if someone else had been asked to help.

A stack of empty aluminum TV-dinner trays, half a package of plastic forks, and an unopened box of paper napkins sat on the counter. In Joan's house? Joan, who had started collecting her china and silver in high school? Laura remembered that Joan had been partial to colorful place mats and matching napkins, and that she kept them in one of the kitchen drawers. She pulled open a drawer and found them still there, undisturbed. Whatever had been occupying Joan's time these last few months of her life must have been engrossing. It had blotted out all her other interests.

Still puzzled, Laura wandered back into the entry hall. She told herself that she had work to do. For starters, she needed to call the moving company, and before that, she had to compile an inventory of what was to be stored. But she was finding it difficult to concentrate. All she could think of was the discussion she'd had with Diane about Joan's strange behavior.

Dazed, she stumbled against a small table in the hall and sent a book crashing to the floor. Suddenly, two men filled the stair landing above her. "What're you doing here?" one shouted as he thundered down the wooden stairs.

Chapter Two

Eyes wide, Laura backed away from the men. As she reached the far wall of the hall, the man who had bolted down the stairs caught up with her, his companion close behind her. The first man grabbed her wrists and pinned her against the wall. With his face close to hers, he demanded, "Who in the hell are you?"

Laura could only stare. At close range his distorted features and hollow dark eyes added to her feeling that she was trapped in a waking nightmare.

Then something snapped in her, and anger boiled up out of her confusion. "What are you doing in Joan Connor's house?"

"I'm asking the questions." The man tightened his grip and pressed her harder against the wall.

A groan escaped Laura just as the man's companion pulled her assailant back and stepped in front of her. "Sorry, my friend was just startled at seeing you here. We're police."

Laura's knees turned to rubber. "Thank God," she breathed. "But why didn't you identify yourself immediately? I don't appreciate being shoved around."

The man who stood before her laughed. At least ten years older than his companion, he appeared to be in his early forties. He had broad, rounded shoulders, and was nearly bald. These two should be in undercover work, Laura thought. No one would ever guess they were policemen. "You took us by surprise," the man was saying. "We're sorry we scared you, but this house is off-limits until the crime report is finished. Can't take any chances, you know."

"Joan's father, Mr. Connor, told me the police had said they would only need a couple of hours in the house." Still angry, Laura glared over at the man who'd first accosted her. He was standing in shadow just inside the living room, and while she could barely make him out, she knew he could see her.

"We're checking for details that might have been overlooked on our first visit," the older man said. "I hate to do this, ma'am but we going to have to ask you to leave now. Who did you say you were?"

"Laura Gibson."

"Mind if I see some identification?"

Irritated, Laura opened her purse and located her driver's license. She held it out. As the man studied it, she said, "Why aren't you in uniform?"

He smiled genially, slipped a hand in his back pocket and brought out a black plastic folder. With a quick motion, he flipped it open, revealing a photo of a man in a blue uniform, then snapped it shut. "Undercover officer. Jake Marshall. What's your relationship to the deceased?"

Laura briefly debated whether she should ask him to show her his ID again, but decided that might be pushing her luck; she'd already irritated the Dallas police enough for one day. "Joan was my friend. Her family gave me the key and asked me to check on her personal belongings."

"You from Houston?" he asked, studying her license as if he were memorizing it.

"Yes, I'm staying at my parents' home here."

"Where's that?" He turned to the man standing in the living room. "Better take down this address for our report."

"Why?" Laura asked.

"Routine. Must I remind you that this is a murder case, Miss Gibson?"

She gave the address, then the phone number when Jake asked for it. Finally she asked, "Do you have any suspects yet?"

"We will." He handed her back her license. "Miss Gibson, please do not come back here for a few days. The lab boys need time to get all the prints."

Fingerprints. That seemed a little strange. Over the years Joan would have had a lot of visitors leaving prints behind that even the most fastidious of housekeeping would miss. Besides, this wasn't the scene of the crime, and the police were sure the murderer was a stranger. So why would they be looking for his fingerprints here? Laura forced herself to stop asking questions for which there seemed no hope of answers. At least the police were doing something, she thought, even if they were being awfully slow about it.

"Hurry with your case," she told Jake Marshall. "The Connors will feel much better when you've caught Joan's killers."

The older man laughed his mocking laugh again. "You can count on us, Miss Gibson."

As Laura headed for the car, she realized her knees felt rubbery. She located the key, slid it in, and started the car with fumbling fingers. Delayed shock from her frightening encounter, she diagnosed.

She shifted into reverse and backed up to avoid two small boys in red coats playing in front of Joan's house. When she reached the curb fronting the house next door she noticed a beat-up blue sedan at the back of Joan's house that she hadn't seen earlier. She tried to see the license plate, but it was angled away from her.

Once again, she found herself wondering what was going on, and why Captain Quill hadn't even bothered to tell her in general terms that his department was actively investigating Joan's murder. She would have been reassured to know he considered the case important enough to be using undercover officers on it.

By the time she got home, Laura's temples were throbbing. It was past six, and she had been caught in rush-hour traffic. That, and the the fright the police had given her, had been enough to trigger a blinding headache.

Lights were on in most of the six condos in her parents' block, she noticed as she parked the car and locked it. The building had a common entrance which led into a long hall lined with lush tropical plants. Laura's parents owned the unit at the far end of the hall.

She'd met their next-door neighbors, or rather, their neighbors' daughter. Like herself, the woman was visiting. When she'd introduced herself she'd explained she was a nun in a nursing order in Chicago. Her mother had been scheduled for surgery, so she had taken leave to be with her. Since that first encounter, Laura had had two brief chats with her, and had found her immensely likable.

Tonight the hall was empty. Laura walked quickly to the end, and was slipping out of her jacket by the time she had locked the door behind her. She went into the bathroom for a headache capsule, and was swallowing it when the phone rang. The sound set off an explosion in the depths of her aching head. Certain it must be either Mrs. Connor or Diane, she hurried to answer it.

A man's voice asked, "Laura Gibson?"

"Yes."

"Go back to Houston."

Laura gripped the receiver. "Who is this?"

"Forget about what happened to your friend, unless you want to end up like her."

"Who is this?" she repeated, her voice little more than a whisper.

Her answer was the hum of a disconnected call.

Laura leaned over the kitchen table and took several deep breaths to steady herself. She had to keep calm, to remember exactly what the man had said. And his voice. Was there anything distinctive about it?

After several moments, she got a notepad from a drawer and wrote down the caller's words verbatim. Then she located the police emergency number and dialed.

A man was working the switchboard. "Homicide," Laura requested.

"Are you reporting a murder?"

"No. I need to speak to someone about a case they're working on."

"You'll have to call back in the morning to have a discussion about a case. Try about eight o'clock."

"I just got a threatening call about the case," she said, her voice rising.

"Oh. You need a dispatcher then."

A man who identified himself as Carl Falls came on the line. Laura told him the details of the call and explained its connection with Joan's case. "Probably a wacko," the dispatcher said. "Lots of cranks out there read about a sensational murder and like to get in on it. They're usually harmless enough. Our policy is to take these reports over the phone. If you'd like, though, I can send a patrol car out to get a statement."

"How could a wacko get my phone number?"

"They're ingenious. They attend funerals and sometimes even pay a visit to the deceased's home and pretend to be an old friend."

Laura remembered the stream of people who had visited the Connors' home to pay their respects in the days preceding the funeral and that day itself. She had been introduced to most of them, and the fact that she was staying in her parents' condo might have been mentioned. It would never have occurred to her to be cautious with Joan's friends.

"You want a patrol car sent to your house?"

"I suppose not. I'll call Captain Quill tomorrow and see what he makes of the call." If he'll let me tell him about it, she added silently.

With her head still throbbing, Laura searched through the kitchen cupboards to find something that looked appetizing. Since Joan's death she'd had no interest in food, but she knew she should force herself to eat. She finally decided on a can of tomato soup. After heating it and pouring it into a bowl, she carried it to the living room. The menacing sound of the man's voice on the phone kept ringing in her ears, so she switched on the TV and settled down on the sofa to eat.

But her mind insisted on replaying the events of the afternoon. As she recalled her encounter with the undercover officers in Joan's house, she suddenly remembered Jake Marshall telling the other man to take down her address. And her phone number. She sat bolt upright, slammed the bowl of soup down and ran to the kitchen phone. When the police operator answered, she said, "I'd like to speak with a policeman named Jake Marshall."

"I'll check and see if he's available."

After several minutes, the man came back on the line. "I'm sorry, we don't show a Jake Marshall on the roll for this division. Are you sure you're calling the right station? You might try one of the outlying districts..."

Laura replaced the receiver with numb fingers. Now what? Who could she call and tell what had happened. Homicide wouldn't talk to her tonight unless she had a new murder to report. The bored-sounding dispatcher would only make a note that she had encountered two men in Joan's house, and that would probably languish in a file forever. If she called Diane, she would insist that Laura come to her house and spend the night, but what would that solve? And the Connors were certainly under too much stress to be given something new to worry about.

Who could she ask to help?

A name sprang into Laura's mind, but she rejected it instantly. Not him. Not Brandon Powell. No.

Sure, he'd offered his help, but probably only out of politeness. Anyway, after the way she'd told him off, he'd be in no mood to hear from her.

But who else was there? He'd said he was a private investigator, after all. Besides, the worst that could happen was that he'd say no.

She forced herself to reach for the telephone directory and turned to Private Investigators. "See Detective Agencies," she read. She flipped back to the *D*s. Dating Services. Dentists. Department Stores. Detective Agencies.

There. Her finger stopped at Brandon Powell, Private Investigator. Former Police Detective. Specializing in Missing Persons. Phone answered 24 hours a day.

Laura picked up the receiver and punched out the number.

A woman answered the phone. "Powell's."

"Laura Gibson. May I speak with Mr. Powell?"

"This is his answering service. If you have an emergency, I can beep him. Otherwise, I'll give him your number when he checks in for messages."

"No. No emergency." Laura read out the number.

Feeling strangely reassured, she went back into the living room and settled on the sofa, then tried to concentrate on what was happening on the TV screen. Realizing it was hopeless, she flipped off the set, lay back on the sofa and pulled an afghan over her. Within minutes, she was asleep.

The harsh jangle of the phone interrupted a dream some time later. Laura was jolted into alertness and jumped up, racing for the phone before she was even aware of where she was. As she caught sight of the kitchen phone, the memory of the threatening call stopped her in her tracks.

She stared at it as it continued to ring, trying to decide whether she should answer. Reluctantly, she picked it up. "Yes?"

"Laura Gibson? Brandon Powell returning your call."

"You returned my call!" she said, her voice breathless with relief.

He sounded wary. "Yes, what was it you wanted?"

"I'd...I'd...like to apologize for what I said this afternoon."

"Forget it."

"And I want to know if you are still interested in helping me."

There was a long pause, and Laura's heart climbed up into her throat.

BRANDON POWELL TRIED to think of a kind way to word his refusal. When he'd checked with his service and learned that Laura Gibson had tried to reach him, he had been delighted. The woman had been filtering through his thoughts since he'd seen her that afternoon. The cool self-possession she had had with Captain Quill was such a startling contrast to her fiery outburst at him that his passing interest had blossomed into an intense curiosity.

He had almost convinced himself to give her a call, but then common sense had prevailed. He didn't want to be the one to try to convince her that her friend had, indeed, been brutally murdered because her employer had sent her out without protection.

Escort services infuriated him, because they preyed on women. He'd been first on the scene at a couple of hellish murders similar to Joan Connor's when he'd been with the police department. The memories of those cases still haunted him, and he had no desire to get involved in another one. "After you left, I asked about your friend," he told Laura, carefully measuring his words so that she could absorb them in her obviously distraught state. "I believe the police are doing all they can."

Her voice sounded lifeless. "Of course. I forgot. You're friends with them. You would take their side."

Something about the call puzzled him. What had happened to make her change her mind about his offer to help? "It's not a matter of taking sides," he said. "I specialize in solving insurance-fraud cases and in locating missing persons. I wouldn't be much use to you."

"Her killers are missing."

Brandon nodded grimly. He remembered the tears he'd seen glistening in her eyes that afternoon. Maybe she just needed someone to share her loss with, someone to listen. Nights are always the loneliest times. "Look, Laura. I know how you're feeling. I lost a police friend when I worked there..."

"I didn't call for sympathy," she interrupted in a low voice. "I called because you're the only one who's offered to help. I got a threatening call tonight."

"What did the caller say?" he asked, alert now.

She ran through it, quietly and succinctly, and then added, "Just before I called you, I thought of someone I gave my phone number to this afternoon besides the receptionist at the police station."

"Who?"

As she described her visit to Joan's home and the men she had met there, he interrupted her several times. "You say Jake Marshall isn't listed in the police directory?" he asked.

"He's not. Is it possible the switchboard operator could be mistaken?"

"Possible, but not probable. The directory is computerized and up-to-date. If a man has official ID, he would have to be in the data bank."

"What about the ID I saw?"

"Easy enough to get. They sell fake ones at local flea markets."

"How could I have been fooled so easily? I suppose it was because I wanted to think the police were still working on the case. I did think it was strange that they weren't through checking out Joan's home. They were scheduled to finish the first day after the murder, her father said."

"The police went to your friend's home the day after the murder?" he echoed.

"Yes, Mr. Connor drove over to see if anything needed to be done. He went inside, but found he couldn't... Anyway, he was preparing to leave just as the police drove up."

"He must have been mistaken. Perhaps the police just wanted to talk to Connor, and his wife told them he had gone to their daughter's house. The police would make a detailed search of the murder scene, but it's unlikely they'd go through her home. There's no reason to believe the murderer even knew where she lived."

"No, I'm not mistaken. Mr. Connor said the policeman took him back inside the entry hall and talked with him a few minutes. He told him how hard the police were working to solve Joan's murder. Do you think that man was pretending to be a policeman?"

"It's hard to tell." There was a pause, and then he asked abruptly, "Are you there alone?"

Laura felt the chill of beginning panic. What did she really know about Brandon Powell? He could have overheard her giving her phone number to Captain Quill and made that call himself. "I'm at my parents'."

He seemed unaware of her growing suspicion. "Good. Frankly, I agree with the dispatcher. I'm sure you just got a crank call. But don't take any unnecessary risks."

Once more, Laura regretted misjudging him. The day's events had obviously unnerved her. She took a deep breath. "Mr. Powell, will you investigate Joan's death for me?"

"I don't think I can help."

"Do you only take cases you're certain you can solve?"

"No, but I wouldn't feel good about building up false hope in you. The truth is, these cases are seldom solved."

"*These* cases, Mr. Powell? Aren't you jumping to conclusions without even hearing the family's side?"

"Perhaps," he admitted grudgingly, impressed by her persistence. "But I still don't think I'm the one."

"I'd like you to try. Will you?"

Again, that long pause. "Let's give the police a little more time. For all we know, they already may be close to arresting the killers. My advice would be to call Captain

Quill tomorrow and tell him about the two men you saw in your friend's house, and about the anonymous phone call. Then sit back a few days and see what happens." He felt like a monster for refusing to help her. Something told him that she wasn't finding it easy to plead with him. If he'd felt there was even a remote chance that the police were wrong about her friend, he would have given the case a shot.

"Nothing's going to happen," she said, her tone laden with sarcasm. "Will you *at least* look into the case?"

There was a moment of tense silence before he replied. "Well, Miss Gibson. Since I can't seem to talk you out of it, I suppose it wouldn't hurt if we met somewhere, to at least talk about it. Mind you, it's against my better judgement, and I'm not making any promises."

She ignored his warning, too eager to pin his acceptance down before he changed his mind. "I understand. Just tell me where and when."

He sighed. "Eight o'clock tomorrow morning at the City Grill, two blocks down the street from the police station."

"I'll be there."

Brandon shook his head as he replaced the receiver. Why hadn't he stuck with his decision? While that incident with the two men claiming to be police officers did seem a bit strange, there was probably a perfectly logical explanation. Grief stricken people frequently got facts wrong and blew things out of proportion.

Just to be sure, though, he would check with Winn to see if the police really had decided to search the victim's home. In the meantime, he couldn't think of anyone he'd rather see across his breakfast table than Laura Gibson.

The problem was going to be keeping his mind on what he knew he had to do. He had to discourage her from wasting any more time trying to second-guess the police.

WHEN BRANDON ARRIVED at the City Grill a little before eight the next morning, he seated himself in his favorite booth at the back of the café, from which he had a good view of the street. At exactly eight, he was taking his first sip of coffee when he saw a gray compact car slide neatly into a narrow parking slot.

The car door flew open, a pair of long, slender legs clad in sheer stockings and a pair of high-heeled shoes emerged from the car. Brandon leaned back and watched appreciatively as Laura stepped onto the sidewalk. A halo of glowing auburn hair encircled her face. It had the shiny, slightly damp look of freshly washed hair and he could almost smell its fragrance.

She was dressed in a dark tailored suit with a white blouse and a dotted maroon bow spilling out at the throat. In her right hand she held a leather briefcase. Ms Efficiency, he thought. All business, except for her walk. That smooth, sensuous glide made him wish they were meeting for a different purpose.

She pushed open the door of the restaurant and paused, scanning the room. He kept out of her view momentarily, studying her. Those green eyes, which had been shimmering with tears the day before, were bright and alert now. Her nose was perfect, her cheekbones high enough to inspire a fashion photographer. Slightly intimidated by such perfection, he noted with relief that her mouth was rather full, and that she had just enough of an overbite to make her seem appealing and approachable.

He waved at her and she started toward him, smiling. He stood when she reached the table, and she held out a graceful hand with long, slender fingers, which he reached out to shake. Her grip was strong and assured. "I hope I'm not late, Mr. Powell," she said in a breathless voice. Before he was ready to release her hand, she slid it out of his grasp and seated herself.

"Just in time. Coffee?"

"Please."

Brandon motioned to the waitress. She came over, turned a cup upright on the table in front of Laura, and filled it. "Need a menu?" she asked.

Laura shook her head. "No, nothing to eat." She turned to Brandon. "I've made a list of everything that I think you may need. Where Joan worked, the names of her friends..."

Brandon glanced at the waitress. "A couple of buttermilk doughnuts for me." Then he turned back to Laura. "Slow down, Laura. You need to eat."

His gray gaze pierced through her and made the blood sing in her ears. He was just as attractive as she remembered, only more so. Glossy brown hair that looked as if he'd just run his fingers through it, casual but expensive clothes, compact body, smoldering eyes. A tough man with a surprisingly gentle way of watching, weighing, tuning in to others that was rare in the self-centered circles she moved in.

"Do you take such a personal interest in all your clients?" she asked.

A smile played around his lips, but his eyes retained their serious expression. "Only those who are spinning out of control. You're too intense about this. You remind me of the Ferris wheel I used to ride at the Texas State Fair. It always started out slow, and then it would gradually accelerate, going faster and faster until I was certain it was going to fly off and sail to the moon."

When she opened her mouth to protest, he said, "Some things you can't rush. In my business, you learn to be patient. It pays off."

Laura leaned toward him. "Most of the time that approach might work. But right now, there's at least one killer out there running free. Some other woman could be murdered tonight. Or do you agree with your friends at the police station that a woman who would go to a hotel room with two strangers just got what she deserved?"

As he watched the anger flare in those deceptively peaceful green eyes, Brandon Powell knew he had just climbed back on that Ferris wheel, and that he was in for a long ride.

Chapter Three

Brandon stretched out a hand and covered hers in a possessive gesture that so startled Laura that she did not withdraw her hand. "Let's get something straight, Laura," he said. "Twice you've accused me of siding with the police. My old police friends would find that very amusing. I resigned from the force because I couldn't agree with a lot that went on. That doesn't mean, though, that I don't think they're doing a great job. Think how upset you are over the loss of a friend. Imagine having to deal with a string of robberies, rapes and murders, and the people who are crushed in their wake. You'd build a mile-high wall around yourself to survive, and that wall is all the public gets to see."

Laura searched his gaze, then reluctantly moved her hand. When she spoke, it was to break the tension his intimate gesture had created. "Maybe I *am* jumping to conclusions. It's just that I'm so frustrated by the attitude I keep running into. Don't the police understand how desperately victims' families need to know that something is being done about the crime?"

"They understand, but they're too overworked to do much about it. That's why I resigned, so I could take cases that the police wouldn't have time for and handle them the way the officers want to, but can't."

She gave him a warm smile. "Then you'll take Joan's case?"

For the first time, he saw her face opening to him, like a rose through a time-lapse camera lens. He thought how comfortable it would be to sit here holding her hand. Just for a few minutes, the two of them, getting to know each other with no unsolved murder, no grief, no misunderstandings between them.

The spell was broken when the waitress arrived with the doughnuts. Brandon took one off his saucer and held it out. "Bet you can't eat just one bite," he said.

Her smile was wry this time as she took the doughnut from him. "It's delicious," she admitted, after her first bite.

He signaled the waitress. "Two more."

"You're not answering my question," Laura reminded him.

He pulled himself back to face the unpleasantness that had brought them together. "Tell me about your friend, and why you're so sure the police are on the wrong track."

Laura wiped the sugary icing from her fingers and opened her briefcase. She drew out a small photo. Brandon glanced at it. The fair-haired woman in the snapshot looked exactly the way one would want one's child's teacher to look.

"Joan was a gentle, shy, loving person," Laura said. "She taught creative writing in junior high school. She was the type of person who enjoyed simple pleasures like preparing a meal for a few friends and then listening to good music on the stereo. In her free time she wrote, mostly poetry." Laura stopped, too choked with emotion to continue.

It took some effort for Brandon not to reach over once more for Laura's hand. "How long had you known her?"

Laura swallowed. "Since I was five. There were three of us. One of our teachers called us The Three Musketeers, and it stuck. We met in kindergarten and went all the way through high school together. After that we went our separate ways, but we stayed in touch. Until last summer, we always held annual reunions and caught up with what had been happening in one another's lives."

"What was different about last summer?"

Laura sighed. "We all got too busy. I got a promotion; Diane, the other friend, was pregnant. Joan was teaching summer school. Maybe we were all growing apart in our interests, too."

"Any romantic entanglements in your friend's life?"

"As far as I know, there was no one special. She was engaged once, but about a year ago her fiancé died in a car accident. Joan's parents said she had one or two male friends, but hadn't really started dating again."

"How hard did she take her fiancé's death?"

"Not so hard that she didn't want to live without him, if that's what you're thinking. Of course she grieved terribly, but she was coping. She loved her job, and in her free time she wrote poems and short stories. The last time I talked to her she was full of plans for the future."

"Any financial worries?"

"No. She was comfortable, and her life-style wasn't showy."

"What about her relationship with her parents?"

"Very close. She visited them often. She was their only child."

"Why aren't they investigating her death?"

"They're not up to it. I lived with them for a year in high school, so they look on me as their second daughter. They desperately want me to convince the police that Joan would never have had anything to do with an escort service. I'm worried about how they'll take it if I have to tell them that the police won't even discuss that with me."

He finished his doughnuts and drained his coffee cup.

"Well," Laura said, impatient. "Will you?"

"Take the case?"

"Yes."

"Based on what you've told me, I can't rule out the escort-service angle. Maybe she was taking her fiancé's death harder than she let anyone know. Maybe she had a male friend her parents wouldn't necessarily have approved of, so she didn't mention him to them. Maybe she decided that the only way to forget was to throw off the traces and get into the fast lane. The pain of losing someone close can make a person skittish about new involvements, and maybe anonymous contact had an appeal..."

"No. Joan was too sensible for that. She would have dealt with the pain, not run from it."

She's got me almost convinced, he thought in surprise. "What exactly do you know about her murder?"

"Very little. The desk clerk allegedly received a call shortly after midnight from a man who didn't identify himself. The caller said to notify the police that there was a body in a certain room, and then hung up. The clerk called the police immediately. When the first policeman arrived, the clerk went upstairs with them and opened the door. Joan—" She stopped and swallowed, then, with a determined look, continued. "—Joan was already dead. She'd been beaten and shot. The room was registered to a Wallace Jones from Cincinnati, but the police haven't located him. Mr. Jones was accompanied by another man. He had told the clerk that they were expecting a visitor later that evening. The clerk said that a woman had come in and asked for Wallace Jones's room number. He identified Joan as that woman."

"Did the men check out?"

"No, they disappeared. The Crown is a large hotel. I understand it would be fairly easy to leave without being noticed."

Brandon sat for several minutes, drumming his fingers on the table. *Say no,* he kept telling himself. At last he looked up. "I'll investigate this case on one condition."

Laura leaned forward, her eyes glowing triumphantly. "What condition?"

Brandon returned her intent gaze. "That you hire me to prove that your friend was working for an escort service."

"What?" The green fire flared in her gaze. "Why? Why would I hire you to prove a lie?" She reached for her briefcase and glanced toward the restaurant door.

His voice cut off her retreat. "Because it's the quickest route. If I try to prove your friend wasn't working for the escort service, I won't know where to start. It'll be much more direct if I see if there is anyway to prove she did work for one."

Laura sagged against the seat, her eyes closing. Brandon noted how pale her skin looked in the harsh sunlight coming through the window. For a moment, he almost regretted confronting her this way; she was obviously under entirely too much stress as it was. But while he was sure that the fire in those eyes was a testament to some hidden strength, some inner resource, he had to get the measure of it now before the nightmare began in earnest.

Her eyes opened slowly. "I still don't like it, but I have to admit your argument makes sense. What are your rates?"

"Expenses only."

She gave an angry shake of her head. "You can't even pay for buttermilk doughnuts on expenses only."

"I can pay for caviar-filled doughnuts on the percentage insurance companies pay me for solving fraud cases. I name my fee, and it's expenses only on this one or no deal," he said harshly.

Silence stretched out between them. She was the first to break it. "When could you start?"

"Now. Nothing else I'm working on is critical. To be perfectly honest, Laura, I think I'll wrap this up before the day's over. Two days, at most."

She gave him a tight smile. "I wouldn't count on it."

Brandon put several bills on the table and scooped up the picture of Joan. "Let's get started. First, you need to file a report on what happened to you yesterday." He guided Laura out of the restaurant, nodding to the uniformed policemen who were seated on stools at the counter.

"Let's walk to the station," Brandon said as they emerged on the sidewalk. He took her hand in his. "Smell that great springtime air. It's perfect for running."

Laura felt a warm thread of pleasure coil through her at his possessive gesture. *You're just pleased that you talked him into taking the case,* she told unconvincingly. "You're right. I guess I haven't been paying much attention," she said, taking a deep breath. The air was crisp and fresh, a reminder that winter was behind her. She hadn't felt so alive in days.

When they neared the station she asked, "Do you think Captain Quill will see me this morning without an appointment?"

"I'll arrange that."

Brandon took her to a side door that led into a long hall that bypassed the reception area. He guided her down to the end and pushed open a door marked Homicide. An older woman in a maroon suit looked up and smiled when she saw Brandon. "What brings my favorite private eye here this morning?" she asked, her tone affectionate.

"My client wants to report a man impersonating a police officer, Leslie."

"Oh, so you're still doing that, are you?" the woman said. She gave Laura a wide grin. "Brandon impersonated an officer the whole time he worked here."

Laura joined in the laughter that swept the room. As the noise died down, she saw Captain Quill emerge from an adjoining room. He gave Brandon a disapproving look, then treated Laura to a similar one. "Good morning, Al," Brandon said. "Laura Gibson needs to see you." He turned to Laura, "I'll meet you at the front entrance when you're finished."

The captain frowned at Laura. She spoke quickly. "I need to report some new developments in the Connor case."

As the door closed behind Brandon, the captain asked, "What's he doing here?"

"I hired him to investigate Joan Connor's murder," she said.

"You're wasting your money. There's nothing he can do that the police aren't already doing."

"It's my money," Laura said.

The captain shook his head slowly. "Well, come on in and let's talk. I've got a busy morning ahead of me."

She reported the incident with the men at Joan's house, and then told him about the threatening phone call.

"This sounds like Burglary's bailiwick, so I'll mention it to them. Have you checked to see if anything's missing?"

"No. I will today."

"If you find anything's been stolen, give me a call. I'll send a patrol car to take the report."

"I don't think the men were thieves, Captain. Why would they allow me to see them?"

"Who do you think they were, Miss Gibson?"

She shrugged. "That's the question I was going to ask you."

"I never make guesses in my work." He stood. "If anything else happens, let us know here in Homicide."

BRANDON MADE HIS WAY to the police lounge after leaving Laura. "Anyone seen Winn?" he asked the group there.

"I saw him in the locker room a couple of minutes ago. He's just going on duty," a man answered.

"Thanks." Brandon went down the hall and entered the locker room. Winn was changing from a long-sleeved plaid shirt into his uniform.

"Got a minute?" Brandon asked.

"I've always got time for an old buddy. What brings you here this morning?"

"I need a little information." Brandon glanced down the row of lockers to see if anyone was within earshot. "About the Connor case."

"No need to lower your voice on that one. I told you it was routine. I'm not officially involved, but I've sat in on a couple of departmental briefings. If nothing turns up soon, it'll be filed with the rest of the unsolved call-girl murders."

"Since when do you search a victim's home when she was murdered in a hotel?"

Winn raised his eyebrows slightly. "Who says it was searched?"

"Joan Connor's father. What do you make of that?"

Winn brushed back his blond hair and took his time to answer. "Maybe they felt there'd be community pressure since the woman was a schoolteacher. You know how paranoid Quill is about public relations. He always makes sure the good citizens think we're doing a thorough job."

"It's not a high-profile neighborhood, but it's possible," Brandon conceded. Keeping the public happy was one of Quill's priorities, even if it was just for show.

"Wait a minute," Winn said, beginning to smile. "I thought I told you not to get involved in this case. What happened? Did being shot down by that pretty little redhead yesterday get to you?"

"I guess. She called me last night and apologized. I agreed to look into the case, but I told her I probably couldn't add anything to the police file. She's pretty persistent."

"And damn attractive. What do you want me to find out for you?"

"Anything you think would help. On the Q.T., though. I don't want Quill to slap your wrists."

"No problem. I'll let you know what's in the file. We're even allowed to tell the press anything we know on this one."

WHEN BRANDON JOINED LAURA in the front reception hall, he asked how her visit with Captain Quill had gone. "Fast," she answered. "He listened, said it sounded like Burglary's responsibility, and then sent me on my way."

"He didn't ask you to go through any mug shots?"

"Nothing. I told you the police aren't interested. What about you? Did you find out anything?"

"I started the process in motion."

She turned to him. "Tell me more than *that*. I want to know everything."

"I can't promise you that, Laura. I do promise to tell you everything when I'm finished. But I can't walk you through it, explaining what I'm doing or what I'm thinking. That's not the way I work."

His take-charge attitude was familiar to Laura. It was how she liked to work, with the freedom to take over an assignment and do it her way, without interference or help, unless she ran into trouble. "I need to feel that I'm involved," she said, hoping he would understand what she was saying.

"You will be. What's your schedule today?"

"The captain told me to check to see if anything is missing from Joan's house. I probably can't be certain since I hadn't been there recently until yesterday. I hate to ask the Connors to check, though."

"Let's go together. If I think a robbery's taken place, then it will be time to call the Connors."

"What about those two men? Do you think they could still be there?"

"I doubt it," Brandon said. "But let's find out."

At Brandon's suggestion, they took his car and left hers parked in front of the restaurant. As she slid into the black leather passenger seat of the shiny red car, she asked, "How could you conduct a surveillance operation in this without being noticed?"

He seated himself before answering. "James Bond drives a flashier one."

"James Bond swings from chandeliers and sets off explosions with a wave of his hand, too."

"Give me time and I'll master those, too."

She leaned back, smiling at him. She gave him Joan's address and relaxed in the seat in silence, enjoying his skillful handling of the car. Then she asked, "Are you a native of Dallas?"

He nodded. "You mentioned last night you live in Houston."

"I moved there five years ago. Now my company's folding, so I'm going to have to decide whether to look for work here or there. Dallas is my hometown."

"What kind of work do you do?"

"Personnel. I interview job applicants and make recommendations for employment."

"You're good at sizing up people?"

"I like to think so. This afternoon I'm going to interview Joan's friends and co-workers. Perhaps one of them will have some information that will help explain what Joan was doing in that hotel on the night of her murder."

Her words reminded them both of their grim mission, and they grew silent again. When they reached the turnoff for Joan's street, Brandon executed a smooth U-turn. Doubling back, he pulled into the crowded parking lot of a nearby grocery store. "We'll park here and walk to the house," he said.

She hurried after him, wishing she hadn't worn the high-heeled pumps when they cut across a lawn and down the alley leading to the back of Joan's house. "Do you think someone might be inside?" she asked.

"Not really. I thought you'd expect me to act this way." He glanced over at her, enjoying the sparkle in her eyes. His answer had been an attempt to distract her and preempt more questions. The truth was that he had a feeling the house would be under surveillance. It was just a hunch, and there was probably nothing to it, but he'd found that more often than not it paid to follow his hunches.

Laura pointed out Joan's house when they neared the back yard. "I have a key, but I don't know if it works on the back door."

"It's time you learned how to open a door without a key," he said. "This is what they leave out of Business 101." When they reached the back door, he took a key chain with a cluster of metal hooks on it from his pocket. After selecting one, he inserted it and jiggled it around. When nothing happened, he chose another and followed the same procedure until a click sounded and the knob turned in his hand.

"It makes one feel so secure," Laura murmured. "Can't you get in trouble for breaking into someone's home?"

"An acceptable risk in my line of work."

Brandon entered first, motioning for Laura to remain at the door. She watched as he made his way into the living room and then ran quickly up the stairs. He was out of sight for several minutes. When he finally reappeared, he said, "No one here. Let's walk through the house together and see if you notice anything missing."

Nothing seemed to have been disturbed since the day before. The book lying open on the kitchen table was still turned to the same page. A dictionary lay on the floor in the living room in the same spot; the lamp she'd turned off was still off. "Everything looks normal in here," she said, turning to Brandon.

He was studying the contents of the bookcase. "Proust. Cervantes. Your friend read these or keep them for show?"

"She loved those books. She was a good writer herself. Someday I think she would have written an important book."

"What was she writing?"

"She usually wrote poetry. But she tried her hand at fiction, too."

"Had she been published?"

"In literary journals."

Brandon rolled up the top on Joan's desk. "Is this where she kept her records?"

"School records?"

"No, financial."

"I don't know. I doubt that you'll find any mysterious entries in her checking account, if that's what you're hoping for." She wanted to work up some anger over the careless way Brandon was riffling through Joan's possessions. It might help keep a little of her grief at bay.

Brandon didn't answer. Instead, he opened each drawer and scanned the contents. Occasionally he would take something from an envelope and read it, but at length he closed the rolltop again. "Nothing interesting here," he said.

"What? No payroll stubs from the escort service?" she said.

"Where did you get your information about the way escort services pay their employees?" he asked, his tone bantering.

"The same place you got yours," she returned.

His only answer was a short laugh. "Let's go upstairs and look around."

Memories of the men rushing at her came back to Laura as she started up the narrow stairs. She was grateful for the reassuring warmth of Brandon's body close behind her. When they reached the upstairs landing, Laura pointed to an open doorway on her right. "That was Joan's room. She used the other one as a study and guest room."

"Let's go to the study first." Brandon led the way inside. This room was Joan's favorite, Laura remembered. Jim Connor had lined the wall with bookshelves, and they were filled now with books, interspersed with knickknacks and souvenirs from trips she had made on her summer vacations. A collection of small ceramic dogs, which Laura remembered Joan had started when she was six, brought back especially poignant memories.

"This was where she did her writing," she said, pointing to an ancient typewriter. Brandon walked over to a four-drawer file cabinet and pulled open one drawer. While he thumbed through it, stopping occasionally to peruse something more closely, Laura went through a letter-sized plastic file holder on the table beside the typewriter.

The first few papers she pulled out were poems. She started to read one, but found her eyes filling with tears and hastily stuffed them back in the folder. "Find anything?" Brandon said.

"What am I looking for?"

"Anything that you wouldn't expect to find in your friend's study."

"There won't be anything unexpected. I knew Joan almost as well as I know myself."

"People change."

Laura glanced up at the serious note in Brandon's voice. "Not Joan. I don't mean she couldn't change, but not in the way you're thinking."

Brandon didn't answer. After a few minutes he asked, "How about an address book? I didn't see one by the phone downstairs or in that other desk. Have you come across one?"

"No. I'm sure she kept one. I vaguely recall seeing a brown one beside the phone in the living room once. It was small."

"Small enough to keep in her purse?"

"No. At least it wasn't there. I looked through her purse when the police returned it to her parents. All that was in it was her wallet, a couple of pens, a lipstick and some tissues."

Brandon finished his search of the file cabinets, glanced around the rest of the room and then suggested they go into Joan's bedroom. He gave her another of the searching looks that made her feel warm all over. "If this is too hard on you, I can check that room by myself."

"No, I'll help," she said quickly.

Joan's bed was neat, its flowered spread decorated with frilly lace pillows. Brandon walked over and picked up a picture from the bedside table. It was a photo of a young man with a beard. "Her fiancé?"

Laura inspected it. "Yes. It's Sean McAble. I never met him, but she sent me several photos of him. They met a couple of summers ago when she took a group of students to London. They wrote for over a year, and then he requested a transfer from his import company to their Dallas office. I talked to him on the phone a couple of times. It's strange to think that both he and Joan were alive not long ago. Maybe there's a connection."

Brandon glanced up, his eyes alert. "I thought you said he died in a traffic accident. Did Joan ever say anything to make you think she was suspicious about his death?"

"Not a word. When I talked to her shortly after his death, she only mentioned that he wasn't the type to be careless. It was a rainy night, and his car was designed for high performance. I think it was a Jaguar, like yours."

"Demons for speed," he agreed. "I'll get a copy of the accident report and see what's listed as the cause of his death."

Brandon pulled open the top drawer of the bureau and went through the lacy undergarments quickly. Laura found it difficult to watch, so she want over and slid open a mirrored closet door. Most of the clothes she saw were unfamiliar, but occasionally she came across some item that she remembered and hurriedly slid its hanger past. When she came to the corner of the closet that held Joan's coats, Brandon said, "Check the coat pockets. People tend to forget what they stick in them."

Laura slipped her hands in the pockets of a camel's-hair coat but found only tissue. She did the same with two jackets, then came to a silver windbreaker, one she remembered well. Each of the trio had bought one at a military surplus store their senior year in high school. The jackets had proved to be indestructible, and Laura had laughed with the others about still wearing hers occasionally.

She searched the first pocket and found nothing, then felt around in the second one. Her fingers encountered a folded square of cardboard she identified as a matchbook.

Curious, since Joan had not been a smoker, she removed the matchbook and glanced down at it. Her hand froze as she read the lavish script: Classic Escort Agency.

Hide it. Don't let anyone see it, a voice inside Laura insisted. She turned with a guilty glance in Brandon's direction. He had dropped to one knee and was searching the drawers of the bedside table. Laura shoved the matchbook into the front of her blouse, her pulse pounding so loudly in her ears that she was certain Brandon had to be able to hear it.

His beeper emitted a shrill sound, and she started guiltily. "My answering service," he said. "Is the phone still working?"

"Yes...yes, I'm sure it must be. I haven't, that is, her parents haven't had the utilities turned off." *I'm babbling like I've lost my senses,* she thought.

Brandon gave her a speculative look but lifted the phone, dialed, and began speaking. Laura willed her weak legs to carry her out of the room and down the stairs.

When she reached the kitchen, she retrieved the matchbook and looked around for a place to get rid of it. Not the cabinets. Too obvious. The trash?

No, Brandon might search that next. If only the weather wasn't so springlike, she could light the gas logs and burn it in the fireplace.

Desperate, she located her purse and dropped the matchbook into a zippered pocket. What was the term for concealing evidence? Obstruction of justice?

She'd risk it, she'd risk anything to keep Joan's parents from seeing this. And she couldn't bear to have Brandon see it, either, although she doubted he was the type to gloat over being right.

BRANDON RETURNED only one call; the others could wait, but he wanted to speak with Winn to find out what he'd learned. As he waited for him to answer, he reviewed what he'd found in Joan's house. Not much of interest. Her bank statements were routine stuff. The personal letters made dull reading. Only one thing intrigued him. Where was her address book? Had someone who had been here before him made certain it wasn't available?

Winn's voice came on the line. "Brand."

"Yes. What's up?"

"Bad news. The file you want's been misplaced."

"Misplaced? What kind of garbage is that?"

Winn laughed. "You know how it is around here. It's holed up in someone's desk at the moment. Anyway, I doubt if the reports are finished. The paperwork's still the worst part of this job. I did get you some information, though."

"What?"

"Doug Young sat in on one of those briefings I was at, and said he was first on the scene. He happened to be in the neighborhood when he heard the call on his radio. He went to the hotel, and the clerk took him to the room."

Doug was one of the force's best undercover agents. But he wasn't attached to Homicide, so it seemed odd that he would get to one first. "What did he find?"

"A female, beaten and shot. It sounds like some weirdo freaked out to me. I'll bet he was just out of jail. I'd like to get my hands on those judges who let criminals roam the streets after we risk our lives arresting them."

"How about fingerprints?"

"The hotel room was filled with them. So far none have told us anything."

"Do you know the name of the escort service where she allegedly worked?"

"Sure. Classic."

Classic. My first bit of luck on this case, Brandon thought. Brandon had worked with Classic's manager, Lee Barber, on another call-girl murder his last year in the department. She was cooperative with the police and tried to run a better service than some, even though the best of the escort services were sleazy operations. "One more question. Who came to the hotel from Homicide?"

"Leslie and her old partner took the call, but everyone who was on duty showed up sooner or later. I was on vacation at the time or I'd be able to help you a lot more."

"You're doing great as it is. Just keep an eye out for that file."

"Sure. What are you paying me for this?"

It was an old joke between them, and it stemmed from more than friendship. Most policemen, whether they would admit it or not, appreciated the work private investigators did. It saved them a lot of time and legwork, and the department always ended up getting credit from the public for the crimes investigators solved. Brandon gave his standard answer. "Send me a bill."

Brandon hung up and looked around for Laura. She wasn't there. He glanced in the study, and then made his way down the stairs.

She was in the living room, sitting on the sofa, her shoulders hunched together as if she were chilled. As he stood there, he saw her body begin to tremble. Giving in to an instinctive impulse, he sat down beside her and put his arms around her lightly.

She leaned her head against him, seeking his warmth. His chest was hard and unyielding, and after a few moments she felt his strength beginning to soak into her. He pressed his face against her hair, and her trembling gradually ceased. In the circle of his arms, she was safe. Nothing could reach her. Nothing could destroy her.

"Laura, you've been here too long," he murmured. His voice echoed through her as his cheek brushed against her hair. What comfort to share her emotions with someone who understood what she needed, Laura thought. And then there was a subtle change.

She heard Brandon's breathing turn irregular as he pulled her closer and put gentle lips to her temple. The touch of flesh on flesh sparked a startling electricity in her.

Almost as quickly as she realized what was happening, she felt him pull back. "Let's go," he said. "I shouldn't have asked you to search your friend's house."

Search. How could she have forgotten? Not trusting herself to look at him, she turned away as she spoke. "You're right. We need to leave. Did you find anything?" Her tone was brittle, the words clipped, staccato.

He frowned. "Laura, what happened?"

She shrugged, palms up. "I thought you'd just diagnosed my problem. It's too much strain for me to search Joan's house."

He reached for her hands, but she clasped them together in her lap. "I'd be a pretty useless detective if I believed that. Laura, talk to me."

Chapter Four

Laura gave Brandon a round-eyed, innocent look. "I don't know what you mean."

"Yes, you do. You found something, didn't you? What is it? If I'm going to help, I have to know everything."

"You're crazy. What would I find?"

For the first time, Brandon understood how difficult it was to handle a case when you let yourself get personally involved with the client. None of the usual rather gruff techniques for extracting information could be used, but the need to have all the information seemed greater. What could he do? She'd been so warm and yielding when he'd held her that he hadn't wanted to let go. His hands had itched to move over her soft, supple skin, and his lips had been drawn to touch that throbbing pulse point. Now she was withholding something and from her reaction, something important.

Her long lashes dropped down to her cheeks, and he could see the trembling beginning again. This time he willed himself to sit still. She looked up at him with the soulful expression he remembered from the day before. Somehow, he had to break through to her, to intervene before she was lost in the fog, the shell she was crawling into.

He mustered his harshest tone. "I have other clients who feel they can trust me. If you won't tell me what upset you while I was on the phone, then I can't accept this case."

He watched her expel a long breath and then square her shoulders resolutely. "I found the proof you were looking for," she said, her head high.

"What proof?"

She picked up her purse from the floor beside the sofa and unzipped a pocket. Then she held up the matchbook. "Send me a bill for your expenses so far."

He took the matchbook from her hands, and his spirits sank when he saw Classic Escort Agency imprinted on it. Winn's information was confirmed. Managing to keep his expression bland, he asked, "Where did you find this?"

"In Joan's coat pocket."

"She smoked?"

"No."

Don't string her along with vague hopes. Just close the case and be done with it, he told himself. The message didn't get through. "Then why would she want a matchbook?"

"Maybe she walked down the street, handing them out to strangers she met." Her eyes glistened as she fumbled for a tissue in her purse.

"Stop torturing yourself, Laura. One matchbook isn't enough reason to throw in the towel."

"Isn't this the proof you wanted?" she asked.

"I keep remembering what you told me about Joan. Don't you think you at least owe it to her to find out why she wanted to work for a sleazy place like that? And why they didn't do anything to protect her? Let's go to the Classic Escort Agency and get some answers."

THE ESCORT AGENCY was headquartered in a multi-storied office building nestled among several hotels near Dallas's Market Center. Since Brandon had said the escort service was sleazy, Laura was surprised when they stepped inside. Obviously he was commenting on the nature of the service they provided and not the surroundings. The reception room was an island of decorator serenity. Beige raw-silk couches and chairs floated on plush beige carpeting, everything blending into the beige grass-cloth walls. Even the discreetly placed phones on the low tables were the same shade of champagne beige.

A tall woman with blond hair pulled back in an attractive chignon and wearing a pale green Ultrasuede dress was speaking on one of the phones. She directed a smile at Brandon and motioned toward an étagère containing an array of cut-glass decanters and crystal glasses.

He shook his head and walked over to a window, staring out at the Dallas skyline. Laura seated herself, trying without success to imagine Joan in this setting.

The woman ended her call and walked toward Brandon. "Liselle Brown," she said, holding out her hand.

Brandon shook it firmly. "Where's Lee?"

"On vacation. May I help you?" Laura studied the woman, fascinated by the low, well-modulated voice, by the level gaze, which seemed flattened out, as though a light inside her eyes had grown dim.

"You can give me a number where Lee can be reached," Brandon answered.

The woman's laugh sounded as false as her long, dark eyelashes. "I don't believe I know you."

"Brandon Powell. I'm a friend of Lee's, and I need to talk to her."

"If you'll leave a number where you can be reached, I'll give her your message. That is, if she calls in. If you're a friend, you must know she is finally taking that long vacation she's been promising herself for ages."

Laura watched as Brandon reached in his pocket and pulled out a business card. "Tell Lee I'm investigating the murder of Joan Connor."

The receptionist's gaze narrowed slightly. "Perhaps I can help you. What did you want to know?"

"How long had Joan been working here?"

She pointed to a chair beside Laura and walked over and seated herself directly across from them. "I've turned all our records over to the police, but I can remember that Joan started in August. She was such a lovely person. It's still hard to believe..." She looked down and swallowed. "This isn't easy to talk about. I was a personal friend of Joan's."

Brandon ignored her patently false emotional distress. "Were you the one who sent her to the hotel that night?"

"I was the one on duty. I have nightmares about it, wondering if there was some way I could have known she was walking into a dangerous situation."

"Who was the man?"

"I told the police the name the man gave me. Wallace Jones. The police think that wasn't his real name."

"No," Brandon said derisively. "Did he ask for Joan by name?"

"You must know we use professional names."

"What was Joan's?"

"I'm not sure I should tell you. But to answer your first question, no, the man did not ask for Joan. He said he wanted someone attractive, a blonde, and on the quiet side. Joan fit that description perfectly, so I called her. She agreed to go right to the hotel." Liselle glanced down again. "That was the last time I spoke with her."

"She didn't check in with you when she reached the hotel?" Brandon inquired in a sharp tone.

Liselle looked confused for a moment, but recovered quickly. "Oh, you're right. She called and said she was there, but that was a professional call. I meant the last time we talked as friends."

"Did she say anything that would have made you suspect she was worried about what she saw when she got to the hotel?"

"Nothing. Really, Mr. Powell, you ought to be a policeman. You ask more questions than they did."

"I used to be a police detective. Were you and Joan friends before she began working here?"

"No, we met here."

"Well, since you were friends, did Joan ever tell you why she decided to work here?"

The woman shrugged. "I suppose she was like the rest of us, wanted to make some money. Isn't that why everyone works?"

"Cut it," Brandon said, his tone harsh. "You're not talking to the press, Liselle. Joan wasn't your typical call girl. She wasn't a drug user. She wasn't in any financial trouble. She had plenty of friends and a close family, so something smells."

Liselle's face hardened, and for the first time she gave Laura more than a cursory glance. "Who are you?"

"My assistant, Laura Gibson," Brandon inserted smoothly. "When did Lee leave town, Liselle?"

"About a week ago."

"Before or after Joan's murder?"

"I don't have time to answer all these questions. I have some calls I need to make."

"And I have some friends in the D.A.'s office who just might think it damned strange that the manager of the

Classic Escort Agency wouldn't even show up at the funeral of one of her beloved employees. Especially since that employee was killed in the line of duty."

"Get lost," Liselle said, two blotches of red marring the perfectly made-up cheeks. She stood and glanced down at the card she was holding. When she spoke, her voice was lifeless again. "I'll tell Lee you were here."

"Do that," Brandon said.

When they reached the hallway Laura asked, "Was it wise to make her mad?"

"I had to jar her so she'd contact Lee soon." He shook his head. "Something's phoney about this."

"What?"

"Lee leaving town about the time of the murder. It doesn't make sense. I worked on a murder case my last year in the department involving one of Lee's girls. Lee took it pretty hard, and she cooperated in every way possible. She wouldn't just go off on a vacation with this up in the air." He grew silent as they entered the elevator. After a brief time, he said, "What did you think of Classic?"

"It wasn't what I expected. Very elegant. Very proper. Why did you call it a sleazy operation?"

"It's only elegant on the surface. The women who work here live rotten lives. Most of them are drug addicts. A few of them sign on for a lark at first or to make big bucks, but gradually it destroys all of them."

"How about Lee Barber? You told that woman she was your friend. Why should she run a business like this?"

"I don't know Lee well enough to know. She probably had a rough time when she was younger, but now she tries to stay out of trouble. I don't know who first bankrolled her operation; probably an old boyfriend who's faded out of the picture by now. She gives me the impression of being a shrewd businesswoman, especially about her customers. They come by referral only, so Liselle's story about the man just calling and ordering a woman like you would a pizza was a lie. Of course, a weirdo could slip through if he used the name of a regular customer who was out of town as a referral. It's happened to Classic before, but it's not like Lee to ignore something like that. The last time she was jumping all over the police to make them find out the identity of the murderer."

"What are the customers like?"

"As a rule, they're successful businessmen; they have to have money to pay the expensive fees. For those fees they expect experienced, sophisticated women their associates will envy. Would Joan have fit in?"

"Not in a million years. She certainly knew what fork to use, if that's what you mean. But she wasn't the type to pretend to be something she wasn't."

Brandon nodded. "That's why I wanted you to go there with me." When they reached the ground floor, he glanced at Laura and saw the deep frown on her face. "Lunchtime," he said, his voice cheerful. "There's a great Greek restaurant in this building."

Laura glanced at him in surprise, her mind still on what they had been discussing. "It can't be time to eat. We just had breakfast."

"Over four hours ago, and you didn't even finish your doughnuts." His gaze ran slowly from her burnished head down the curved line of her breast, waist and thigh, to the long slender legs. "A good wind would blow you away. Let's order the house salad for two. It's loaded with feta cheese, great anchovies, and the best Greek olives in the city."

Tension made Laura's stomach rebel at the thought of food. "I'm not hungry, but I'll drink something cool while you eat."

Brandon smiled wryly. "Don't bother. I'll run you back to your car and pick up a hot dog near my office. That ought to keep my expense sheet low."

Laura caught his smile, but wondered if underneath it he thought that was the reason she'd refused him. Embarrassed, she protested, "You're making me feel terrible."

"If you don't start forcing yourself to eat, you're going to feel worse." They reached his car and he helped her inside. Within moments they were driving down the street toward her own car. "This afternoon I have several people lined up to see."

"Concerning Joan's case," she asked hopefully.

"I hope so. At this stage I'm just guessing."

"Can I help? After all, I am your 'associate.'"

He grinned. "I didn't want Ms Professional Name to know you were Joan's friend. The people I want to see this afternoon might not talk freely in front of you. Why don't you interview some of Joan's friends, and we'll meet at my office around six and compare notes. Is that convenient?"

"Oh, it is." She had hated turning down Brandon's invitation to lunch. She enjoyed being with him immensely, but her head had started to throb again, and even the thought of food made her feel sick. Finding the matchbook and then seeing the woman who claimed to have sent Joan to the hotel brought the reality of Joan's death home to Laura, made it more real than even the funeral had. Maybe talking to Joan's friends, people who knew her and loved her, would help put things into perspective. When they reached her car, Brandon waited until she was safely inside before he left.

Laura drove directly to the school where Joan had taught. It was a rambling one-story structure in the middle of a large tract of land with only a few trees breaking the monotonous landscape. Rows of bicycles were lined up in racks, and over on one side was a staff parking lot. Laura parked in front of the building in a slot designated Visitors Only.

Following the signs that gave directions to the school office, she pushed open the door and went inside. The school secretary, Pat Turner, came from behind the counter and hugged Laura when she saw her. Pat was a thin, bright-eyed woman that Laura remembered meeting at the Connors' home a few days earlier. "I'm so glad you stopped by," Pat said. "Did you hear about the car wash Joan's students held on Saturday? They're going to use the proceeds to start a scholarship fund in her memory."

Laura's eyes squeezed shut momentarily. "What a wonderful tribute. Pat, do you think I could talk to a few of Joan's closest friends during their breaks this afternoon? I'm trying to find out if any of them know anything that could help solve the crime."

"I'm sure you can. I'll let them know you're in the lounge so they can stop by. One thing you'll find out is that not a single one of them believes that story the police are telling. Joan did *not* go to that hotel for the purpose they say."

"I know she didn't. Now all I've got to do is find out why she *was* there. Did you talk to her much?"

"Every morning and every afternoon," Pat said. "First thing every morning she would come by and check her box and chat for a few moments. She did the same every afternoon before she left."

"Those last few days. Did she talk about anything in particular?"

Pat nodded. "How tired she was. She was staying up late to finish something she was writing."

"What?"

Pat shrugged. "I really didn't ask. Joan had been writing ever since I knew her. She wrote me a poem for my birthday, and last year one of her short stories won a contest in a writers' magazine. Lately she seemed very pleased with her work, as if she thought it was her best yet."

"Do you know anyone who might know what she was writing?"

Pat tilted her head to one side. "Perry Hill might. He's a music teacher. His classroom is next to Joan's, and they were close friends. Not dating or anything like that, just friends. He came to work here shortly after Joan's fiancé died. Perry's wife died a couple of years ago, so there was a special bond between them. They shared a lot of interests, too. Both of them had season's tickets to the ballet, and I think Joan was teaching Perry how to cook some of those fabulous dishes she used to make." She stopped and called out to a young girl who was entering the office. "Cheryl, would you got to Mr. Hill's room and tell him that Laura Gibson wants to talk to him in the lounge when he goes on his break?" After the girl left, Pat turned back to Laura. "One of our student helpers. I like to keep them busy."

Laura remembered Perry from the funeral. The fortyish, silver-haired man cried without restraint during the service. Afterwards he had apologized for his show of emotion, and had offered his condolences to the Connors. His name was the first one on the list of people she wanted to see today.

A small plump man, bald on top with a fringe of short brown hair above his ears, came out of an adjoining office. "Mr. Morton, our principal," Pat said. "This is Laura Gibson, Joan's friend."

"Yes, I met her at the funeral. Sad occasion. We're finding it hard to get along without Joan these days. Her students are devastated."

"I heard about the scholarship. What a great bunch of kids you must have here," Laura said.

"Junior-high students can surprise you. One moment they're children, the next, adults. A challenging age to work with."

"Could I ask you a few questions about Joan? I'm working with a private investigator to try to solve the case."

"Certainly. Come right in," Mr. Morton said.

Except for a glass case full of trophies on the wall behind him, the office was as unpretentious as the man. When they were seated, he asked, "What did you want to know?"

Laura tried to remember what Brandon had asked her when they were searching Joan's apartment. "Was there anything different about Joan in the past few months?"

He glanced down. "Joan was an outstanding teacher. Her classes were innovative, and she was always well-prepared." He cleared his throat before proceeding. "However, the last few months she was not exactly on top of her job. I wouldn't want her friends to know this, but I was worried about Joan."

"Worried?" Laura wasn't certain she wanted to hear what he would say next.

"She had always been punctual, but at least seven times in the last month she arrived after eight o'clock."

A smile tugged at the corners of Laura's mouth. School principals hadn't changed much. "Did she offer any excuses?"

"Oh, yes. She said she had been up late nights working on a writing project. I believe she told me she didn't hear her alarm."

Up late nights? Laura tried not to think about the implications of that.

"There were other problems. She handed in inaccurate attendance reports, and didn't get her grades in on time, either."

Laura conceded that that didn't sound like Joan. She forced herself to ask, "Do you think she was working at another job, moonlighting?"

"Not as a streetwalker," the principal said, his face turning beet-red. "The problem was her writing. Now, I encourage my teachers to have hobbies and to improve their skills. But she was carrying it a bit too far. When I pointed that out to her, she promised that as soon as she finished her current writing project, she would have no more problem."

Laura leaned forward, "Surely she told you what she was writing?" Joan had never discussed her projects, explaining that she had an irrational fear that if she talked about them, something would happen to keep her from finishing them. But confronted by her principal, Laura thought, she might have broken her rule.

"I didn't inquire. I'm sure it was something for one of the journals where she'd been published before."

"The police are convinced that Joan was working for an escort agency," Laura said flatly.

"I think the media must have started that lie. They're so irresponsible, always looking for something sensational to report. I'm sure the police will uncover what really happened soon."

"Let's hope so," Laura said, standing. "Thanks so much for your time. If you think of anything else, or hear anything that might help me, I'd appreciate your giving me a call."

When she came out of the principal's office, Pat Turner met her at the door. "Perry's on his break now. He's waiting for you in the teachers' lounge. It's the third door on the left."

Laura hurried down the hall and pushed open the lounge door. Perry Hill, dressed in a navy blazer and a pair of checked pants, sat on a green vinyl couch. He stood and came toward her. "Miss Gibson, I'm so glad to have the chance to talk to you." He was obviously struggling to maintain his composure. "The other teachers here loved Joan but they didn't know her the way I did. Joan and I had become very close friends. I don't know what I'm going to do without her."

"I know what you mean," Laura said, concerned by the extent of his distress. "Please call me Laura. I feel someone who was such a good friend of Joan's will be my friend, too."

He hunched his shoulders and moved back to the sofa. Laura sat down on a chair beside it. "Pat tells me you've hired a private investigator," Perry said. "Don't you think the police are doing their job?"

"They have a lot of cases to work on. Brandon Powell, the investigator I contacted, hasn't promised to take the case yet. He said he'd start by finding proof that Joan was working for that escort agency."

"Why, that's ridiculous! It's a damn lie."

Laura found herself defending Brandon. "No, he merely thought it was the place to start. He hasn't been able to convince himself yet, so he's following up every lead he can. I'm trying to help. I thought the best place for me to begin was with her friends. Do you know anything, Perry? You and Joan were very good friends."

"Her closest." He gave Laura an apologetic smile, "Except for you and Diane, of course. Joan told me all about 'The Three Musketeers.'"

"We didn't see much of one another over the last year. I'm grateful she had you, Perry. You can probably be of more help than anyone else."

"How? I can't forgive myself for what happened. I keep feeling that if I'd done something differently I could have prevented it."

"I know that feeling. When was the last time you saw Joan before that night?"

"At work the same day. The evening before, I went by her house, but she told me she was too busy for a visit. I teased her about writing the great American novel..."

"Is that what she was writing? A novel?"

"She didn't say, and I certainly didn't ask. I knew how superstitious she was about it. I suspect, though, that she was working on a story based on Sean's life. He died before I met her, and at first she seemed to be handling her loss quite well. But then the delayed reaction set in and over these last few months, she had become obsessed with him."

Laura's expression betrayed her surprise. "I had no idea. I thought she was handling her grief as well as could be expected."

"It wasn't grief, exactly. She seemed almost elated about something. On several occasions when we were out together, she had me drive by places that reminded her of him."

"Just drive by?"

"Yes. Slowly. Sometimes we'd circle the block. I think it gave her comfort. I didn't question her about it. After my wife died, I used to go to the places we'd gone together and just sit, recapturing those moments."

Laura had trouble imagining Joan giving into that kind of morbidity—or tolerating it in someone else. It was hard to believe she had been close to Perry. The friendship must have been based on the compassion Joan had always felt for those in need. "Did she talk about Sean constantly?"

"No, that's not the way it works. You just want to relive the moments you've spent together. For instance, Joan got a call from a Jaguar dealer when I was at her house a few weeks ago. That's what Sean drove. I think she wanted to buy one."

"On a teacher's salary?"

"Sure, it was just a dream. But it was important to her. I saw a brochure listing Jaguar parts and their prices on the desk in her study just a week before she died. I think she was trying to decide if she could afford the upkeep."

Strangely, the brochures weren't there now. "Joan was always so sensible about money," Laura protested. "Maybe she thought she was going to be paid well for this writing project she was working on. Tell me what you know about it."

"It kept her busy. She quit inviting me for those delicious home-cooked meals, and started eating frozen dinners to save time for her writing."

"So I noticed, when I was in her kitchen. That doesn't seem like Joan."

"Like I say, when you're obsessed, you do things differently. I know. I've been there myself."

"Obsessed sounds like a strange way to describe Joan. She was always so well-adjusted, so in control of herself."

"Then how do you explain her behavior?"

Laura thought about his question, and had to admit she had nothing to offer in the way of an explanation. Remembering her talk with Brandon that morning, she knew what she had to find out. "Would you say this obsession of Joan's could have changed her so radically that she'd take a job with this escort service?"

"Never," Perry said. His eyes brimmed over, and his voice hoarsened. "Over and over again I ask myself why I didn't insist on seeing her that night. I knew she needed a break from all the writing she was doing, but I didn't try hard enough. If I'd been there, she wouldn't have ended up in that hotel room."

"You can't blame yourself," Laura said, attempting to console him. She knew he would soon be returning to a classroom full of lively seventh- or eighth-graders and would need to be in control of himself again. She stood up and went over to him, placing a comforting hand on his shoulder. "We're going to learn the truth soon, and then we all can stop speculating about why Joan was in that hotel room that night."

He placed his hand over hers and looked up with a grateful expression. "I think I know why," he said quietly.

Chapter Five

"What! Why do you think Joan went to the hotel?" Laura asked Perry eagerly.

"I think she went there to see someone who had known Sean, a friend of his perhaps, who was passing through town and gave her a call. I'm sure she would have leaped at the chance to talk to someone who had known him. Have the police contacted Sean's friends to see if they recognize the name of the man who was registered in that room?"

Laura thought over Perry's theory. "You may have something there," she said with cautious optimism. It was the first explanation she'd heard that made any sense, but it left a lot of unanswered questions. Why had that woman at the escort agency said that Joan worked there, and why would one of Sean's friends want to kill her? Still, she'd mention the possibility to Brandon.

The bell that signaled change of classes sounded, and Perry stood up. "That means my free period's over. Miss Gibson—Laura—this has meant a lot to me to have a chance to talk things over with you. Maybe we can get together and come up with some more answers."

"I'd like that, Perry." She wrote out her parents' phone number on a slip of paper. As she handed it to him, she wondered for a moment if she should give her number after her anonymous phone call, then flushed guiltily.

THE TEMPERATURE WAS in the low eighties, and the sun was bright as Brandon made his way to the police station after letting Laura off at her car. He stopped first at the traffic desk and filled out a form requesting the printout on the accident that had taken Sean McAble's life. Although he considered it unlikely that there was any link between the two deaths, he'd learned never to overlook any detail. Sometimes the most unlikely clue was the one which solved the case.

While he waited for the accident report, he wandered from room to room looking for Doug Young. He finally located him in Ballistics. Doug was dressed in his usual low-slung jeans and a knit shirt with a tasteless catch phrase printed on the front. His chin was covered with stubble, as if he'd forgotten to shave that day. Brandon knew it was all merely a part of his disguise.

Doug had the reputation of being the department's most savvy undercover agent. More than once he'd received citations for the dangerous operations he'd conducted. While Brandon had been on the police force, their relationship had been cordial. Now it was adversarial and remote, based on a grudging mutual respect.

Brandon suspected that Doug resented it whenever an investigator solved a case the police had given up on. Whenever it was to his benefit to exchange information, though, he was willing to swallow his resentment. "What's up?" he asked Brandon.

"Got time for a cup of coffee?"

"If you're buying," Doug said with a grin.

They went outside and crossed the street to a small diner. Once they were seated, Brandon said, "I hear you were the first on the scene of the Connor murder."

"Why is that any of your business?"

"A friend of hers hired me to make it my business."

"I was there, all right," Doug said.

"Why?"

"I was just going off a stakeout down the block when I heard it on my car radio."

Brandon shook his head skeptically. "Since when does an undercover officer show up at a murder scene? Both of us know you'd never risk blowing your cover unless a lot was at stake. Come on, Doug. The Connor woman's murder is connected to one of your operations, right?"

Doug took a long gulp and wiped off his mouth with the back of his hand. "I wasn't too worried about blowing my cover. Murderers don't usually hang around the scene of the crime, so who would know I was first at the scene? For that matter, how do you know?"

"You know I have my sources. What kind of connection were you looking for that night? Is Lee Barber involved in something besides running a call-girl operation?"

"Could be. If I knew, we'd move in and everything would be over. I'm in the middle of something, and if you're smart, you'll stay out of the way."

"I'm staying in until I find out what's happening. At least give me a motive for the murder. Was it a psycho killing?"

Doug shook his head decisively. "No, it was a professional job. A few pieces of furniture were overturned to make it look weird, but I'd say it was well-planned."

Brandon showed his surprise. "Does Homicide agree with you?"

"How would I know? Quill's mum as a clam on this one."

"Do you think they're still working on it?"

He shrugged, grinning. "What does Winn say?"

No answer was expected.

SEAN MCABLE'S REPORT revealed nothing unusual. Sean was alone, driving over the speed limit, though not dangerously so, in a rainstorm. He went around a curve, lost control of the car and hit a brick wall. According to the coroner's report, he died instantly.

As for personal facts, McAble was a resident alien from the United Kingdom, working for a British importing firm on a green card. He was 31 years old. His car, a late-model Jaguar, was totally demolished.

Brandon folded up the report and put it in his pocket. Back to square one now.

LAURA HAD TIME to go by the Connor home and report to Mrs. Connor that she had been to Joan's school. She also mentioned that she had engaged a private investigator to work on the case. Mrs. Connor seemed surprised. "Is that necessary?"

"The police are busy, and Joan's case is just one of many to them," she explained.

"Is the investigator expensive?"

"No, he's... a friend," Laura said lamely.

Mrs. Connor, an older version of Joan, with the same lively blue eyes and the same blond hair, streaked now with gray, gave her a smile. "Then that's different. I hope he can find out the truth soon."

"He will," Laura said. "How is Mr. Connor feeling?"

A shadow passed over Mrs. Connor's face. "He doesn't complain. The doctor is trying out a different blood-pressure medication on him. He is still cautioning against getting upset about anything, but I'd like to know how we're supposed to make sure he follows that order."

Laura patted Mrs. Connor's hand. "Perry Hill said to give you his love."

"Perry is nice," she said. "Joan was always trying to cheer him up. His wife was ill for a long time before she died, and Perry cared for her at home. Last Thanksgiving we invited him for dinner. Diane and Bob came, too." Her eyes began to fill with tears.

Laura broke in quickly, "Several people mentioned to me that Joan had been working very hard on a writing project lately."

Mrs. Connor glanced up, forcing a smile. "Yes, she was. Spending hours on it. I hadn't seen her that happy in months."

"What was she writing?"

"Don't you remember her superstition?"

Laura nodded. "When I was with her a lot, though, she usually let something slip. A few months ago she mentioned something to me about publishing a book of her poems."

Mrs. Connor grew thoughtful. "Yes, she still wrote poems, but this was something different. She said something once, I'm not certain what, that made me think she was writing a magazine article."

"Non-fiction?"

"She could write anything she wanted to. Don't you remember that she worked on the high-school newspaper?"

"That was because journalism was the only writing course our high school offered. Joan always preferred creative writing."

"I'm probably just mixed up," Mrs. Connor said, her voice suddenly dispirited again.

Laura looked at her watch, then leaned over and kissed Mrs. Connor. "Time for me to meet with the investigator now. I'll talk to you soon."

AS SHE DROVE TOWARD Brandon's office, she tried to organize what she'd heard so that it would make sense when she reported it. She was looking forward to seeing the look on his face when his able assistant checked in. The truth was that she was simply looking forward to seeing him again. There was something so satisfyingly right about him. The right eyes, the right gestures, the right voice, as if she had known him before, or half-remembered him from her dreams. How ridiculous, she decided. Surely she didn't believe in that business of love at first sight.

The address Brandon had given her was on the fringes of the downtown area. She double checked it to make certain she was in the right place when she drove by it the first time. It was a five-story building, made of the rough limestone popular at the turn of the century and set at an angle so that its entrance faced the corner.

She parked in the rear and walked around to the main entrance. Inside, she stopped to admire the dark, wood-paneled lobby and the black-and-white tiled floor. When it was new, nearly a century earlier, it must have been a showplace.

The lobby was empty except for an elderly man presiding over a small newsstand. He greeted her as she walked toward the elevator, and then returned to a magazine he was reading.

Laura had no difficulty locating Brandon's office when she reached the third floor. She pushed open the door and walked inside. There was something about the room that made her feel she'd stepped back in time into a doctor's office from a past generation.

Brandon entered the room. "Hi. Have any trouble finding me?"

"Your directions were great."

"I have a fresh pot of coffee. Want a cup?"

"No, thanks." She already had a case of caffeine jitters from a cola she'd drunk at Joan's school.

"Come to my office while I have one, then. You can tell me what you learned."

She followed him into a larger room that looked down on the parking lot. This room, too, gave her the feeling that she was about to be ministered to by a kindly old family doctor. "Was this once a doctor's office?" she asked.

Brandon finished pouring himself a cup of coffee and pointed to a chair as he perched on the edge of his desk. "My dad and his father before him were both doctors. This was their office. I inherited it, but as you may have guessed, I don't spend much time here. My car's really my office, and the only secretary I have is the answering service. How did your afternoon go?"

She settled into the worn leather chair he'd indicated and was swallowed up in its dark coolness. "I went to Joan's school and talked to some people. How about yours?"

"So-so. Did any of Joan's friends say anything that might help?"

She felt a flash of irritation that he didn't intend to share what he'd learned, but she hid it quickly, remembering what he'd said about his methods. "I think I'm on to something, but I'd like to hear your reaction. Let me tell it just as I heard it."

"Good," he said, his gray eyes intent.

Laura filled him in on the principal's report of Joan's recent actions, and the writing project everyone had mentioned. Then she described her meeting with Perry and his belief that Joan was obsessed with thoughts of Sean. When she was finished her green eyes glowed. "What do you think?"

"I think I'd better check out this Perry character."

"Oh, great! I have a real future in this business, I can tell. I report to you that Joan is absorbed in a writing project, obsessed with her dead fiancé and thinking of buying a Jaguar, and you think poor Perry is more important? Either you need a refresher course, or I need a crash course in how to spot a suspect."

A slow smile spread across Brandon's face. Laura was irresistible when she was all agitation and energy. He found it hard not to give in to the temptation to send her into orbit at every opportunity. "I heard every word you said. Maybe I've missed something, but what's the connection between Joan's murder and these other events?"

"I don't know yet. For one thing, Perry wondered if perhaps Joan was writing a story about Sean. And he had a theory that the man in the hotel room might have been a friend of Sean's who called Joan to invite her over for a chat."

"That's assuming she wasn't involved with the escort service. Otherwise, this friend of Sean's would have had to go through them."

"None of Joan's friends believe she was involved with Classic. Talking to them has made me even more certain that there's some other reason why that matchbook was in her coat pocket."

"What reason?"

"You're the detective," Laura said with sarcasm. "At least I found out *something*."

"Ouch," he said. He set down his cup, stood up and walked over to a table across the room. "I'm not giving you a hard time, Laura. I just want you to get in the habit of thinking through everything you're told about Joan. From what you've told me, Perry sounds like he's just taking wild guesses so he won't have to feel guilty. The guy sounds a little strange to me, talking about obsessions. You said Joan was normal."

"She was normal, and so is Perry."

He grinned. "Have it your way." He had to admit that he was taking an instant dislike to Perry Hill, sight unseen. Perhaps it was because it sounded like the guy was trying to play on Laura's sympathies instead of offering her support in her own grief. Besides, Perry had been a little too quick to come up with a theory. It wouldn't hurt to check him out. "Want to help me start putting these clues together?" he asked Laura.

"That's why I'm here," she said, her tone cool. Brandon's failure to be impressed with her findings was still irritating her.

"Then I'll show you how I work." He took a roll of white paper from a shelf under the tabletop and rolled it out. "I tack this on a wall when I'm working on a complicated case. Then I write every clue I get on it, even if I think it's probably worthless. When I have enough of them, I draw lines between the ones that have connections. Eventually the answer jumps right off the paper."

She joined him and held one end of the paper while he tacked it to the wall. He handed her a pencil. "Now write everything you know that might help us."

"What?"

"Names. Places. Events. Whatever comes to mind."

"Okay." She scribbled: Jake Marshall. Classic Escort Agency—August. Crown Hotel. Wallace Jones. Writing project. Joan—tardy. Jaguar. Sean McAble. Matchbook—coat. Seeing the clues listed, she felt discouraged.

What possible connection could all these unrelated items have with Joan's murder?

Brandon moved closer and took the pencil from her hand to add a few items. As their hands touched, he fought the urge to turn her around and place his lips on hers. He dropped his hand and moved back, reminding himself that she was a client, with a case that was beginning to baffle him.

Laura sighed. "I thought this was going to be easy, but it's getting more complex by the minute. Why doesn't someone come forward and tell the truth about what Joan was doing?"

Brandon longed to comfort her, but he knew there was nothing he could say at the moment. "I think we've worked enough today. How about dinner at a place near here where there's a hot trumpet-and-piano duo on Monday evenings?"

Shaken by his nearness, Laura started to say yes. She enjoyed Brandon's company, and being with him kept her grief at bay, but she wondered if he was only being kind. She'd already sensed how much empathy he had for other people's sorrows. Anyway, she wasn't hungry. Her appetite had disappeared the night she'd learned about Joan. Maybe it would never return. "Thanks, but I should go to Diane's tonight."

"What have you eaten so far today?" he asked, his tone gentle.

"Diane will have dinner," she said defensively. There was that concern again. It made her feel vulnerable and off balance.

"You haven't answered my question."

Although he had moved back across the room, she could almost feel his warm touch. She cleared her throat and answered, "A doughnut with you. And I had a Coke at

Joan's school." She hadn't realized how little she'd eaten. "Mrs. Connor made tea. I had milk in it," she added quickly.

"Oh, well, as long as you put milk in your tea, I don't know why I'm worried," he mocked.

She smiled. Why was she refusing his invitation? "On second thought, I will go with you," she said. She glanced down at the suit she'd been wearing all day. "Should I change and meet you somewhere?"

"You look great." He picked up his jacket from the rack where it was dangling and slipped it on. Then he rebuttoned the top button of his shirt and tightened the knot in his tie.

"I'll call Diane and tell her I won't be over," Laura said. She went to the phone and dialed Diane's number. When her friend answered, Laura told her she was going out to dinner with a private investigator who was interested in Joan's case.

"Aha," Diane said. "When Mrs. Connor called and told me about your friend, I knew something was up."

"Diane! We're going to be discussing the case." She glanced up and saw Brandon smiling at her. "Actually, you're right," she said into the phone. "I guess you could say he's okay to look at."

Brandon removed the receiver from Laura's hand. "Hi, Diane. Brandon Powell here. I hope you don't mind that I talked Laura into going out with me tonight."

"I'm delighted, Brandon. Just be certain you get her home early," Diane said.

"Yes, Mother."

Laura snatched the phone from Brandon. "Goodbye, Diane. I'll call you later, when I'm alone."

THE RESTAURANT BRANDON had mentioned was in a downtown hotel. He parked his car in the garage himself, explaining that he hated waiting for the valet when he was ready to leave.

It was a small, intimate place, so dark that it took a moment for Laura's eyes to adjust before she could make her way across the room. The individual tables glowed with soft pools of candlelight, and the music Brandon had promised flowed out, mellow and sweet.

There was no printed menu; the waiter recited several mouth-watering specialities in enough detail that a cook could have reproduced them at home. "Just soup. Something creamy," Laura said, giving Brandon an apologetic smile.

As Brandon turned to give the waiter their order, Laura studied his profile. The shadows cast by the candlelight made the planes of his face seem almost geometric, and showed his jawline to be firm and strong. When he turned back to her, she glanced away, hoping he hadn't noticed her interest.

When their wineglasses were filled, Brandon touched the rim of his to hers, his eyes on her face. She took a sip to cool the heat rushing to her cheeks. His relaxed manner unnerved her, making her own hurried efficiency look awkward.

He was a study in contrasts. She'd already seen how fast he drove and how much he could accomplish in a short time. His calm easiness was an illusion, she decided, watching how his long, lean fingers lay still on their table. There was a deliberateness of purpose in him, a centered energy. She knew intuitively that he wasn't a man anyone would want to thwart.

Laura found herself facing more than soup for dinner. Brandon had requested a basket of warm, fresh bread and a buttery pâté to accompany her soup. A fruit plate with succulent green grapes, ripe raspberries and crisp golden slices of pear sat temptingly between them.

As she nibbled, Laura felt her racing inner clock slowly readjusting to match his even, paced motions. She'd read somewhere that people who spent time together tended to breathe in tandem. At the time, she'd thought that sounded dull. Now it seemed the most natural thing in the world.

"What attracted you to police work?" she asked, after coffee was served.

"I wanted to annoy my father." He smiled, as if the memory was a good one. "The Powells have always been a medical family. My father, his father... I think it goes back to Hippocrates. I intended to be an attorney, but I got sidetracked by a criminology course that fascinated me, so I joined the police force after college."

"Was your dad disappointed?"

"My sister became a doctor, so he accepted my defection. I think he secretly admired it. He'd be pleased to know I'm using his office now. How about you, Laura?"

"There's not much to tell. I'm an only child. My dad was in the oil business, but now he's retired. He and my mother are in Europe at the moment."

He frowned. "I thought you told me you were with them last night."

"I said I was staying at their place."

He gave her a hard look. "There's a crucial difference. You knew I was asking if you were alone."

She gave him a wry smile. "What did I know about you?"

"Gee, thanks." His laugh was humorless. "You said your employer was going out of business. What will you do?"

"I'll look for another job."

"In Houston?"

She shrugged. "I haven't made up my mind. I share an apartment with a friend. I told her not to look for another roommate for another month. I may find out how the job market is here."

"It's good. Especially for women with red hair." His eyes lingered on her hair.

"But can she type?" Laura said sardonically, acutely aware of his interest. "I take my career seriously. I'm a personnel generalist."

He arched his eyebrows, and she laughed.

They lingered over coffee after they'd eaten, both of them reluctant to break the mood of the evening. More relaxed than she'd been in ages, Laura made her way out of the restaurant, Brandon at her elbow, lightly guiding her. In the elevator, she hummed one of the tunes the duo had been playing, aware of Brandon's eyes on her.

The elevator door opened and they stepped out into the concrete-and-steel garage. Laura said, "I'm glad you invited me..."

The words died in her throat as she felt Brandon grab her arm and shove her to the rough, cold floor.

"What...?" She half lay on her side, staring around her in astonishment as she searched for an explanation for Brandon's actions. Almost simultaneously, she heard a sharp explosion nearby.

Brandon was bending over her, positioned on one knee. She had no idea where it had come from, but he was holding a gun at chest level and his finger was squeezing the trigger.

Chapter Six

"Stay down. Behind the post," Brandon ordered before making a dash down the concrete corridor in the garage.

Laura heard more shots being fired and half rose, peering around the post. She could see Brandon crouching beside a car. At the far end of the garage, a man stood in the shadows. His features were impossible to make out, but she estimated him to be over six feet. Glancing toward the elevator, she wondered if she should try to run for help.

Another round of shots was exchanged, and she saw Brandon leap up and run to the shelter of a concrete pillar. The man at the far end had disappeared into the shadows. Just as she made up her mind to run for help, the elevator door swished open and a couple stepped out. The woman cradled a baby in her arms, and the infant was laughing and holding out its arms to the man.

Without thinking, Laura jumped to her feet and ran toward them. She pushed the elevator button and shouted, "Get in."

"But..."

Shots echoed in the hollow concrete cavern, and the woman screamed. As the elevator doors opened, the woman pulled on her husband's arm. He had turned to see where the sound had come from. Laura gave him a push, and he almost fell into the elevator behind his wife and child. "Send help," Laura said as the doors closed.

She stared at the metal doors, her hands shaking, her breath catching in her chest, and wondered why she hadn't gotten in with the couple. The sound of a vehicle roaring up beside her made her turn in panic. "Jump in," Brandon said, the passenger door swinging open. "I can't leave you behind. I don't know who's still out there."

With the car still in motion, she climbed in and frantically lunged for the door handle to pull it shut. Brandon was driving with one hand, and holding the weapon in the other. Ahead of them she caught sight of a set of taillights just disappearing around a curve. When they neared the exit, she saw a man in a bright yellow coverall standing outside the toll booth. His back was to them, and he was shouting and gesturing. The wooden bar that blocked the exit until the parking fees had been paid lay in splinters on the pavement. Brandon didn't slow down, and the tires crunched over the wood. Laura turned back and saw the attendant shaking his fist at them, his mouth working convulsively.

When they hit the street, the car bounced and Laura's head bumped against the roof. "Get on the floor," Brandon said.

"But..." She felt him grip the back of her neck and push her down toward the floor. She gritted her teeth and crouched down, and a feeling of giddiness overcame her, as if she couldn't get enough oxygen to her brain. The car swerved and swung from side to side, and she could hear the screech of brakes as other cars tried to get out of their way. Brandon was muttering to himself.

Terror struck when she thought they had gone into a spin. A strong smell of hot rubber reached her nose, and she closed her eyes, prepared for the crash she was certain was coming. Instead, she heard Brandon let loose a string of curses, and then the car slowed down to what she supposed was normal speed.

"They got away," he said.

"Can I get up now?" she asked, her voice stronger than she had expected.

"Yes."

She unfolded herself gracelessly from the floor and fell into the seat with a yelp.

"My gun," he said, holding out his hand.

Laura arched up out of the seat and gingerly retrieved it. It felt cold and heavy in her palm. He took the gun and leaned over to slip it into an ankle holster.

"Do you wear that all the time?" she demanded.

He kept his eyes on the road. "Sometimes I take it off in bed."

"Don't try being funny with me," she said, enraged now, adrenaline turning her fear into anger. "Do you know how many people could have been killed? There was a baby in that garage."

He continued to watch the road, ignoring her outburst.

"Brandon," she said, her voice growing louder. "You're fired. I don't want any more to do with this violence."

Still no answer.

"Didn't you hear me?" she said, turning in the seat. "You're off this case."

His eyes narrowed to gray slits. "No one takes me off this case until I find out who was taking potshots at you tonight."

"Me?" The word came out shrill.

He nodded grimly.

She refused to believe him, couldn't imagine what she'd do if she did. "No, it couldn't have been me. I don't know anyone who would want to shoot me."

He glanced at her. "Believe me, Laura. That first shot was fired in your direction. That's why I shoved you to the floor. Did you get a good look at either man?"

"There were two?" she asked, the anger leaving her voice as she thought about how she'd panicked and hadn't even checked out their assailants. A lot of help she'd been.

"Yes. Could the man you saw have been one of the men in Joan's house?"

She tried to think. "He was standing in the shadows, but I think he was taller than either of the men at Joan's. Did you get a license number?"

"Yes, but it won't do us any good unless they're amateurs. By now they've already stopped and switched plates or abandoned the car. It could have been a stolen vehicle."

The enormity of what he was saying began to sink in. "Brandon, I'm sure you're mistaken. Those shots couldn't have been aimed at me."

"If it's any help, I don't think they were trying to kill you. They had ample opportunity and didn't take it, so I think they only intended to frighten you."

Her voice was little more than a whisper. "But why?"

"You've been asking too many questions."

"Only at Joan's school..." She stopped, her eyes growing wide. "You think someone there is involved?"

"I don't know. Yet."

She digested his answer in silence for several minutes, then a thought struck her. "But how would anyone know where I was tonight?"

"That's what I intend to find out."

She melted against the seat, boneless, all the fight gone out of her. Until a little more than a week ago, she'd never thought about murder except in the abstract. Now, her friend had been murdered and she was being shot at. *It is too much to take in,* she thought, shuddering.

When they reached his office, Brandon pulled into the parking lot and stopped beside her car. He turned off his lights and glanced around the parking lot. A car with a security company's sign on it pulled up beside then, and a uniformed man waved. Brandon rolled down his window. "See anyone hanging around here tonight?"

"No one, Mr. Powell," the man said. "It's been a quiet evening."

"Good." Brandon rolled his window back up and turned to Laura. "Would you like me to drive you to a friend's house?"

She roused herself from her lifeless state. "I'd like to go home. You said you thought someone was just trying to warn me."

His voice was comforting. "I think you're safe, but you shouldn't be alone."

"No, I'm fine. There's an alarm system in my parents' condo." She straightened her shoulders and took a deep breath. "I can drive, but I would appreciate it if you'd follow me." After a pause she added, "Shouldn't we go by the police station first to report this?"

"I'll report it, all right," he said. "There's no hurry. No one is going to send out an APB when neither of us can describe the guys."

"But you got a good look at the car...."

"Which is probably hidden in someone's garage by now. Trust me, Laura, I know how the police operate. If you went in to report this, you'd just get another lecture from Quill about leaving the case to the professionals."

"It's just not fair. I..." A sense of futility stopped her protest.

Brandon's gaze, full of kindness and understanding, rested on her face like a caress. He reached out, and with one finger drew her hair back behind an ear, his finger softly touching her neck. His touch was as potent as if he'd drawn a line of fire across her skin. "You were great in that garage. You risked your life to get the couple and their baby back in the elevator. Why didn't you go with them?"

"And leave you?" She felt her cheeks burn the moment the words were out.

He reached over and took her hand. It felt like a low-voltage current suffusing her. For several moments he rubbed his thumb in slow circles in her palm. She kept her eyes on his, drowning in their depths.

Then he laid his hands on her shoulders, lightly, before leaning over and brushing her temple with his lips. It was little more than a feather touch, but it sent shock waves through her. She reached for his arms and ran her hands up his sleeves.

His tweed jacket felt pleasant in her hands, its roughness reminding her that he was with her, as solid as a rock. As her hands neared his shoulders, her fingers encountered a rip in his left sleeve. She stopped and investigated, running a finger into the rip. When she felt moistness, she drew back abruptly.

He jerked his head up with a surprised expression in his eyes. She held out her hand to catch a ray of light from a street lamp and stared at Brandon's blood on her finger. The enormity of what had happened in the parking lot hit her like a ton of bricks. "My God, you've been shot," she said.

He took her hand and looked. "You're right." He felt his arm. "Just a graze. I wasn't even aware of it." He reached for a tissue from a leather case under the dash, and wiped the blood from her finger.

"I'll drive you to the emergency room," she said, regaining her composure and some good sense with it. She reached for the car door. "Let's take my car. I'm not too familiar with standard shifts."

He laughed. "Slow down, Laura. I'm not going to any hospital. This is no more than a nick, and I'll take care of it when I get home—in my car."

At least let me look at it when we get to my house."

"If it'll make you feel better," he said in an indulgent tone.

ADRENALINE WAS STILL running high in her as she sped down the street, hoping that a patrol car would stop her so she would have help persuading Brandon he needed medical attention. Naturally, there wasn't a police car in sight.

When she pulled into the parking lot behind her condo, Brandon swerved in beside her and swung out of his car. He reached her car just as she was stepping out, and his face was dark as a thundercloud. "What in hell were you trying to prove with that wild driving?" he demanded.

Relieved to see that he still had the strength to lose his temper, she gave him a sweet smile in reply. "I was just practicing driving like an investigator."

The corners of his mouth lifted slightly, but he didn't answer. When they reached the entrance to the building, he insisted on going in first. "The last door on the right," she told him, trailing along behind.

"Who lives there?" he asked, pointing to the door next to hers.

"Sister Martha. Actually, her mother lives there. She's visiting while her mother's in the hospital."

Brandon took the key Laura offered him and motioned for her to step aside. He unlocked the door, waited several moments and then shoved open the door with a burst, leaving Laura outside to stare after him. She waited nervously, but after several minutes he returned. "It's safe," he said.

"I thought you said there wasn't anything for me to worry about."

"I don't take unnecessary risks."

"So I see," she said. She flipped on a light. "I'll get the first-aid kit. Take off your jacket and shirt."

"I'd rather have a cup of coffee. Can I make us one?"

"Sure, in the kitchen," she said. "There's some coffee I ground this morning in a canister on the cabinet. I hope you like it with cinnamon, because that's the only kind I have."

"Right now I'd like it any way," he said.

When she entered the bathroom, Laura reached for the door to the medicine chest and stared in dismay at the mirror. She brushed through the russet tangles quickly and located the first-aid kit.

Coffee was already streaming through the coffee maker when Laura reached the kitchen. Brandon had slung his coat and tie over a kitchen chair and was removing his shirt.

She paused in the doorway, acutely aware of the muscles rippling in his naked back as he settled himself on a kitchen stool. She inhaled deeply and forced herself to walk across the floor. He smiled at her, seemingly unaware of the effect he was having on her. "See, it's only a graze. I think the assailant intended to singe your hair, but when I shoved you down, he got me instead," he said.

Careful not to make eye contact and reveal the effect he was having on her, she dampened a sponge with antiseptic. "This may hurt a little," she said.

He chuckled. "You sound like my dad now." When she pressed the sponge against his skin, he winced slightly.

Later, as Laura patted medicinal cream on the wound, she had to hold her breath when her fingers brushed his velvety skin. The urge to stroke the curve of his spine almost overcame her. She was aware of a pressure in her chest as though her heart had grown to heavy for it, cutting off her air, and she knew that one touch from him would make her spin out of control.

BRANDON FELT THE TENSION aroused by the shooting incident slowly ebb and be replaced by a new tension, this one pleasant, triggered by the soft touch of Laura's fingers on his skin. He felt as if they were enclosed in a warm intimate cocoon, spun out of the sweet, spicy aroma of cinnamon and coffee intertwined with the scent of Laura's hair as it brushed against his face. His gaze drifted to her soft, unpainted mouth, and he felt his body rise to the unconscious invitation she offered.

She was just as intoxicated by it as he was; he could hear it in her raspy breathing, could see it in her determination not to look at him and in the deliberate way her fingers lingered on his arms. All he had to do was reach out for her, show her he wanted her, how he was inflamed by her.

No, he told himself firmly, pulling himself back from the brink only with the greatest effort. It was one thing to embrace a woman in her grief; another entirely to read something into her response. He knew she was relieved that the danger had passed and that she was grateful for his help. When he made love to Laura he intended it to be because that was what was wanted. By both of them.

BRANDON CHECKED the alarm system before he left to see that it was working properly. "If anything bothers you during the night, even the slightest noise, give me a call." He wrote down his home phone number for her.

Laura seemed detached, remote. She hoped that Brandon had not been aware of her response to him in the kitchen. He'd certainly given no indication that he had been. "I'm going to be fine," she assured him. "Diane's husband, Bob, would be over here in a jiffy if I needed him. And Perry gave me his number in case I needed anything."

"Be careful who you call. You don't know who's involved," he warned her.

"I have to trust friends," she said. "Brandon, I'd like to help tomorrow. What can I do?"

"The best thing would be to return to Houston but I doubt you'll do that," he said, smiling at the way she'd deflected his concern about her.

"Right. I had planned to go to the Crown Hotel and interview the desk clerk before you took the case. Maybe if I know what really took place that night, I will be able to come up with a reason why Joan might have been there."

"You're not going to that hotel without me," Brandon said. Then he chuckled. "I think I just fell right into your trap. Okay, we'll go there together. I'll give you a call in the morning after I've checked out a couple of other things, and let you know when I can pick you up."

"I'll be ready," she said, walking him to the door.

"Lock it behind me," he said, and was gone.

The phone rang moments after Brandon left. Laura's hand hovered indecisively over the receiver, and then she picked it up. "Gibson residence."

"Laura? I'm sorry to bother you, but Perry called to say he hadn't been able to reach you." It was Jim Connor, Joan's father.

"I was out with a friend," Laura said. "How are you feeling?"

"As well as can be expected. The doctor changed my blood-pressure medicine today, and I hope that'll do the trick. I was surprised when Millie told me you'd hired a private investigator. Do you think the police aren't doing their job?"

She ran through the same explanation she'd given Millie Connor. "Having an experienced investigator follow through on obscure leads can't hurt, can it?"

"No, I appreciate it, but I was wondering if we can afford his fees."

"Didn't Mrs. Connor tell you he's a friend of mine?" Laura said. She'd given out that explanation so often she was almost beginning to believe it herself. "He's working for expenses only."

"That's great. Let me know what they are. I want to pay them," Mr. Connor said quickly. There was a hopeful note in his voice.

Before the conversation ended, she found herself promising to give Perry a call to reassure him that she was fine. He answered on the first ring. "Perry, it's Laura Gibson. I hate to call so late, but Mr. Connor said you wanted to talk to me."

"I tried to reach you all afternoon and evening. Was anything wrong?"

"No, I was with a friend. What did you want?"

"Well, mainly I wanted to talk to someone who understands but I didn't want to burden the Connors. The principal called me in at the end of the day and suggested I take a leave of absence until I can get a handle on my grief. I have an appointment with a counselor for tomorrow, but just being with you this afternoon helped me so much." She heard the choking sound beginning in his voice, but he continued, "Joan told me a lot about you, so I feel we already know each other."

The urgency in Perry's voice left Laura feeling uneasy. "I'm glad you're going to see a counselor, Perry."

"Maybe we can get together soon now that I'll be free during the day. I'd like to help you with your investigation."

Laura had no desire to spend time with Perry, but she tried to be tactful. "Your counselor may not feel that's wise," she said. "Let me know how your first session goes."

When she replaced the receiver she was left with a strange feeling about Perry. The man seemed devastated by Joan's death. Or was he merely covering something up, as Brandon had suggested?

THE NEXT MORNING Laura went out in the hall to water one of the potted palms she'd noticed drooping the day before. As she was kneeling beside the heavy brass planter with her watering can, the door next to her parents' opened, and she heard a familiar voice. "Just the person I wanted to see," Sister Martha said. "I've just taken some sweet rolls out of the oven and can't eat them all myself. Would you like some?"

"I'd certainly enjoy a cup of tea if you have one," Laura said. She followed Sister Martha into the apartment. The sister was dressed in a shapeless skirt and a white blouse. It was hard to pinpoint her exact age, but Laura guessed her to be somewhere in her early forties. She wore a pair of sturdy oxfords, and she gave the impression that she could cover a lot of ground quickly if she wanted to.

The apartment layout was similar to that of Laura's parents' unit, but it was furnished in a more formal style. Sister Martha led the way to the kitchen, poured a cup of hot water for Laura, and handed her a tea bag. "How's your mother?" Laura asked.

"Better. She'll have to stay in the hospital another week, and I plan to remain here with her for at least two weeks after that. It will be the longest I've ever been away from my order. How are the parents of your friend?"

"They're still in shock."

"No wonder. You mustn't expect them to be themselves yet. I do a lot of grief counseling, and people need to be given time to deal with their loss."

Laura remembered Perry. "I'm worried about a friend of Joan's," she said. "He teaches at her school and says they were good friends, nothing more, but he's grieving as if she had been the most important person in the world to him." Laura went on to explain about Perry's wife and Joan's fiancé. "I guess there was a strong bond of understanding between them."

Sister Martha nodded her head. "Now, it sounds as if he's trying to forge that same bond with you, since you share his sense of loss over Joan's death. Subconsciously he's transferring the affection he felt for her to you. You'll have to handle it carefully, and it won't be easy. Naturally you'll want to be kind to him, but it may seem to you that he's out of line. Try to remember that he's very vulnerable right now and couldn't take much in the way of a rejection."

"I feel like I'm walking on eggshells around him."

"A good description," Sister Martha said, laughing. "Maybe the counselor you say he's going to will help him see that he can't latch on to you as a substitute for Joan or his wife."

The doorbell rang, and Sister Martha jumped up. "It must be the cleaner's. I packed in a hurry and have to get one of my habits cleaned."

Laura drained her tea, worried she might miss Brandon's call, and went into the living room just as the sister emerged from the bedroom with folds of dark gray cloth draped over her arm. A young man lounged at the front door. "Would you mind holding this while I get the wimple?" Sister Martha asked Laura, handing her the heavy bundle.

When she returned, she instructed the man from the cleaner's to come inside. "Now handle this carefully," she told him. "The habit must be dry-cleaned, not washed, but the wimple—" she held up the headpiece "—needs to be bleached, washed, starched and ironed."

Laura was fascinated. "What holds it on?" she asked.

Sister Martha slipped the white form over her head and adjusted the linen bands under her chin. Then she positioned the coif. "You have to get used to it," she said. "At first it's a little difficult to move your jaw, but after a while you learn how."

"It looks uncomfortable to me," the deliveryman said.

"It keeps you on your toes," Sister Martha assured him, in the determinedly cheerful voice that is the hallmark of the helping professions.

After he left, Sister Martha went out in the hall with Laura.

"I thought nuns no longer wore long habits," Laura said, curious.

"It's up to each order. My order is very traditional, so we prefer to wear them." She glanced down at the short skirt she wore. "When I'm on leave, I wear whatever I like. This belongs to my mother."

When Laura returned to her parents' apartment, she perched by the phone for a few minutes, then, deciding she was behaving like an adolescent with a crush, stood at the window, watching a man washing his car. She could see that it was a beautiful day. The clear blue skies and the gentle wind that barely ruffled the tops of the trees did nothing to give credibility to the weather forecast of afternoon thunderstorms that she'd heard on the radio. But it was Dallas, after all.

Hindsight and sunlight made the sinister events of the evening before seem unreal, and she wondered if perhaps Brandon had overreacted. It was possible that the men had been in the garage for some other reason, perhaps to steal or strip a car, and had fired at her because she was a witness. Slim comfort, she thought, but preferable to thinking she was a target.

The phone rang, and she raced to answer it, then waited to let it ring again before picking up the receiver. The message was short. Brandon would pick her up in five minutes.

When Brandon arrived he didn't mention the episode of the night before. "The desk clerk who was on duty the night Joan died has been transferred to the morning shift. If we hurry we can see him," he told her.

"I'm ready," she said. She had managed to throw on a yellow knit dress in the five minutes he'd given her, and she was relieved and pleased to note the admiring sweep of his eyes when she opened the door.

"I checked out Perry," he said when they reached his car.

Inwardly glad, she still chided him. "Isn't that an invasion of privacy?"

"Not if he's a suspect."

"I thought there had to be just cause before anyone became a suspect."

"It pays to be careful. He's clean as they come. He's from Oklahoma City, forty-two, single. His degree is in music education, and he drives a Volkswagen."

"Is that all you could find out?" she asked, playfully sarcastic.

"I didn't have long," he said, countering. "I know I'm being unreasonable about the guy. He's probably just what he seems, but until I solve this case, no one's off the hook."

Laura paused before replying. There was no purpose to be served by telling Brandon about the strange tone of Perry's call the evening before. "He's taken a leave of absence from school and is getting grief counseling," she said.

Brandon nodded his head sympathetically. "It's tough to lose a friend."

The Crown was in what Brandon described as the third tier of hotels in Dallas. While it was far from being as luxurious as the newer ones, it was still listed in the convention guides as a quality hotel. Brandon found a parking space on the street and put his police sign in the window. "How did you manage to keep that after you resigned from the force?" she asked.

"It's a privilege extended to some private eyes after they solve enough cases," he said. "Especially if they give the police the credit."

When they neared the lobby, a tumult of feelings assailed Laura. The grief, which had begun to seem almost bearable, flared, and she again felt her eyes brim and her chest ache. Brandon took her arm and guided her into the revolving doorway as if he sensed that she might need encouragement.

They walked toward the check-in desk where a man with curly brown hair smiled expectantly at them. No other customers were in sight. Brandon leaned over the counter and spoke softly. "I'd like to discuss the Connor murder with you."

The man stepped back, his expression changing to one of alarm. "Who are you?" he asked.

Chapter Seven

Brandon took his ID from his pocket and showed it to the man. "I understand you were on duty the night of the murder."

"The police told me not to discuss it with anyone."

"That doesn't sound like the police," Brandon told the clerk. "I used to be a police detective. You were probably requested not to give interviews to the press since you'll be a key witness in the trial."

"Trial?" His eyes shifted nervously over to Laura and then back to Brandon. "Has someone been arrested for the crime?"

"They will be," Brandon said. He slid a bill from under his ID and moved it toward the clerk. "The victim's family has asked me to look into the case. Naturally they'll want to reward you for helping them."

The man stared at the money as if it were a scorpion about to sting him. "I don't have anything to tell."

Brandon leaned closer. "You might as well talk to me. I'm not leaving until you do. The police say you made a statement about the murder victim. I'd like your version of what you said about her."

"I just told the truth."

"Then you won't mind repeating it to me," Brandon said.

After a pause, the man said, "What do you want to know?"

Brandon showed him the photo of Joan that Laura had given him. "Ever see this woman?"

"Yeah. She's the one."

"The one who did what?"

"The one who went to Wallace Jones's room that night," the clerk said.

"How do you know that was his name?"

"He showed me a driver's license. Or maybe it was a credit card. I don't remember. Anyway, he had a reservation. It was a call-in from the day before. He said he was from Chicago and wanted to reserve a room for two. I didn't see the other man, but Jones said his name was John Davis. I gave Mr. Jones the key, and just before he left he told me a woman would be coming from Classic later that evening and to send her up to his room. I was a little surprised. We don't get too many high-class women visitors here, but I didn't say anything."

"Then what happened?"

"About nine these women arrived. The one in the picture came to the desk."

Laura opened her mouth to ask who "these women" were, but Brandon gave her a warning signal. The clerk pointed to the photo. "She asked for Mr. Jones's room number just like he said she would. I told her it was 701 and directed her to the elevator. The last I saw of her, she was getting in it."

"With the other woman?" Brandon asked.

The clerk looked up, fear in his eyes. "What other woman? I told the police there was just the one. This one."

"You said 'women,'" Brandon said, leaning toward him.

Beads of moisture broke out on the man's forehead. "No, I couldn't have. Or if I did, I made a mistake. There was just the one. Sometime in the night, after midnight, the phone rang and a voice told me there was a dead woman in room 701. I called the police, and within minutes this guy dressed in jeans arrived. He showed me his police ID so I took him up to the room. I let him in, but I didn't go inside with him. After that police swarmed all over the place. It was a madhouse."

"The guy in jeans," Brandon said, "did he stay until the other police arrived?"

"I don't think so. At least I never did see him again."

"What else can you remember about Wallace Jones?"

"Nothing. That's all I know. Honest."

Brandon's eyes narrowed. "You better be telling me everything," he said. "If I find out that you're holding something back, you're going to be hearing from me again."

"I told you everything," the man insisted, his voice shaky.

Brandon laid his business card on top of the bill. "Give me a call when you're ready to talk about the woman who was with Joan Connor. I'll make it worth your while."

When they walked away, Laura said, "He's lying. Joan didn't come here alone."

"I know. He's scared, too."

"Do you think the police know that?"

"No doubt."

"Why don't they give him a lie-detector test, make him tell what really happened?"

"It's not that easy. The police have to follow guidelines laid down by the legal system. A witness who looks scared isn't necessarily withholding evidence. There has to be more proof of guilt."

"What you're really saying is that a call girl's murder isn't important enough," she said, her tone bitter.

"I can't say that if Joan had been murdered in her home her case would be getting the same attention. Things aren't always fair, Laura."

They had reached the door. Laura exhaled deeply, her shoulders sloping in defeat. "I feel like we're running into roadblocks everywhere we turn."

Brandon noted her pale color. "Did you eat anything this morning?"

"Yes, I ate ... food." Laura stopped. "That's it, Brandon."

He gave her a worried glance. "Food is what people usually eat," he agreed. "Let's stop at the hotel's coffee shop and get you something more to eat."

"Not me," she said, laughing. "I was wondering if Wallace Jones ordered any food from room service."

Brandon's expression changed to one of approval. "Good point. Let's find out."

When Brandon asked a porter how to find the room-service office, the man directed them to the basement. They rode the elevator down and located the door marked Food Service and entered.

A woman with long, straight blond hair gave them an inquiring look from the behind the desk. Brandon put his ID card down with a twenty-dollar bill tucked under it. "I'm here to investigate the murder of the woman the other night. Could you tell me if there were any room-service deliveries made to room 701 that night?"

A furrow appeared between her brows, but she glanced down at the money. "I can't see how that could hurt," she said slowly. After she hit a few numbers on her keyboard, a series of entries appeared on the computer screen. "Yes, there was an order. Just a minute and I'll find out what it was."

After a pause she read off, "Four steak dinners were ordered and delivered."

"Four?" Laura repeated, leaning over the counter.

"Yes. Two steaks medium, one medium-rare, one rare. Four baked potatoes and four garden salads. There was a bar order, too, but you'd have to find out what it was from another department. The order was called in at 6:22. The delivery was made between 7:15 and 7:30."

"Did they sign for the bill?" Brandon asked.

"They paid at the time of delivery."

"With a credit card?"

The woman checked. "No, they paid cash. Manny Alvarez delivered it and brought cash back with him."

"Where would we find Manny?" Brandon asked.

"I don't know if he's working today, but you can look. The people waiting to take deliveries have a lounge right inside those swinging doors leading to the kitchen. Check with them."

"Thanks," Brandon said.

"Anytime," the woman said. She slipped the money into her pocket.

Brandon led the way into the kitchen. The room the woman had mentioned was lit only by the flickering light from a television screen. The program was in Spanish. Several young men were lounging on chairs, and no one looked up when Laura and Brandon walked in. "Manny here?" Brandon asked.

One boy glanced their direction. "He's off for a few days."

"Do you know where he lives?"

The boy's eyes swept over Brandon and he shook his head. "No idea."

Brandon took Laura by the arm and guided her outside. "Why didn't you offer him money to tell us Manny's address?" she asked.

"From the look he gave me, I'd say he suspects I'm with Immigration. Let's ask our friend in the office. This may be the break we've been looking for."

The woman in Food Service told them that employee addresses were kept in the personnel department. She didn't make any promises, but said she'd try to give Brandon a call if she could find it out.

At Laura's suggestion, they drove to Joan's house after leaving the hotel. "I want to search her files again and see if I can find out what she was working on. Unless she wanted to keep it hidden, it should have been in a file on her desk."

"I'd like to look at the mail that's been coming since her death, too. Who's been collecting it?" Brandon asked.

"I don't know," Laura said, surprised that she hadn't considered the mail. "I don't think the Connors have even thought of it. I certainly haven't, and I should have. I saw the postman down the street the other day when I was there."

"Maybe it's stuffed in a box on her front porch."

"No, she had one of those old-fashioned mail slots in her front door. I remember once when I was visiting her I almost jumped out of my skin when some letters plopped on the hall floor right by my feet."

"I didn't see anything on the floor yesterday."

"Me either. I'll call Mrs. Connor and find out when we get to Joan's."

THEY ENTERED THROUGH the front door this time. No one appeared to have been in the house since their last visit.

Laura dialed Mrs. Connor. She answered on the first ring, but her voice was dull, lifeless.

"This is Laura. I hope I didn't disturb you."

"I was trying to nap, but I'm glad to hear from you."

"This will only take a minute. I was wondering what's been done about Joan's mail."

"I hadn't thought of it." She sounded dismayed.

"You're certain Mr. Connor hasn't stopped it or had it rerouted to your house?"

"I'm sure he hasn't given it a thought. We're not functioning too well yet. I don't know what we would do without your help. What should I do to get it sent here?"

"I'll check at the post office and pick up any necessary forms," Laura said. "Now try to get some rest."

Brandon had been listening to Laura's side of the conversation. "I'll go next door and check with the neighbors. Maybe someone has been taking the mail in until they see one of the Connors," he said when she hung up.

After he left, Laura went upstairs and started going through the files systematically. She found a couple of short stories, but their dates indicated that they'd been written more than a year earlier. One drawer held creative writing done by Joan's students, and the third drawer contained miscellaneous notes, but nothing that appeared current.

Discouraged, Laura was ready to give up her search when she heard voices downstairs. She hurried to the railing and saw Brandon standing in the doorway talking to a mail carrier. When she joined them, he handed her a stack of letters. "Mr. Thomas says he's been putting mail through the slot regularly," Brandon said. "I told him we'd get Joan's parents to sign the necessary forms to have it delivered to their house."

When the door closed, Brandon turned to Joan. "Now who in hell has been coming here every day to pick up the mail? And why?"

Laura thumbed through the letters. An electric bill. A book club notice. She paused when she reached a long white envelope whose return address was that of an editor of a Texas magazine. She held it out. "Do you think I should open this and see what an editor is writing to Joan about?"

"You've been authorized by Mr. Connor to handle Joan's affairs."

She ripped it open and scanned the letter quickly. "Brandon, this is our first solid lead. Joan had evidently written this editor wanting to know if the magazine would be interested in running an exposé of a ring of car thieves."

"Car thieves?"

She glanced up. "I guess Mrs. Connor was right. I didn't know Joan had aspirations to be an investigative journalist, but this looks like proof. And everything Perry said about Joan being interested in cars fits now."

Brandon took the letter from her and whistled. "This is it, Laura. Now we've got somewhere to start in our investigation."

"If only the letter had more details. I know!" She sounded excited now. "I'll call the editor to find out what else Joan said in her letter."

"Do it," he urged.

He stood by while she dialed. The editor was in and answered her phone. Laura introduced herself and explained about Joan's death. They exchanged polite remarks, and then Laura got to the point. "We've hired a private investigator, and he's interested in knowing if Joan gave you more details about her article. The sources she would interview, that sort of thing."

"The proposal was quite detailed," the editor said. "Hang on while I locate it in my files."

She returned to the phone in a brief time. "According to the letter, Ms. Connor's fiancé, Sean McAble, was killed in what she thought was a normal auto accident. About six months after his death she was going through his personal papers and found notes he'd written concerning a foreign-car-theft ring involving high-ranking businessmen and some public officials."

"Did she say the cars were Jaguars?" Laura asked, remembering Perry's remarks about the brochures he'd seen.

"No, she wasn't that specific. It seems that when she found the papers, she went to the police and asked them to reopen the investigation of her fiancé's death. She felt that he might have been murdered because he knew too much. One policeman showed some interest, but he told her that she didn't have enough proof. She set out to find proof, following through on some of the leads in Mr. McAble's notes. When the policeman was still unconvinced, she wrote us and asked if we'd be interested in publishing her findings. I'm certainly sorry to hear of her death, and I hope it wasn't connected with this. If you'd like, I'll send you a copy of her letter."

When Laura got off the phone, she told Brandon what the editor had said. "It ought to be easy now. All we have to do is locate the policeman Joan was in contact with, and he'll be able to tell us who she was investigating. I can't wait to see Captain Quill's face when I tell him I really do have some new developments in this case."

Brandon was frowning. "Don't get your hopes up, Laura. The editor said the police didn't take Joan seriously, so what makes you think they'll believe there's a connection between her death and this magazine article? We need to find her research notes."

"And what if we don't find them? Do we just let all of Joan's work count for nothing? Or are you afraid to find out which of your police friends refused to take Joan seriously? Which of them couldn't be bothered to save her life?" She turned away, not wanting to let Brandon see her angry tears.

Brandon touched her shoulder gently. "I know how frustrated you're feeling, but let's take this one step at a time. We've got a good place to start now. Let's add this to the chart in my office and then start making the connections. I'll ask in the auto-theft department and see which policeman talked to Joan. I hope it wasn't just a phone call, or there may not be any record of it."

"Surely the police will remember."

"Do you know how many calls they get a day?"

"I guess you're right," Laura conceded. "Remember what Perry said about Joan being interested in Jaguars? That's what Sean drove, so there must be a tie-in there."

"I was already planning to visit the importing company where McAble worked this afternoon. Also, I'll stop by a couple of Jaguar dealers and do a little snooping."

"I think I'll stay here and search some more. Joan had to have kept her research notes somewhere."

"If you find anything, give my answering service a call. And keep those doors locked!"

AFTER AN HOUR Laura gave up in defeat. She'd searched every drawer in the house and even some boxes stacked in a closet, but there was no sign of Joan's notes. Now what? she thought. She couldn't go home and sit, waiting for Brandon to turn up something. She decided to head back to the hotel and see if the woman in the food services offices had been able to learn where Manny lived.

When Laura arrived, she was told the woman had gone off duty. Dispirited, she pushed open the door to the kitchen and once again saw several waiters watching TV. She went over to one and asked if he knew Manny's address.

The young man grinned at her. "What do you want with Manny?"

"I just want to talk to him."

"You better not let Anna hear you say that."

"Who's Anna?"

"She's Manny's girl. Hey, you ought to know Anna if you work here. She's a maid."

"Oh, that Anna," Laura covered quickly. "Are you going to tell me Manny's address?"

"I don't know it."

Laura left and started down the hall. She stopped when when she passed a door marked Housekeeping, and retraced her steps. Inside she saw a counter and rows of shelves containing linens. "I'm looking for Anna," she told a plump woman who was counting out sheets.

"Anna," the woman yelled. "Someone here to see you."

A slight, dark-haired girl emerged from a back room. "Yes?" she said.

"Anna, I'm Laura Gibson. I need to ask Manny a few questions, but he's not on duty. Could you tell me where he lives?"

"Is he in trouble?"

Laura laughed reassuringly. "Not at all. He delivered a room service order to 701 the night that girl died, and we need to clear up a few details."

"He didn't see anything. He told me so."

"This is just routine. We can't close our files until we ask him a couple of questions," Laura persisted. "Do you have his address?"

Anna still looked unconvinced, but she walked around the counter toward Laura. "He lives in the Bluebird apartments on Thirty-Second. It's the building on the corner, but I don't know the name of the other street."

"What's his apartment number?"

"I'm not sure. I've never been inside, but we passed it one night and Manny pointed it out. It's in the last building facing Thirty-Second, upstairs near the end. Does that help?"

"I hope so. I suppose I could ask the apartment manager." Remembering how careful some managers were to preserve their tenants' privacy, Laura added, "Do you have a picture of Manny that I could borrow so I can ask around for him in the complex? I promise to bring it back to you this afternoon."

Anna smiled. "Yes, in my purse. Come with me to the lockers." She led Laura down the hall to her locker and took a snapshot out of her purse. Anna was still worried. "You're sure Manny's not in any trouble?"

"Absolutely," Laura said. "And thanks for your help. I'll be back in no time."

Laura stopped at a phone booth, checked for the address of the apartment complex and hurried out to her car, which she'd left around the corner from the hotel entrance. Proud of her detective work she headed for the apartment.

Her mind was racing with thoughts of how she'd locate Manny when she glanced at her rearview mirror. There was something familiar about the car behind her. It was old, with dents and scratches and a damaged grill. A blue car.

Then she realized it could be the one she'd seen behind Joan's house the day the two men had startled her.

With her heart in her throat, she made a quick turn and then sped up. The car reappeared behind her within seconds. In the mirror she could see two men in the front seat, but they were too far away for her to make out their features clearly. When she slowed down to force them closer, the driver of the blue car slowed down also, keeping his distance.

Well, Laura, she told herself, *you're the great deputy detective. How do you go about losing a tail?*

Chapter Eight

With determination taking over from fear, Laura squared her shoulders and turned back to the main street, playing for time while she decided what to do. She could drive to the police station and tell Captain Quill she was being followed. An image of the bored look on his face formed in her mind, and she vetoed the thought.

Spotting a fast-food hamburger place ahead, she changed lanes and turned into its parking lot. As she braked, the blue car passed by. She was almost certain she recognized Jake Marshall. She craned her neck to read the car's license number but the rear plate was bent and caked with mud.

Suddenly bravado deserted her, and with rubbery knees she went inside the restaurant and ordered a cup of coffee, taking it to a booth that gave her a clear view of her car and the entrance to the parking lot. After a half hour and two refills of coffee to keep the waitress happy, Laura went back outside. There was no sign of the blue car.

As she resumed the drive to Manny's building she kept a close watch on the rearview mirror, but saw nothing alarming. That was not true of what she saw through the windshield when she turned into Thirty-Second Street. The apartment complex was in a low-rent neighborhood. Trash was piled high in the dumpsters, and the few bushes that were growing against the brick buildings were stunted and anemic. Laura parked, with some misgivings, located the manager's office and went inside. A middle-aged man sat at a desk. "Could you tell me Manny Alvarez's apartment number?" Laura asked.

"Who wants to know?"

"Laura Gibson. I need to question him about a hotel customer."

"You from the police?"

"No, I'm with a private investigator's office. It will be worth your while to tell me his number." Was that her talking? Next thing she knew, she'd be speaking out of the side of her mouth.

He turned his back on her and thumbed through a card file. "I don't have any Manny Alvarez listed." There was regret in his voice.

"But his girlfriend told me he lived here." She took the photo out of her purse. "This is his picture."

"I don't recognize him. Sorry, lady. He may be living with someone else in the complex. That's what some of these people do. They move in and then let all their friends live with them without telling me."

Discouraged, Laura walked out of the office and was about to head toward her car when she remembered that Anna had given her a general location. She turned and hurried up the rusty metal steps leading to the second floor of the building facing Thirty-second. When she neared the end, she knocked on one of the apartment doors. Getting no answer, she tried the door beside it.

On Laura's third try, someone answered. A young woman with a baby in her arms and a toddler peeking from behind her skirt, came to the door. Laura showed the woman Manny's picture. "I'm looking for Manny Alvarez. Do you know which apartment he lives in?"

"Are you a bill collector?"

Laura shook her head firmly. "I just need to talk to him about work."

The woman shifted the infant to her other arm. "I think he has a job, but maybe not. He lives down there. Apartment 223." The door closed before Laura could thank her.

Laura knocked on the door of apartment 223. Within a short time the door opened, and she recognized Manny Alvarez. "I'm Laura Gibson," she said. "I wonder if you'd mind helping me by answering a few questions about the people you saw in room 701 the night Joan Connor was murdered."

A twitch in his left eye betrayed his nervousness. *"No Inglés."*

Laura almost gave up in despair. *"Por favor, Señor Alvarez,"* she said in her halting Spanish. *"Mi amiga muerta..."* She stopped. "Damn, I think you're just pretending. My friend was murdered the other night, and you may have seen her killers. Please, I need their descriptions."

"I already told the police I didn't see a thing," he said angrily. He started to push the door closed, but she wedged her foot in the crack and stopped it.

With one hand on the door, she started in. "You don't have to be afraid of me. I'm not with the police."

"I'm telling the truth," he insisted. "Waiters are trained not to see hotel guests. We're told to keep our heads down and never to look directly at anyone. I didn't see anyone's face."

"You delivered enough food for four people, but there were only supposed to be two in there at that time. How many were there?"

"I don't know. I just pushed the cart in and left. I didn't look. Now leave me alone." He shoved her hand off the door. She moved her foot just in time to keep it from being crushed, and stood staring at the door, the harsh echo of its slam ringing in her ears.

She'd blown it. Her first real attempt to get some evidence without Brandon and she'd made a mess of it.

WHEN SHE ASKED for Anna at the hotel, the plump woman in Housekeeping glared at her. "You made Anna cry," she said. "What do you want want with her this time?"

"She wasn't crying," Laura said, bewildered.

"She is now. Anna," the woman shouted, "that lady's back again."

Anna came out, her eyes red-rimmed and puffy. Laura held out Manny's picture. "What's wrong, Anna?"

"He's mad I told you where to find him."

"Have you seen him?"

"He called. I shouldn't have told you anything."

"I didn't mention your name, so how did he know you were the one who told me where to find him?"

"He must have guessed. Now he's mad at me."

Laura gave her a sympathetic look. "I'm really sorry, Anna." She reached in her purse, pulled out her wallet and flipped it open to a picture of Joan. Holding it out to Anna, she said, "This was the girl who was murdered. She and I were best friends since we were little girls. Manny may be the only person who can help me get her killers. Why won't he help me?"

Anna stared at the picture. "Your friend was very pretty," she said in a soft voice. "I'm sorry she died."

"Do you think you can talk Manny into helping me? I'm not from the police. I only want to find the men who killed my friend so they can be punished."

"I don't know what I can do."

"Try. Just try to talk Manny into helping." She wrote her name and phone number on a piece of paper she found lying on the counter. "Take this, and give me a call if Manny will talk to me. Tell him I'll make it worth his while."

"I'll try." Anna said.

BRANDON'S CAR WAS just pulling away from Laura's building when she arrived. She honked her horn and he drove back into the parking lot and got out. "I went by Joan's house, but you'd left," he said.

"I found Manny," she said, climbing out of her car.

Anger flashed in his eyes. "What do you mean?"

Expecting praise for having located Manny, Laura stared at him in astonishment. "Just what I said. I met Manny's girlfriend at the hotel, and she directed me to his apartment complex."

He stepped in front of her, blocking her way. "Don't ever go off like that without discussing it with me."

"Excuse me, but did I miss something? When were you given the right to decide what I'm going to do?"

"Right now. I'm in charge of this investigation, and I don't intend to be responsible for what happens to an amateur sleuth."

"Amateur sleuth? Is that what's bothering you? I hate to mention it, but I'm the only one who's come up with any clues so far. Most of the things on your precious chart are mine. I found out that Joan was working on a writing project. I found out it involved a car-theft ring. I thought of checking room service. Now you're upset because I'm the one who located Manny."

He snorted in disgust. "Quit trying to change the subject. We're talking about your safety. The closer we get to the killers, the more dangerous this may get. So, you don't go anywhere without my permission."

"Dream away," she said. "I'm willing to listen to your advice, but I'll make my own decisions where I go."

"And you accuse me of being stubborn."

She smiled ruefully. "I think both of us qualify in that area. But, Brandon, I have to decide what's right for me to do. I promise to be careful. Now, as I said, I found Manny, but I didn't have any luck getting him to cooperate."

He walked to the apartment with her as she told him what had happened. "I blew it, didn't I?" she asked.

"It's too soon to tell. You may hear from Anna yet. You think Manny saw more than he's letting on?"

"Yes, he's frightened. I believe someone's threatened him."

"Or paid him off," Brandon added thoughtfully.

When they reached her living room, he took off his jacket.

"How's the arm?"

"Almost healed. If it's any consolation, I didn't have much more luck than you did at the importing company McAble worked for. They handle Jaguar parts, along with some other British imports. According to them, Sean was a former race-car driver, so they weren't too surprised when the accident was attributed to speeding."

"Did you think they were trying to hide anything?"

"Not really. The man who was manager when Sean worked there has been transferred back to England. I have his phone number. I'll give him a call, but it doesn't look promising."

"Did you find out which policeman Joan talked to?"

"I checked. No one remembered, and there didn't seem to be any record of it. As I said, that's not unusual. Those kinds of phone calls aren't logged, and someone calling to say they want a death that's on the books as accidental investigated, even if they talked to a policeman a couple of times, would not be remembered. These things happen all the time. I left a notice on the bulletin board in case someone who wasn't around today remembers Joan. If she was as quiet and retiring as you say, she may not have made much of an impression. You saw yourself how hard it is to get anyone there to listen to you when you're related to the victim."

"What should we do next?" Laura asked.

"I need to make a phone call. I'm going to get in touch with a former undercover officer and see if he can find out what operation Doug Young is working on. If it concerns car thefts, we may be getting closer to some answers."

"You keep coming back to Doug Young," Laura said thoughtfully. "Do you think he's involved in Joan's murder?"

Brandon's voice dropped. "I don't want to talk about it." He sat down on a bar stool and put his head in his hands.

"Don't shut me out," Laura said. It was all she could do not to walk over to him and put her arms around him. "I thought we were working together on this."

He lifted his head and smiled. "I made it plain I wasn't going to fill you in on everything until the case is over. The less you know, the better for you."

"Why don't you let me decide that? Please tell me what you're thinking."

He sighed and swiveled around on the stool. "I have a hunch, but hunches aren't worth a damn in court. Ever since I heard Doug was the first at the crime scene, I've had this uneasy feeling. I hope I'm dead wrong. He may just be involved in uncovering the operators of the car-theft ring, but if so I don't know why he wouldn't let me in on it. He knows I'd never blow his cover."

"If he were...a part of the ring, what would his role be?"

"I don't think he'd be in charge of it. If anything, I'd say he's being paid off to divert suspicion from the real leaders. It's happened before. A policeman sees a criminal getting away without any punishment and he gets disillusioned. It's only a small step for that policeman to decide that he's underpaid and overworked, so why shouldn't he pick up some of the easy money that's floating around. The temptation's there every day. It's to their credit that most cops stay clean and turn down the offers they get."

"How does Joan's death fit into this?"

"That's the part I can't figure. I can't see Doug having anything to do with her murder. Maybe he didn't know it was going to happen. Maybe the leaders of the ring called in some hired killers to do the job, and Doug learned of it when he heard the police call that night." He slammed his fist down on the bar. "There's got to be a way I can either prove or disprove this theory. It's driving me crazy."

"How about that police friend of yours? Can he find out if Doug's operation has anything to do with foreign-car theft?"

"Winn? He's snooping for me, but so far no luck. That's why I'm going to call Frank Overman. He used to be Doug's boss, but he's retired now. He still has some contacts, and he enjoys getting his nose back into departmental business occasionally."

BRANDON TALKED on the phone for over twenty minutes. When he turned back to Laura, he was rubbing his ear. "Frank's lonely, and it's hard to get him off the line. I think he'll help if he can, though. Now I think it's time we got our minds off this case. How about a night out?"

"I don't feel like it," Laura said apologetically. "I relaxed last night at the restaurant with you, and look what happened. What did Frank say?"

"Uh-uh." Brandon came over and stood by her. "You wormed my hunch out of me, but that's all I'm telling you tonight." His expression grew sober. "It's beginning to look as if Joan was killed because she knew too much. I don't want that happening to you. Now how about going to a movie tonight, for my sake? I need to get away from the case for a little while."

Laura knew when it was time to quit arguing.

The movie was a mindless farce about a couple of computer nerds, but she found herself laughing until her sides ached.

Brandon downed three hot dogs and a chocolate shake. When Laura refused food, he held a hot dog against her mouth until she gave up and ate it. It tasted wonderful. But then, everything was wonderful when she was with Brandon.

When they returned to the apartment, Brandon walked her to the door and then stood looking down at her. Her hair was loose around her shadowed face. Slowly, he put his hands on her shoulders. "See you in the morning?" he asked.

Trying to be casual, Laura nodded, unable to take her eyes off his mouth, so near, smiling faintly.

He moved nearer. Two inches...one...then his lips met hers. Not a comforting gesture this time. Not a reassurance that she wasn't alone. No, this was a deliberate, claiming kiss that sent the foundations of her world crumbling.

Later that night, long after he'd left her at the door and she lay in bed, she kept remembering that kiss. There was something so strong, yet sweet, so dazzlingly unfamiliar and yet known, about it. She wondered if he too was sleepless with the memory of it.

LAURA WAITED RESTLESSLY for Brandon's call the next morning. Diane dropped in for a quick chat, and Laura filled her in on what had been happening. "I can't imagine Joan being involved in a crime investigation," Diane exclaimed. "Her poems and stories were always about love and nature. There's got to be some mistake."

"That's what I thought at first, but evidently she was so upset when she learned Sean's death might not have been accidental that nothing else mattered."

"But why wouldn't she have talked about it to me or to you?"

"What would we have told her?"

Diane nodded. "You're right. We would have told her to forget it, that it was too dangerous to try to investigate herself. I wish I had time to help you. I feel so useless, letting you do everything. Even the Connors seem to have resigned themselves to never learning the truth about that night. You're the only one who won't give up. Promise me you'll be careful. I couldn't handle losing another friend."

"I promise," Laura said. "Diane, there is one way you can help. Would you call Perry and talk to him?" She told Diane about her conversation with Perry two nights earlier. "I feel guilty just deserting him, but the sister next door feels it's best if I keep my distance while he's working through his grief."

"He seemed nice enough when I saw him with Joan," Diane said sympathetically. "Joan told me he's a very talented musician. I think he plays in a chamber-music group.

I'll bet he was in love with Joan and didn't have the nerve to tell her."

"There you go again," Laura said.

"While I'm on the subject, tell me more about this detective of yours. Is he as attractive in person as he sounded on the phone?"

"Definitely," Laura said, smiling broadly.

DIANE HAD BEEN GONE only minutes when Brandon called. "Did you sleep late?"

"Not too late. I've been anxious to hear from you so I can get started today. What have you been doing?"

"Snooping where I'm not welcome."

"What did you find out?"

"I'll tell you at our picnic."

"What picnic?"

"The one I'm inviting you to in White Rock Lake Park right now. It's a beautiful day outside. The flowers are bursting into bloom, the wind is soughing through the tall grasses, the birds are singing."

"Gosh, you sure have a way with words."

He laughed. "I'll be by to pick you up about eleven-thirty, if that's okay with you."

"It's perfect, as long as you promise to give me something to do on the case this afternoon. There must be people I can shove up against walls or records I can steal when clerks turn their backs. I know what to do; I watch detective shows."

She enjoyed the rich sound of his laughter.

THE SPRING DAY WAS perfect, just as Brandon had painted it. They drove to White Rock Lake, and Brandon chose a spot far from the main entrance area. His was the only car in the parking lot when they got out. After wandering around for several minutes, they chose a grassy knoll overlooking a sparkling blue lake.

The picnic lunch he'd promised consisted of a bottle of a fruity white German wine, some fried chicken in a red striped bucket, a package of corn chips, and some oatmeal cookies still warm from the bakery oven.

"Such elegance. I must admit I'd pictured one of those antique wicker hampers filled with food you'd stayed up all night cooking," Laura said. She settled down on the grass while he fought with a newspaper that refused to lie still long enough for him to set the food on it.

"I knew this would impress you," he said.

She was wearing a pale pink silk blouse and a pair of cream trousers. A small gold locket gleamed on a thin chain between her breasts where the neckline of the blouse formed a V. Her hair had that freshly washed look again, and it looked burnished in the sunlight. Brandon thought of a hundred reasons why he ought to take her in his arms, but none was the right one.

"A detective leads a nice life," she said. "You're not wearing your gun, are you?"

"Would it bother you?"

"Frankly, yes. I've never been out with an armed man before."

"My gun's in the car," he said. "Feel better?"

"A little more civilized. Any new ideas about how we're going to link Joan's article with her murder? I feel more frustrated than ever now that we know what she was involved in. Don't you think it's time to tell Captain Quill?"

"Soon. If I can learn anything from Frank, I may be ready to have a talk with the captain. Laura, we do have to face the possibility that there may be no link between the article and her death."

"But that leaves us where we started, with no explanation for her being in the hotel. I wish Anna would call and say that Manny's ready to talk. I have a hunch that he's going to tell us something that will pin down the identity of the killer."

"You're beginning to sound like me." He held out the package of chips, and she took several.

"Do you think Jake Marshall and his friend are part of the car-theft ring?" she asked.

"They're probably only hired help. If our theory holds true, then I'd guess they were there to search Joan's house for anything connected with the operation."

"They did a good job. There's nothing in the house that shows she was writing anything lately." She leaned back against a tree. "It's nice here."

"Perfect. Better than anything Houston has to offer."

She laughed. "I remember coming here as a kid. Do they still rent canoes?"

"I saw the rental stand when we were driving in. Do you like to canoe?"

"I love it. I went canoeing down the Rio Grande once during spring break from college." The sun and the half-glass of wine she'd drunk had combined to make her drowsy. As she spoke, her words came slowly. "I remember how we just drifted down this bend in the river between tall rock walls. It was so incredibly peaceful. We'd dip our paddles in the water and gently stroke. It was as silent as the inside of a cathedral."

He smiled over at her as her eyelids drifted downward and then lay still. "I'll take you canoeing when this case is cleared up," he promised her softly, even though he doubted she could hear him.

He was pouring himself another glass of wine when a shaft of sunlight glanced off a metal surface and almost blinded him. He looked up and saw that a car was pulling up about a hundred yards across the grass from them, in blatant disregard of the No Parking sign.

Shading his eyes with his hand, Brandon studied the car. It was blue and old and had seen a lot of use. Two men were in the front seat. The man on the driver's side started to get out. He was in his forties, slightly overweight, and was losing his hair on top. He didn't look their way, but Brandon was almost certain he was aware of them. Suddenly the penny dropped.

With his attention still partially trained on the man, he reached over and gave Laura a quick, hard shake. She opened her eyes resentfully. "Yes?" Her voice had a drowsy, indistinct quality.

"Glance to your right without seeming to and let me know if you recognize that man. Quick."

"Huh?" She slid her gaze to the right and then glanced back at Brandon, her eyes wide. "It's Jake Marshall."

Chapter Nine

Brandon kept his head low and pretended to be gathering up the remnants of the picnic. "Start talking and laughing as if everything's normal," he ordered.

Laura's mind went blank for a moment, but she forced herself to laugh. "Are you really going to stuff yourself on some more cookies?" she asked in a voice that sounded strident to her own ears.

"I've only had ten." In a whisper he said, "When I tell you, get up and run for the car."

"Leave you?"

"Now," he said, grabbing her arm and pulling her to her feet.

She hesitated, and he said, "Run." She turned and started running the opposite way from the men, toward the pavement where the Jaguar was parked. It was locked when she got to it, and she realized she had no way of getting in it and going for help. The parking lot was still deserted, and as far as she could see, there were no park attendants in the area. She leaned against the side of the car, her breath coming in short gasps.

Brandon was standing, facing the two men, and she saw the light glint off something metal in the hand of the man with Jake. He was the same man who had been in Joan's house.

A cry escaped her as she saw Brandon step forward and arc his fist into the man's face, taking the man by surprise. A shot was fired, but appeared to miss Brandon as he struggled with the man for possession of the gun. Brandon seemed to step past the man and pull him into his hip. There was a thud, and the man and his gun hit the ground separately. Jake Marshall lunged toward him, but Brandon rolled to the right, out of his reach.

No longer stunned, the man on the ground rose and started toward Brandon, but Brandon whirled and threw him to the ground again. Laura watched, her horror tempered by fascination, as Brandon kept both men off balance like a trained acrobat.

When the man on the ground again rose to his knees, Laura closed her eyes, wondering how long Brandon could hold out. She knew she should run and try to flag down some help on Buckner Boulevard, but, as in a bad dream, her legs refused to move.

She squeezed her eyes shut in an effort to regain control of herself and when she opened them, she saw Jake's companion stretched out on the ground. Brandon had a tight grip on the front of Jake Marshall's shirt. Laura willed herself to approach them to look for the gun. When she located it, she picked it up gingerly and carried it over to Brandon. "Who sent you?" Brandon was asking Jake, his mouth close to the man's ear.

"Nobody. We were going to mug you," Jake answered.

"Liar. Who sent you? Tell me now before I really get mad."

Jake groaned. His nose was bleeding, and one eye was swollen shut. "I don't know. Honest. We just got a call and were told to come to the park and rough you up. Scare you. Warn the lady to go back to Houston. We weren't supposed to kill you. Bill always goes crazy when he gets scared. That's why he shot at you. He wasn't trying to kill you."

"Who called you?"

"I don't know."

Brandon shook him, and Jake let out a cry and clutched his shoulder. "How are you going to get paid?" Brandon asked.

When the man refused to answer, Brandon gave him another shake. "Okay, I'll talk. We're supposed to pick it up at Classic. We've done jobs for Lee Barber before. I don't ask questions."

"What were you doing in Joan Connor's house the other day?"

Jake glanced over at Laura. "We were told to put a matchbook in a coat pocket. I don't know why. It was just a job. We didn't hurt your lady when she sneaked up on us."

"What else did you do in the house?" Brandon asked, his tone quiet but menacing.

Jake clamped his lips together, but the glacial stare from Brandon made him sputter. "We took the mail out of the house a couple of times."

"Who did you deliver it to?"

"The desk at Classic. We didn't steal anything for ourselves. It's just a job. We got to eat."

"Did you take any papers from the desk?"

"No. Nothing in the house, except for the mail off the floor by the front door. I swear it's the truth."

"Where's Lee Barber?"

"I heard she's out of town."

"Who shot at us in the parking garage the other night?" Brandon said, his voice tight.

"Not us. Honest. Man, we won't go back to that house again, and I'll tell Classic I don't want any more work where you're concerned."

"You're wise," Brandon said. He gave him another vigorous shake. "If you come near her again—" he nodded toward Laura "—you'll never take another job anywhere."

Brandon let go of him abruptly and Marshall fell to the ground, clutching his shoulder and moaning. "Tell Lee to send some men the next time she wants to scare me," Brandon said.

He walked over and picked up the bucket of chicken and the wine bottle along with the newspaper, then turned toward Laura. She held out the gun limply and he took it.

"What about these men?" she asked, staring at the man who lay still on the grass.

"They'll live." Brandon started toward the car, and she hurried along beside him. His breath was still coming in short rasps.

"Are you hurt?" she asked.

He shook his head, unlocked her side of the car, then went over and dropped the trash in a container. Laura wondered if he was even aware of what he was doing. As he started to get in, she said, "You're not going to just let those men get away, are you?"

"I'll have the police watch them. Jake won't admit to the police what I shook out of him. I'd rather have him on the loose until I know more. They won't do any more damage."

"You don't know that," she said, her voice rising in frustration. "Who do you think you are? The Lone Ranger?"

He got into the car, started the engine, and smiled over at her. He knew it would make her furious, and as long as she was angry with him she wouldn't ask questions that he didn't want to answer yet. She was too quick at finding missing pieces, and she could get herself in trouble if she caught on to the truth before it was time to make a move.

Not that he knew the whole truth yet himself, but he knew he was getting close. His mind was whirring with questions. What was Lee Barber's connection? She'd supplied information to the police more than once in exchange for being left alone to run her business. She'd even participated in a highly successful sting operation once—an operation commanded by Doug Young.

Always the circle kept coming back to Doug.

Another question. How had Marshall and his friend found them? He was certain no one had been following them on their way to the park. That meant either Laura had mentioned where she was going to someone, or his phone call to her had been overheard.

He had used a phone in the police station to call her. He'd borrowed an empty office, and when he'd hung up the phone he'd caught a glimpse of someone hurrying down a hall. Someone who could have been Doug Young. "Could have been" wasn't good enough, though. He'd have to have an airtight case against Doug before going to Quill.

LAURA WAS SLUMPED in the bucket seat, her heart still pounding rapidly. Something was wrong here. Why was Brandon so determined to keep the police out of his investigation? When he'd taken on the case, she had assumed they would hand over the information they uncovered directly to Captain Quill. Now Brandon was up to something quite different and, maddeningly seemed determined not to explain.

She glanced over at him. His face was set in grim lines as he maneuvered through the traffic. She longed to reach out and touch the red welt that was swelling on his face. Watching him fight with the two men had terrified her, and had made her aware of how much she cared about him. Now that it was over, that terror had changed into an overwhelming desire to put her arms around him, to feel his heart beating against hers, to make certain nothing more was going to happen to him because of this case he was trying to solve for her.

As desperately as she wanted to see Joan's killers behind bars, she wasn't willing to have Brandon hurt because of it. It seemed to her that it was time to turn over all the evidence and let the police do their job. With their manpower and equipment and their network of contacts, they were in a much better position to handle the risks involved than Brandon was.

After a few minutes, she said, "I suppose it wouldn't do any good to ask you to drop the case, would it?"

"The same good it would to ask you to return to Houston and wait until the case is resolved."

"I don't want you hurt any more," she said huskily.

He glanced toward her, his expression softening. "I know what I'm doing, Laura. I'm just sorry you had to be there."

"I'm worried, Brandon. What's going on?" she asked in a low voice.

"I don't know," he answered harshly.

"You must have some ideas," she said, the anger she always felt when he shut her out beginning to surface.

"Remember, I don't share ideas," he said. By the shake of her head, he knew he'd managed to make her angry again.

She was angrier still by the time he pulled away after dropping her off at home. She had insisted he come in and have a cup of coffee, but he'd refused. Then, to make matters worse, he'd given her a stern lecture about staying home until she heard from him. The best assurance he could extract from her was that she was just going to the Connors' for a visit.

AFTER BRANDON LEFT Laura seething with anger in the parking lot, he drove directly to his office and called Frank Overman, the retired undercover officer, again. Frank's wife told him her husband was having his daily jogging session around the neighborhood.

Brandon sped to the street where Frank lived. He circled the block twice before he spotted the elderly man turning the corner. Dressed in a pair of gray sweats and a jersey left over from his days on the police force, he was running doggedly down the street. Brandon slowed down, realizing as he looked at the man that he had aged considerably in the year since he'd last seen him. Brandon pulled to a stop a little ahead of him and called his name.

Frank loped up beside him, smiling. He slid into the Jaguar's leather seat. He was breathing heavily. "How far do you run?" Brandon asked.

"Three miles on my good days," Frank said. "I think I found out what you want to know. There's an Operation Back Roads going on."

"Back Roads? What's it about?"

"Something to do with cars."

Brandon was careful not to show that this information was important to him. "Cars. That covers a lot of territory."

"Best I can do. From what I could learn, it's a big one. Involves some movers and shakers. It's got to go right or heads are going to roll around the department. I know I can trust you not to mention it to anyone."

"Is Doug in charge of it?"

"Yeah, he's the best one I ever trained," Frank said with pride.

JUST AS LAURA WAS getting in her car to go to the Connors', Sister Martha came out of the building and started across the street. Laura called over to her, "Need a ride?"

Sister Martha wore another dark skirt with a plain white blouse. More clothes from her mother's closet, Laura surmised.

"I can catch the bus," she said, pointing to a bus stop across the street from their parking lot.

"If you're on the way to the hospital, I can take you. I'm going within a block or two of it."

"In that case," Sister Martha said, "thanks." She settled herself in the seat. "How's the investigation coming?"

"I really don't know. We're learning things we didn't know about Joan, but we can't put them together yet."

"Sounds interesting. I'm a great fan of detective stories." Her hazel eyes brightened. "Let me know if I can help in any way."

DIANE OPENED THE DOOR at the Connor house when Laura arrived. In a low voice, she said, "I could wring that Perry's neck for getting Mrs. Connor upset. He just left."

"What did he do?"

"He wouldn't stop talking about how wonderful Joan was and what a tragedy it was that her life had ended so young. The guy's a creep. He ought to know that mentioning Joan's name every second isn't going to help her mother right now."

"He must have really cared for Joan," Laura said.

"He cared for the attention she gave him," Diane said in a disgusted tone. "I think he's hoping you'll do the same. He mentioned several times how beautiful he thinks you are and how much better he feels when he's around you."

"I've only seen him twice. Once on the day of the funeral, and once at Joan's school," Laura protested.

"Who's there, Diane?" Mrs. Connor asked from the living room.

"It's me. Laura." Laura hurried into the living room and hugged Millie Connor. "I came by to take you for a ride on this beautiful afternoon."

"That's a wonderful idea," Diane chimed in. "The children are with Bob's mother, so I'm free to go, too. We could show Laura how Dallas has changed since she lived here."

"I'm too tired," Mrs. Connor said. She pointed to a chair beside her. "Laura, I think you need to have a talk with Perry. He's grieving so much."

"How can I help him?"

"He feels you're the closest thing to Joan he has left. The way you talk reminds him of her. Such a dear, dear man." Her eyes filled with tears, and she leaned back against the couch. "I've got to get control of myself before Jim gets home. He worries if I've been crying."

Laura silently agreed that she was going to have a talk with Perry. He had no right to come here and upset Mrs. Connor this way. "Why don't you and Mr. Connor get out of town for a few days? Maybe visit your sister in Ohio."

"Or take a trip to somewhere restful...like a beach or mountain resort," Diane added.

"It's strange you mention a trip," Mrs. Connor said, sighing. "We're scheduled to take a trip to Hawaii for our thirtieth anniversary. It's this coming Saturday. I need to call and cancel it. It was Joan's gift to us."

"Joan would want you to go," Laura urged.

"She'd insist," Diane agreed. "Think how much good it would do you to get away for a while. You wouldn't have to go places with the tour group. You could just sit on the beach and rest in the sun."

"It does sound pleasant, but I don't think we ought to," Mrs. Connor said, shaking her head. "It just wouldn't seem right somehow." She closed her eyes.

Diane glanced over at Laura and grimaced. Laura shook her head sadly, remembering how Sister Martha had told her not to hurry the Connors through this intense mourning phase.

Mrs. Connor opened her eyes and leaned forward. "I just remembered something, Laura. The library downtown called today. They said to tell Joan that the reference librarian had located the information she had requested."

"What information?" Laura said.

She shrugged. "I didn't ask. I couldn't bring myself to tell them what happened to Joan, so I just said I'd relay their message. Maybe one of you should return the call."

"I will," Diane said quickly.

"Wait," Laura said. "Why did they call here instead of Joan's house?"

"Oh, that's not unusual. Joan was always giving out this phone number for people to call during the day. She knew I didn't mind taking messages. It's not easy for a teacher to leave her class," Mrs. Connor explained.

"Who called from the library?"

"I didn't ask for a name. It was a woman, maybe a receptionist."

"Did Joan tell you to expect a call?"

"Not that I remember. It wasn't necessary."

Seeing how important the call seemed to Laura, Mrs. Connor put her hand against her forehead as if it hurt her to think. "I'm sorry, I didn't ask for details, Laura. All I could think of was getting off that phone before I broke down. Do you think it was important?"

"I don't know," Laura admitted. "Let me call the library and see what I can find out."

Laura went into the kitchen and located the phone number in the yellow pages. The switchboard connected her to the research department after she explained about the earlier call. A young man answered and listened while Laura went through her story again. "Gosh, there are a lot of librarians who do research here. Hang on, and I'll see if I can locate the person you need."

He was gone for several minutes. When he returned, he said, "No one knows anything about it, but I can leave a note on the message board. Where can you be reached?"

"I think I'll come to the library," Laura said.

Diane was looking at her quizzically when Laura replaced the receiver. "I couldn't locate the librarian who did the research," Laura explained.

"You must think it's important if you're going there."

"I really have no idea. It may concern a class Joan was teaching at school. But Brandon says that sometimes the most insignificant things supply the missing answers."

"Brandon," Diane said, imitating the way Laura had said the name. "When am I going to meet this new man in your life?"

"Soon," Laura said, smiling.

Before Laura left, she gave in to Mrs. Connor's pleas that she give Perry a call. "I promised him you'd get in touch with him," the older woman said.

Perry answered his phone on the first ring. When Laura identified herself, he immediately asked her if she would meet him for a cup of coffee. "I'm on my way to the library. The main branch downtown." She explained about the call from the research department.

"Would you like me to go with you?" he asked eagerly.

"Thanks, but I'm on my way now."

"Your friend came by my house a few minutes ago and asked me a lot of questions. I didn't appreciate his attitude."

"Who?" Laura asked sharply.

"Mr. Powell. Did you send him?"

"I told him you were a close friend of Joan's. He's talking to everyone who knew her." She wondered why Brandon hadn't told her he was going to grill Perry. Still keeping everything to himself, she thought.

"I'll give you a call soon, then, to see if you found out anything important," he said.

WHEN BRANDON LEFT FRANK, he drove by the address Laura had given him for Perry Hill. He suspected he was wasting his time, but he wouldn't know for sure until he'd talked to the man.

Perry lived about six blocks from Joan's house, Brandon noted as he pulled up in front. He went up to the door and rang the bell. No answer. Brandon rang again and waited, then started back to his car just as a Volkswagen pulled into the driveway. A silver-haired man got out and came toward Brandon. "I'm not in the mood to talk to a salesman today," he said. The man's eyes were red-rimmed and puffy, as if he'd been crying.

Brandon handed him his card. "I'm investigating Joan Connor's murder, and I understand you were one of her closest friends."

"Laura told me about you. I'm sorry, but I really can't talk about Joan right now. I've just come from seeing her mother."

"I'll only take a moment," Brandon said. "Laura tells me you have a theory about why Joan was in that hotel room."

"It's just a theory. The truth is, Mr. Powell, Joan wasn't herself for the last month or two before her death." He took out a tissue and dabbed at his eyes. "I haven't mentioned this to anyone, but Joan and I argued the day of her death. I told her she was making a mistake neglecting her work and her friends, but she wouldn't listen." He stopped, too choked up to talk.

"You're feeling guilty about arguing with her?" Brandon asked in a quiet voice.

"Yes, of course I am. I shouldn't have lectured her the way I did. Maybe if I'd been more understanding she would still be here." He turned toward the house. "I'd invite you in, but as you can see I'm in no state to talk to anyone. The only person who seems to understand how I'm feeling is Laura, but she's too busy trying to find out what really happened to Joan to have any time for me."

Brandon stood on the sidewalk, watching Perry as he went into his house. The man worried him, especially his interest in Laura. He'd only known her a few days, and his interest in her seemed too intense. That thought made Brandon smile. He'd only known Laura a few days, too, and she was on his mind constantly.

After returning to his office, Brandon made a call to the police station to see if his inquiry about anyone remembering Joan investigating Sean's death had brought any results. Myra Trent was on duty in the auto division. "Sorry, Brandon," she said. "No one's responded to your message yet. Have you checked to see if Sean McAble was ever involved in an accident before his fatal one?"

"Yes. There wasn't anything. You might try Auto Theft," he said. It was a long shot, but he had to find the link between Sean McAble and Joan's query to the editor.

Myra was back to the phone within minutes. "McAble didn't report an auto theft, but his name's come up on the computer as reporting a theft of auto parts. Want me to read the report to you?"

"Definitely."

Myra read the report quickly. Sean McAble had reported the theft of the leather seats from his Jaguar several months before his death, shortly after he arrived in this country. The thief had never been apprehended. "There's a notation here," Myra said. "It seams McAble called back in after the seats were installed to say that he believed that the replacement seats were the ones that had been stolen in the first place."

"How would he know?" Brandon said.

"It doesn't say. He was advised to discuss it with his insurance agent and to warn them against using that auto-parts place again in case the place was fencing stolen goods."

"And then the case was closed? No investigation of the auto-parts place?" Brandon asked.

"None mentioned here." Myra's tone became defensive. "You know how it is, Brandon. We're short of staff. We can't investigate everything. Evidently McAble didn't offer enough proof that the leather seats were his original ones."

"I know," Brandon said. "Does the report state which insurance company McAble used?"

"Quality."

"Great. I've done work for them. Thanks a million, Myra."

As soon as Brandon got off the phone, he drove to the main office of Quality Insurance. The reception recognized him from a previous case, and greeted him warmly. "Did you get that bruise on your face doing work for us?" she asked.

Brandon felt his cheekbone. "I bumped into a door," he said.

"Sure. Who do you need to see today?"

"Records. One of your former customers interests me."

"I'll buzz down and tell Records you're on the way."

The woman presiding over the front desk in the records department was less friendly. "You'll need authorization to see anything here," she said frostily.

"Call Howard Miller and he'll give me authorization," Brandon said.

The woman dialed the number, spoke into the phone, then got up from her desk. She managed a smile. "Okay, what record are you interested in?"

"Sean McAble. Theft of auto parts."

"There's an epidemic of that," she said, sighing. "Especially foreign cars. And the parts are as expensive as if they were made of pure gold." She went over to the bank of beige filing cabinets that lined the wall, found the drawer she needed and pulled out the record on her first try.

Brandon read over the file. It stated that Sean McAble had not only reported the similarity between his original car seats and the ones that had been installed to replace them, he had become angry when he felt the insurance company did not take his complaint seriously. He had made several trips in to see his agent and a notation indicated that at one point he had made some pointed remarks about what he believed was a tie-in between someone in the insurance agency and the auto-parts store that had replaced the seats. According to him, the insurance agency was charged at least three times the value of the seats. Overseas Auto Parts, the company his insurance company had sent him to when he'd reported the theft, was not only involved in fencing stolen property, it was guilty of cheating the insurance company, too, McAble had alleged.

When Brandon finished reading the report, he returned it to the woman at the desk. "Who's the CEO of Quality?"

"James Comal," she said. "He's in charge of the Dallas Charities Fund Drive this year. You've probably seen his picture in the paper a lot in recent months." There was pride in her voice.

"I've heard of him. One or other of the Comals seems to be in the local news every day." Brandon was not personally acquainted with the Comals, but he knew they were a prominent family. One brother was an aide to the mayor. Another was an attorney. It was unlikely they were involved in anything shady, although you never could tell. He'd do a little snooping on the streets this afternoon.

WHEN LAURA REACHED the vicinity of the library, she circled the block three times trying to find a parking space on the street. Finally she gave up and turned into a city parking garage. When she stepped from the car, she felt a rush of panic as she remembered the moment when she'd first realized Brandon and she were being shot at in that other garage. Determined to get a grip on her nerves, she walked through the shadows toward the elevator, cringing as each footstep echoed off the concrete, creating a phantom stalker who was just one pace behind.

Chapter Ten

Once she reached street level, Laura took a long breath and relaxed. It felt good to have something definite to do, something that might unearth some clues she could discuss with Brandon when they met again.

That reminded her of Brandon's stern lecture about her not going anywhere this afternoon. For a moment, she wondered if she should call and let him know where she was, and then decided she was being foolish. This chance to find out what Joan had been researching was too important, and what possible trouble could she get into in a library?

She asked for the man she'd spoken with on the phone earlier. When she told him her name, he said, "I located the librarian for you. Her name's Sara Prinz." He pointed over to a row of desks. "The fifth one down. She's expecting you."

Sara Prinz was close to Laura's age. She had a pencil stuck behind one ear, and enormous horn-rimmed glasses which magnified her eyes to cartoon proportions. "Lloyd told me about Ms Connor," she said, rising when Laura reached her. "I couldn't believe she was the woman who was murdered. I heard about the tragedy on the TV, but I guess I missed the name or just didn't connect it. You never think these things could happen to someone you know. What can I do to help you?"

"I'm working with a private detective trying to sort out this case. I understand she had asked you to do some research for her. Could you tell me what it was?"

"I don't see any reason why not. Ms Connor wanted me to track down the owner of Overseas Auto Parts. It's a large auto-parts company that works out of a warehouse here in Dallas. I thought it would be a simple thing to find out, but I was wrong. The owners are listed as unknown because it's operated through a holding company."

"Isn't that illegal?"

"Not at all. It means an attorney is the contact person if someone needs to reach one of the owners. As long as a company is privately owned, it's legal enough."

"Why would an owner want to work that way?"

"To protect his privacy would be my guess. There are other reasons too, having to do with state and federal regulations. I could research the specifics for you if it would help."

"Thanks, but I'm not sure I need that kind of information. Who is the attorney?"

"Joseph Comal. Head of a big law firm here."

"If I went to him, would he tell me the name of the owner?"

"He couldn't unless you got a court order first. And you'd only get that if you could present evidence of malfeasance."

"Did Joan tell you why she wanted this information?"

Sara seemed distracted for a moment, as if searching through some huge mental data bank. Then she said, "Something about a magazine article she was writing, I believe. I remember she was in a hurry that day. I think she'd come here during a free period and needed to be back before her next class started. I'm having a hard time believing she was working for an escort agency."

"None of her friends believe it," Laura said abruptly. She stood, and held out her hand. "Thanks so much for your help. I'd like to leave my phone number so you can give me a call if you remember anything else."

WHEN LAURA CAME OUT of the library she checked her watch. It was a little after four. The sunny sky had changed to one of the stormy ones Dallas is famous for in the spring. Dark, sinister gray clouds overlaid with long green bands of light hung over the horizon. Rain threatened, thunder rumbled; everything reminded Laura of the tornadoes that raked the area every spring.

A sudden sharp gust of wind tore at her, and she wrapped her arms around herself as she hurried down the street toward the parking garage. She had only gone a short distance when she thought she heard footsteps behind her. Her shoulder bag slapped against her hip as she turned quickly to see who was there. She saw no one.

She began to walk faster. The footsteps sounded in her ears again, but this time she decided not to give in to her foolish fears. Just one more block and she'd be passing the parking booth where she'd seen a muscular man sitting on a stool her first time by it.

When she reached the corner the light turned red, and she waited for the person behind her to catch up. The footsteps had stopped and no one came. Her eyes searched desperately for a policeman she'd seen near this corner earlier. Where were the other pedestrians? At this time of day, she decided, everyone was inside the large office buildings. There were no stores in the area, and anyway, why would shoppers be out in this kind of weather?

With no cars in sight, she headed rapidly across the street. The footsteps followed.

Panicked now, Laura began to run. The footsteps clattered behind her, and she could hear them gaining. This was no phantom, she thought. Her heart pounded so hard it made her chest burn. It seemed that her whole life had speeded up in the last few days. Faster, faster, like a top spinning out of control or like that Ferris wheel Brandon had told her about.

When the footsteps reached her she tried to scream, but an arm shot around her and at the same time a hard, wiry hand came down over her mouth. She kicked and tried to wriggle away from her attacker, but felt herself being dragged sideways until she was facing a brick wall in what she thought must be an alleyway.

When she attempted to bite the hand over her mouth, she felt something cold against her throat. "This knife is going to slash you if you don't stand still," a low voice said. The blade of the knife grazed the side of her neck as if to emphasize the words.

He is going to kill me, she thought with detached clarity. This must be the man who killed Joan. Or perhaps he was totally unconnected with the case. A rapist who had seen a woman alone on the street. *Stand still,* she told herself. *Try to give yourself time to think.*

When she appeared to acquiesce, he murmured, "That's better."

She tried to speak against his moist palm, and he pressed the knife against her neck again. "Laura Gibson. This is your last warning," he said. "There are people who are tired of you. They want your promise you'll be back in Houston by tomorrow night. What am I going to tell them, sweetheart?"

She swallowed, and he laughed. "Can't talk with this knife against your throat? Just nod your head."

Tell him what he wants to hear, her mind said. She nodded, and felt the cold blade touch her throat again. "Good. Now let's rough you up a little so you won't forget." In a flash he moved the knife down her sweater, slicing it open to the waist. She felt the cold sting of the blade against her exposed skin and thought she might faint.

Laura struggled to get away from him, but he only laughed. "Maybe you need a little more convincing. How's this?" he asked. "If you're not on your way to Houston by tomorrow night, your dead friend's mother is going to be the next victim. You wouldn't want that on your conscience, now would you?"

Laura heard voices in the distance. Without another word, the man shoved her to the pavement in the alleyway and ran toward the opposite end, away from the way they'd entered. Laura fell to her knees, her body shaking and her breath catching in her chest, her heart pumping hard. She gritted her teeth and gripped the wall to help pull herself to her feet.

She stared in the direction he'd disappeared. Nothing. She hadn't even gotten a look at him, she realized.

A chill overtook her and she looked down, realizing why she was cold. She clutched the edges of the sweater together and tied them as best she could.

She stumbled toward the street, and when she reached the sidewalk she saw two men in business suits walking toward the library. She started to call after them, but decided against it. She hadn't the energy to explain her state and appearance to strangers. Staying close to the walls of the buildings, she walked toward the garage. Her mind replayed the man's threat over and over until she thought she'd scream.

The man in the booth gave her an odd stare when she reached the garage. She stared straight ahead and hurried past him. When she got to her car, she fumbled her keys but finally was able to unlock the door and climb inside. She slumped into the seat, then hit the button on the door in a panic. Everything that had happened to her in the last few days came back in a flood and she gave way to a bout of trembling. The thought of Mrs. Connor bothered her the most. What kind of animal would threaten her?

Suddenly she realized she had to warn Mrs. Connor. And she had to get to Brandon and tell him what had happened. She ignored her trembling hands and started the car.

When she reached the booth she had her money ready, and she handed it to the operator along with her ticket. His eyes took in her torn sweater, but instead of offering an explanation Laura deflected his curiosity with a hostile look.

Rain blurred her view of the road as she pulled out into the street, and she turned on the windshield wipers. She drove slowly through the heavy downpour, talking to herself, reviewing what had happened, wondering if she had the strength to go on.

By the time Laura reached Brandon's office, she had found some hidden reserve of strength. She parked the car behind the building, checking to make certain no one was lurking in the alley before she got out. She ran across the lobby to the elevator, ignoring the friendly wave of the man at the newsstand. At the moment she trusted no one.

She pushed open Brandon's door. The outer office was empty, so she ran into the back room. He was sitting at his desk, and he glanced up in surprise. At the sight of him, she crumbled, murmuring his name.

He was on his feet instantly and hurrying toward her. "What's wrong, Laura?"

She swallowed. "Someone..." She swallowed again, trying to dislodge the lump in her throat, but couldn't go on.

He put his arms around her, and she leaned her head against him. His palms made circles on her back, kneading the tense muscles. "What happened?" he murmured. His heart pounded in rhythm with hers.

After a few minutes she stepped back. Brandon's gaze swept over her torn sweater and his eyes grew stormy. "Who did this to you?" he demanded.

"A man. Downtown." Her voice was giving her trouble again, and she felt herself begin to shake. He helped her into the leather chair, then went over to the coffeepot and poured her half a cup. He topped it off with brandy and then added sugar.

Seating himself on the arm of her chair, he said, "Drink this." As much as he wanted to find out what had upset her, he knew the shock, the vagueness, the trembling had to be cared for first. He could wait. All that mattered was that she was safe and with him. From now on he had to keep her close and protected.

She took the bracing drink, her hands shaking so badly it almost sloshed over the rim. "It's to drink, not just to stare at," he said gently.

She took a long gulp, shuddered, and handed it back to him. "I got another warning," she said. "Get out of Dallas by tomorrow night or..."

"Or?" he probed. Her voice had returned, and he knew that he'd been right not to give in to the urge to cradle her in his arms. Inside, he was seething. Whoever had done this was going to have to pay.

"A man dragged me into an alley. He was holding a knife against my throat. He said Joan's mother would be the next victim if..." She stopped, finding it difficult to go on. *Pull yourself together,* she urged herself. Squaring her shoulders, she continued. "He warned me to back to Houston."

His eyes grew darker, but his voice was gentle. "Start at the beginning, Laura. Tell me everything that happened since I last saw you."

She told him about the library and the confrontation in the alley with a semblance of coherence. As soon as she finished, he said, "Let's go to the police immediately."

"No," Laura said, tightening the knot in her torn sweater. She'd been through enough for one day. She couldn't bear the thought of being questioned by the cynical Captain Quill, especially since he'd already told her to mind her own business. "What good would it do? I didn't even get a glimpse of him. All I know is that he wasn't much taller than me and he had on a gray jacket."

"Laura, we've got to report this."

"I can't. At least not right now. You told me yourself that the police couldn't help without a description."

He stared at her for several moments, then reached for the phone. "I'll call Winn and have him take the report here. You remember him, don't you? He's the friend who was having the birthday celebration the day we met."

"What can he do? I thought you said he's with Homicide."

"All policemen are trained to take reports." He dialed, spoke briefly on the phone and then turned back to her. "I think I've got an extra shirt in the storeroom. Let's get that sweater off of you and see if you're hurt."

Brandon muttered an oath under his breath when he saw a thin line of blood on her shoulder as he helped her out of the sweater. "It's not deep," she protested, slipping into the large cotton shirt he handed her. It came down to her knees. She buttoned it and sat down in a chair. "Brandon, I'm worried about Mrs. Connor. Do you think they'll harm her?"

"Warnings are given to frighten people. If someone really wanted to hurt Mrs. Connor, they'd never issue a warning in advance. But I think you may have to return to Houston tomorrow."

"I can't just sit in Houston waiting to hear what's happening."

"Maybe you won't have to. I'm getting close now. That's why they're trying to get us to stop. But if I don't have enough for the police to move in and make some arrests by tomorrow afternoon, I'm putting you on a plane for Houston. Tell me what you found out at the library again."

When she finished telling him, he repeated grimly, "So Overseas Auto Parts is owned by a holding company administered by Joseph Comal, James Comal's brother." He stood up and went over to the wall. "The pieces of the puzzle are beginning to fall into place. It won't be much longer now."

Laura followed him with her eyes. The chart was covered with scribbles now, and she saw lines crisscrossing the entire sheet of paper. She wanted to read it, but didn't trust her legs to carry her that far. *Maybe when I quit shaking,* she told herself.

"Do you have enough to go to the police yet, Brandon? I think it's time to get some help. These people are vicious."

"All I need is a little more time, a few loose ends to tie up, before I accuse anyone of anything. Remember, we still don't have the faintest idea why Joan went to that hotel room."

Laura closed her eyes. It always came back to that, and she had to admit that they seemed to be no closer to answering that question than they had been the day they started.

The outer door opened and Brandon walked into the reception area. "Winn," Laura heard him say. "Thanks for getting over here so quickly. Laura's in here."

Laura recognized the man in the police uniform immediately. He shook her hands and sat down in the chair Brandon pulled up for him. "Take your time answering my questions," Winn said. "I'm in no hurry."

As she talked, he filled out a form. She liked the way he managed to sound professional and concerned at the same time. "Who knew you were going to the library?" he asked after she finished her account.

Laura thought back. "I told a librarian on the phone. And Mrs. Connor and Diane Hastings, a friend, knew." She paused while he wrote that down, something buzzing at the back of her mind, nagging her memory.

"That's all?"

"I think so," she said. She frowned, and Brandon took her hand.

"Was there someone else?" he urged.

"Let me go back over my visit with Mrs. Connor."

"Did anyone call while you were there?" Winn asked.

"Not that I remember. I called the library and then..." She stopped, her eyes growing wide. "Perry. Perry Hill knew. Mrs. Connor insisted I call him, and he wanted me to meet him for a cup of coffee. I told him I was on my way to the main library." She looked over at Brandon. "He said you'd questioned him this afternoon."

Brandon was frowning. "I tried to. He said he was too upset to talk."

"Want me to pick him up for questioning?" Winn asked.

"Not yet," Brandon said quickly. "Give me until noon tomorrow. In case there's a connection, I don't want to send him into hiding."

"How about Mrs. Connor? Do you want us to notify her that she could be in danger?" Winn asked.

"It will frighten her out of her wits," Laura said. She bit down on her lip. "I'm not sure Mr. Connor's health could survive something like this either."

"Get a patrol car to cruise her neighborhood tonight. If nothing breaks by tomorrow, we'll have to warn her," Brandon said. "I've got this case almost wound up. I don't want any slipups now."

When Winn left, Laura reached for her purse to leave. "You're coming home with me," Brandon said. "I'm cooking dinner, and I'm going to see to it that you get a few bites down before I let you go home."

"Is that a threat?" she asked, feeling as if a weight had been lifted from her chest. The last thing she wanted was to go home and spend a lonely evening reviewing what she'd been through that day.

"You better believe it," he said, his tone teasing.

BRANDON'S HOME WAS located in Highland Park, that enclave of old money north of Dallas's downtown area, where houses that had been built more than fifty years earlier were still gaining in value. "Another inheritance," he explained as they pulled into the driveway. "When my dad died, my mother decided to move back to the small town where she grew up. My sister and her husband live in

Minnesota. No one wanted to sell the house, though, so I became its caretaker."

"It's a fantastic house," Laura said. A house that looked as if it had played host to many happy occasions, she added to herself.

When they went inside, he directed her to the downstairs guest suite so she could freshen up. "You'll probably find something to wear in one of the closets," he said.

After he left, Laura located a silky white robe and decided to take a shower. She could still feel the imprint of her attacker's hands on her, his moist hand on her mouth, his body pressed against hers. She stood under the hot spray for a long time, letting the water wash away all but the memory of the experience.

When she finished her refreshing shower and was drying off, she heard Brandon's voice. Did he have a visitor? No, she realized she was hearing only his voice; he must be on the phone. Slipping into her robe, she located the kitchen and found Brandon there.

The kitchen was a massive room, with a cooking island in the center with a hammered copper hood above the burners. Next to it was an enormous butcher-block counter. All sorts of exotic pots, baskets, and gourmet utensils were dangling from a metal rack attached to the beamed ceiling. The tiled counters had rounded corners, and there was a triple stainless steel sink with a built-in draining rack for fruits and vegetables.

Brandon was removing food from the refrigerator. "Pull up a stool and make yourself at home," he said.

"What a kitchen," Laura said. "Are you a great cook?"

"I like to experiment. My mother had a food show on a local TV station, so she had the kitchen there duplicated in our home."

"Lucky you."

"Not really. She was always into some fad. One month it was high protein foods; the next it might be tofu or brown-bread-and-sprouts time. At least things didn't get dull."

He moved over to the rack and took down a large copper-bottomed pot and filled it with water. "How does pasta sound?" he asked.

"Good."

"I'm glad, because that's about all I have."

She laughed, feeling at home. There was no awkwardness between them, no what-am-I-doing-here-dressed-in-nothing-but-a-robe-in-a-man's-house, no compulsion to fill in the silent gaps while he worked.

He set out two wineglasses and filled them with white wine, and put a plate of crisp, buttery crackers in front of her. She sipped from her glass, watching his tanned hands turn in graceful, easy movements as he fluted mushrooms, made radish spirals and cucumber flowers, and then arranged them with thin asparagus stalks on a bed of Bibb lettuce. When the water in the pot came to a boil, he added a sprinkling of salt and a refrigerated package of pasta swirls.

After lowering the flame on the burner, he pulled up a stool and sat down across from her. "Do you entertain often?" Laura asked. Only an arm's length away from her, he radiated such smoldering intensity that she felt his heat deep within her. Lifting her head, she stared into a pair of dark gray eyes burning with desire.

"No, I'm too busy." His voice was soft and compelling, caressing and unleashing an almost unbearable tension in her. "Laura," he said, twirling the stem of his wine glass. "I'm not involved with anyone. Are you?"

Brandon cursed himself silently for asking the question. It had been a mistake to bring her here, especially after what had happened to her today. He was still furious and shaken over the way she'd been threatened, the way her sweater had been slashed, the trail of blood the knife had left on her delicate skin.

He longed to take Laura in his arms, comfort her, promise to protect her always. But he knew he wouldn't be able to stop at that; he wanted to make love to her, too. And he sensed that she wanted it as much as he did.

He still couldn't be sure that her responsiveness was a matter of personal chemistry. Danger, he knew, was a powerful aphrodisiac. Her adrenaline level was still high; she'd rushed to him as her rescuer and now she was showing her gratitude in a time-honored way. Gratitude wasn't what he wanted.

"No, I'm not involved with anyone," she said.

He stood up. "I better check the pasta."

The abruptness of his reply startled Laura, and she felt herself grow warm over what she had been thinking. "Need some help setting the table?" she asked.

He pointed to a drawer. "There should be some place mats and napkins in there."

Laura bent her head as she made two napkin fans and slid them through the ivory rings she found in the drawer. She selected silver, and arranged the settings on a table that looked out over a spacious backyard complete with a swimming pool. By the time she finished, he was tossing the pasta with thick cream and cheese.

Over dinner, Brandon kept the conversation light. He told her more about his family, and asked her questions about hers. Laura found his determined attempt to steer the conversation away from anything intimate almost amusing.

After dinner he started gathering up the dishes from the table. "Why don't you stay with your friend Diane tonight? I think you'd be safe enough in the condo, but there's no need to take chances. I'll run you over to Diane's house."

Laura couldn't resist teasing him. "Why is it I get the impression you're eager to get rid of me?" she asked. "Are you expecting company, Mr. Powell?"

He didn't laugh. Walking over to the sink with a stack of dishes, he said, "Laura, your life has been threatened today. I'm concerned that you stay somewhere safe and somewhere you can relax until we see if you need to return to Houston tomorrow."

She looked away from the impatience in his eyes. "I feel very safe here."

The blood started to pound in his chest. In self-defense, he kept his words blunt and cold. "How safe are you with me?"

Chapter Eleven

Laura could feel laughter bubbling up inside her as Brandon stood there trying to look menacing. "Let me be the judge of that," she said.

The corners of his mouth curved slowly into a smile. He walked over to her and stood, smiling down at her, his eyes revealing his doubts. She reached up and touched the bruise on his cheek, and he clasped her hand tightly in his, his gaze darkening. She nodded in answer to his silent question, and his hand slid into her hair, caressing it softly.

She was aware of his mouth hovering above hers, of wanting it to press against her lips, and she knew she had never felt such intense desire before. Her lips parted involuntarily as he lowered his head, tasting her lips with his in long velvet strokes. He moved gently, reassuringly, at the unhurried pace she had come to recognize as a part of his very being.

She whispered his name, loving the sound of it as his mouth slipped from hers and trailed across her throat and upward to her temple, igniting her sensitive skin. His hands moved from her hair to her back, pulling and pressing her against himself, molding her soft curves against his hard, lean length.

His mouth returned to hers, his kiss warmer, smoother, more life-sustaining than air itself. His tongue probed, slowly searching, expertly seducing, demanding total possession, while his lips crushed hers, his breath her breath, his pulse, hers.

His hands found their way to the sash of her robe, and she felt it open and fall from her. He tore his mouth from hers and moved her back, allowing the robe to fall free. His eyes took in the full white breasts spilling over her lacy half-bra. His hands traced every inch of her body, discovering its slender softness, her small waist, her slim, strong thighs, her curving hips. One hand reached up gently to cradle a straining breast as he deftly unsnapped her bra and let it drop to the floor.

His hands left her body only long enough to shed his own clothing, then returned, trembling with eagerness and hunger, burning her with their touch. He pressed her against him, molding flesh against flesh as his lips returned to hers, his tongue exploring and discovering, all doubts dissolved.

SOMETIME LATER he found himself in bed with her, not certain whether he'd carried her there or if they'd moved together, lost in their close embrace.

He took his time, exploring, touching, caressing, inciting her to soft, sweet moans. Fiercely denying himself the urgent passions coursing through him, he felt himself on the brink of losing control before moving over her, gently probing, his mouth and his hands and his body delighting her, possessing her fully.

She melted under the onslaught of his agonizingly slow, considerate seduction, which was turning her to honey and oil, mellowing her as it inflamed her, opening her like a flower to face the sun, fulfilling her in a crescendo that seemed to go on and on and on until she was lost inside it.

She awoke hours later, pinned by his arms, but instead of feeling trapped she felt comforted and safe, as though nothing could ever harm her as long as she stayed in the shelter of this man. She reached up and kissed his shoulder. He moved slightly, then settled back down, and she snuggled against him, content.

THE NEXT MORNING Brandon sat on the edge of the bed, looking down at Laura. She was curled in a tight ball, clutching her pillow in her arms, her hair tumbling over the sheets. He brushed several strands away from her cheek, careful not to disturb her deep slumber.

It was that dream he'd had last night, he told himself. Or rather, that nightmare. He's awakened, drenched with sweat, his heart pounding, remembering only that someone had been trying to hurt Laura. Then he'd found her there, cradled in his arms, her face turned to his, her lips parted in that vulnerable curve that tore at his heart.

Even now, in broad daylight, after a shower and a cup of coffee, he couldn't shake the memory of that nightmare. Damn. That's why he shouldn't have made love to her. She was too important to him now, consuming his thoughts, throwing him off balance when he needed to be razor-sharp.

Unless he could wrap up the case this morning, he was putting her on a plane for Houston by early afternoon. Or maybe he could talk her into flying to Minnesota to visit his sister. After taking care of a few matters, he'd give his sister a call and see if she was going to be home. No one would think of looking for Laura there.

The people involved in Joan Connor's murder were a sinister bunch. Not underworld types. They used that class of scum to do their dirty work, hit men to murder a young woman like Joan, thugs to try to steal information and to threaten Laura and himself. How had Joan learned that the Comal brothers were involved in fencing stolen car parts from their auto-parts store at the same time that one of them was a prominent CEO of the insurance company? It was a nice little scam, and the money was laundered through Quality Insurance and stayed in the family. Slick. Sean McAble's notes must have told her enough to make her suspicious. After his death, which no longer could be considered accidental, she'd started investigating the Comals. Now she was dead, murdered, her reputation smeared. But he was still missing the evidence that would tie all these events together, and time seemed to be running out on him.

The call he'd taken last night while Laura was in the shower might provide the clue he was missing. A woman who had once worked for Classic had heard on the street that he was investigating Joan's murder. She owed him a favor. When she'd been working for Classic, one of her clients had gotten pretty rough, and Brandon had helped her get out of the business, lending her enough money to set up a new life. She had told him on the phone that she knew a woman who still worked for Classic who might be willing to talk about what had happened to Joan. No promises, but if the woman was willing, she'd leave a message with his answering service where he could meet her. In return, the woman wanted him to help locate her missing husband and their son. Brandon had agreed, and today he was waiting for her call.

While he was waiting, Brandon had a few more leads to follow up on. He intended to find out if Lee Barber was connected with the Comals in any way. And he intended to find out more about Perry Hill. Of all the people who had known that Laura was going to that library, he was the one who didn't check out. It would have been easy for him to call someone and tip him off.

What was bothering Brandon most, though, was the identity of the policeman Joan had gone to with her suspicions. There was always the possibility, of course, that she had only made one phone call, been told that she would have to have irrefutable proof, and had never called back. But from what Laura had told him about Joan, it sounded as if she wouldn't have told an editor that the police wouldn't take her seriously until she'd made several attempts to get their attention. Was there someone in the department who had wanted to make certain her reports never came to light? Someone such as Doug Young, who might be even more deeply involved in Operation Back Roads than anyone suspected? The thought sickened Brandon, but he had to find out the truth.

Today he intended to have a meeting with Doug and ask him some very pointed questions, questions that would either tip Doug that he was a suspect or make him help Brandon in his investigation of Joan's murder.

Laura stirred in her sleep, and Brandon reluctantly left her side. Before leaving the house, he wrote her a note and placed it in the middle of the kitchen table where she'd be certain to see it. If all went well, he'd be back by noon with the good news that he had a case strong enough for Captain Quill to take action.

WHEN LAURA AWOKE, she knew it was late from the amount of light in the room. She reached over and touched the pillow beside her, but it was empty.

A pleasant warmth suffused her as she lay there, remembering the previous night's passion. She knew if there was one moment she'd remember over and over again, this would be it. There was still so much she wanted to learn about Brandon, so much time she wanted to spend with him, so many ways she wanted to show him she loved him.

Love? Her mind stumbled on the word. How could she be so certain so soon? The answer was quick in coming. There were certain things you accepted without analyzing them. What she felt for Brandon was one of those things.

She luxuriated in her memories for a while, then she got up and checked the rest of the house for any sign that Brandon might still be there. When she reached the kitchen she saw the note on the kitchen table propped against the coffee machine which was keeping a pot of the brew warm.

The note was brief, telling her to stay there until he called. Or was *ordering* a better word? She realized then that his manner no longer irritated her, because she accepted that it was only a reflection of his concern for her safety. The note reminded her she needed to get a reservation for a plane bound for Houston that evening, but he was hoping it could be canceled. If all went well, the case would be virtually wrapped up that day.

Laura reread the note several times as she drank her coffee. Each time, her eyes lingered on his signature: "Love, Brandon." She liked his handwriting. Like him, it was bold and incisive. But his words warmed her more than the coffee did.

She poured another cup of coffee, enjoying the kitchen and the love that had gone into its design. Finally she realized she couldn't possibly spend the morning in his home waiting for his call. If she had to return to Houston this evening in order to keep Mrs. Connor out of danger, she'd have to close up her parents' condo. The few things she'd put in the refrigerator would have to be given away, perhaps to Sister Martha. And she'd like to wash the sheets and do some vacuuming so everything would be in tip-top shape when her parents returned from Europe.

She called Brandon's answering service to leave a message that he could reach her at her place. His number was busy when she dialed, and she was almost relieved. She didn't want him worrying about her when his mind was on the case.

She took a quick shower and dressed in Brandon's shirt, letting it hang out over her slacks. Her car was parked at the rear of the house as Brandon had indicated in his note. A man wearing a straw hat was there pruning a bush, and Laura waved at him as she drove away.

When she reached the condo, she parked behind it and walked into the outer hall. Mr. Connor almost bumped into her. "Here you are. I rang your doorbell, but I decided you must have gone out for a late breakfast."

"Come in," Laura said. "What brings you here on a workday?" She didn't like to admit it, but she was glad she wasn't going to have to enter the apartment alone. She was still a bit edgy from all that had happened the day before. But seeing Mr. Connor reminded her of the threat that had been made against his wife. She fervently hoped he wouldn't have to be told.

He followed her into the apartment. "I wanted you to know that Millie and I have decided to leave for Los Angeles this afternoon. We're going to Hawaii after all. She told me you and Diane convinced her that Joan would have wanted us to go. Joan had paid for it as our anniversary present, and we'd waited so long to cancel we would have lost most of her money. Of course it won't be the same, but it might do us some good, remind us how grateful we should be for the years we had with Joan."

"Oh, it will do you good," Laura said, hugging him. "I think it's a perfectly wonderful idea. You need to get away from here for a few days. I bet your blood pressure will return to normal while you're lying on those fabulous beaches."

He looked a little puzzled by her effusiveness. "I feel bad about running out on you when you're working with that investigator. Are you sure there isn't anything I can do to help?"

"Everything's going great. By the time you return from Hawaii, my detective friend may have some news for you. News that will prove Joan didn't go to that hotel room on her own."

"That would help Millie," Jim Connor murmured. He reached in his pocket. "I have something I'd like to leave with you." He took a small handgun out of his pocket. "I keep wishing I'd insisted Joan take some self-defense courses. It would make me feel better if you had this."

Laura recoiled instantly. "I don't know how to shoot. Anyway, isn't it illegal to have a handgun?"

"Not in one's home. Of course, if there are small children around it's not safe, but you're all alone here. You can carry it in your car, also, since you're not in your hometown. Otherwise you'd need a permit. I called the sheriff's department and asked about city and state gun laws."

"If it makes you feel better," Laura said hesitantly. "I might keep it in my car. Is it loaded?"

"Yes, but it's got the safety on." He spun the barrel around and showed her the bullets, then demonstrated how to remove the safety and cock the hammer.

Laura shuddered inwardly but took the gun, checked to see that the safety was on, and dropped it in her purse so she'd remember to put it in her car. "When do you leave?" she asked.

"Our plane leaves for L.A. at one this afternoon. Millie is getting her hair done now, and I'm on my way to my shop to give them some last-minute instructions. I hope we're doing the right thing."

"You are," Laura assured him. If he only knew what a wise decision he was making, getting Mrs. Connor out of town.

As Laura was reaching in her closet for a change of clothes a few minutes after Mr. Connor left, the phone rang. Anna, the maid at the hotel, was on the line. "I talked to Manny, Laura," she said, her voice low. "He's scared, but he finally promised to tell you what he remembers about that night."

"Oh, that's marvelous," Laura said.

"You must promise not to tell anyone, though. He'll be killed if you do."

"Who will kill him?"

"I don't know. Come to the hotel and maybe Manny will tell you himself."

Laura grabbed a dress from the closet and slipped it on. She ran a brush through her hair, reached for her purse and rushed down the stairs and across the parking lot to her car, her mind racing with thoughts of how delighted Brandon would be that her efforts to reach Manny through his girlfriend had worked. It wasn't until she was driving down the street that she remembered that she'd promised Brandon not to conduct any more solo investigations. Well, this time it couldn't be helped, and he'd have to understand. Maybe if he'd told her a little more about where he planned on being for the day, she could have included him in the visit to Manny.

She left her car with the valet at the hotel and went to the housekeeping office in the basement. Anna was waiting for her just inside the door. She smiled shyly at Laura.

"Manny is in the lounge. Let me get him and then you can meet in the laundry room. No one will notice us there."

She came back within minutes, Manny walking beside her. The expression on his face was sullen, or perhaps frightened. Laura went down the hall and followed them into a large room filled with washers and dryers, all of which seemed to be churning and whirring at the moment. She passed the bill she was concealing in the palm of her hand over to Manny. "I appreciate this more than you'll ever know."

He pushed her hand away. "I don't want any money. They said they'd kill me if I told anyone what I saw."

"Who said that?"

"One of the men in the room."

"How many were there?"

"I saw three when I walked in. Then another came in."

"What did they look like?"

"I really don't know. Just like I told you before, I've been trained not to look at hotel guests. From what little I saw, two of them were tough. The had on suits, but their shoes weren't nice. One man was dressed fancy. Very good shoes, polished nice. He didn't speak. This is what I told the police."

Laura was disappointed. "Were they tall? Fat? What color was their hair? Manny, this is important."

"I'm sorry," he said, hanging his head. "I barely glanced at them. I rolled the cart in, and the man in the good shoes paid me in cash. I was getting ready to leave when another man came out of the bathroom. I wouldn't have noticed him, but he started yelling at the other people. He told them they were fools to be seen, and he yelled at me to get out of there fast and not to tell anyone what I'd seen or I'd be sorry."

"Did you notice anything about him? What was he wearing?"

"I did see something. He didn't have a coat on, and his sleeves were rolled up. On his left arm, he had a tattoo."

"What kind of tattoo?"

"A ship."

"A yacht?"

"No. It was an old-fashioned sailing ship."

"Did you tell the police about the tattoo?"

"I was afraid to. That man meant what he said."

Laura got a piece of paper and a pencil from her purse. "Manny, sketch the tattoo for me."

He shrank back. "That man will kill me if he finds out I talked."

"I promise I'll never tell anyone except the detective, and he won't tell anyone else. He'll just use this to help him locate the killer. Please, Manny." She held the money out to Anna. "Anna could use a new dress. Do this for Anna."

Manny stood there for a long moment, the frown on his face growing deeper. Laura held her breath, sensing that this was too vital to walk away from without giving it her best shot. Finally Manny reached for the paper and drew a rough sketch of a tall sailing ship with a number of sails. "It was something like that. I only got a glimpse of it. I was backing out of the room as fast as I could get the cart to roll."

Laura took the paper and slipped it into her purse. "Thank you, Manny. And Anna. You may have saved some other young woman's life."

Elated, Laura went to the front of the hotel and waited until her car was brought around. She considered driving to Brandon's office to show him the sketch, but there was little hope he'd be there in the middle of the morning.

Instead, she returned to her apartment and called his number. The woman at the answering service sounded weary. "I'd like to have you reach Mr. Powell for me," Laura said.

"I'd like to be able to reach him. The phone hasn't stopped ringing for him this morning, and everyone seems to think it's an emergency."

"Have you paged him?"

"Three or four times. The first time he called in, but since then he's been ignoring me."

Laura frowned. "Has he done that often in the past?"

"Not when I've been on duty. He always gets back to me within a short time."

"Maybe his pager's out of order. Is there any way to check that?"

"No. It's never happened before. I think it has a red warning light to let him know if it's not working. Maybe he's in a meeting and can't be disturbed."

"Well, that's a possibility," Laura said. "But try him again and when he calls in, tell him Laura Gibson really needs to speak with him."

BRANDON FELT THE buzz of excitement he always did when he was near the end of a case as he made the rounds that morning. He was still waiting for the call from the woman who was going to set up a meeting with the call girl from Classic, but he had tracked down another man who was on file as having reported an experience similar to Sean's with the theft of some Jaguar parts. The man had told Brandon that he was willing to testify that the parts replaced on his car were grossly overpriced and that there had been no waiting period to get the parts. He had written a letter to the insurance company telling them that he suspected the body shop was purchasing stolen car parts and then charging the company at least double their worth. Quality Insurance had never answered his letter.

After leaving the man, Brandon had stopped by Doug Young's office. As much as he dreaded it, it was time to confront him. Brandon had to find out which side Doug was really working for.

Doug wasn't there. A man in the office across the hall told Brandon that Doug had called in sick. It could be true, or unofficial code to say that Doug was going back under cover.

Brandon left a message with the receptionist asking her to tell Doug the next time he called in that Brandon needed to talk to him.

At loose ends while he waited for Doug's call, Brandon decided to drive to the hotel and see if Manny was back at work. He'd done his homework, and had learned that Manny was in the country illegally. Although Brandon had a lot of sympathy for the young people who swarmed across the border between Texas and Mexico looking for a better way of life, he intended to use this information to try to get the truth out of Manny. With luck, one of those steak dinners had been delivered to a man fitting a Comal's description and Captain Quill could have an arrest warrant issued.

Brandon was still a few blocks from the hotel when his pager sounded. He pulled over to the curb and located a pay phone. The woman at the service told him he'd had a call from Doug Young. "He said to tell you he's ill today but he would like to talk to you. He's at home." She gave him Doug's address.

Brandon turned at the next corner and headed for the eastern part of Dallas. Alarm bells were clanging in his head, warning him that he might be being set up, but he'd have to chance it. Besides, he still had a few cards he could play that would shift the odds in his favor.

He parked down the street from Doug's apartment building. After checking to see that his gun was loaded and that he had an extra clip of ammunition under his jacket, he started down the sidewalk.

It took him several minutes to locate the building that matched the address he'd been given. Then he walked up the end stairs. There was no one around. Probably an adult building. They were usually deserted on weekday mornings.

The corridor was empty and as silent as a cave. Brandon's footsteps echoed softly in the hall. When he spotted Doug's number, he walked past the door to the staircase at the opposite end of the hall. He leaned against the door and waited to see if anyone would get impatient and check to see who had been in the hall.

After several minutes without any action, Brandon once again made his way back to Doug's door. He stood beside the door, back to the wall, and took out his gun. With the gun chest-high in one hand, he knocked and waited for the explosion and splintering wood that would answer his question before he could ask it.

Chapter Twelve

A door across the hall opened, and Brandon turned and met the eyes of a woman whose unkempt appearance suggested she had just gotten out of bed. She spotted the gun, her eyes widened, and she backed into her apartment, slamming the door shut.

Brandon waited several more seconds and then knocked softly on Doug's door with his free hand. This time the door moved backwards a slight distance. Surprised it wasn't locked, Brandon froze. He moved to the right of the door, out of sight of anyone who might be in the room, and waited, the hammer cocked on his gun.

Nothing happened.

After what seemed like an eternity, Brandon decided to make his move. Swiftly, he dived through the door, holding his gun with both hands. He deliberately landed on his shoulder and rolled past a sofa until he reached a crouching position against the opposite wall. He only had time to make one visual sweep of what appeared to be an empty room before he felt an explosion going off in his head.

Face down, he slumped to the floor.

LAURA GREW EDGY as morning became noon and then turned into early afternoon. She got out the vacuum cleaner and made a start at tidying for her parents, but stopped when she realized she might not hear the phone ring over the noise when Brandon returned her call. At two o'clock, she called the answering service again and learned that Brandon still had not reported in.

Impatient by nature, she found herself growing more and more tense as the afternoon wore on. Should she stay put, or go to Brandon's office and wait there? But then another possibility occurred to her. Perhaps Brandon was calling his home, where she was supposed to be waiting for him.

She kept telling herself to stay calm, that nothing had happened to him, that he was capable of taking care of himself. He'd told her so in no uncertain terms on several occasions.

When her doorbell rang at three-thirty, she hurried to it and peered through the peephole, expecting to see Brandon. Instead, she recognized the uniform of the cleaning man who had picked up Sister Martha's habit earlier that week. The man was holding the plastic-draped habit in his hand now.

Laura opened the door. "Hi," the man said, recognizing her. "Your neighbor doesn't seem to be at home. I rang her doorbell several times."

"She's probably at the hospital with her mother."

"May I leave her cleaning with you?"

"Certainly. How much are the charges?"

"Seven dollars."

Laura got her purse and paid the man, giving him a tip as well. She took the habit and hung it carefully on the door frame between the living room and the hall leading to her bedroom so that she wouldn't forget to take it to Sister Martha that evening. Realizing she might have to drop it off on the way to the airport made her anxious again. There was nothing left to do but wait, and patience had never been one of her stronger virtues.

WHEN BRANDON CAME TO, he groaned and tried to get up. His head felt as if a dentist's drill had gone berserk inside it. After several attempts, he managed to sit up and look around. For a moment everything seemed normal, and then he spotted a leg sprawling out from behind a large chair.

Half crawling, he made his way toward it, then stopped when he recognized the man lying there.

Doug Young. Although he knew from the size of the wound in the center of Doug's forehead that it was useless, Brandon reached for Doug's wrist and checked for a pulse that wasn't there.

Feeling as if he'd been kicked in the chest, Brandon had to fight to keep from passing out again. Although he'd seen a number of murdered people during his years in the homicide department, he'd never grown hardened to it. And especially not when it was someone he knew.

He tried to stand, but his legs gave out and he half fell, half sank onto the floor. His knee nudged something hard, and he looked down and saw his gun lying there.

Damn. He didn't need to sniff it to know it had been fired recently. He'd been set up, all right, and he'd walked into it like a rookie.

He struggled to get to his feet once more, and by groping his way along the wall managed to reach a phone. His vision blurred momentarily, but when it cleared he dialed a number that connected him directly with Homicide without going through the switchboard.

Brandon recognized the voice as belonging to a policewoman named Leslie. He identified himself and asked to speak with Winn. The way he felt right now, he only wanted to deal with someone whose methods he was familiar with.

"He's just leaving. Want me to try to catch him for you?"

"No, you can take the report, Leslie. An officer's been murdered. Doug Young."

Leslie's voice faltered. "Doug? Are you sure?"

"I'm in his apartment right now." He gave her the address.

"I'll be right there. Are you all right, Brandon?"

"Except for a busted head, I'm fine."

Brandon hung up and stumbled into the bathroom and splashed cold water on his face. He looked at himself in the mirror. There were no outward signs of what he'd been through. Then he felt the back of his head, where he vaguely remembered feeling something immovable make contact just before he'd passed out.

Not a mark. His assailant must have used a rubber club to make certain there'd be no proof that Brandon had been unconscious during Doug's murder. Clever bastard.

He was about to call his answering service when he came out of the bathroom, but he decided against it. He wasn't up to returning calls at the moment, and he didn't want to be on the line when Leslie and the others from Homicide started arriving. He'd take a few moments to search through the apartment and see if he could locate anything that might lead to the murderer.

The apartment was furnished in what appeared to be one of those three-rooms-of-furniture rental packages: a tan couch and two matching chairs, two tables, two lamps, and a garish picture of a sunrise over a beach. The closet held clothes that would have suited Doug's cover. He'd never thought much about Doug's personal life, but he wasn't surprised that Doug was such a loner. Not many women could deal with a man who had a new identity every time a new assignment came along.

In the kitchen, Brandon saw a phone number scribbled on the wallpaper above the phone. Probably just a pizza parlor that delivered, but he scribbled it down anyway.

Leslie walked in moments later. With her was a man Brandon had never seen before. Leslie came over to Brandon first. "You need medical aid?" she asked, giving him a concerned inspection.

"I'm okay."

The young man who had entered with her was kneeling beside Doug's body. From the expression on his face and the way he gingerly picked up Doug's wrist, Brandon surmised that this was his first homicide. "What happened?" Leslie was saying.

Brandon ran through the events of the morning. When he mentioned asking the receptionist to give Doug a message when he called in, Leslie's eyes brightened. "I'll check and see what Doug had to say when he called in. Do you know what kind of case he was currently working on?"

"He told me it was a big one. I have reason to believe it involved a car-parts theft ring, but he didn't say."

"What did you want to see him about this morning?" Leslie asked.

"The Joan Connor murder. He was the first officer on the scene."

The young officer finished checking Doug and then turned. "He's dead, all right."

"Brilliant," Brandon muttered.

Leslie flashed a smile at Brandon. "My new partner. He's a rookie. Bernie Steele."

The rookie officer stood up and faced Brandon. "What made you enter the apartment if the man didn't come to the door?"

"You should have listened when I told Leslie," Brandon said. His head was throbbing painfully.

"I was busy. Tell me again."

"For God's sake," Leslie interrupted. "This just happens to be one of the best private eyes in the city, Bernie. Don't treat him like a suspect."

"Thanks," Brandon said. His head was buzzing as if a colony of bees had decided to settle in it. He sat down.

Leslie came over and looked at the top of his head. She felt it gingerly, then began running her fingers over it. "Where were you hit?"

"The back of the head. There's no evidence. Someone must have used a rubber sap."

"Here's the murder weapon," Bernie said, pointing to the gun lying on the floor where Brandon had left it.

"It's mine," Brandon explained wearily. "I'm sure my fingerprints are the only ones you'll find on it. It's pretty evident I was set up."

"You think Doug set you up?" Leslie said, her tone incredulous.

Brandon shook his head. "I'm trying to sort it out. The murderer must have known I was looking for Doug this morning and was waiting for me. My guess is that Doug was forced to make that call, but I doubt if he thought he'd be murdered when I got here."

Leslie turned from her inspection of the room. "Who knew you wanted Doug to call you this morning?"

"The receptionist, and a guy across the hall from Doug's office. I didn't mention it to anyone else."

They looked at each other for a long moment and then turned away. Neither wanted to have to voice what they were both thinking, that someone in the police department must have let Doug's murderer know that Brandon was waiting for Doug's call.

After wandering around the room and studying its contents, Leslie turned to Brandon. "There's a third possibility. Maybe Doug wanted to see you, but by the time you arrived someone else had come here to kill him. Then you showed up, and they saw it as the perfect opportunity to make it look like you killed Doug."

"It's a long shot, but it's possible," Brandon said. "I've already had a few warnings to get off the Connor case."

"Have you found out anything?" Leslie asked.

"Lots. I don't have an airtight case yet, but I'm getting damn close." He didn't mention that he'd had suspicions that Doug was involved. Doug's murder meant some rethinking of that theory.

"Too close, if you ask me," she replied.

Footsteps sounded in the hall, and in moments several police officers materialized in the doorway. After brief greetings, they started work, moving around the room, chalking the outline of Doug's sprawled body on the floor and marking the location of the weapon.

Two medics arrived and bent over Doug. A photographer positioned his lights and began taking photographs. Bernie Steele went out into the hall, and Brandon heard him knocking on a door, beginning the hard tedious work of tracking down potential witnesses.

Brandon felt useless as he sat there staring at them. A few years ago he would have been part of this team. It was only at times like this that he felt a twinge of regret at having left the department.

A few minutes later the rookie returned. Accompanying him was the woman who had seen Brandon outside Doug's door when he'd arrived. She had changed into a dress now, and her hair was combed. Her eyes still showed her fear as she glanced toward Brandon and then looked away quickly. "Tell my partner what you told me," Bernie said.

Leslie came over to the woman. "Yes, tell me anything you know."

The woman swallowed hard. "I saw a man standing outside this door with a gun in his hand."

"Can you describe the man?" Leslie asked.

The woman glanced at Brandon and then looked away again.

"Tell the police officers who you saw," Brandon said.

"Him." She pointed at Brandon.

Leslie gave Brandon a puzzled look. "Why was your gun out, Brandon?"

Explain this one without speaking ill of the dead, Brandon said to himself. "I had a hunch something was wrong."

"A hunch!" Bernie Steele said, sneering. "Leslie, we've got to take him in. We have a witness saying she saw him with a gun out before he entered. A gun that he admits was the murder weapon."

"Hold on," Leslie ordered. "Brandon doesn't have to be taken in. He'll go on his own and tell Captain Quill what happened."

"Did you hear anyone else in this apartment either before or after you saw this man?" Bernie asked the woman.

She shook her head, her eyes fixed on Brandon's face as if she expected him to rush toward her with violent intent.

"You left out something, rookie," Brandon said. "My gun doesn't have a silencer. Why wouldn't the woman have heard the shot being fired?"

"You had plenty of time to get rid of a silencer before we arrived."

"Stop this," Leslie ordered. "Brandon, I think it would be a good idea for you to drive in to the station now. Bernie, take down this woman's account and explain to her that she may be called on to testify."

Brandon rose from his chair and made his way through the door, past Bernie, who gave him an angry look. Brandon had to admit that from the rookie's perspective, it looked as if the murderer was being allowed to walk away from the crime. That's what separated the rookies from the experienced cops. The old guys seldom accused the wrong person.

The sunlight made his eyes burn as he walked outside and started for his car. He was still numb from the blow on his head and from finding Doug sprawled on the floor. He needed time to sort out what had happened and see how it fit in with the Connor case.

As he got inside his car, he saw several more patrol cars arriving and a group of neighbors huddled together, staring up at Doug's building. A yellow rope had been positioned around the entrance to the apartment, warning the onlookers not to try to enter. Brandon flipped on his car radio automatically, tuning it to the police band. He heard a man's voice, saying, "The suspect, Brandon Powell, is driving away now. Tail him to the station to be certain he reports in.''

Suspect! Brandon's felt himself growing angry. Leslie must have changed her mind after he walked out, and let Bernie radio in the call to the department. With his eye on the rearview mirror, he saw an unmarked car ease away from the curb and move along behind him.

He was damned if he was going to allow himself to be stopped. The was exactly what Doug's murderer had counted on. It was one thing to drop by the police station and explain to Quill what had happened, but if he was considered a suspect, he'd be held up for hours. He'd have to be booked officially and then interrogated before he could be released on his own recognizance. In the meantime, the car-theft ring and the murderers would have time to bury evidence and plug any leaks.

No, he couldn't allow that. He'd have to dodge the tail and go underground for twenty-four hours or so until he could check out the rest of the leads he had. He made a wide swing around and pressed the accelerator to the floorboard. The two men in the unmarked car stared at him blankly for a moment, and then Brandon heard a squeal of brakes and tires as they attempted to follow him.

Brandon glanced around. This was a tree-lined residential neighborhood. Young mothers were out walking their babies in strollers. Children were riding bikes on the sidewalks. An elderly couple was taking a leisurely stroll. There was no way he could risk a high-speed chase here.

Reluctantly, he continued down the street and then turned into an alleyway leading to an area he knew. He gave his car one regretful glance before he abandoned it and began to run down the road.

LAURA PACED THE FLOOR in her apartment, wondering what she should do. It was nearly four now, and still no word from Brandon. Another woman had taken over at the answering service, and she had requested that Laura not call her any more. "I'll let you know the moment he comes in," she had said, her tone indicating that she thought Laura was harassing Brandon and might even be the reason why he was avoiding everyone that day.

Laura thought of calling the police station, since she was becoming increasingly convinced that Brandon was in trouble. But the thought of what he'd say if she involved the police unnecessarily kept her from dialing the number.

A little after six, she flipped on the TV to get her mind off her worries. The gray blankness of the screen dissolved into a shot of an apartment building. Standing in front were dozens of police cars, their blue lights revolving. Policemen, in and out of uniform, were milling about. The camera zeroed in on a man who said in a hushed voice, "As you can see, the police are out in full force here. One of their own has been murdered. Doug Young, a police veteran of fifteen years, was found shot to death here this morning. We have been receiving conflicting stories from police officers ever since, and no department spokesperson has yet come forward."

Doug Young. Laura slumped in her chair and took a deep breath. A cold shudder chased across her body. Was this what had kept Brandon tied up all day? He had told her the evening before that he wanted to see Doug first thing this morning.

The reporter's face faded, but his voice continued as a picture of Brandon filled the screen. "The police are looking for this man, Brandon Powell, a former police detective and currently a private investigator. He was at the scene of the murder but disappeared on his way to the police station. Anyone having information concerning his whereabouts should contact police at the number on the screen immediately."

Laura's shock at hearing about Doug Young's murder had given way to overwhelming bewilderment. What had happened to Brandon on his way to the police station? As she stared at the telephone number at the bottom of the screen, she felt as if she'd walked into a a waking nightmare. Surely this didn't mean they thought Brandon had killed Doug?

With that thought came a surge of anger compounding her confusion and fear. She went over to the phone and dialed the police station. "Captain Quill in Homicide, please. Tell him it's Laura Gibson, a client of Brandon Powell's."

Captain Quill sounded even more world-weary than usual. "Yes, Ms Gibson?"

"What are you doing to find Brandon?" she demanded.

"We've put out an APB. Why?"

"I'm worried about him." She quickly described the shot that had been fired at them in the parking garage and the two men who had accosted him in the park. "You must find him before it's too late."

"Brandon can take care of himself," the captain said. "It's your role in this I'm concerned about. Doug Young was one of our best police officers. If you have any information that might help us solve his murder, I suggest you come forward with it now."

"The first I heard about it was on the TV. I'm worried about Brandon."

"Very touching. Let me warn you that if you know where he is and you withhold that information, you'll be charged as an accessory to a crime. If you'd followed my advice and left your friend's case to the police, things might be different now."

"And who knows how many more people might have been murdered," Laura shot back. "You've been letting Brandon do your job, and you're only interested now because a policeman has been killed. Joan was ignored by the police, too. Did Brandon tell you that she was investigating a car-theft ring that involved important people in Dallas?"

"Really?" he said coldly.

"Furthermore, I think it may have involved the police. Someone has known every move Brandon has made. Why don't you investigate your own house before you go casting stones elsewhere?"

"That's quite enough, Ms Gibson. Let me repeat that you are to report any calls you get from Brandon immediately. We'll be keeping a close watch on you."

When Laura replaced the receiver she glanced around her apartment, more frightened than she ever remembered being in her life. There had been nothing reassuring about Captain Quill and the thought of being under surveillance made her skin crawl.

She needed to get out. But where to go? She hated the thought of leaving here where Brandon might try to reach her. But what if the police put a tap on her phone line and his call to her led them to him?

She leaned her head against the wall, moaning. *Brandon, where are you? Why didn't you let me go with you this morning so you'd have a witness to prove you didn't kill Doug Young?*

After a few moments, she straightened up and went into the bedroom. She chose a few clothes from her closet and packed her suitcase. She couldn't stay here much longer, but where could she go? Houston? No, then she wouldn't know what was happening to Brandon.

The Connors'? They were out of town. Diane's! She and her husband would welcome her with open arms, she knew. That way she'd still be in Dallas where she could hear the news. Brandon would be able to figure out where she might be, since she'd mentioned Diane to him more than once.

She tried to reach Diane by phone, but there was no answer. Well, she'd drive over and wait for them to return. With two small children, they seldom went anywhere for more than a couple of hours.

She lugged her suitcase to the back door and then went back to see that the blinds were adjusted the way she'd found them. She was heading for the back door again when the phone rang.

"Laura." As soon as he spoke she recognized Brandon's voice. "If anyone's there, hang up and pretend it was a wrong number."

"I'm alone," she said. "Do you think my phone is tapped? Captain Quill said I'm being watched."

"He hasn't had time to get a court order to tap your phone."

"Where are you?"

"I'm safe. You've heard about Doug?"

"Yes. What happened?"

Brandon ran through the morning's event. "I walked right into a setup."

"Are you all right?"

"I'd rather be having a rerun of last night, darling."

Laura's voice dropped. "Please, Brandon, just give up and come in. I'm sorry I ever got you into this mess."

"Someone had to be in it," he said grimly. "I'm almost there, and it's too late for me to stop now."

"Do you still think Doug was involved with Joan's murderers?"

"No, I think I was wrong about that. I've learned a few more things, and I hope to have enough to bring in the evidence by tomorrow."

"Evidence on who?" Laura asked.

"The less you know, the less danger you're in. I still have a few chunks missing, but not for long."

"Can I help? Please, Brandon. I'm so worried about you."

"No, you should go back to Houston and wait like you promised me you would."

"I can't do that now. I'm not leaving Dallas until I know you're safe. Please let me help you. Do you have a car? I heard they found your Jaguar where you abandoned it."

"I'm without a car, a weapon, and money. But it's too dangerous for you to try to help me. Anyway, you'd lead them to me since you're being watched. Probably watched by two groups of people who would like to get their hands on me."

Laura felt a jolt of apprehension. "Who? Besides the police?"

"The murderers. I don't think you're in any immediate danger. They don't kill anyone unless they're certain that person knows enough to endanger them. As was evident this morning, they still think I'm just guessing, or they would have killed me, too. Instead, they hoped to tie me up with legal proceedings while they laundered their businesses. My escaping must have them in an uproar, and they'll be out looking for me. Your best bet is to call Captain Quill back and ask him to send someone to escort you to the airport and onto a flight to Houston."

"Never. I don't trust the man." She paused and then continued, "Please, Brandon. I want to help you."

"How?"

"I'll think of a way. I was just on my way to Diane's house to spend the night. Maybe Bob, Diane's husband, can think of a way to help you."

"You don't want to involve them."

"They will want to help. You're going to need us if you're going to wrap up this investigation. Until then, none of us are safe." She told him about the Connors going to Hawaii. "At least I don't have them to worry about Mrs. Connor now."

Brandon was silent for a moment. When he spoke again, Laura had to strain to hear him. "I'm desperate enough that I'll take your help if you can give it without risking yourself. If you think of a way, I'll meet you in two hours at the corner just west of the entrance to the State Fair grounds. Do you know where that is?"

"Yes, but won't there be too many people around?"

"Nothing's going on at the fairgrounds or the Cotton Bowl tonight. I'm near there now, and the carnival's not even open."

"What can I bring you?"

"While I'm dreaming, how about some cash and a rental car? I can drive you back to wherever you need to go."

"Okay, I'll try," Laura said. "How will you know it's me if I'm in a rental car?"

"Blink your lights twice when you come around the corner. But if you think you've been followed, just keep going. Promise you won't take any chances?"

"Yes," Laura said.

"One more thing, darling. I love you."

Laura tried again to reach Diane, but there was still no answer. As she stared around the apartment, trying to think of a way to slip past the police and whoever else might be watching her building, she saw the habit hanging from the door frame.

Laura started to laugh. It was perfect, and she wondered why she hadn't thought of it before. The news of Doug's murder had made her forget to listen for Sister Martha's return so she could give the habit to her.

As she ripped the plastic off the garment, Laura raised her eyes to the ceiling in a silent plea for forgiveness. Mysterious ways, indeed, she thought.

Chapter Thirteen

Laura stared down at the various mystifying pieces of her disguise, trying to fathom how they fit together.

After struggling for what seemed like an eternity, she stared at herself in the mirror. Her slender body was lost in the voluminous gray folds. Only a small triangle of face showed, framed on all sides by stiff white linen. Curving wings curled out on either side. All that was missing was a rosary, which she remembered having seen around the waist of the sisters she had observed.

She went into the bedroom, located a heavy beaded necklace that belonged to her mother and roped it around herself. She changed into a pair of dark, unobtrusive shoes whose tips just showed under the robe. Her purse was small enough to hold under one of the heavy gray folds.

As she started down the hall, Laura began to formulate a plan. It hinged on Sister Martha not coming out into the hall as she walked by her door. Laura could only hope she was still at the hospital. Not until she reached the entrance to the building did Laura realize she had been holding her breath.

Once outside, she didn't glance to the right or the left, but kept her head high. One hand fingered the beads as she walked briskly, trying to ignore the awkward feel of the swirls of material brushing against her legs and ankles.

It was just after sunset, and only a soft glow of light lingered in the western sky. She passed her car in the parking lot without glancing at it and continued on across the street to the bus stop. Two teenaged boys were sitting on the bench, but one got up and offered her his seat. She thanked him softly and sat down, trying to peer around the wings on her wimple to see if she could spot any cars lurking in the area. The minutes seemed like hours before a bus finally rolled up to the stop.

Once on the bus, she settled quickly into a seat near the back where the light was dim. No one appeared to notice her. The bus made several stops to pick up and discharge passengers, and after nearly thirty minutes it reached the heart of the city.

Laura spotted a large, luxury hotel and pulled the cord. When she stepped out, she quickly scanned the area for anything suspicious, but saw nothing.

Inside the hotel, she asked at the desk where a bank machine was located. The clerk pointed to an alcove, and she went over to it. Once there, she removed a plastic charge card from her wallet and inserted it, requesting the maximum allowed for one transaction. After a few minutes, she repeated the operation with another credit card, just to be certain she had enough for Brandon.

With the money safely in her wallet, she went over to the car-rental desk. A young woman with brown eyes was leaning on the counter. "I'd like to rent a car," Laura said. Just as Sister Martha had said, it was nearly impossible to speak with the linen band constricting her jaw.

"We have a medium-sized tan sedan available. If you don't mind waiting, we can send for another model."

"I'll take the sedan," Laura said quickly. She removed her driver's license and a credit card from her purse.

The woman took it and glanced at the picture, then looked up, clearly puzzled. "You're not in . . ." she said.

"We don't wear these all of the time now, dear," Laura said, trying to get the sound in her voice that she'd noted in Sister Martha's.

The woman laughed self-consciously and returned to the task of completing the forms. She handed a paper over for Laura's signature. "I guess I just never think about anyone my age being a nun," she said.

"We're all ages," Laura explained as she signed.

She went outside to wait for the car to be brought around. Under the habit, her skin crawled with the feeling of being watched, but she couldn't see anyone nearby who gave her more than a normal curious stare.

When she slid behind the wheel of the car, the doorman accidentally slammed the door on her trailing skirts. He reopened it, apologizing profusely, and Laura gave him the most forgiving smile she could muster. She drove quickly, her mind already going over the route she should take to reach the fairgrounds quickly before Brandon gave up on her. Her eyes darted back and forth between her rearview mirror and the road ahead.

She slowed down when she saw the fence surrounding the amusement park. October was the month of the Texas State Fair, but parts of the park operated year-round. Tonight everything was closed and deserted, just as Brandon had said.

Grotesque metal skeletons rose against the evening sky, and there was an eeriness to the place that heightened her uneasiness. When she spotted the corner where Brandon had said he would be, she made a sharp turn, checked her rearview mirror and flashed her lights.

BRANDON LOOKED AT HIS WATCH for the third time that minute. Laura was already five minutes late. He prayed that that didn't mean she'd run into trouble. He shouldn't have allowed her to talk him into letting her help, but he'd been desperate.

With a car and money, he'd be able to get another gun and meet with the woman from Classic. He'd heard from a source on the street that Lee Barber might be ready to talk, that she was in deeper than she'd bargained for, and he had a number where he might be able to reach her in Florida the next morning. Things were breaking fast now. Someone had become desperate, and was beginning to make mistakes. Doug Young's murder had been the biggest one, unless you counted trying to set him up to take the blame for it.

Almost certain now that he would have enough evidence to get a grand jury to bring in an indictment, Brandon still had a nagging feeling that he was missing something. Doug Young's death had thrown a new element into the case. If Doug wasn't involved with the car-parts ring, then there was another policeman on the take. Another undercover officer? Tomorrow he would call Frank again. Even with an APB out for him, he knew he could trust Frank.

Lost in thought, he jerked his head up at the sound of an approaching car. In the eerie light from the street lamp, he saw it was a late-model tan sedan. There appeared to be a lone person inside, his head draped in a strange hood. Expecting to see several armed men pour out of the back seat where they'd been crouching, Brandon slipped back

No Easy Answers

into the bushes just as the lights blinked twice. He hesitated but stayed where he was, a sinking sensation in his stomach as he wondered what methods they'd used to get this signal out of Laura.

The car went around the corner, and Brandon flattened himself against the fence and began walking toward the entrance to the fairgrounds. It was a perfect place to hide.

He was almost to the entrance when the car came around the corner again. It blinked its lights twice, then the driver pulled against the curb and opened the door on the passenger side, calling out softly, "Brandon."

He recognized Laura's voice, ran toward the car and slid into the passenger's seat. "Accelerate," he said.

She obeyed, and the car lurched forward. He pointed toward a corner. "Turn here."

Once again she obeyed, and then came to a halt in an alley. Laura slumped over the wheel, totally exhausted.

He touched her shoulder softly. "Laura? Is this really you?"

She lifted her head. Brandon had a look of astonishment on his face. She began laughing softly, and pulled off the wimple and pitched it into the backseat.

"Where...?"

"My neighbor's. She wasn't home, and the cleaners left it at my place so I borrowed it."

His face relaxed, and he moved toward her. "I've been so worried about you, darling."

His words were drowned out as he pulled her to him and lowered his mouth to hers. At the first taste of him, her response overwhelmed her. After all the worries of the day, to see that he was safe, to feel his tongue probing, his lips crushing hers, his hands claiming her breasts with soft pressure, she knew this was what she had needed.

He tore away from her at last with a groan, and she stifled a small cry. Her hands still clung to him, and her eyes were misted over with desire. "I've never kissed a sister before," he said, trying to get her to smile.

She shook her head. "Jokes, Mr. Powell?"

"I've got to get you out of here. It's not safe. Where do you want me to take you?"

"Let me stay with you," she pleaded. "I can help."

"You've already helped me enough." He checked outside the car and then got out, walked around and opened her door. She slid over to the passenger's seat, and he got in. "Where am I taking you?" he asked.

"Diane's. Unless you think it's too dangerous for her children."

"It's not, unless someone is following us. I'll keep an eye out."

She gave him the address and then sat silently while he backed out of the alley and started down the street. "How much longer do you need before you go to the police?" she asked after several minutes.

"One day. Maybe two at the very most. Lots of things are coming together. Tomorrow I'm going to see someone who may give me the hard evidence I need."

"Who is responsible for all of this, Brandon? Where is it going to end?"

"Three people, mainly. They're prominent people I think Joan was referring to in her letter."

"Who?" Laura said. "Surely you can trust me enough to tell me their names. One of them is probably that attorney, Joseph Comal, that Joan was investigating. And you mentioned his brother's name. James Comal, I believe it was. So who is the third?"

"You know it isn't a lack of trust. It just that I don't want to put you in any more danger than you're already in."

Laura grew silent, knowing it would be useless to press Brandon on this point. As they neared Diane's house, he said, "I want you to know where I'm going tonight. It's a summer cabin on Lake Lewisville, north of Dallas. With luck I'll come in sometime tomorrow, but if not, I'll have to return to the cabin."

"I've heard of the lake. Are you sure you're safe there? Whose cabin is it?"

"It belongs to a client I completed a case for last year. He gave me the key and told me I could use it anytime I want. The little resort area where it's located is usually deserted during the week, and I know the owner won't be around. I got a card from him from Switzerland a few days ago." Quickly, he detailed the directions. "The cabins don't have numbers on them, but you can't miss it. It's a fake Swiss chalet, right down to the brightly colored carved decorations in front. It's on the back row, along the lakeshore. But don't try to find me until you hear from me."

"Brandon..." she murmured. How could she see him drive off when his life was in danger?

He gave her a warm smile. "Nothing's going to happen to me, darling. Soon this will all be behind us, and I'll take you for that canoe ride."

She gave him a slight smile in return, pleased that he remembered their conversation in the park. "Is there anything I can do tomorrow that might help?"

"Stay with Diane. Don't go anywhere until you hear from me." He turned onto the street where Diane lived. "Which house?"

"The fifth one on the left." Where would she find the strength to walk away from him?

When he stopped in front of the house, he turned to Laura and touched her chin. "Promise me you'll stay inside and not let anyone know where you are until you hear from me?"

She hesitated, but finally nodded her head. He brushed his thumb along the curve of her lips. "Laura, I promise we'll spend time together soon." He wanted to hold her, but was terrified someone would see her with him. "Don't forget your neighbor's headgear in the backseat."

She took the wimple and coif when Brandon handed them to her and slipped them back on her head. "I've got to get this back to Sister Martha."

"Don't return it to her until you hear from me. She'll have to wait until it's safe for you to be seen."

"She won't need it for a while," Laura said. "I hope she doesn't call the cleaner's to find out why it hasn't been delivered."

He leaned over and his lips met hers. "I love you, Laura."

"I love you," she said softly. It took all of her willpower to open the car door and get out. She was adjusting the long skirts so she could walk when she remembered what she'd heard from Manny that morning. When she tapped on the window, Brandon leaned over and rolled it down with an inquiring look.

"Manny finally talked," she said. "He didn't see much that night. There's one thing that might be a help." She started fishing in her purse for the napkin and then held it out. "Manny said that one of the men had a ta—"

"Go," Brandon said as a car turned onto the street. He took the paper out of her hand and stuffed it into his shirt pocket. "Walk to the front porch without looking back. Keep your face toward the door as you ring the bell. And remember, don't go anywhere until you hear from me."

Laura straightened and walked briskly toward the front door. She heard the vehicle that had worried Brandon put on its brakes and then turn into a driveway several doors down. When she reached the porch, she rang the doorbell without looking back. Footsteps approached, and the porch light came on.

Laura shielded her face from the street, her heart pounding. The front door swung open, and Bob was framed in the doorway. "Yes?" he said, no sign of recognition in his eyes.

"It's me, Laura. Let me in," she whispered.

"Laura?"

"I need to stay here."

He pulled her inside and slammed the door shut. "What in the world is going on? We just got home and turned on the news. Your detective friend's wanted for murder."

Diane hurried into the hall, then stopped in surprise. "I thought I heard Laura's voice."

"It's me," Laura said, removing the headgear. She put it down on a hall table and slipped the robe off. "Can I have a hanger? I'm in enough trouble now without getting a nun mad at me."

Diane started to laugh. "Laura Gibson. What is going on? Bob and I have been worried sick about you, and here you've been going around masquerading as a sister."

"Maybe we better all sit down," Laura said. "It's a long story."

WHEN LAURA AWOKE the next morning, it took her a few seconds to remember where she was. Then she recognized a rocker Laura's parents had given Diane and Bob when their first daughter was born.

No wonder she'd overslept, she thought, remembering how the three of them had stayed up most of the night while she told them all that had been happening.

Almost all, she amended, stretching contentedly. She hadn't told them about the night she'd spent with Brandon, even though Diane had long ago guessed that Laura's interest in him was more than professional.

The house was abnormally quiet, and Laura felt a moment's alarm. She got up quickly and went out into the living room. It was empty.

She went into the kitchen and found a note from Diane on the table. "The kids and I have gone for our morning romp in the park. Help yourself to whatever you find for breakfast."

While Laura fixed herself a piece of toast, she read the morning paper, which Diane had left on the table. It had a front-page story about Doug Young's murder, accompanied by a photo of Brandon, identifying him as a prime suspect. Diane had circled the photo and written "Approved" at the bottom, bringing a smile to Laura's face.

The smile turned to a grimace as she read the evidence against him. Her stomach clenched with worry, and when the toast was ready she couldn't force it down.

When Diane came in a short time later, she reported that she'd met a woman at the park who claimed she'd seen Brandon at a grocery store that morning and was wondering if she should report it. "All of Dallas is buzzing about this."

"Brandon wouldn't wander into a grocery store," Laura said. Not even Diane or Bob knew where he was staying.

"I hope he gets the evidence he needs today. I'm not sure how much more of this suspense I can stand."

"Is he going to be able to prove that Joan didn't work for that escort agency?" Diane asked.

"That's been the hardest part of this whole case. Everything else is beginning to fit in, but we still don't have any answer as to what made Joan go to the Crown Hotel."

"Brandon will find out today," Diane said. "We'll have a party and celebrate when all of this is over."

"It can't be over soon enough for me," Laura said.

The rest of the day was spent in an agony of suspense. Having the children around helped. Laura offered to entertain them after their naps while Diane caught up on her paperwork. That evening, Bob rented several video movies, comedies only, in an attempt to get Laura's mind off the news they'd heard on TV concerning the search for Brandon.

The night was the hardest to get through. Laura lay awake worrying about Brandon until past three o'clock. Once she was tempted to call Homicide and find out if he'd been apprehended, but she was almost afraid to find out.

The next day was equally tedious. Around three in the afternoon, Laura felt she had to get outside. "Let me take the children to the park," she said.

"You know what Brandon told you," Diane said.

"Park. I want to go to the park," Diane's three-year-old, Betsy, began to chant.

"Now look what I've started," Laura said apologetically.

"I'll take her. And the baby. They sleep better if they've been outside. Why don't you look through the books that came today from my book club? I'm sure you can find something interesting," Diane suggested.

After she and the children had left the house, Laura wandered around trying to decide how long she was willing to remain a virtual prisoner. As she crossed the hall, she caught a distorted glimpse through the leaded glass in the front door of a man walking toward Diane's house.

Chapter Fourteen

Laura froze, hoping she couldn't be seen from outside. Her hopes were dashed almost immediately. "Laura, it's me. Open the door." Laura recognized Perry's voice as he began to pound on the door.

She tried to decide if she should ignore him. But that was ridiculous. Any minute Diane would return, and she might bump into Perry. Taking a deep breath, Laura went to the door. "I'm not feeling well, Perry. Today isn't a good time for visitors."

He pressed his face against the glass. "I won't stay a moment. I've got a book for Betsy. One I promised Diane I'd bring her the other day at Mrs. Connor's house."

Her excuses exhausted, Laura reluctantly opened the door, and Perry came inside. "I've been so worried about everyone," he said. "I tried calling the Connors, but they haven't answered. When I went by there, no one was at home. Then I went to your place several times, but you weren't there. Your next-door neighbor is worried about you, too. She said the man from the cleaner's said he delivered something of hers to your place but she hasn't been able to find you in."

"For heaven's sakes," Laura said. "I've been right here at Diane's."

"I heard about that detective friend of yours," Perry said. "Do you think he really killed that policeman?"

"Of course not." She hurriedly changed the subject. "The Connors decided to take that trip to Hawaii, after all."

"Oh, I'm glad. It was a present from Joan, you know." He glanced around the room. "Where's Diane?"

"She took the children to the park." Reaching for the book, she said, "I'm not feeling too well, Perry. I think you should leave before you catch what I've got."

"Nonsense. I never get sick." Perry walked into the living room. "I like Diane's house. It's so warm. I always felt sorry for Joan in her house."

"But it's a nice house," Laura protested.

"It was a lonely house. People aren't meant to live alone."

"I don't agree," Laura said. She moved away from Perry, wanting to keep some distance between them. "Joan was very content with her life."

"If Joan had lived, we might have married. At least, I thought that at first. But then things started to change between us. Joan didn't seem to have any time for me at the last. She got angry with me."

Laura glanced over at him, alarmed by his tenseness. "I'm sure she was just too busy with her writing, Perry."

"That's what I like about you," he said. "You always try to make me feel good. I feel very attracted to you, Laura. I hope you won't laugh, but the first time I saw you I felt there was going to be something special between us."

Laura found it difficult to breathe. "We don't know each other, Perry. We've only seen each other for a few minutes. You're just lonely for Joan, and I'm a link with her."

"No, you're wrong there. I didn't feel this way about Joan when I first met her. In fact, I was just sympathetic with her and tried to help her through her grieving. But there was a spark between us that I haven't felt since my wife died. Mrs. Connor said you're not involved with anyone."

Laura walked over and stood in the doorway. "I don't feel well, Perry. This isn't a good time to talk."

He moved to her side. "I won't stay long, but I just want you to know how I feel about you." He ran his hand down the side of her hair and then began caressing her shoulder. "My wife's hair was auburn. I loved the feel of it."

His intimate tone and his touching her worried Laura. She stared at him, remembering Brandon's first reaction when she'd told him about Perry.

Perry seemed to take her silence for agreement. He smiled at her. "I may not go back to my job at school. The principal seemed to think I was having mental problems, but now I don't care. It means I can move to Houston to be near you."

Perry's face was too close, his body pressing against hers. Was Perry really disturbed, or was this just part of the grieving process, as Sister Martha had suggested? More important, though, was whether he could have had anything to do with Joan's murder. He'd sounded angry when he'd said that Joan hadn't had time for him. Maybe her neglect had pushed him over the edge. Brandon had tried to warn her that there might not be any connection between Joan's death and the magazine article she was researching. How ironic it would be if Brandon was running from the police now trying to find the murderer when he was standing here staring at her.

The phone rang. Laura glanced at Perry, wondering if he'd make a move to keep her from answering it.

He was still smiling at her. She talked softly as she moved toward the phone. "This may be for Diane. I should answer it."

Perry's eyes had a glazed expression, and he watched her every move. Laura picked up the phone. "Hastings residence."

"This is Winn Johnson. I'm looking for Laura Gibson."

"Winn! This is Laura." Her knees grew weak with relief.

"Are you alone?" Winn asked.

"No, there's a friend here. Perry Hill. I think I mentioned him to you the other day." She looked over at Perry to see if he was upset that she had mentioned him. He was still smiling at her in a way that made her skin crawl.

"Don't say anything to him, but I have a message for you from Brandon."

Her heart beat wildly. "Where is he? Is he all right?"

"Shh. He said to tell you he has all the evidence he needs now. He's going to come in tonight."

"That's wonderful!"

"Maybe. I'm a little worried. According to Brandon, there's some police involvement in this case. I'm afraid there'll be an accident when he tries to come in. You know, someone will claim they were just trying to arrest him."

Laura bit her lip in frustration. "What should we do, Winn?"

"I'm thinking about going to him and seeing if he won't let me take him in."

For a moment, Laura felt a frisson of alarm. What if this was just a ploy on the part of the police to recapture Brandon? "What did he say when he called you?"

"He told me he was worried about you. He gave me your phone number and the address where you were staying with the Hastings. He told me to call and let you know he was okay."

"Did he tell you where he was staying?"

"Good Lord, no. He called me at the police station, and you never know when someone is going to pick up one of the phones and listen in. Especially now. Everyone knows Brandon's my buddy. He told me you knew and I could find out from you."

Was he telling the truth? Confused and more than a little worried, she glanced up at Perry. He had moved closer to her, and she could feel his warm breath on the back of her neck. "I don't know, Winn. Brandon told me not to tell anyone where he was staying. Why didn't he just call me?"

"He said he tried. The line was busy, and he couldn't risk being seen at the pay phone he was calling from."

Laura tried to remember whether Diane had been on the phone, and realized she had talked to her mother several hours earlier. "When did he try to call me?"

"He called me over an hour ago. I didn't want to arouse anyone's suspicion, so I waited until it was time for me to go off duty. Then I drove to this neighborhood. I was just going to knock on the door, but I decided that might make you think something had happened to Brandon."

Perry was stroking her hair again. "You're near here?" she asked, torn between fear of Perry and worry that she shouldn't tell anyone from the police department where Brandon was.

"About two blocks away. I was just thinking. Maybe it would be best if you drove out to Brandon's hideout with me. That way you could help persuade him to come in with me. He won't believe me when I tell him that it's not safe for him to just drive into the police station by himself."

Laura shuddered, remembering how much trust Brandon put in the police force. "Even though he knows there's a bad cop?"

"You know Brandon. He says it's an isolated incident, but I'm beginning to wonder. There was a definite attempt to cover up the facts in your friend's case."

"I knew it," Laura said triumphantly.

"Then you want to come with me?"

She took a deep breath. "Yes."

"Can you get rid of that Hill guy without letting him know where you're going? Tell him you're going to the police station."

"I think so."

When Laura replaced the receiver, Perry was frowning. "That was a policeman, Perry. He's on his way here now. Maybe you better leave."

"What was it all about?"

"Joan's case. I'm still working on it."

"I don't think you ought to be involved with Brandon Powell, Laura. He's a suspect in a murder."

"I'm going to the police station with a policeman," she told him.

"Can I go with you?"

"No, Perry." His chin trembled and she added, "We can be friends, Perry, but that's all. Mrs. Connor didn't know, but I *am* involved with someone else. Why don't you talk to your counselor about how you're feeling? He can help you."

Perry was just leaving as Winn pulled up in front. Laura was watching out the window, and noted that Winn sat in his car until Perry drove away. That was a good sign. It meant he didn't trust anyone not to follow them to Brandon's hideout.

She held the front door open as Winn walked toward the house. There was something different about him today. His clothes, she supposed. Instead of the blue uniform she'd seen him in before, he was dressed in a tan sports coat over an open-necked striped shirt. His smile was just as genuine, though, and she invited him inside.

"That man who was leaving was Perry Hill," she said. "He's been acting strange. Brandon was suspicious of him from the beginning. Did he mention Perry today? Or is his evidence related to those who are involved in the car parts ring?"

Winn's eyebrows shot up. "Brandon told you about that?"

"Actually, I'm the one who called the editor and found out the details after that letter from the magazine editor came to Joan's house."

"Brandon mentioned the letter, but I thought he'd kept it to himself so you wouldn't be in any danger." His smile broadened. "I have this feeling that Brandon and you are sharing a lot these days. He talks about you constantly."

Laura returned his smile. "Let me leave a note for the Hastings and get my purse."

After writing the note, she went into the bedroom and located her purse in a dresser drawer. It felt heavy when she lifted it. Then she remembered that it held the gun Mr. Connor had given her. She had been berating herself for not giving it to Brandon that night, but in her haste to get to the door she hadn't thought about it. Since then she'd kept her purse hidden in this drawer, because it was too high for Betsy to reach.

Afraid to leave the gun behind without telling Diane, she decided there was nothing to do but take it with her. She'd hand it over to Brandon when she saw him, even though she knew he wouldn't need it with Winn to protect him.

When they reached the car, Laura settled into the passenger's seat beside Winn. "Where to?" he asked.

"Lake Lewisville."

"I would never have thought of that. Leave it to old Brand to throw everyone off his trail." He pulled out and began moving down the street. "He has a client who owns a cabin up there, doesn't he? Now what was that client's name? I met him once, but it's slipped my mind."

"He didn't tell me."

"What's the address?"

"I don't have one." At the frown that appeared on Winn's face, she added quickly, "He gave me a complicated set of directions, but I'm sure I'll be able to take us there."

"Good. The more I remember how livid Quill is over Brandon's disappearance, the more concerned I get about his safety."

"You don't think Captain Quill is the policeman who's involved?"

Winn laughed. "I doubt it, but I'd never rule out any possibility. Brandon didn't name his police suspect on the phone, so we'll have to wait until we get there to find out his identity."

They grew silent as Winn drove through the late-afternoon traffic. As they neared the expressway, the main arteries were clogged with people on their way home from work. To Laura's taut nerves, it seemed they weren't even moving ten miles an hour.

Winn punched on his radio. A newscaster began recounting the day's news. Laura closed her eyes and leaned back. When no mention was made of Brandon, she felt herself exhaling and realized for the first time how tense she actually was.

After the news, it was a welcome relief to listen to a musical program as they made their way across Dallas, through the outlying suburban communities and then into the countryside. The sun was just going down in the west, but the heat of the day had built up in the car, leaving the interior of the car warm.

"Sorry about the heat, but the air-conditioning's been acting up lately," Winn apologized.

"I'm fine, but I wonder how you can stand that warm jacket."

"I think I'll take it off." He pulled over to the side of the road, opened his car door, got out and shrugged off his jacket. Leaning inside, he handed the jacket to Laura, and she folded it and laid it on the back seat. Winn stayed outside until he finished rolling up his shirt-sleeves.

"Whew! That feels a hundred percent better," he said as he climbed back into the car.

"I can imagine. How much farther is it to the lake?"

He grinned over at her. "Getting anxious to see him?"

She nodded, smiling back at him. The radio crackled with static and she leaned forward to tune in the station more accurately. As she reached for the knob, something drew her gaze to Winn's muscular forearm. Her hand froze in midair as she stared at the tall sailing ship outlined on his left arm.

She felt her chest tighten. Her stomach knotted. Her mind was racing, trying to make sense of what she'd seen. Perhaps tattoos of sailing ships were fairly common, or maybe Winn had been in the navy and that was a tradition there. She practiced swallowing, trying to get some air into her lungs, telling herself she was the victim of an overactive imagination.

It didn't work. The rational side of her mind was telling her not to be stupid. Anyone with eyes could see that this tattoo was the exact replica of the one Manny had drawn for her.

She forced herself to register the unthinkable in her mind. Winn was the policeman who was involved in Joan's murder. With his strong muscular arms, he must have beaten her and then drawn his gun and shot her.

Her eyes strayed to Winn's leg. Was his gun in a holster strapped to his ankle? For endless seconds she sat staring, her brain barely functioning.

"Nice song," Winn said. He started humming along with the music on the radio.

She swallowed, trying to moisten her mouth so she could speak. "Lovely." Stifling down an hysterical laugh, she remembered how relieved she'd been when Winn had called while Perry was there. Talk about jumping headlong into danger.

Her mind turned to Brandon, and she realized for the first time that she was revealing his hideout to the one person who was the most dangerous to him.

Stay calm, she told herself. There were decisions to be made, and she couldn't afford to panic. *You mustn't let on that you suspect him*. She had only to keep herself tightly under control and stall for time until she could think of a way out.

"What's the name of the resort area where Brandon's staying on the lake?" Winn asked.

Her throat felt as if a golf ball had lodged in it. "He didn't say. I know where it is, though."

"Sure you can locate it in the dark?"

"Yes." She forced herself to sit up straight, fighting to keep the fear out of her voice. "I promise I won't get us lost, Winn. I have the directions in my head."

He smiled over at her. "Good girl."

What was he planning to do? Brandon wouldn't be an easy target, even for someone as experienced as Winn. But he would use her as bait, just as he had used her involvement with Brandon to trap her into going with him.

How was she going to get out of this? She studied him covertly and realized there was absolutely no chance of overpowering him. She'd seen a self-defense video once, and remembered that she was supposed to get him in a vulnerable position where she could kick him in the groin. But even if she found an opportunity when they were getting out of the car, suppose she missed? She had no experience with this sort of thing, and certainly no real training. All she'd managed to do would be to infuriate him.

"Brandon's a great guy," Winn said suddenly.

"How long were you partners?" she asked, her own voice sounding far away.

"A little over a year. I'd just moved here from a town in central Texas after a divorce. Brandon had just witnessed his partner getting killed. We took to each other immediately. There's nothing we wouldn't do for each other."

"Brandon told me how much he thinks of you," Laura said automatically. Then she felt her body grow even more tense as another thought overtook her. Was Winn telling her that Brandon was on his side?

No! It was unthinkable! But images raced through her mind, fragments of conversations. Brandon with his arm around Winn at the birthday celebration... Brandon refusing to tell the police about the attack in the garage... The news accounts that Brandon's gun was the weapon used in Doug Young's murder... Brandon driving a Jaguar, the kind of car Joan had been investigating... Brandon refusing to tell her what he'd learned about the case... Brandon stepping forward in the police station after her first meeting with Captain Quill, offering his help. What an ideal way to keep her under his control, to allow her just enough leeway to see what she could find out about Joan's murder but insist that he would keep the police informed.

She shivered uncontrollably and squeezed her eyes shut, as if she could shut off her mind. Nausea rose in her and she felt dizzy.

She had little doubt that she was slated to be the next victim. There was a roaring in her ears, and her heart began to pound with slow, shaking thuds. The sides of the car seemed to move inward toward her. Winn turned to her, a smile covering his face as it blurred before her eyes. "Brandon sure is lucky to have met a woman like you," he said.

She fought to clear her vision as he continued. "I bet you're pretty good to him." His insinuating words sent sparks through her brain, like water thrown on a glowing light bulb. Her hands curled involuntarily into fists, and she knew than that she wasn't going to be a passive victim.

"You'd have to ask him that," she said, trying desperately to keep her tone light.

Her only chance was to get away before Brandon joined him. There was a strong possibility that Winn knew the way to Brandon's cabin and had only told her he didn't as a pretext to get her to go with him.

Or perhaps there hadn't been any contact between the two of them since Brandon's escape from the police. Perhaps Brandon had been so certain of her cooperation that he'd arranged for her to be the go-between if he and Winn got separated. The thought left a bitter taste in her mouth, but it added steel to her spine.

"We're getting near the lake," Winn said. "Where do we turn?"

Laura leaned forward alertly. "It's beginning to look like Brandon described." Should she open the door and roll out? Anything was better than the torture she was going through. As she tried to make up her mind, she saw a lighted sign ahead that read Information Center.

"Stop there," she said.

"The Information Center?" He sounded skeptical.

"There's a map I'm supposed to look at." Her voice had an amazingly cheerful ring to it. "Gosh, it's going to be great to see Brandon again." She felt as if a part of her were outside her body, watching herself act a part in a melodrama.

Winn chuckled. "Not half as glad as he will be to see you, I bet."

"I hope so," she managed huskily.

He seemed pleased with her answer as he pulled into the graveled parking lot in front of the small wooden building. She reached for her purse, and its heaviness was suddenly a comfort.

"You don't need to take that with you," he said. "I'll stay in the car."

Was he going to search her purse? Then, suddenly, relief flooded her as she realized he trusted her. He was letting her get out of the car and walk inside without him, which could only mean that he didn't suspect she knew the truth. It should be ridiculously easy to escape from him once she reached the safety of the information center. "I'll be back in a jiffy," she promised.

The wooden steps made a loud noise as she half ran up them. When she entered the building, she saw a small, silver-haired woman sitting behind a desk. The woman looked up, "All the salesmen have gone home, but I'll be glad to answer any questions you have about the subdivisions around the lake. I have some brochures you can take, which will tell you the price of lots."

Dismay filled Laura. There was no help here. If she stayed too long, Winn would investigate. It was unthinkable to involve this frail, elderly woman in the fracas. She glanced at the phone on the wall, and remembered she had left her purse in the car. Was that why Winn had insisted?

The woman was staring at her with a puzzled expression. "I need to look at the map for a moment," Laura said, wondering if she could ask to use the phone on the woman's desk. But the building was glass-fronted. Winn would see her on the phone and come inside.

She walked over to the map just as the sound of footsteps climbing the stairs cut across her nerves like a whip. Winn filled the doorway a minute later. He smiled at the woman as he walked over to Laura. "Find what you're looking for?"

"I think so." Laura's gaze focused on the map, and she saw that the information center was directly across the road from the subdivision where Brandon had said the cabin was located. She placed her finger on the map in the opposite direction from Brandon's location. "It's right here. Holiday Haven. Down this street. One. Two. Three." Her finger stopped. "There. That's it."

Winn took her arm, exerting slight pressure on it. "Good. Let's go."

Laura shrugged free of his grip, smiling at Winn. "I need a rest room." She turned to the lady. "Is there one here?"

"Right there," the woman said. "Down that short hall. The women's rest room is on the left."

As Laura started toward it, she heard Winn moving along beside her. Did he intend to follow her into the women's rest room?

When they reached the door, she pushed it open and entered. Winn's footsteps stopped, and she could almost feel his presence hovering outside the door.

Anger flooded Laura, and she felt a surge of determination like none she'd never felt before. Nobody was going to do this to her. She made a sweeping survey of the layout of the room. Two toilet stalls. A counter with a sink in it. A wastebasket with a window directly over it.

She walked over to the sink and turned on the water. Then, as quietly as possible, she unfastened the latch on the window and slid it open, thanking God there was no screen on it.

For a moment she stopped and listened, but heard nothing from the other side of the door. Had he guessed what she was doing? Was he now standing outside the window, waiting for her?

"Laura, what's holding you up?" Winn's voice sounded through the door. Although there was a new edge of menace in it, Laura took strength from it. She knew now what she must do.

Chapter Fifteen

"Just a minute," Laura answered Winn impatiently.

He chuckled, and the wall shook as if he were leaning against it. She tiptoed to one of the toilet stalls and after a few moments flushed the toilet.

Then she hurried over to the window, scrambled up on the metal wastebasket and wriggled through the opening. The distance to the ground was greater than she'd estimated, and she fell in a heap. Without allowing herself time to see if she'd been hurt, she jumped up and began to run across the road in the opposite direction from where she'd pointed on the map.

When she reached the other side, she ran into the shelter of some bushes and stood trembling, trying to decide what to do next.

Within seconds, Winn came stomping down the front steps of the building. From the determined set of his broad shoulders, Laura could see that he was angry. He strode around the small building and then stood at the back, studying the area. When his gaze finally settled in her direction, she felt her hands shaking, her breath catching in her chest.

After several moments, he stalked toward the car. She sagged in relief, realizing she had a few minutes. Should she go back to the information center and call the police? No, that might be what he was expecting. She'd try to find an occupied cabin and ask to use their phone.

She turned and started through the bushes. Twigs tugged at her blouse, and she had to stop to untangle herself once. She heard something behind her and began to run. Her foot hooked in a vine, and she fell halfway to the ground but clung to a bush. Inhaling deeply, she forced herself to stand still and look around. There was nothing behind her. Her imagination was working overtime again.

Before starting out again, she tried to orient herself to the location of Brandon's cabin so that she wouldn't blunder into it. In the growing darkness, she could see only two lighted cabins. The roads were curved, and it was difficult to decided just how the subdivision lined up with the squiggles on the map. One cabin was across the road, and it seemed a certain bet that that must be the lake side, since she hadn't caught a glimpse of water yet. She started toward the other one.

As she neared it, she realized she was approaching from the rear. A light shone dimly inside, and she could make out a figure of someone standing at a sink. Let it be a women preparing a meal or cleaning up the kitchen, she prayed. As she started forward, she heard a car's engine in the distance. Frightened that Winn had seen through her ruse, she sprinted across a cleared space into a stand of pine trees and slipped stealthily along a tangled row of bushes.

When she neared the back steps, she opened her mouth to announce her presence. To her horror, she saw Brandon silhouetted against the light.

For one shocked moment, she couldn't move. Her mouth worked frantically, but the scream didn't come out.

"Who's there?" Brandon called out.

He started toward the door. As he neared it she felt her strength returning, and she twirled around and began to run. Her only thought was to put as much distance as possible between them.

BRANDON FLIPPED ON the porch light and tried to see outside. He was almost certain he'd heard footsteps and seen someone poised outside his door. Although he was wary of someone from the Dallas police finding him, he doubted they'd run up to his back door and then disappear.

No, the shadow he'd seen was a woman's. A woman who resembled Laura. He shook his head at the way his thoughts were wandering. He'd been thinking about Laura all day, wishing he could see her, wondering if she were missing him as much as he was missing her. No wonder he thought he'd seen her.

He returned to the sink and picked up another dish to dry when he heard what sounded like someone stepping onto the pier. Only one other cabin was occupied in the subdivision. A couple had arrived the day before with their two small children. The children had spent half their time on his side of the road, playing too near the water for their own safety. He'd seen them outside just before dark, and he'd told them it was time to go home. Maybe they hadn't and the figure had been their mother looking for them.

He dried his hands on the dish towel and picked up the flashlight by the door before walking outside. It was quiet and peaceful, and as far as he could see, no one was around. He was ready to go back inside and dismiss the whole incident as a figment of his imagination when he heard a soft plopping sound. The sound of something breaking the surface of the water.

One of the children falling in? He ran down the path toward the water's edge, calling, "Who's there?"

WHEN LAURA HAD found the strength to flee from Brandon's cabin, she had plunged down a path, hoping it would lead her into the woods. As she continued on, she saw the dull gleam of water ahead and realized she had been mistaken as to which side of the road the lake lay on.

A sharp pain jagged through her chest and her side. When she reached a wooden pier, she glanced around frantically, trying to decide which direction to take to skirt the lake. Then she spotted a canoe beached on the shore.

Without stopping to think, she grabbed one end of it and began to tug. It was a lightweight cedar-and-canvas craft, and once she had turned it over it moved easily into the water. Inside it, she saw that the paddles were in place.

She slipped into the canoe and sat down on the center seat before picking up a paddle. As quietly as possible, she dipped it into the water and began to stroke. The only sound as she glided forward was the quiet music of the rippling water's surface and the pounding of her pulse in her ears.

Then she heard Brandon calling. Her shoulders tensed into tight knots and she redoubled her efforts, pushing and pulling the paddle in rapid strokes designed to move her away from the shoreline and danger. Instead she moved jerkily, the bow of the canoe dipping up and down as the craft fought to go in circles.

She glanced up and met the beam of a bright light. It almost blinded her. "Laura, is that you?" Brandon was shouting, his tone incredulous.

She ignored him and tried to paddle even faster. He lowered the light, and she could see him standing on the end of the pier, staring at her. "What are you doing?" he demanded.

"Go away," she screamed, brandishing her paddle in the air.

"I know you wanted to go canoeing, but this is ridiculous. Have you gone mad?"

When she didn't answer, he began to pull off his shirt. His shoes followed. As Laura tried to move faster, she only succeeded in moving the canoe in a semicircle.

Frantic, she tried to straighten out as she saw Brandon dive into the water and begin swimming toward her with long, smooth strokes. In her panic, she prepared to fight him off with her paddle.

As he neared the canoe, she struck out at him but missed. His hand grabbed the edge of the canoe. She raised her paddle again, aiming at his hand, but he managed to pull over the canoe. She let out an anguished cry as she felt herself toppling into the water.

Bewildered, Brandon steadied himself and began treading water as he watched Laura plunge in beside him. When she surfaced, he positioned himself behind her and took hold of her chin. She struggled to get away from him, but was dragged down by the weight of her wet clothes.

"It's okay, Laura," he said soothingly when she resurfaced. "It's Brandon. I'm here to help you."

"No," she gurgled, flailing her arms briefly before slipping under the surface again.

This time he dived under, put a hard lock around her neck and pulled her to the surface. Her sudden stillness worried him as he swam with single-arm strokes back to shore.

When they reached shallow water, he stumbled to shore, pulling her with him. She was choking and gasping. He gave her a firm slap between her shoulder blades. After another bout of coughing, she caught her breath and stood, staring at him wild-eyed.

He surveyed her tenderly, and after a long moment the fear in her eyes gradually diminished. "Brandon?" she said softly.

He put his arms around her, the water dripping onto the pebbles along the shore. "It's me, darling. Who did you think it was?"

She made soft noises for a few minutes and then jerked away abruptly. "Winn," she said.

His eyes became alert. "Winn? Where is he? He's with the car-parts ring."

"I know," she said, sobbing. "For a little while I thought you were, too."

"Me?" The shock in his voice was all the reassurance she needed.

"Brandon, I'm sorry. I know now that it was crazy, but nothing in all of this has turned out to be what it seemed." She buried her head against his bare chest, wrapping her arms around him.

He held her close. "How did you get here?"

"Winn called me. He said you had enough evidence on the criminals to get an indictment."

"I think I do but I haven't talked to him." He pulled back slightly and gave her a disapproving frown. "I thought you promised me you wouldn't leave Diane's."

"Until I heard from you. Winn said he had a message from you."

"Poor darling," Brandon said, holding her against him again. "How did you find out he was part of the ring?"

"He rolled up his shirtsleeves, and I saw the tattoo."

"Yeah," he said grimly. "I didn't look at Manny's sketch until I reached here the other night. Then I tried not to believe it could be true, but all along the evidence had been pointing toward Winn. I let my friendship with him blind me. This morning I talked to a woman from Classic. She described Winn so exactly I knew I had to accept the truth about him. How in the hell did he find out where you were staying?" His hand was making comforting circles on her back. Then his hand stilled. "But what happened to make you think I was in on it, and where is Winn now?"

Laura pulled back, suddenly realizing they weren't out of danger. "I rode with Winn, but when I saw the tattoo I got confused. He kept talking about what a great guy you are and how close you'd been and I started to think about you not wanting to go to the police, refusing to tell me things, and driving that Jaguar. I was imagining all sorts of crazy things. I escaped from Winn through a rest-room window at the information center. I wanted to avoid you, but I had to come this way because I'd shown Winn another subdivision where I told him you were staying. He's looking for us now."

"Damn." He let go of Laura, steadied her and then knelt down to put on his shoes.

"He remembered you had a client who owned a cabin on Lake Lewisville, but he couldn't remember the name. Let's get out of here, Brandon."

Laura squeezed the water out of her hair, her blouse, and her slacks as best she could. She removed her shoes and poured water out of them. "Why did you pull over my canoe?" she said.

"Sorry, but you were attacking me with that paddle," he said, shaking his head to get the water out. He slipped on his shirt. "Let's get back to the cabin. I've got a gun there. Then we'll make a dash for the car. There's no phone in the cabin."

They had only gone a few steps when they both raised their heads at the sound of tires crunching over the pine needles on the road. "Hide here," Brandon said, guiding her into the underbrush.

They crouched down and watched as Winn parked his car and opened the door. He climbed out and began to walk down the path to the cabin, which was set far back from the road. It seemed an eternity before he reached the front door and knocked on it.

After a brief wait, he called out, "Brandon, it's Winn. Laura told me how to reach you. I've got some good news." Laura could feel Brandon's muscles tense as he knelt beside her. She reached over and took his hand.

After a few minutes, Winn knocked harder. "Brand, I know you're in there. I remembered the name of that client who loans you his cabin, and I asked the lady at the information center where it was located. Come on out, buddy."

Laura saw a grim expression in Brandon's eyes as he watched Winn's efforts. After a pause, Winn reached down and removed the gun from his ankle holster. He held it out and then kicked at the door. The door refused to budge.

"Come out with your hands up," Winn ordered. "I'm tired of playing games. I've got Laura out here with me, and if you want to see her alive, you better walk out slowly."

"Would he really kill you?" Laura whispered against Brandon's ear.

He nodded grimly. "And he could come out looking like a hero since I'm wanted for murder. I don't know how he intended to explain your death, though. He'd have to convince them that you tried to help me escape and were armed and dangerous."

Winn left the porch and started around the cabin. Laura shrank closer to Brandon. When Winn reached the back door, he pulled open the screen door and disappeared inside. Brandon rose and grabbed Laura's hand. "Let's run for the car. I can get it started without a key."

"Let's go to Winn's car. I have a gun in my purse," she said.

Brandon gave her a surprised look, but he didn't argue. When they reached Winn's car, he said, "Get in the driver's seat. Release the hood latch. When the engine catches, press down on the accelerator until I can slide in and take over."

Laura nodded. She got inside and located the hood release. It was stiff, but she gritted her teeth and tugged until it gave. Her breath caught at the clang it made, but a glance toward the house revealed nothing. She was glad it was so far from the road.

Brandon lifted the hood, and within seconds she heard the engine start. Glancing back at the cabin, she tapped down lightly on the accelerator until the engine made a smooth purring sound.

A shout came from the direction of the cabin. Laura saw Winn burst out of the front door just as Brandon reached her side of the car. One foot still on the accelerator, she slid over and then moved her foot as she felt Brandon's take over.

He accelerated, and the car sped down the road. "He'll be after us in the rental car," Brandon said. "Where's your gun?"

Laura groped around on the floorboards and found her purse. She opened it and took the gun out. "The safety's on."

"Take it off and hand it to me. Then fasten your seat belt."

She obeyed and then crouched down in the seat as Brandon swerved down a narrow lane and sped around a corner. "He's coming. Hang on," he told her.

The car plunged down the lanes and then pulled onto a paved road. They passed the information center in a blur and moved onto the highway. In the rearview mirror she could see the blinding beam of Winn's headlights. Brandon turned abruptly onto a side road, sending a spray of gravel into the air. The headlights followed, still close behind.

The sound of metal hitting metal made her glance at Brandon. He seemed to sense her question, even though he didn't look her way. "He's firing now. Keep your head down and brace yourself."

Before she had time to react, she felt the car make a one-hundred-and-eighty-degree turn and come to a jarring stop beside the road. Brandon leaped out with the car still running, and she heard the sound of shots being fired as Winn's car roared past.

After an interminable moment, Laura heard a resounding crash. Winn's car came to a shuddering stop against a tree down the road.

Brandon was running toward the car Winn had been driving, his gun held high. Laura leaped out and ran around to the driver's side, ready to run Winn down if he came after Brandon.

She heard a shout from Brandon and watched as he pulled Winn from the car. Winn was cowering, his face dripping blood. "Against the car," Brandon ordered.

Winn turned toward the car. "Can't you see I'm hurt?" he said, his voice trembling.

"Spread-eagle," Brandon answered, breathing heavily. He searched him with one hand and removed a gun. Glancing toward Laura, he said, "Come here and get the gun."

She walked toward them as if in a haze and reached out for the gun. To her surprise, he handed her both his and Winn's.

"Drive to the nearest phone and call the Dallas police. Tell them Brandon Powell is here and they'll send out the troops."

"But..."

He ignored her confusion and took hold of Winn, moving him closer until they stood nose-to-nose. "Now, you bastard," he said, "you're going to tell me what's going on."

Laura was rooted to the spot, staring in horror at the dark anger on Brandon's face. "I'm here to help you, buddy," Winn said, oozing friendliness.

"Liar," Brandon shouted. "Tell me everything or you'll never be able to talk again."

"I wasn't going to hurt you or Laura," Winn answered. His hair was hanging in his eyes. Blood was dripping down his forehead and onto his shirt. "Can't you see I've been shot?"

"I didn't shoot you. The glass from your windshield cut you up some. Now tell me the truth. How long have you been involved with the Comals?"

"My arm is broken."

"Tell me how long you've been working for the Comals."

The answer was raspy and difficult to understand. "A little over a year."

Brandon's eyes narrowed. "I'd never have pegged you for a dirty cop. How did they recruit you?"

"I owed some money. Racetracks in Louisiana. Then I arrested a man who was harassing one of Lee Barber's girls. She acted real grateful and insisted on paying off my debts. Then she started to blackmail me." He closed his eyes. "Brandon, I'm hurt. Get me an ambulance."

Brandon grabbed his chin. "Start at the beginning. Tell me who's involved. I know about Joseph Comal. He's the attorney who covers for his brothers. James is CEO at Quality Insurance. He sends foreign-car owners to Overseas Auto Parts, which I suspect is owned by their other brother, Roy. Then James has the insurance company pay off the inflated claims. They've got a crew of car thieves stripping cars and then recycling the parts, some of them to the very same owners they stole them from. The brothers collect from both ends and the middle. Am I right?"

Winn opened his eyes. "I think so. I just did a few odd jobs here and there for them. They never let me know the extent of their operation. Let me go, Winn. For old times' sakes. I won't get into any more trouble. I've been going through hell since all this happened."

Brandon ignored his pleas. "Don't give me that. This morning I talked to a woman at Classic, and she told me

Lee Barber is Joseph Comal's mistress, has been for years."

Winn decided to try to make some points with Brandon. "Yeah, Joe Comal financed Classic and still owns it. Lee didn't want to get into any trouble, but he forced her. Once you tangle with him, you can't get away."

Brandon glared at him. "Now the truth is finally coming out. But using Classic was Comal's biggest mistake. Tell me what happened to Joan Connor."

Winn cut his eyes over to Laura and then looked away. "She came to Homicide one day and said she wanted an investigation into her boyfriend's death. I overheard the guy who was talking to her promise he'd look into it. After she left, I offered to do the legwork myself, said I'd always been suspicious about the case."

"You're lying. Who was the man and why wouldn't he have come forward with this information when Joan was murdered?"

"He left the department. I swear I'm telling the truth. You can check for yourself."

"I will. What did you tell Joan?"

"I reported her to the Comals since I knew they'd been responsible for McAble's death. I don't know the details. I just heard them mention it once. Anyway, Joe Comal told me to pretend to work with Joan on the case. I dropped by her house several times and discussed it with her."

"The beer! That was what was buzzing around in the back of my head all along. The beer in Joan Connor's refrigerator was your favorite brand. You brought it over."

"I didn't know any was left. I didn't kill her, Brand. I didn't even know she was in danger. No one would have gotten hurt if she and her boyfriend hadn't poked their noses into things that weren't any of their business." He glanced over at Laura. "And if she hadn't insisted on getting you involved, things could have been different."

"Why did you cooperate with me, tell me things about the case?" Brandon said, coldness in his eyes.

"If I had refused, you would have become suspicious. Brand, let me go now. I'll leave town."

Brandon continued, "How did you get Joan to that hotel room?"

"I just followed Lee's orders. She told me to tell Joan that a man was going to make a full confession that he had tampered with McAble's brakes to silence him. Joan fell for it, and Lee Barber pretended to be an undercover officer and picked her up. I didn't know they were going to kill her."

"Then Joan never even knew about the escort agency. The Comals used Classic to set her up because Lee Barber was on the payroll and they could count on her to back them up!" Laura said. "Who murdered her?"

"A couple of hit men Comal called in from out of town. I wasn't anywhere near when it happened."

"You were seen in the hotel room. Someone described your tattoo to me. When you took your jacket off, I knew who you were," Laura continued.

"I swear I left that room with Joseph Comal before Joan and Lee even showed up. Lee left, too. She told me she didn't know Joan was going to be murdered, just roughed up a little to warn her off the investigation, like you were. I didn't find out about her murder until the next morning."

"Who threatened the help at the hotel?" Brandon asked.

"The Comals took care of that. They own a piece of the hotel."

"And Doug Young?" Brandon said. "Did you set that up?"

"Not on purpose. I'd been ordered to call one of the Comals and report when you planned to meet with Doug. That's all I did. Doug was like a bulldog. He was sniffing too close to the Comal operation. He tipped his hand to them when he showed up at the murder scene. Then you came along and got them worried. I warned Joe Comal nothing serious better happen to you or he'd answer to me. If you let me get away, Brandon, I can find out more. We can finish solving this case together, like old times."

Brandon snorted in disgust. "You had every intention of killing Laura and me tonight. You knew about the threats being made on her life. You knew about the man who assaulted her on the street. You don't really think I'd turn you loose."

He turned to Laura. "You better get the police here quick. This animal isn't safe with me much longer."

AFTER LAURA MADE the phone call, she returned to the gravel road where she'd left Brandon. A local police car was parked beside the road, and Brandon was talking to an officer. Another policeman handcuffed Winn and seated him in the back seat.

When Brandon turned from the car, she went over and touched his hand. "I'm sorry it turned out to be your friend, Brandon."

He appeared not to hear her as he walked away. She repeated what she'd said, and he turned. "You couldn't know how I feel," he said savagely. "I almost let you get killed tonight." He noticed that her clothes were clinging damply to her body. "Why don't you go home and get into some dry clothes? It's finished here. You've done enough."

Chapter Sixteen

Laura did not know how to respond to Brandon's abrupt dismissal. "I'm sure the police will want to question me. I've been a witness to a lot tonight, some of which you didn't even see," she said.

"Tomorrow will be soon enough for you to give your statement. There's plenty of evidence without involving you any further."

"Brandon, I'd like to see this thing through...now that it's about over...." She struggled with her confusion and shock at his unexpected brusqueness.

Go ahead, get rid of her, he told himself. *You saw the strained look on her face when she saw that you were ready to strangle Winn with your bare hands.*

She doesn't deserve a guy who could do that to someone he thought was his best friend. A guy who didn't even have enough sense to see what his best friend was doing when it was staring him in the face all the time. And on top of everything else, you almost got her killed. Way to to go, hero.

He resorted to the one ploy she hadn't yet seen through. If he could make her mad enough, she'd walk away with no regrets. "What are you waiting for?" he asked. "There aren't going to be any rewards handed out for exposing a bad cop."

Her head came up and her shoulders stiffened. "I didn't expect any," she said, quietly.

Several more police cars came to a stop beside them. Lights were flashing, and men and women came tumbling out and walked over the policeman who had handcuffed Winn. "Is he injured?" one said.

"Yeah. I've called for an ambulance. He's in no danger, though."

"Is it true he's a policeman?" another asked.

Brandon's face was pale in the lights. "Can anyone run this woman home?" he interrupted. "She lives in Dallas."

A uniformed policewoman stepped forward. "I'll be glad to. Right this way."

Laura cast one last look Brandon's way, but he refused to meet her gaze. He stared straight ahead, and she went over to the patrol car and climbed in.

The woman smiled over at her. "Looks like you had a rough night tonight. Want to tell me about it?"

Over the sound of the crackling police radio, Laura ran through the significant details of what had happened. The policewoman nodded her head sympathetically when she learned Winn had been Brandon's partner.

"That's a tough break. You have to learn to trust your partner with your life."

Laura recognized Captain Quill's voice on the radio, and she heard Brandon speaking with him. From what she could make out, it appeared the captain had been suspicious of Winn for some time. An internal investigation was being conducted, but until tonight they hadn't been able to gather enough proof.

There was no mention of Joseph Comal or Lee Barber. Laura asked the policewoman about that. "They're probably issuing arrest warrants for them now. It's best to surprise them so they don't have a chance to plan an escape."

When they arrived back in Dallas, the policewoman insisted on accompanying Laura into her parents' condo. Laura turned on all the lights and offered her a cup of coffee. She refused, saying, "Thanks, but I've got to get back. Take care of yourself now. You've had quite a shock."

That was the understatement of the year, Laura thought. After the door closed behind the policewoman, Laura showered, washed and blow-dried her hair and changed into a dress to go out again. She had no intention of playing a walk-on in this particular drama.

First, though, there were people she needed to contact before the news broke in the morning papers. She called Diane's house.

Diane answered, and hearing Laura's voice, started a monologue. "I've been worried sick about you. What happened? If Perry hadn't called to see if you'd gotten back from the police station, I would have thought you'd been kidnapped. You could have at least left me a note..."

"Hold on," Laura said interrupting her. "I did leave you a note. On the kitchen table."

"It wasn't there."

"Winn must have destroyed it while I was in the bedroom getting my purse," she said. "I'm sorry I frightened you, Diane." She ran through a brief synopsis of what had happened. Diane gasped from time to time but kept silent.

When Laura finished, Diane said, "You did it, Laura. You proved Joan didn't work for that escort agency. I'm so proud of you. Think how the Connors will feel when they hear the news. Are you going to call them?"

"Tomorrow, after I check to see what time it is in Hawaii, we'll call them together. I feel bad for thinking Perry was so disturbed he could have murdered Joan."

"That is a laugh," Diane said. "When he called he told me he'd made a fool of himself in front of you. He said you told him you were involved with someone else."

"He needs help. He's emotionally upset, and I hope he keeps going to that counselor."

"If every guy who finds you attractive needs help, counselors' offices would be filled," Diane joked. Her tone sobered then. "But you're right. I'll have a talk with Mr. Connor when he returns and see if we can't all encourage Perry to get the help he needs. Joan would have wanted that. Aren't you proud of her, though? I never dreamed she'd have the courage to try what she did."

"Yes," Laura murmured. With all the violence and pain, she'd almost forgotten that at least some good had come out of this tragedy.

LAURA'S NEXT STOP was a difficult one. On her way to the parking lot, she stopped at Sister Martha's door. It was past ten, but she could hear what sounded like voices on a TV. She knocked and heard Sister Martha's brisk footsteps. "Who's there?" the sister asked.

"Laura Gibson, your neighbor."

The woman opened the door. "Laura, how good to see you. When did you get home?"

"Tonight. I just wanted you to know that I'll get your habit to you tomorrow. I hope you haven't needed it."

"Not at all. The deliveryman told me he left it with you. How much do I owe you?"

"We'll settle that tomorrow," Laura assured her. After the news broke tomorrow, she'd tell the sister how it had been used. She could only hope she'd be understanding.

"How's the investigation coming?"

"I wish I had time to tell you the good news, but I've got to rush now. It should be on the news in the morning."

"Wonderful. I'll look forward to it."

WHEN LAURA REACHED her car, she realized she had no destination in mind. She pulled out and then headed for police headquarters. No matter what Brandon thought, she had a responsibility to report what she'd witnessed.

She entered through the side door and went straight to Homicide. It was deserted except for a woman sitting at a typewriter, her back to the door. Laura recognized her as the woman Brandon had called Leslie.

She cleared her throat and the woman turned. Her face lit up with a warm smile. "Laura Gibson. I've just heard about your harrowing experience tonight. Pull up a chair."

When Laura was seated, Leslie said, "Can I get you a cup of coffee?"

"Thanks, no. Have they brought Winn in?"

The woman's expression sobered. "He's at Parkland Hospital. Nothing serious, just a few cuts and bruises. They're keeping him overnight to make certain there aren't any internal injuries." She put her hand to her chin and shook her head. "First we lose Doug, and now we find out Winn was involved. This place is like a morgue."

"Then I suppose Brandon has been cleared of all charges."

"We never believed for a minute he was involved! At least, not those of us who had worked with him. Of course, the captain had no choice but to search for him since he was found there and his gun was the murder weapon. I'll bet Brandon is broken up over Winn. Brandon's always ready to believe the best about anyone. He's so pure at heart himself he can be a little too trusting."

"Where is he?" Laura asked hesitantly.

"At the hospital with the captain. I understand Winn is giving a full confession tonight. Naming names and places. Brandon is filling in the details he's learned in his investigation. It's such a shame about your friend, but at least her killers aren't going to get away with it. They were two hit men brought in from out of town, but with Winn's description we already have identified them and we hope to arrest them before morning."

"How about the Comals?"

"All three brothers have been arrested, but Lee Barber hasn't been located yet. The Florida police are looking for her."

"How about those creeps I saw in Joan's house, the ones who came to the park? One called himself Jake Marshall."

"He and his friend were picked up yesterday on a traffic violation. The officer recognized them from the report Brandon filed the other day, so he brought them in. At first they denied everything. Then tonight, after they heard that Winn is turning state's evidence, they started falling all over themselves, offering to squeal in exchange for a lesser charge."

"Did Winn say how he found out where I was staying?"

"Your friend's address book was found in the trunk of his car, along with some of Joan Connor's research notes. You'd think he would have destroyed them, but I guess he thought they might be valuable to him if the Comals decided to get rid of him. To find you, he must have called every number in the address book until he got the right one. It's hard to believe he was involved in this. Even worse, that he might have gotten away with it if he hadn't started to panic. He's admitted being the one that your friend's father encountered at Joan's house. He'd gone there to get the notes that morning as soon as he heard about the murder."

"He forgot his beer. I knew something was wrong as soon as I saw that, because Joan detested beer."

"It's usually the little things like that that trip criminals up," Leslie said. "This is a fascinating business. Ever though about becoming a policewoman?"

Laura shook her head. "No, I don't think I'm cut out for it."

"Maybe you'd prefer working as a private detective," Leslie continued, her eyes twinkling. "There's one I know of who might be interested in training an assistant."

Laura smiled weakly. She couldn't discuss Brandon with anyone at the moment. "One more thing," she said. "Who were the men who shot at Brandon and me in the parking garage?"

"We're not certain yet. Winn thinks they're the two hit men."

"The same men who killed Joan?"

Leslie nodded. "And one of them probably roughed you up near the library. The Comals were getting desperate. They made a mistake murdering Joan. She probably wouldn't have been able to prove her allegations, and I doubt if that magazine would have published an article without proof. The Comals probably realized their mistake, and that's why you weren't their next victim."

Laura shuddered, realizing how near she'd come to suffering the same fate as Joan. "Will I be asked to give a statement?"

"Haven't you yet?" Leslie pushed back her chair. "Captain Quill's set up a base at the hospital. Let me call there and tell him you're on your way. If you don't feel like driving, I can get a squad car to take you over."

"I can drive." She reached for her purse and then said, "The rental car! I just remembered. It's wrecked."

Leslie smiled. "Give me your rental papers, and I'll see that the agency is informed that the car will be impounded as state's evidence. You won't be charged for it. Oh, and tell Brandon that he can pick up his Jaguar when he's ready. It's been kept for him in the police parking garage."

"Thanks for all your help," Laura said, rising.

"Thanks for all *yours*. Without you, your friend's case might never have been solved." She walked to the door with Laura. "Give Brandon lots of tender loving care tonight. He's going to need it."

AN AMBULANCE PULLED INTO the emergency entrance just as Laura reached the hospital. She got out of her car, the swirling lights playing tricks with her vision as she walked to the entrance. When she reached the information desk and asked for Captain Quill, she was directed to the sixth floor.

A group of uniformed men and women were hovering at the far end of the hall when she stepped off the elevator. As she neared the group, Captain Quill detached himself and came toward her, holding out his hand. "Leslie said you were on your way," he said. "Come with me and

I'll show you the room where you can give your statement."

Laura shook his hand. "Is Brandon still here?"

"Yes, he's finishing up in the room with Winn. Bad night around here."

He stopped outside a door and knocked. A male voice said, "Come in."

"Ms Gibson here to give a statement."

"Send her in."

Laura spent a little less than half an hour answering a series of rapid-fire questions which left her exhausted. When she finished, she was asked to sign the statement. She had agreed to being videotaped, and only hoped her answers had been coherent and accurate. Some of the events had blurred together in her mind, but she'd done the best she could.

"That'll be all," the police officer said. "Thanks for coming in."

When Laura left, she scanned the hall and saw Brandon sitting in a chair outside a door. His shoulders were slumped, his hands clasped between his knees, and he was staring up at a man who was talking to him. She was shocked by his disheveled appearance, by the dark circles under his gray eyes. She wanted desperately to go to him and put her arms around him.

She started toward him, but someone called his name and he stood up and went through a door without seeing her. She leaned against a wall and tried to decide what to do. Nothing was going to make her leave until she'd at least tried to clear the air between them.

She felt she understood Brandon now. At his core he was all sympathy, compassion, caring. Like a knight of old, he saw himself on a quest for justice, and she loved him deeply for it. Although she knew that loving him would mean moments of anxiety and worry, there was nothing about him she would have changed.

She walked around a corner and sat down on a chair near the elevator to wait for him. After a few minutes she heard footsteps coming down the hall. "You look like you could use a little rest now, Brandon. You've had quite a shock tonight," Captain Quill was saying. "Thanks for all your help with this case."

The footsteps stopped. "I'll be seeing you," Brandon said. his tone terse.

Laura rose and reached in her purse for one of her business cards. She heard one pair of footsteps coming toward her and prayed they belonged to the right person.

Brandon rounded the corner and she stepped out, "Mr. Powell. My name's Laura Gibson. I'm an assistant to a private investigator, and I wondered if you needed any help. I'm trained to squeal during car chases and to investigate things that go bump in the night."

He stopped, his smile rueful. "Haven't I brought you enough grief, Laura?"

"You've brought me happiness," she said softly.

He shook his head. "I think you need to have your head examined. Since you met me you've been threatened, shot at, and almost killed by a man I thought was my best friend. What are you? A masochist?"

She spoke to the sorrow in his eyes. "I know this won't help, but I'd still like to say I'm sorry about Winn."

He brushed back a lock of hair from his forehead. "I keep thinking it was my friend who led your friend to her death. That's not going to be easy to live with."

"Tragedy never is," she said.

"What if it's a tragedy I could have prevented? There were things about Winn that bothered me from the beginning, but I overlooked them because we worked together so well."

"You couldn't have known what Winn was doing." She put her hand on his arm. "Remember what you told me about Joan? You said people change."

He shook off her hand. "I was wrong about Joan. She hadn't changed. She just trusted my friend."

"She *had* changed. In lots of ways. I would never have thought her capable of gathering evidence on her fiancée's murderers, especially since she didn't breathe a word to any of her family or friends. Your friend changed, too, but in the wrong direction. At least he's turned state's evidence instead of trying to plead innocent. Don't make it any worse than it is."

"I don't know how you do it, but you're making it sound so simple."

"Love is simple. It's people who make it complicated," she answered in a low voice.

She saw him swallow. "My life's complicated." He grasped her wrist and then dropped it as if he'd touched a firebrand. "I should never have let you get under my skin. Do you know how I felt when I realized it was my fault you'd gotten in that car with Winn, that you were an inch away from being murdered tonight?"

She wrapped her arms around his waist. "Once someone gets under your skin, I've heard it's impossible to get rid of them."

He stood, looking down at her. "Don't, Laura. I saw your face those times you watched me roughing up people. You went through hell when I was a fugitive, stealing a nun's clothes, racing through dark streets, cowering in the shadows. You deserve better than that."

"Try again," she said. "I didn't buy that one."

The corners of his mouth twitched briefly before he managed to pull his brows together in the frown she knew so well. "I can't change, Laura. I might promise but it wouldn't work."

"Who said anything about change?" she said, nuzzling her chin against his chest. "We're both stubborn, Brandon. I've always known that someone would be right for me. I just had to meet you to find out who."

His eyes grew dark and smoldering. "Laura." The word shuddered from him as he bent his head, his lips covering hers with a hard, bruising contact. "I love you, Laura," he murmured. Her mouth parted under his, responding fully to the slow caress of his hands on her body.

His kiss deepened, his tongue a sweet and swift invasion, and she melted into it. She could feel his heartbeat settling into that steady, strong, reassuring rhythm that she had adopted as her own.

He pulled back, whispering, "I couldn't have let you go anyway. I would have followed you anywhere you went."

She nodded, laying her head on his shoulder. "I know. You have to check to see if I'm eating enough."

He laughed and pulled her against him, his lips seeking hers again. It was as if all the passion and desire she'd ever known were concentrated in that one touch of lips. She pressed closer and clung to him, faintly aware of male voices passing close by.

Captain Quill's words broke through her dreamy state. "I don't know what I think of this client-investigator behavior," he was saying, laughing. "Seems a little irregular to me."

Laura pushed back reluctantly and faced the thin man just as the doors of the elevator started to move together. "I'm just getting my money's worth," she said, smiling sweetly.

**Enemies by birth, lovers by destiny!
Now in mass market size,
that richly authentic romance set during
the reign of the Roman Empire in Britain.**

Lynn Bartlett
Defy the Eagle

The beautiful daughter of a Roman merchant and a rebel warrior of Britain must deny their opposing loyalties and heritage when the ultimate passions of love become too overwhelming to ignore.

Available in MAY or reserve your copy for April shipping by sending your name, address, zip or postal code along with a check or money order for $5.70 (includes 75 cents for postage and handling) payable to Worldwide Library to:

In the U.S.

Worldwide Library
901 Fuhrmann Blvd.
Box 1325
Buffalo, NY 14269-1325

In Canada

Worldwide Library
P.O. Box 609
Fort Erie, Ontario
L2A 5X3

WORLDWIDE LIBRARY

DEF-1

All men wanted her, but only one man would have her.

Desert Storm
Nan Ryan

Her cruel father had intended Angie to marry a sinister cattle baron twice her age. No one expected that she would fall in love with his handsome, pleasure-loving cowboy son.

Theirs was a love no desert storm would quench.

Available in JUNE or reserve your copy for May shipping by sending your name, address, zip or postal code along with a check or money order for $4.70 (includes 75 cents postage and handling) payable to Worldwide Library to:

In the U.S.
Worldwide Library
901 Fuhrmann Blvd.
Box 1325
Buffalo, NY 14269-1325
Please specify title with book order.

In Canada
Worldwide Library
P.O. Box 609
Fort Erie, Ontario
L2A 5X3

WORLDWIDE LIBRARY

STM-1

ATTRACTIVE, SPACE SAVING BOOK RACK

Display your most prized novels on this handsome and sturdy book rack. The hand-rubbed walnut finish will blend into your library decor with quiet elegance, providing a practical organizer for your favorite hard-or soft-covered books.

Only $9.95

Approximately 16" x 8" when assembled

Assembles in seconds!

To order, rush your name, address and zip code, along with a check or money order for $10.70* ($9.95 plus 75¢ postage and handling) payable to *Harlequin Reader Service*:

>Harlequin Reader Service
>Book Rack Offer
>901 Fuhrmann Blvd.
>P.O. Box 1325
>Buffalo, NY 14269-1325
>
>*Offer not available in Canada.*

*New York residents add appropriate sales tax.

Take 4 best-selling love stories FREE
Plus get a FREE surprise gift!

Special Limited-Time Offer

Mail to **Harlequin Reader Service®**

In the U.S.
901 Fuhrmann Blvd.
P.O. Box 1394
Buffalo, N.Y. 14240-1394

In Canada
P.O. Box 609
Fort Erie, Ontario
L2A 5X3

YES! Please send me 4 free Harlequin American Romance® novels and my free surprise gift. Then send me 4 brand-new novels every month as they come off the presses. Bill me at the low price of $2.25 each*—a 10% saving off the retail price. There is no minimum number of books I must purchase. I can always return a shipment and cancel at any time. Even if I never buy another book from Harlequin, the 4 free novels and the surprise gift are mine to keep forever.   154 BPA BP7S

*Plus 49¢ postage and handling per shipment in Canada.

Name _____ (PLEASE PRINT) _____

Address _____ Apt. No. _____

City _____ State/Prov. _____ Zip/Postal Code _____

This offer is limited to one order per household and not valid to present subscribers. Price is subject to change.   AR-SUB-1A

**For the millions who can't read
Give the Gift of Literacy**

One out of five adults in North America
cannot read or write well enough
to fill out a job application
or understand the directions on a bottle of medicine.

**You can change all this by joining the fight
against illiteracy.**

For more information write to:
Contact, Box 81826, Lincoln, Neb. 68501
In the United States, call toll free: 800-228-3225

**The only degree you need
is a degree of caring**

"This ad made possible with the cooperation of the Coalition for Literacy and the Ad Council."
Give the Gift of Literacy Campaign is a project of the book and periodical industry,
in partnership with Telephone Pioneers of America.

LIT—A—1